D0734248

# RAVE REVIEWS FOR
# DAWN THOMPSON AND
# *THE RAVENCLIFF BRIDE*!

"A seductive, brooding tale of dark love. Victoria Holt, move over!"
—Bertrice Small, Author of *The Last Heiress*

"For a novel that will entertain and give you chills, grab a copy of *The Ravencliff Bride*; it is guaranteed to appeal to fans of gothic and paranormal romances."
—*Romance Reviews Today*

"With its delicious Gothic overtones, haunting suspense and thrilling climax, Thompson's tale sends just the right amount of chills down your spine…Thompson creates such appealing characters that you'll be hooked…. A novel that will entertain and give you chills."
—*RT BOOKclub*

# Myth, or Destiny?

"Once each generation, during the mating season, the *Fossegrim* crosses over from the Otherworld to inhabit his earthly waterfall, there to lure a mortal maiden and seduce her. Though he may live apart, just as a mortal lives, he cannot stray far from his waterfall. From it, he draws his strength. He has one month to accomplish his mission and fulfill his destiny, or forever remain in the mortal world, unable to return to the astral realm. Failure dooms him to live and die as a mortal dies. All privilege comes at a price."

Fascinated, Becca hung on the count's every word. She had not heard this fable, and his delivery was so impassioned that the woodland creatures had crept close along the forest curtain, as if they were just as enthralled with the tale as she.

"And if the lady resists him?" she asked.

"The lure of the *Fossegrim* driven by mating lust is irresistible, *mitt kostbart*," he said. *"Irresistible."*

Other *Love Spell* books by Dawn Thompson:
**THE RAVENCLIFF BRIDE**

# Dawn Thompson

# THE WATERLORD

LOVE SPELL  NEW YORK CITY

LOVE SPELL®

March 2006

Published by

Dorchester Publishing Co., Inc.
200 Madison Avenue
New York, NY 10016

ISBN 0-505-52673-5

The name "Love Spell" and its logo are trademarks of Dorchester Publishing Co., Inc.

Printed in the United States of America.

Visit us on the web at www.dorchesterpub.com.

*First and foremost, this book is dedicated to my editor extraordinaire, Chris Keeslar, whose patience, insights, and willingness to listen to a new voice has made my dream a reality.*

*Thanks and applause to all the talented authors of GOTHROM, Hearts Through History, the Beau Monde, and LIRW, for cheering me on, and to the Red River Romance Writers, who started the ball rolling. Heartfelt thanks to Candace Goldapper for her friendship, encouragement, and for being there to help me iron out the technical difficulties when the computer misbehaves.*

*And last but not least, thanks to the inimitable Bertrice Small, for her enthusiasm and gracious support of my work.*

# Chapter One

Cornwall, England
Midsummer's Eve, 1815

It happened in the blink of an eye. One minute the post chaise was tooling over the moor through the pouring rain at Becca's insistence, the coachman making a valiant attempt to escape the imminent pursuit of her father . . . or worse. The next, she lay dazed, upside down on top of her unconscious abigail, crushed against what seconds before had been the roof of the now upended equipage. The wheels were still spinning crazily, shooting out water like fountains as the rain sluiced down into them. The groaning sound they made, mingled with the shrieks of the horses, struck her with terror.

Lightning speared down now, in rampant flashes snaking through the night sky visible through one of the carriage windows. The other window was blocked. By what, Becca couldn't tell, though it had an earthy scent about it, detectable through a crack in the glass. She dared not try to right herself. The carriage wasn't stable. Each time the horses' shrill cries broke the awful silence, it shuddered and slipped a bit more. Had it gone into a ditch? Where was the coachman?

Becca groaned. The slanted view of her predicament was still in motion due to her vertigo. Everything around her seemed to undulate, like the pattern in her watered silk traveling costume fetched up in tangled disarray about her middle. She tried to free her hands to pull it down for the sake of modesty, but she had landed on one arm and couldn't reach the hem with the other.

"Do not move," said a deep, authoritative voice from somewhere above.

It certainly was not the coachman's voice. This voice was cultured, with traces of an accent Becca couldn't place.

She squinted toward the window, trying to make his image come clear. He seemed a phantom in that eerie setting. The carriage lanterns were extinguished in the crash, and stormclouds had swallowed the moon. Yet there was an eerie luminosity about him, like a fluid silver aura in the ghostly lightning flashes that lit his face through the rain-spattered glass.

"Th-the coachman . . . ?" she murmured.

The phantom shook his head, spraying water from the brim of his beaver hat. "Dead," he replied. "He has broken his neck in the fall."

Becca uttered a strangled gasp.

"You must stay still," he cautioned her. "Your carriage has overturned on the edge of a steep-sided gorge above the River Fowey. If you thrash about it will go over, and you will surely perish. My man and I will free you, but you must remain calm and do exactly as I say."

"W-who . . . ?"

He smiled, and uttered something in a foreign

tongue. "Count Klaus Lindegren at your service, my lady," he said, tipping his beaver.

He was gone in a flash, barking orders to another. Where had they come from? She hadn't heard a carriage approach, and they certainly couldn't have come on foot in such a storm, and in such a desolate place. Cold chills gripped her as she listened to his deep, mellow voice issuing commands. There was something comforting in the sound of it, like the music cool water makes while rushing over pebbles in a stream. It was soothing . . . almost hypnotic. In any other circumstances it would have been a welcome sound.

"Set the right leader free!" he commanded. "Easy, Sven! Hold the ribbons! Cut the tack if needs must, else he drive the chaise over! See how the ground crumbles? *Quickly, man!*"

"I cannot hold him, your excellency!" cried the other.

"Cut him loose and let him go, then! We shall deal with him later."

"What of the other?"

"I shall attend to the other. Quickly, I say! Can you not see? The coach is slipping!"

Becca scarcely breathed. Her heart was thudding against her ribs, and she had begun to tremble so much that she feared the vibration alone would cause the chaise to fall into the abyss. A shot rang out, and she screamed with a lurch in spite of herself. The cry had scarcely left her lips when the count appeared at the window again, a smoking pistol in his gloved hand.

"All is well, my lady," he said, in that captivating accent. It was like balm to her frayed nerves. "It was necessary that I put one of the horses out of its misery. Its leg was broken, and its floundering was undermining the carriage. You are not alone in there?"

"My maid, your excellency."

He raised his hand. " 'My lord' will suffice," he said, nodding past her toward the inert servant. "Is she . . . ?"

"I do not know. She is not conscious."

"Look into my eyes, and listen carefully to what I am about to say," he charged. It was like drowning in a silver sea. At least, those piercing eyes looked silver in the lightning's glare, but then, so did the rest of him. All at once she realized she must appear naked to him from the waist down, but for her thin summer hose, the way her frock was hiked up, barely covering her personals. His gaze riveted to hers, he seemed not to notice. "Are you injured?"

"N-no . . . just shaken about."

"Good!" he said. "I shall open the door. When I reach inside, grab fast to my hand and let me pull you clear."

"Only one of my hands is free," she cried.

"As I raise you off the other, grab fast with both, but do not move otherwise. Let me do the work. I will not deceive you; the carriage is unstable. With the horses removed, it has stopped pitching, but their floundering has loosened the earth beneath you, and if you rock it . . ."

"What of Maud?"

"I beg your pardon?"

"My abigail! What of my abigail?"

He was silent apace. "First things first," he said. "Let me free you, my lady, and then I shall see to your maid."

With no more said, he thrust his pistol and gloves toward a shadowy form at his side that Becca hadn't noticed until that moment, and eased the staved-in carriage door open. It was sprung in the crash, and the dreadful sound it made ran Becca through like a javelin. His hand appeared, the arm behind it sheathed in soggy black superfine. She gripped it, and it was as though she had suffered a lightning strike. His strength was unexpected, and her breath caught in her throat as he lifted her through the gaping door with ease and set her on her feet.

Becca's knees gave way, and she sagged against him. Her frock had fallen back about her ankles as was proper, thank the stars and gravity, but not before he'd glimpsed what lay beneath, she was certain. He smelled clean, of the rain, of sweet cress, wild herbs, and the ghost of recently drunk wine. The whole was threaded through with his own distinct male essence, mysterious and evocative. It was a pleasant scent. She drank him in deeply.

"Thank you, my lord," she murmured against his saturated lapel. The weather was warm, and he wore no topcoat or mantle over his frock coat. It was heavy with the weight of the rain slamming them in horizontal sheets. She gasped. "You are soaked through, sir!"

He popped a dry grunt. "I have no fear of water, my lady," he said. Was there a hidden meaning there . . . some private irony? His mildly sarcastic tone suggested such. It gave her pause for thought, but not for long. Catching a glimpse of the chaise, and the dead horse unhitched beside it, she gasped again. "I have weathered many storms," he went on, leading her away from the edge, "but you shall catch your death in such a . . . thin costume. Step inside my carriage. There is a warm robe in the boot." He snapped his fingers. "Sven!" he said. "Fetch the fur robe for the lady."

The coachman scrambled toward the count's carriage, but Becca dug in her heels. "What of Maud?" she asked.

"I shall fetch your maid," the count answered, handing her into a well-appointed brougham. Snatching the carriage robe from Sven's outstretched hand, he tucked it around her. "Forgive the familiarity, my lady," he said. "Extreme circumstances call for bold measures if I am to see to your comfort. I shall be back directly."

"What are you going to do?" Becca called after him.

"I am going to climb inside and fetch your abigail," he said, "before the chaise goes over the edge and takes her with it. Forgive me, but we have no time to spare."

"You cannot climb into that carriage!" Becca shrilled. He was tall and slender, a fine figure of a man, but far too muscular to attempt such a feat. "You will both be killed!"

"And if I do not, who then?" he returned. Standing arms akimbo in the pouring rain, he didn't even seem to notice it—at least, he made no sign that he did. "She cannot climb out on her own, and Sven here is far too portly. I do not see any other about, do you?"

Just then, the chaise shifted on the spongy ground, and Becca cried out again.

"Fear not, my lady," he assured her. "All will be well." Then, with a nod toward Sven, he sketched a bow in her direction, clicked the heels of his mud-spattered Hessians, and strode off toward the teetering chaise, his man in tow.

Becca watched with breath suspended as the count thrust his beaver hat toward his driver and disappeared inside the gaping mouth of the carriage, which was poised like a wounded beast ready to gobble him whole. Lightning speared down all around them, and streaked across the moor. The storm was stalled overhead, and in the glare of white light flashes she saw what must have caused the chaise to go over: A large blackened tree limb, evidently sheared off by lightning, was blocking the road. It must have spooked the horses. She gave it only passing notice. It didn't matter anymore. The only thing that mattered was that her strange, hypnotic savior was risking his life for a total stranger. Her father and the debacle she had left behind were forgotten then, as she sat wrapped in the sumptuous fur robe, pleading with the darkness inside the chaise teetering on the brink to give birth to the count's handsome head emerging.

She wasn't made to suffer long. Minutes passed, seeming like hours, before movement stirred the blackness that had swallowed him. It was not his strong silhouette but Maud's that cleared the door first, and then he eased her into Sven's arms. The count had no sooner gotten clear when the chaise, groaning like a living thing, slipped and pitched and tumbled over the edge into the ravine in the midst of a mudslide of loose earth raining down. Then came the thunder of impact, as it bounced off the rocky wall—once, twice—and the thud and splash of displaced water, as it crashed into the river below. The rumble echoed after it, and Becca buried her face in the fur robe and shuddered, realizing how close she had come to death on this lonely stretch of land on Bodmin Moor.

Sven laid the unconscious abigail on the brougham seat, and the count climbed in beside Becca across the way. He wasn't even winded for the exertion, and she marveled at his stamina, getting a good look at him for the first time without the hat casting shadows that not even the lightning could chase away. He seemed a man in his mid- to late-thirties. The wavy hair plastered to his forehead was chestnut in color, except for a broad streak in front that appeared to have been bleached nearly white by the sun. His eyes, deep-set and mesmerizing, were not silver as she'd first thought, but a steely, shimmering blue, the color of clear seawater, tucked beneath sun-bleached brows. All else paled before those dazzling eyes. They seemed to see into her soul.

"My cottage lies there"—he gestured—"at the edge of the wood." How odd. The chaise had passed right by that stretch of road before the accident and she hadn't noticed a cottage . . . but there was one now. She saw it clearly in the lightning's glare. Cottage, indeed! It was a rambling, three-story Tudor at the edge of the grove. How could she have missed such a structure? "I shall conduct you there safely," he went on, "and then, while we see to your maid, my man shall return to deal with your coachman and the poor horse I have shot, and retrieve the other that we have set free." It wasn't until then that Becca noticed the bulk of a corpse beneath a tarpaulin by the side of the road. She shuddered again, and he wrapped his arm around her. "You are cold . . . more due to shock than the climate, yes? Hmmm." He took up his walking stick from the floor—something else she hadn't noticed— and thumped the brougham roof. "Home, Sven!" he called.

"*Hyaahh!*" Sven shouted, and the restless horses pranced off with a clatter of jingling tack and hooves clopping in mud.

"My lord, I cannot allow—"

"Nonsense!" he interrupted. "How can you not? This woman here needs tending, and I have a fine staff at your disposal, at least until you are both fit to travel. Now, then! You have me at a disadvantage, my lady. Who, may I ask is it that I have just had the pleasure of rescuing upon my fortuitous journey . . . home?"

"Becca . . . Lady Rebecca Gildersleeve, my lord," she said, low-voiced. "And my abigail, Maud Ammen."

He gave a satisfied nod. "Well, Lady Rebecca Gildersleeve, you will be happy to know that my man was able to retrieve one of your portmanteaux earlier, whilst distributing the weight on the chaise. The night is young. We shall deliver your maid into the capable hands of my housekeeper, Anne-Lise—the next best thing to a surgeon in these parts, by the way—and I shall have one of my maids help you change into something dryer. Then we shall talk, hmm?"

Becca nodded. There was no use to protest. Where else was she to go? Besides, her father would never find her tucked away in the wilds of the Cornish moors. She suffered a bittersweet pang thinking of him. But no, she wouldn't dwell upon all that now. She'd made the only decision she could make if she were to escape his plans for her future. There was no turning back. She was safe enough . . . for now, and she couldn't very well leave Maud.

Leaning back against the plush squabs, she shut her eyes to the vertigo that hadn't left her and pulled the carriage robe closer. It held her savior's scent as well— clean and fresh, with the fragrance of herbs and sea grass. She inhaled, and a soft moan escaped her throat. When she'd first set eyes upon her strange host through the chaise window, she'd feared, in her semiconscious haze that he was the specter, Death, come to collect her. But, no. And it was good to be alive.

# Chapter Two

An hour later, dressed in a dry peach muslin frock, Becca was seated on a comfortable chaise longue in the count's sumptuous though sparsely furnished salon. She was sipping an herbal draught his housekeeper had prepared. Across the way, in a matching wing chair, her host sat nursing a brandy, swirling it in slow revolutions until it threatened the rim of his snifter.

He, too, had changed clothes. His wet hair had been slicked back, and he was dressed casually, wearing black satin inexpressibles, an Egyptian cotton shirt, and a flawlessly tied neckcloth beneath an indigo brocade lounging jacket. How long his legs were, stretched out on the Aubusson carpet in a manner that left little to the imagination in the area of his well-turned thighs. It was not deliberate, Becca was certain; he was simply relaxed, while they waited for word of Maud, in the housekeeper's charge. And he was no doubt exhausted, though he showed no sign of it. His mood seemed more contemplative than weary.

"So, Lady Rebecca Gildersleeve," he said, his voice lifted, as though he'd emerged from a trance. And not a moment too soon, thought Becca. The liquor in his glass was on the verge of spilling over onto the carpet. "What caused you to take to the highway on such a night as though the King's men were in pursuit?"

Should she confide in him? He had a right to know he harbored a fugitive, for that was what she had become, albeit not without good cause. She studied the tea in her cup, deciding.

"Oh, now, why such a face?" he asked. "You must excuse my poor attempt at levity. I meant only to lighten your spirits until that there in your cup can ease your cares, my lady."

"What is this tea?" she said, glad of a chance to avoid the issue. "It is quite delicious."

"Lavender flowers steeped with honey . . . to calm you, my lady, after your ordeal. You cannot tell the scent? Curious. The blooms grow in great profusion in your country."

"Forgive me, your ex—*my lord*," said Becca. "Your accent, it is unfamiliar to me."

"Sweden is my homeland," he said. "I have not seen its shores in . . . many years. England is my home now. You might say that I am in exile, but that boring tale is for another time, when I have drunk many more of these"—he exhibited his snifter—"and you are not so overset with other matters."

Becca wanted to say *I shan't be here long enough for that,* but smiled instead, and took another sip from the cup. Already it was making her drowsy. She couldn't help but wonder if there weren't other mysterious herbs in the brew. Something was overpowering the lavender. She couldn't quite place it.

"You have not answered my question," he said in the deep, mellow voice that so unnerved her. It crackled with seductive fire, and gooseflesh snaked along her spine. "What drove you out on the highway in such a tempest, hmm?" he prompted, inclining his head in a provocative tilt. The look of him then was so endearing that her defenses melted, and she took a deep, tremulous breath.

"I was traveling south to Plymouth," she said, "to book passage on a ship there."

"Sea travel, in these troubled times? Is that wise, my lady?"

Becca gave a bitter laugh. "Not wise, no," she agreed. "But necessary, my lord."

"I would hear more of this," he said. Drawing his legs back from their outstretched position, he leaned forward in his chair. "Please, my lady, continue. I cannot imagine what calamity could cause so lovely a creature to flee her homeland."

Becca ignored the obvious compliment. It wasn't his words that moved her. His body spoke far more eloquently—every nuance of expression, every motion as he shifted position in the wing chair, was speaking now. He seemed almost alarmed. His silver-blue eyes had all but disappeared beneath the jutting ledge of his brow, which had become pleated in a frown. His lips had lost their color of a sudden, and the muscles had begun to tick along his angular jawline. It was clear that somehow he viewed her escape in the same light as his exile. The sudden genuine sorrow in him brought a lump to her throat. The look alone was an embrace. Yes, she would confide in this man. What harm could it possibly do? But she needed to know more about him first.

"When you hear my tale, you may think twice about harboring me, my lord," she said, "even for this brief time needed to have my abigail on her feet and for me to take my leave of your kind hospitality." She hesitated. "Do you not think we should include the countess, your lady wife, in this conversation? She may certainly object to having houseguests forced upon her so soon after arriving. I know it would certainly rattle me." Truth be told, she was curious to know if he had a wife, having seen no one save the count and his servants since they'd arrived.

His right eyebrow lifted, and she averted her gaze. She was not skilled at subtleties, and he had obviously seen right through her awkward attempt at nonchalance.

"Alas, I have no lady wife," he said, clearly amused. "I have yet to find the woman who will have me."

"Oh," Becca said, embarrassed. "I assumed . . . That is to say . . . Oh, dear, I beg your pardon! I didn't mean to pry." What she couldn't say—dared not say, though she was on the verge of it—was that she found it hard to imagine why such a dashing gentleman as himself was still unwed. What tied her tongue was the little flutter of gladness that came over her with the knowledge that he was still unattached. What sent hot blood racing to her temples was that she had such thoughts despite the impropriety of her being there alone with him in that guise, albeit due to circumstances quite beyond her control.

He waved off her apology with a gesture. "There is no pardon to beg," he murmured. "Please continue, *mitt kostbart.*" Though she did not understand their meaning, the words seemed like a caress the way he'd spoken them.

"I did not mean to chance the Continent in such times as these—"

"Two women traveling alone in wartime?" he cut in. "Surely no reputable captain would allow it!"

"No, and I am not foolhardy, my lord, just desperate. I meant to sail to the Channel Islands. It is safe there—neutral ground."

"And do what?"

"Enter an Anglican convent, perhaps . . . at least for a time. They could not touch me under the protection of the Church."

"One so young and vital, such as yourself, shut up in a nunnery? But why? 'Tis unnatural."

Becca's posture collapsed. She had been thinking out loud and said more than she'd intended. Now she had no choice but to continue. One fleeting glance toward those riveting eyes told her he would not let it rest until she did.

"You were not far from the mark when you suggested that the King's men were in pursuit of me . . . except that neither the poor mad King nor the Prince Regent knows I exist, unless my father has called in the soldiers. It is Father who will surely follow after me, and it shan't be difficult for him to do so once he learns I hired that chaise. . . ."

"You had best commence at the beginning, my lady," he said. "You have lost me."

"You are entitled to know the sort of trouble you have invited into your home, my lord," agreed Becca. "My father, Baron Gildersleeve, fancies himself an 'ivory hunter.' I believe that is the term. He spends his time, and his fortune, in the gaming hells. It wasn't always thus. Once we were a happy family. Mother and Father were a devoted couple. Games of chance always intrigued Father, but he was hardly an inveterate gambler. That all changed when Mother died three years ago. It was then that gambling became an addiction with him. He has wagered away our horses, our unentailed lands. . . . Only our Cornish estate at Boscastle and a modest townhouse in London remain. When all else of value was gone but those, he wagered *me*—in a game with a man whom I would rather die than wed, sir. It would have put things to rights for him had I been willing, but nothing would have been served in such a sacrifice. He would have only begun the gaming all over again."

"What sort of man would—"

"Compulsive gambling is a sickness, my lord," she said, "a sickness that has infected far too many in this country of late. And there was more than one attraction in such an arrangement. I am not yet of age by one year, you see, and such a betrothal would have saved him the expense of my introduction into society, and given him more blunt to squander. Cedric Gildersleeve is a practical man in all save his gambling endeavors. I love my father, and it breaks my heart that I shall never see him again—but I could not countenance being trapped in a loveless marriage when I have not yet begun to live. My come-out is inconsequential. It means nothing to me. My freedom is quite another matter, sir. I hired the chaise at the coaching inn near our home on the coast. Father would not do the London Season, you see, else I might be snapped up by another and spoil his plans. He kept me here in Cornwall—as far from Town as possible, to avoid any chance of that occurring."

"And you know that he is in pursuit?"

"I know there will be pursuit, my lord. There is only one coaching inn in Boscastle. He will follow, and he will more than likely not be traveling alone. Sir Percival Smedley will no doubt be with him . . . the man I am supposed to wed. I must away beforehand or he will drag me back, and I will not bear it. I would rather have gone over the edge of that gorge in the chaise than be forced into a marriage I do not wish."

"No wonder you were traveling at such a speed."

"That is the only thing I regret. If I had not urged the driver on, he would be alive."

"You are not responsible for the driver's death, my lady," he said. "I saw what occurred. If he had been traveling at half the speed, it could not have been avoided. Lightning sheared off the tree limb you saw in the road. It came too close to the nervous right leader—already spooked by the storm—and he bolted, tipping the carriage on the sloping shoulder of the road. That you and your maid are alive is a miracle, my lady. The chaise would have rolled over twice but for the fallen horse preventing it. The driver panicked and was thrown clear. He was inept, my lady. You must not reproach yourself for the man's death. He alone was the cause of it."

If he were only trying to ease her conscience, she warmed to him for it, but no, this was a man who meant what he said. He was passionate in his convictions and self-confident to a fault; he had proven that at the edge of the gorge. He was not unlike the knight in shining armor of her young dreams, whom she'd prayed would come and carry her away, sweep her off her feet and save her from the looming marriage. Becca had never encountered such gallantry—such bravery. She was in awe of it. It was almost as if he secretly harbored a death wish, or he simply did not credit that he could come to harm. But that was ridiculous.

"I cannot thank you enough for coming to my rescue, my lord," she said, "but I shall be away just as soon as Maud is fit to travel and I can arrange for another coach."

"You are welcome to remain at Lindegren Hall as long as you wish, my lady," he said. "You are safe here . . . safer than you know."

Something in the tone of his voice delivering the last chilled her to the marrow. She shuddered visibly, and he surged to his feet. A teapot stood on the gateleg table alongside the lounge. He reached it in two strides and refilled her cup despite her protests. What she'd already drunk had made her woozy, and she wondered at the wisdom of taking more.

"I shouldn't," she said. "I fear it has already had its way with me."

"Anne-Lise's remedies never fail," he replied. "What

you need is rest. Do not fight the tincture. There is nothing to fear inside these walls."

"And . . . if they come . . . ? My father, or others?"

"You must leave them to me," he said. "You are under my protection. No harm will come to you."

Just then, a knock at the door turned them both toward it.

"Come!" the count said.

The door came open in the tiny hand of a short, stout woman dressed in black twill. An angular white lawn cap hid nearly all of the gray hair braided in a crown beneath. Becca had never seen one quite like it. The woman sketched a curtsy, and folded her hands over her apron, like a quaint mechanical toy that had run down. She appeared more elfin than human, as though she'd stepped off a page from a tome of fairy tales Becca recalled from her nursery.

"Beggin' your pardon, your highness," she said, "but the lady's maid is restin' comfortable. She should be right as rain in the mornin'."

Becca's eyes flashed toward her host. "*Your highness?*" she said.

He waved the notion off with a gesture. "No, no," he said. "Anne-Lise is sometimes carried away, what with your . . . confusing forms of address in this country." Though his lips smiled, his eyes—those incredible, riveting eyes—bore down upon the servant with such intensity that the woman backed up a pace. "Is that not so, Anne-Lise?" he prompted.

"Y-yes, m'lord. Beggin' your pardon, m'lord." She offered another curtsy.

A wry smile creased his handsome lips. "But then, the staff at Lindegren Hall does tend to look upon me as a prince among men, do you not, Anne-Lise?" There was a playful twinkle in his eyes now, but the housekeeper's odd expression hadn't changed. She almost seemed afraid.

"Yes, m'lord," she said. "About the maid—I've put her in the yellow suite. Ulla's sittin' with her till m'lady is ready to retire. Then she'll tend them both. We've set up a cot for her in the dressing room between. 'Tis all done up proper—just like ya said, m'lord."

"Excellent!" he replied. "You may retire, then. We shan't have need of you again tonight."

"Yes, m'lord," she murmured, offering an awkward curtsy as she backed toward the threshold.

Becca rose to her feet, a close eye upon the woman's clumsy exit, which was almost as if she were leaving the presence of royalty. "I think I shall retire as well, with my lord's permission," she said. "I really am quite worn to a raveling, and this wonderful tea has done its work."

The count held up his hand to stay the housekeeper as she was about to quit the room. "One last duty, Anne-Lise," he said. "Kindly show my lady to her apartments." Turning to Becca, he took her hand and raised it to his lips. The kiss was long and lingering. His moist breath puffing on the back of her hand sent little shivers of pleasure coursing through her innermost regions. This enigmatic man was skilled in the subtle art of seduction. She was no match for his prowess.

"My lord," she said, easing her hand out of his.

There was no impropriety. He released her trembling fingers at once, offered a heel-clicking bow, and stood while she accompanied the housekeeper out of the room.

Becca followed the odd little woman up a freestanding spiral staircase to the third level of the strange cottage, then to a door on the left side of the corridor, where she was shown into a large, well-appointed sitting room with a view of the forest through the leaded panes. The woman quickly drew the draperies and lit the candles, then floated through another door and prepared the bedchamber as well. At last, with a pert curtsy, she was gone.

The housemaid, Ulla, entered from the adjoining sitting room to prepare Becca for bed. Similarly attired to Anne-Lise, though younger, she wasted no time laying out Becca's nightdress and wrapper. To Becca's surprise, her portmanteau had been unpacked and her clothes hung neatly in a towering oak wardrobe. Toiletries had been laid out on the vanity—rosewater, talc, and hand-milled soap that smelled of citrus and rosemary. Her every need had been anticipated, but she dug in her heels when the maid attempted to undress her. She would see Maud first . . . just to be sure.

"Ya mustn't wake her, m'lady," said the maid, leading her through the sitting room to the yellow suite.

Becca stared down at her sleeping abigail. She seemed peaceful enough, but a blue-black lump on Maud's brow beneath a strong-smelling poultice was evidence of a serious injury. Flecks of some anonymous matter clotted on the cloth. Becca couldn't recognize it.

"What is that?" she asked, pointing.

"Oh, 'tis just sage seeds crushed in water. It will take the swellin' down by mornin'."

Judging from the size of the lump, Becca doubted it, but she let the maid lead her back to her suite and help her into the waiting nightdress. Her empty portmanteau in the corner caught her eye, bringing to mind her other luggage lying at the bottom of the gorge in the Fowey, with the broken chaise. If her father were to find it, mightn't he think she had perished in the crash and been carried away by the strong current? It was so close to Lindegren Hall, he would surely come to inquire. No! She wouldn't think about that now. The thought evoked the sound of running water, and she strained her ears to listen.

"Is that the river I hear?" she said, padding toward the window. "It cannot be. The river is below us. Could it be a stream, perhaps, or a beck in the forest?" When she attempted to pull the draperies back, the maid took them out of her hands.

"No, m'lady," she said. "We leave these shut at night."

It seemed an odd response, and Becca studied the maid who smoothed the draperies back in place.

"I *do* hear running water," she persisted.

" 'Tis a . . . waterfall, m'lady, deep in the wood," Ulla said. "When the wind's just right ya can hear it plain."

"A waterfall," Becca mused. "I should like to see it. We have one near my home . . . at Boscastle, and there is a grand one at Tintagel. My father took me there when I was still in leading strings. I shan't ever forget the sight. It was magical, and so tall! But then, I was little, wasn't I? It would have seemed so to my child's eye, wouldn't it?" Her eyes misted, recalling those happier times. How had it all come to this?

"Yes, m'lady," said the maid. "Ya won't be seein' this one, I'm afraid. It's too deep in, and there's no lane, only rocks all slimed with moss. 'Tisn't safe. The master would skin me if he knew I told ya about it."

"I cannot fathom why. But no matter. Your secret is safe with me, Ulla. And now, if you will allow, I should like to retire. Between Anne-Lise's lavender tea and that wonderful waterfall music, I think I shall drift off to sleep before my head touches the pillow."

"Yes, m'lady," said the maid. Sketching a curtsy, she disappeared through the dressing room door.

*Closed at night, indeed! What nonsense,* Becca thought. Crossing to the window, she snuffed out the candles and parted the heavy portieres. The moon shone down upon the forest, bathing the trees in a silvery haze. What did the silly chit mean, there was no lane? The moonlight showed it clearly, a narrow footpath wending its way through the trees. Beyond, like a shimmering ribbon, the waterfall was visible tumbling below, singing as it spilled down over an all but invisible ledge hidden from view but for brief glimpses through the trees. Why had Ulla lied?

Transfixed, Becca gazed down at the scene. It bore the same ethereal aura she'd seen about her strange host, when she'd first glimpsed him through the coach window. All at once, motion caught her eye, and she gasped. The count was strolling along the path toward the falls. Strange lights floated around him, roaming the forest floor as if they were leading or accompanying him on his jaunt. A fugitive mist had risen, but only where he walked. It seemed to move with him. His feet were hidden by it.

Mesmerized, Becca stared. Were her eyes deceiving her? Was this some trick of the herbal draught she'd drunk? The count stood on the brink, his arms raised to the heavens. She blinked to clear her vision and gasped again. He was stark naked.

# Chapter Three

Becca blinked, and the count was gone. It was as if he had vanished into thin air. Had she imagined him? No, never; he was real enough, but where was he now? He couldn't have jumped or dove off the ledge. The sound of the water rushing below suggested a significant drop, and then there were the rocks. Midsummer's Eve. All manner of strange phenomenon were reputed to be afoot on Midsummer's Eve, and Cornwall was rife with strange tales of unexplained and unexplainable happenings. Becca shuddered and shut the draperies. What was happening to her? She had never taken Cornish superstitions to heart. It was definitely time she took herself to bed.

Her dreams were no kinder, however. They were fierce, troublesome visions, threaded through with her strange host's evocative scent. It seemed stronger somehow, ghosting its way through those dreams, as if he stood in the room beside her bed, gazing down upon her as she slept. Try as she would, she couldn't open her eyes to see if he really was standing there. Not until first light spilled in the window, when Ulla pulled back the draperies in the morning.

Though the dawn was gray with cottony fog pressed up against the panes, it was blinding, and Becca narrowed her eyes against the glare. A hipbath had been set before the gaping hearth. No fire was lit in it, but then, why would there be? As dreary as the day looked, the heat was oppressive, even inside the drafty old house. Steamy water rose from the tub, fragrant with rosemary and lavender. Becca threw back the counterpane and swung her feet to the floor, only to jerk them back again. She had stepped in a puddle of water.

"Oh!" she cried. "The floor is wet here!"

Ulla glanced toward her from the tub, where she was sprinkling attar of roses into the bathwater, but made no reply.

Upon close examination, Becca saw that there seemed to be a trail of water leading from the door. The floorboards were black where it had seeped into them.

"Ulla?" she prompted.

"We musta spilt it bringin' the water up, m'lady," the girl said with a shrug.

Becca scrutinized the distance between the bed and the hipbath. "How could that be?" she said. "See how far the bath is from this bed?"

"I see, m'lady," Ulla said, "but how else could it have got there? The help in this house are a clumsy lot. They musta slopped it over some way. You'd best slip on this bathin' dress and climb in while the water's still warm. There'll be no benefit from the herbs once it's grown cold. The master was most particular about the herbs, and about a good soak ta soothe your aches."

It wasn't until then that Becca felt the soreness in her muscles. It was as though she had bruised every one while being tossed about like a broomstraw in the chaise. All at once, hot blood surged to her temples.

Her mind's eye glimpsed again the sight she must have presented to her host, with her traveling frock twisted up about her hips and thighs and then some. He was a gentleman and hadn't let on that he'd noticed, but there was no doubt that he had viewed more of her naked anatomy than he had any right to see. But then, so had she, of his. She could only imagine the color of her face, recalling that. How perfectly the man was formed. How narrow his waist and broad his shoulders. How his muscles had rippled in the moonlight as he stood on the brink of the waterfall, communing with the stars alone knew what, standing there in the altogether . . . .

"Haven't ya heard me, m'lady?" said Ulla, breaking her trance. "The water's gettin' cold!"

Klaus had bathed and was nearly dressed to go down to breakfast. He stood with his arms bent back to receive the ivory brocade waistcoat Henrik was holding out for him. He shrugged it on, and Henrik stepped around in front of him to execute his neckcloth in the intricate Oriental wrap.

"Have you decided, your highness?" Henrik asked, negotiating the first and most critical fold.

"Do not call me thus!" Klaus snapped. "You will slip and do it before the ladies. Anne-Lise has already done so, and I had to cover her blunder by excusing it as ignorance of English protocols. Is it so difficult to remember to address me as 'my lord,' Henrik? It isn't as though all this is new to you, being an elder, and considering that we're camped here more often than we are in the Otherworld of late. Or had you forgotten in your new situation as a gentleman's gentleman?"

"I know who I am," said Henrik. "I merely want to be certain you do not forget who you are . . . *my lord*."

"Yes, well, there isn't much chance of that, considering."

"Time grows short."

"I know that, Henrik."

"You need to decide."

"It is not all that easy. I am damned if I do and damned if I do not. What would you do if you were in my place, old friend?"

"Me, my lord? How could I know? I am full-blooded astral, no half-breed like yourself. There are no human ancestral voices calling me. Besides, who am I to counsel you, Prince of the *Fossegrim*, in such matters? Now, if you were one of the lower forms—"

"Shhhh!" Klaus hissed. His hands clenched, and he slapped his thighs with white-knuckled fists. "There are mortals in the house, or had you forgotten?"

"You have crossed the line and joined their ranks, I'm thinking."

"I have done what my kind has done since time out of mind. I have come of age again, Henrik, and you know I must cross the line to fulfill my destiny." Crossing the line wasn't the hard part. Traveling between worlds was second nature to him now, considering his obsession with the human half of his heritage. Remembering on which side of that line he belonged was the difficulty. Remembering, and obeying an axiom older than time. It went beyond breaking tradition and approached disobeying an edict from the astral gods— from the great god Syl himself.

"Do you not think it fortuitous that you happened upon a suitable subject at the exact moment of your arrival . . . or was that not coincidental?"

"You know as well as I that our worlds exist on a parallel plane. While I can only exist in one or the other at a time, I see quite clearly in both."

"So, your 'sight' saved the lady's life. Is that what you're saying?"

"Two lives were saved, Henrik."

The elder waved his hand in a gesture of dismissal.

He was of an indeterminable age, slender and gray-complexioned, with sparse hair to match, and a wisdom that Klaus had always depended upon. "The other is of no consequence," he said. "She is too far beneath you."

"Ahhh, but without her, my clever fellow, Lady Rebecca would have no reason to stay, would she?"

"What are you about, my lord?" Henrik gasped, as if a light had gone on in his brain. "You wouldn't . . . ?"

"Take ease, old friend. Have you ever known me to cause harm to anyone—in this realm or the other?"

"No, my lord."

"I am surprised at you!"

"What then, my lord?"

"Let us just say that Anne-Lise's remedies, while imparting long-lasting properties for the good, will keep Miss Maud Ammen in a state of condition unfit for travel until I have made up my mind. My lady will not leave without her, and however I decide, she will need the woman."

" 'Tis a dangerous game you play, my lord."

Klaus's eyes flashed, and bored into on the elder. " 'Tis no game, Henrik," he said, "and there are consequences either way. I can take her and fulfill my obligation in this time as I have done in the past so many times before, or I can defy you and the other elders, forsake my birthright and my passage between realms, and be condemned to live and die in this one."

The elder's jaw fell slack. "Die? You would tamper with your immortality?" he asked, incredulous. "I thought it was just a matter of selecting a suitable host."

"If it comes down to it, yes," said Klaus. "That is what I must decide. The option has always existed, Henrik. It is just that I have never . . . contemplated it before."

"What makes this time so different from all the others, my lord?" asked the elder. Having finished wrapping the neckcloth, he stood back to scrutinize his work. His enthusiasm for his new avocation was amusing. Klaus would have laughed if the situation weren't so grave.

"I do not know," he said. "It might just be that I am . . . tired at last or that I see something in this creature that I have not seen in any of the others. Something worth risking my immortality to savor. Coming here so often, I have grown . . . comfortable in this realm, Henrik. Yet though I walk among these, I am not one of them. I am so . . . lonely."

"Hah!" the elder scoffed. "Vanity is all this is. You have the undying devotion—the physical and mental companionship—of any member of the female species of your own race at your disposal, and your command. Any among them would be only too glad to stroke your pride."

"But not my heart," Klaus snapped.

The elder wagged his head. "You have lived too long among mortals, my lord. This fascination you have with your human side will be your undoing, you mark my words. Your first obligation is to us of the astral. You know that."

"Ahhh, but the ultimate decision is still mine to make, old friend," said Klaus, a sad smile on his lips. "And I alone must make it."

"There is another option, my lord," the elder suggested. "Another possibility."

Klaus's smile faded. "Possibility, yes. Probability . . . no. But we shall put it to the test, eh?" His smile returned. "Are you with me no matter what I decide?"

"Always, my lord."

"Good, then! Now fetch me my coat. I have a houseguest awaiting me in the breakfast room."

\* \* \*

"Do you not find the fare to your liking?" the count asked, nodding toward the untouched food on Becca's plate. Her head shot up at the sound, that mellow resonance invading her thoughts. Why was it having such an effect upon her? Why was *he* having such an effect upon her?

"Forgive me, my lord," she said. "The food is most delicious. It is just that I am not encouraged in regard to my abigail's progress. The swelling on her brow is subsiding, but she drifts in and out of consciousness. I'm worried. Perhaps a surgeon should be sent for."

"She is needing rest to mend, my lady," he said. "Believe me when I say that she could not be in better or more capable hands than Anne-Lise's. If there were need of a surgeon, she would be the first to insist upon it. As you said, the swelling is subsiding. Surely that is a good sign. These things take time, my dear."

"That's just it, my lord. I have no time. My belongings and Maud's are sitting in the river below in the boot of that chaise. They will surely be found and—"

"My man retrieved them at first light," he interrupted. "You will find them in your chamber . . . a bit soggy, but nothing that cannot be repaired. My staff will see to it."

Becca's jaw dropped. "I . . . I do not know what to say, my lord," she murmured. "I am in your debt again."

"Nothing of the kind," he returned. "I have simply done what any host would do to make his houseguest comfortable. Now! Let us speak of it no more. You have my word—if there is need of a surgeon for your maid, I will fetch one personally. Do you trust me, my lady?"

How could she not, after his daring rescue? How could she doubt his sincerity, when he had gone to such lengths to prove himself? At the root of it, she was attracted to this enigmatic man across the table. She hadn't wanted to admit it before, but there was an endearing quality about him that was hard to resist—especially for one such as she, who had virtually no experience with members of the opposite sex. Perhaps it was his foreign charm, or that he was the first man to treat her with such gallantry. Or was it the elusive sadness that she'd glimpsed in those penetrating eyes? Whatever it was, something shocking throbbed deep inside her whenever he spoke, whenever she met his riveting gaze. He was having a dangerous effect upon her, and she made a bold attempt to steel herself against the lure of his charm. She would be gone as soon as Maud was fit for travel, after all, never to see Count Klaus Lindegren again. Why did that thought dampen her spirits so?

"My lady?" he prompted.

"O-of course, my lord," she said, low-voiced. "You have been most kind. You must forgive me. It is just that I am unsure of the proper protocol for such a situation as I find myself in, and I shan't be at ease until I am beyond my father's reach."

"Is that all, then? You have been beyond your father's reach since you set foot inside Lindegren Hall, *mitt kostbart*."

"That is twice you've used those words addressing me, my lord," she said. "What do they mean?"

He flashed a handsome smile, and sunbeams broke over her soul. "A mere term of endearment," he said. "Forgive me for taking the liberty, but I could not help myself. Since your etiquette in this country is so rigid between the sexes, I did not want to offend. It is not so where I come from. It seemed less a liberty spoken in a foreign tongue, but since you have caught me out, I must confess, and I do so with the utmost respect. You are what the words suggest . . . *precious*, my lady. I speak it in the Norwegian, however; the words in Swedish are not so pleasant to the ear."

Hot blood rushed to Becca's temples. She wished she hadn't asked. No one had ever called her precious before. That involuntary flutter started deep inside her again, sending a flurry of shockwaves rippling through her most private regions. She shifted uneasily in the chair in a vain attempt to quell the feeling. When she braved a glance in his direction, his warm smile broadened. He looked like a little boy who had just been caught with his hand in the biscuit tin. Embarrassed through she was, her heart threatened to melt.

"O-oh," she murmured, swallowing a dry gulp.

He laughed outright, tossing his head back, quite pleased with himself, she thought. How handsome he was when he laughed, but the absence of laugh lines on his angular face testified to the fact that he did not do so often. It wasn't until then that she realized the sun-bleached wave that streaked through his chestnut hair in front, like in color to his eyebrows, was not gold, or gray, but something more akin to silver. It more closely resembled the strange aura she'd seen shimmering around him when he peered through the window in the chaise. It was striking. She had never seen the like.

"Now you're making fun of me," she pouted.

"No, *mitt kost*—my lady," he said, the words riding a chuckle. "I assure you not. You are too charming. It has been some time since I have so enjoyed the company of one so—how shall I say—unassuming? I believe that is the word I seek . . . at least, the only word I dare say to express myself. My English is not all that accomplished."

"It is most definitely that and then some, my lord," said Becca. The heat rising in her cheeks narrowed her eyes. She could only imagine their color, which made matters worse.

He was about to reply when the appearance of a liveried footman in the breakfast room doorway turned their heads. The fingers of a cold chill inched along Becca's spine at the sight of the man. The servants at Lindegren Hall seemed to have a habit of appearing out of nowhere. She'd noticed it with Ulla and Anne-Lise and now this stone-faced person, but that was not what turned her skin to gooseflesh and caused her fork to slip from her fingers. The man's very bearing flagged danger.

"What is it, Olav?" the count queried. His handsome smile faded, and Becca began to tremble.

"There is a person to see you, m'lord," the footman said. "A Baron Gildersleeve. I have put him in the salon."

Becca stifled a strangled gasp and surged to her feet. Her host rose also, staying her with a gesture.

"I knew he would find me!" she cried.

The count skirted the table and slipped his arm around her shoulders. "You are not found, my lady," he said. "Look at me, *mitt kostbart*." He tilted her chin up to meet his gaze with his forefinger. How mesmerizing his water-colored eyes were. She was content to drown in that shimmering sea. "We both expected this. Now comes the time that you must trust. All will be well, you will see." He led her to the footman and handed her over the threshold. "See her up the back stairs to her apartments," he charged the man. Then, to Becca: "Shhh, not a sound! Go with Olav. I will see to our visitor, hmm?"

# *Chapter Four*

Klaus squared his posture and entered the salon to face a portly man impeccably dressed in the fashion of the day, and who bore little resemblance to his daughter. But for the color of his hair, like golden fire, albeit faded with gray at the temples, and eyes that were neither green nor brown but something in between, he saw no resemblance whatsoever.

Baron Gildersleeve turned from the view he'd been scrutinizing through the leaded panes in their diamond-shaped fretwork, his hands clasped behind him.

"You wish to see me, sir?" said Klaus.

"If you are the lord of this manor, I do, yes."

"I am Count Lindegren, at your service." Klaus clicked the heels of his Hessians together, offering a shallow bow. "And you are . . . ?"

"Baron Cedric Gildersleeve. I shall come directly to the point: I seek my daughter Rebecca. She is traveling with her abigail and would have passed this way a short time ago, according to the calculations given me at the coaching inn where she hired a chaise. She is under age and a runaway, sir, and I mean to have her back before she does herself a mischief and comes to serious harm, traipsing about the wilds of the moor with no male supervision."

"I am sorry for your trouble, but I fail to see how it involves me, sir," Klaus replied.

"I've just told you," the baron barked. "I have it on good authority that she would have passed this way. It is the road the chaises take, and since your cottage is the only residence in the immediate vicinity, naturally I would be remiss not to inquire if you had seen her."

"I wish I could say that I had," said Klaus, "but I'm afraid I cannot. I've only just arrived, myself—from abroad late last evening, with my staff—to open the manor for the summer. Won't you take a seat? Forgive me, but you look a bit flushed. Might I offer you refreshment—tea, or something . . . stronger—before you resume your search?"

The baron waved him off with a gesture. "Thank you, no," he said. "I must away. She is bound for Plymouth, according to the station master's list, to book passage, I would imagine, the foolish chit, to God alone knows where, and I must reach her before she sails."

"I am sorry that I cannot be of more help to you, Baron Gildersleeve," said Klaus silkily, "but as I've said, I have just arrived and—"

"Yes, yes, I shan't detain you further," the baron interrupted. Surging past him, he stopped in the doorway and turned. "You are sure you haven't seen her?" he asked, his eyes narrowed.

Klaus bristled and his posture clenched. "You insult me now!" he said. "I offer you—a total stranger, mind—hospitality in my home in sympathy with your cause, and refreshment in genuine concern for your well-being, and you as much as accuse me of being a liar, sir?"

The baron raised his hands. "Hardly that," he said.

"I have a deep-seated mistrust of . . . foreigners, my lord. With good cause, but that is another tale, and I've no time to tell it. I am a distraught father. I fear for my daughter's safety, and I fear I shan't be reasonable until I have her back again. Have you children, my lord?"

"None that I can claim."

"Well, if you had, you would understand. Rebecca is promised in marriage to a fine, upstanding gentleman. The bird-witted goose could not do better, though she obviously thinks otherwise, and means to prove it by defying me. Well, all she will prove, sir, is her stupidity. I mean to see that she does not lose her virtue or her life in the process, no matter who I must insult along the way."

"Then I shall not detain you. My man will see out, sir." Olav appeared, his arm swept wide, and the baron gave a surly bow and followed.

Klaus waited on the threshold until he heard the front door slam. Streaking to the window, he watched through the diamond-shaped panes as Baron Gildersleeve climbed into his coupe and signaled to his driver. The carriage sped out of the circular drive and onto the highway without giving way to another coach tooling along at a steady pace. Screaming wheels and loud shouts fractured the morning quiet as the two carriages halted. Both drivers' fists were raised toward the heavens, and to each other. The baron's walking stick, protruding from the coupe window and carving wild circles in the air, was agitating the horses.

Neither carriage gave quarter, and Klaus held his breath. The last thing he needed now was another houseguest recuperating from a mishap. Especially not *that* individual, and certainly not while Klaus was secretly harboring his daughter upstairs. The man was a typical *Sassanach*, to borrow a disparaging reference for the overbearing English which he'd picked up on his sojourns among the Scots—one of many words and phrases he'd added to his vocabulary over time. Klaus did not blame the girl for trying to escape her father. He punctuated the thought with a string of expletives in Swedish.

The carriage horses had begun to mill and prance and complain. Both drivers were hard-pressed to control them, until a third carriage, carrying toward the skirmish from the south, forced the issue. The baron's coupe swerved and bolted. Its left wheels on the road, its right gouging a trench in the soft shoulder alongside, it skirted the confrontation and disappeared around the bend, splattering the other two coaches with the mud of its hasty departure.

Klaus's gave a sign of relief. He waited while the other drivers got their carriages back on course and went their separate ways, then left the window. It wasn't likely that the baron would be returning now, but it was almost a certainty that he would return once he learned Rebecca had not reached Plymouth. The chaise in the river below would be found, and it was too close to the cottage. There would be an investigation—the last thing he needed. It had to be disposed of, but there was only one way to do that, and nothing could be done about it until nightfall. One thing was certain: There was no time to lose. He had to make his decision, and he had to make it quickly.

Becca had no view of the drive from her chamber windows, since they faced the forest, and the suspense was overwhelming. She had visions of her father bounding up the spiral staircase and dragging her bodily out of the house. Her heart was hammering against her ribs and her throat had gone dry. Would her host betray her? Her father was a very persuasive man. There was no telling what he might say. What if he was able to convince the count that *he* was in the right and the count should hand her over to him? It was a distinct possibility, considering that she and the count were on such short acquaintance. In her limited experience with the opposite sex, the one thing she had learned from her observance of her father's gambling cronies was that men inevitably tended to stick together. She'd begun to pace, and when the knock came at her sitting room door, she froze. It came a second time before her feet would carry her across the room to answer.

No, this wasn't her father's knock. He would be hammering the door in, his hoarse bark bouncing admonishments off the rafters. She threw it open to face Klaus Lindegren, an infectious smile up-tilting the corners of his handsome mouth. He sketched a bow and extended his arms toward her. She went into them with a sigh of relief, not giving a thought to the impropriety of the embrace. It was clinical, after all, meant to put her at ease. She wasn't prepared for the firestorm of emotions that washed over her in those strong arms, however. His muscles were flexed, hot and hard against her. The vision of him standing naked on the brink of the waterfall crept across her mind, just as it had so many times since she'd seen him there the night before. Something thrumming at her very core would have undermined her balance if he weren't holding her so tightly . . . soothing her so gently . . . bringing her to awareness of her femininity in a way no one had ever done. Suddenly, she was like a flower opening its petals for the first time. Such feelings were scandalous, forbidden. So was the unmistakable pressure of his swelling manhood pressed against her. She strained against it, both hands firmly planted on his chest.

"You see, *mitt kostbart?*" he said, holding her at arm's distance as though he weren't aroused, as though he hadn't just aroused her in the bargain. "I told you all would be well."

"H-he's gone?' she asked, braving a glimpse of those seawater eyes. She almost gasped. They were flecked with silver!

He nodded. "All gone, my lady."

"He will return—I know it!" she said. "When he doesn't find me—"

"Shhhh . . . if he does, I will send him on his way again." A frown creased his brow. "You're trembling," he said. Sliding his hands the length of her arms, he gathered her hands in his and drew them to his lips. It was a slow, reverent kiss that he bestowed, sensuous and deep. She should pull away, but she did not— could not. His warm breath upon her skin turned her knees to water. It was a long moment before he lifted his lips and met her eyes. Could he read her thoughts? *Yes!* He must have done. He frowned again, and she did not know where to direct her eyes.

"I am too bold. Forgive me," he said, releasing her hands. "I tend to forget your . . . customs are so rigid here. Not so in my . . . homeland. I have embarrassed you. Such an embrace in my country does not have the connotation you English place upon it. Why, where I come from, you would be addressing me as Klaus by now—an acceptable intimacy, especially since I have saved your life."

"Oh, but I *couldn't!*"

"Would you consent to think it?"

" 'Think it,' my lord?"

"Yes . . . when you think of me . . . will you say my name in your mind?"

It seemed an odd request, but she nodded, avoiding his eyes. Why did it seem that she had committed herself to something scandalous?

"In some cultures, the saving of a life means that one owns that life, that he is . . . responsible for its safety and comfort, and bound to it for as long as he lives. It is a comforting thought, is it not, that you could have someone to look after you—a guardian of your body and soul for all time?"

"It seems a bit . . . possessive to me," said Becca. "I have just fled from such a 'guardian.' "

"Oh, now, *mitt kostbart*, I do not mean to suggest that I—"

"Of course not, my lord," she said. She didn't want to give him the wrong impression. "That would be rather inappropriate, don't you think?"

He laughed outright. "Do not ask that of me," he said. "My answer might shock you. But enough sparring. I mean no offense. I speak thus only to put your mind at rest. I know this . . . situation is difficult for you, and I am simply trying to put you at your ease. I see my jabbering is having the opposite effect. Pay me no mind. Credit it to my euphoria at having sent your father on his way so easily. It is curious, you are . . . unalike in every aspect. But for the way your hair flames and your eyes flash green in some lights and brown in others, I would be hard-pressed to finds a resemblance."

"We are alike in one other way, my lord," she said. "In our determination. It has always been so."

"Well, then, I, too, may join your company—though I would much prefer to limit it to *your* company, having met your father. It was determination that lifted you out of that chaise, my lady, and determination will see us through all this together."

Becca spent most of the day sitting beside Maud's bed. The swelling was nearly gone, though the bruise remained. The abigail slept much of the time, but she did rally once long enough to recognize Becca before drifting off into a deep sleep again, once Anne-Lise dosed her with one of her tinctures.

Becca didn't see Klaus again, not even at nuncheon or dinner. He disappeared after their strange encounter on the threshold of her sitting room, and she dined alone the rest of the day.

Ulla drew the draperies at dusk, but Becca cried off when she offered to ready her for bed. She had something else in mind, and she needed to be fully dressed to do it. Using a tome she had borrowed from the library downstairs as an excuse to stay up awhile, she told the maid she would dress herself for bed when she tired and dismissed her. As soon as the girl left, she set the book aside, snuffed out the candles, and went to the window.

Parting the draperies just enough to view the forest in the moonlight, she fixed her eyes upon the silvery path, and the waterfall rushing musically over the rocks to the river below. Waiting. Would he tread that path again? If he did, she meant to follow him—unseen, of course—and discover just exactly what sort of ritual he practiced there.

Some time later, when she grew weary of standing, she dragged a Chippendale chair alongside the window and sank into it. More than once, she began to nod off to sleep, surging to her feet each time to revive herself. It was nearly midnight when her vigil bore fruit. Just as he had the night before, Klaus appeared on the path, his feet hidden in the mist, strange lights bobbing all around him. Wasting no time, she snatched her pelisse from the wardrobe, for the nights were cool and damp, and stepped out into the hall. It was deserted. All was still, and she tiptoed down the stairs and out of the house unseen.

It was a moment before she got her bearings, never having traveled the grounds before. Following the sound of the waterfall, she soon found her way. Pacing herself at a discreet distance, she crept along the path, a close eye upon Klaus through the trees. Moonlight playing upon his naked skin gave him a silvery aura. It defined his broad shoulders, narrow waist, and the arrow-straight indentation of his spine. It picked out his taut buttocks and lean, corded thighs as he strode along through the ground mist that hid his feet.

There was an otherworldly look about him there in that primeval setting. Hot blood raced through Becca's veins at the sight, and a wave of chills almost made her lose her footing on the slippery moss. She was observing something very private, meant for no one's eyes to view, least of all hers. That was obvious. It seemed almost sacred, the way Nature seemed to bow in awe. Not even the woodland creatures spoke. All was still, until a twig snapped beneath her feet.

Becca stood stock still as Klaus stopped and turned, his head cocked, his ears pricked to the sound, affording her an unexpected and alarming view of his manhood. She checked a gasp. How magnificent he was! Even in a flaccid state, and at such a distance. She held her breath and didn't draw another until he turned back and moved on again. It would not do to be caught out here, in this magical place, with him in the altogether. Not after what had occurred between them earlier. Treading softly, she stayed well behind.

Flat tables of moss-covered stone formed a natural descent from the edge of the falls. Klaus started down with ease, but Becca hesitated. She would be out in the open if she followed him then, and much of what lay ahead was hidden in the mist, the slippery rocks underneath only visible in brief glimpses. She had already come a good distance from the house. If she were to fall or lose her way, how could she return?

Straining her eyes, she searched what lay ahead, beyond the place where the falls sluiced down into the river. Through the gauze of spray and foam rising from the riverbed, something dark caught her eye farther on. Klaus was moving toward it. *The chaise.* It was. She blinked, and it was gone. Klaus had disappeared as well, and so had the eerie little lights that had flickered about him. Could it be the Will-o'-the-Wisp of her nursery tales that she was seeing? Impossible! She could not credit superstition. Had she imagined it all? No. A moment ago he was there and now he wasn't, plain and simple. The mist had vanished as well, showing her a clear path. It only took a moment for her to decide, before she began scrambling over the moss-clad rocks to the edge of the river below, where seconds ago the broken chaise had rested.

Becca strained into the moonlit darkness ahead, but the broad, flat ribbon of silvery water gurgling past was vacant as far as the eye could see. It was shallow there, where the chaise had gone over—too shallow for the current to have carried it downstream. That accounted for the fact that her portmanteau was only mildly water-damaged. But where had the chaise gone?

She stood staring for some time before turning to climb back up the way she'd come, only to pull up short before Klaus, inches from her at the river's edge. The mist had returned, climbing his naked body like vines. He did not speak, but gazed down with reverent, hooded eyes at her face in the moonlight, his sensuous lips parted. For a moment she was certain he was about to kiss her.

A gasp blossoming into a raw scream spilled from her throat at the suddenness of his appearance—at the wraithlike look of him. The bobbing lights were all around her: flashing, blinking—almost touching her! They were all tangled into the white pinpoints of light brought on by the vertigo starring her vision as consciousness failed. Another gasp escaped her throat; then she swayed and spiraled, unconscious, into his waiting arms.

# Chapter Five

Becca groaned awake in the Chippendale chair at first light, her head resting on the hard windowsill. There was a strong taste of apples in her mouth, like chamomile. It was almost bitter. She shook her head to chase away the last dregs of sleep. It ached from resting on the narrow windowsill, and she groaned, trying to focus her eyes.

Had she dreamed it all? No, she couldn't have! She'd been there, in the forest, with Klaus. Her heart leapt. His name was coming unbidden to her mind now, whenever she thought of him, just as she'd promised. Nonetheless, it was jarring. It couldn't have been a dream. It was too real—*he* was too real, standing naked in the mist, catching her as she swooned from fright when he appeared out of nowhere. What was happening to her? She had never been prone to fainting spells before.

She flexed her neck, stiff from resting so long there, and soothed it with a trembling hand. The sunlight streaming through the window hurt her eyes. It couldn't have been a dream. But if it wasn't, how was it that the sun was shining when she had gone below at midnight? Could she have been so long in the forest? And how had she gotten back to this chair? Her mind was blank. She couldn't remember.

She wasn't given long to dwell upon it. She'd barely stretched her stiff limbs when Ulla entered from the dressing room, a bundle of fresh linen in her arms. The girl pulled up short and stared. Her eyes oscillated between the un-slept-in bed and Becca, seated in the chair beside the window, still dressed from the night before.

"Oh, m'lady!" she cried. "Ya haven't slept in that hard old chair?" She gasped. "The draperies are open! Oh, fie, m'lady, I told ya the draperies are always ta be closed at night."

"The moonlight was so lovely shining upon the trees," said Becca, rising. "I couldn't resist the sight. I . . . I must have fallen asleep." She didn't believe it for a minute, though there was no other explanation. She was exactly where she had been when she last remembered watching Klaus tread the path below through the mist. There was no mist now, only the fine, delicate particles of water ghosting about the distant falls in soft, diaphanous clouds.

"Have you looked in on my abigail this morning?" she queried, hoping a change of subject would put the matter of open draperies to rest. Now, at least, she knew why that rule was enforced. If the master of Lindegren Hall was accustomed to bathing in the nude in warm weather, he certainly wouldn't want an audience.

She'd heard that the Swedes practiced strange bathing habits—that they even constructed outbuildings where they poured water on heated stones and bathed in the steam. Rumor had it that they flayed themselves with birch branches beforehand to open the pores and plunged into icy water afterward to close them again. She had evidently happened upon Klaus indulging himself in some such practice in the forest. She had also heard that Swedes were skilled seducers. That, she could attest to well enough.

"I've just come from your maid," said Ulla. "She's awake this mornin', askin' for ya. I was just comin' ta fetch ya."

"Thank you, Ulla. I shall go to her at once. Then, after I've changed, I shall break my fast with a tray in her chamber, if you please. Make my excuses to the master, will you?"

"Yes, m'lady," Ulla said, sketching a curtsy.

The girl went about her business then, returning the Chippendale chair to its proper place at the edge of the Persian carpet and pulling the draperies all the way open. Becca left her to her chores and skittered into Maud Ammen's sleeping chamber through the adjoining dressing room.

The abigail seemed dwarfed beneath the counterpane. Only a slight swelling remained on her brow, but the bruise was ugly and black. Becca stifled a gasp. The mousy little maid looked half asleep, as though she'd been drugged, her brown eyes hooded and glazed, though she tried to manage a smile. She appeared older than her thirty years with the color drained from her face. Becca beamed at the recognition in that smile, in a bold attempt to mask her concern.

"What's happened ta us, my lady?" the abigail murmured, her voice like gravel.

"The chaise went over in the storm," Becca replied. "You took a nasty spill. I made it worse, I'm afraid, landing on top of you as I did, my frock twisted up around my middle like a Penzance roundheels for the count to view."

"The count?"

Becca nodded. "Count Klaus Lindegren. He is a Swedish nobleman. This is his cottage. He brought us here after the chaise went into the gorge. After he pulled me out, he climbed back inside, while it teetered on the very brink, to pull you to safety, Maud. I have never seen the like. He no sooner climbed out of it that it went over. Then he brought us here. His housekeeper—Anne-Lise is her name—has been tending you. Father has been and gone, seeking us. The count sent him packing, but he will surely return when he learns that we never reached Plymouth. We are safe here for the moment. The count has offered us his protection. But you must rest and mend now, Maud, so we can be on our way. We cannot impose upon his hospitality forever."

"My head hurts terrible bad, my lady," said Maud. "And I'm so tired . . ."

"Then rest, and mind Anne-Lise, and you shall be on your feet again in no time."

Klaus paced before the vacant hearth in his bedchamber, his hands clasped white-knuckled behind him underneath the tails of his superfine frock coat. Rebecca hadn't come down to breakfast or nuncheon. It was nearly time for the evening meal. Across the way, Henrik stood watching, his gray head wagging. Klaus didn't have to look at him directly to read his dour expression. The elder's deportment spoke louder than any words he might have uttered, and always had done.

"If she doesn't come down, I shall have to face her," said Klaus.

"I should think you would have done that already, my lord, and spared yourself this anxiety."

"Yes, well, I was hoping I would not have to."

"Would you care to tell me what you've done?"

Klaus threw his hands into the air. "She must have been watching from the window when I went down to dispose of the chaise," he said. "At any rate, she followed me to the river. She must have seen me cross over with that carriage. When I emerged again without it, I startled her—no more than she startled me, I might add—and she swooned."

"Outstanding!"

Klaus scowled. "She evidently thought her eyes were playing tricks on her. What else would she think? Carriages do not vanish into thin air, do they? Counting upon that, I brought her back to her chamber and dosed her with some of the chamomile and poppy sleep cordial Anne-Lise is dosing the abigail with. I propped her up in the chair she'd evidently been sitting in observing me below, and left her there, hoping she would think she had fallen asleep and dreamed the episode. That is what bothered me most . . . leaving her in that stiff, inhospitable chair, with a bed made with quilts of down so close at hand."

"And the chaise . . . ?"

"Is on the other side," said Klaus, finishing his sentence.

The elder rolled his eyes.

"Well, what else was I to do with it, Henrik? It could not remain where it lay, and where would we conceal it here? Baron Gildersleeve will return. Aside from that, when that chaise does not reach Plymouth, there will be an investigation. The coaching company will send their agents searching for it. They would have found it sitting in that river below, and we would have them swarming all over the grounds in search of its occupants. Not to mention the coachman we have buried. You know as well as I that my anonymity must be preserved at all costs. The chaise is gone. They will not find it in the Otherworld."

"The young lady is no fool, my lord. You shan't easily convince her that what she saw was a figment of her imagination."

"Once she has experienced several more . . . *dreams,* she will be quite content to credit them to her imagination, I assure you. Once she has had a glimpse of my world, how could she attribute it to anything but imagination and not be accused of madness? The sight of mortals has narrowed since the war, Henrik. The Otherworld has been lost and forgotten—swallowed up by the mists of time. We are naught but fable, no more than fodder for legend and myth now. No sane mortal would attest to belief in the astral realm anymore, but in dreams . . ."

Henrik gasped. "You would not!"

"I would, and I will if needs must . . . when the time is right."

"You are going to tell her, then?"

Klaus smiled. "Dreams are curious things, old friend," he said. "They exist in the gauze between the real and the unreal. Once the veil is parted all things are possible, and you yourself reminded me that I have not two but three options."

Becca deliberately avoided Klaus that whole long day. Now she sent her excuses and cried off the evening meal as well, opting for another tray in her apartments. There would be consequences. He would never accept delayed fatigue after the accident as a reasonable excuse for her to absent herself from the dining hall so long. But she feared facing him, because if it hadn't been a dream she would know, and she would surely die of mortification.

The knock came all too soon at her sitting room door. She knew whose knuckles rapped on the ancient wood, and her heart took a tumble. Even the way he knocked on a door was a caress.

When she opened the door Klaus stood on the threshold, bearing a cordial glass filled with a shimmering plum-colored liquid on a silver salver. A sprig of rosemary was immersed in it.

"Something special for . . . fatigue," he said, through

a lopsided smile that thrilled her soul. There was nothing in his bearing that suggested anything untoward had occurred between them. Still, she couldn't help feeling that it had occurred. It had seemed so real. She could still feel the slippery moss underfoot and the cool mist from the waterfall sifting over her face.

"What is it?" she asked, nodding toward the glass. Stepping aside, she let him enter. There was no impropriety. Ulla was next door, laying out her nightdress, drawing the infernal draperies and turning down the bed, and the door between was open, after all.

"An old Gypsy remedy," he said. "Honey mead, with several drops of sweet wine, rum, vinegar, and water steeped with rosemary. Taken before bedtime, it is most beneficial. Come, sit with me and drink. This is an herbal house, *mitt kostbart*. There is no greater hand with the herbs in your land or mine than Anne-Lise. Her cures are the stuff of legend." He set the salver on the drum table at the edge of the carpet and removed the sprig of rosemary from the glass. "May I?" he said, striding to her bedchamber door.

"My lord?"

"I wish to place this under your pillow," he explained, his smile broadening. "It is said that a branch of rosemary steeped thus and placed under the pillow will bring pleasant dreams of a lady's true love."

Becca stood in the doorway watching as he placed the sprig of rosemary beneath the feather-down pillow on her bed with not a little flourish, meanwhile nodding to Ulla, who was looking on.

"There!" he said, joining her again. "Pleasant dreams, *mitt kostbart*. Perhaps that will encourage you to rest your head upon fine linen and soft down instead of the cold, hard woodwork, hmm? Now we sit, and talk a bit before I leave you to those dreams."

The cordial glass was in her hand before she realized she'd taken it. Sinking down on the chaise, she watched him take his seat in the wing chair opposite, his long legs stretched out as they had been when they'd first talked in the salon. The muscles in his corded thighs rippled beneath the faun-colored breeches. She'd seen what lay beneath them . . . at least once. That first time hadn't been a dream; that was a certainty. It had probably prompted what had happened last night. However, she didn't want to think about it now. Those images had already sent the blood rushing to her temples. She could just imagine the color of her cheeks. Blushing was the curse of her fair-skinned coloring.

"Drink, my lady," said Klaus. "That will give you none of its benefits while still in the glass."

Becca took a sip. "My stars! This is *strong*, my lord!"

"When did something weak as water ever cure anything?"

"I suppose . . . it is just that . . . I am unaccustomed to strong drink, my lord."

"I would hardly call that cordial 'strong drink,' 'tis medicinal—not a libation drunk for pleasure. Oh, now, such a face!" He laughed outright at her grimace. "How like a child you are, unspoiled by the world . . . unjaded by life. You are a delight, *mitt kostbart*. Do not let life taint you. Innocence comes at a price above gold."

Whether it was the effects of the cordial or just the inherent curiosity that had always been her undoing, Becca decided to draw him out . . . just to be sure. If one could ever be entirely sure with such a smooth-talking, enigmatic man as Count Klaus Lindegren.

"I'm worried that Father will return," she said. "You do not know him as I do. He will leave no stone unturned . . . and that chaise at the bottom of the gorge will not stay hidden forever. It is certain to be found, and—"

Klaus raised his hand. "It shan't be found," he said. "My stable hands removed it from the river yesterday morning, as soon as your father was on his way. It has been . . . dismantled. What parts they could not use as spares for my own vehicles have been burned or buried. The coaching company can well afford to take the loss, but you cannot afford the consequences of discovery. I told you that you can trust me, my lady. You need never fear coming to harm at my hands. Klaus Lindegren may be accused of many things, but he has never failed a lady in distress."

He sounded so sincere, yet she distinctly saw . . . something impossible. She shook her head to clear her vision, already fuzzy from the cordial, and her doubts, despite his smooth oration, still lingered.

"Th-thank you, my lord," she murmured. She would not let on that she suspected him of anything. Still, she did not fear him. Was that because of her attraction to the man that she could no longer deny? Possibly, but be that as it may, she'd felt safe in his presence from the start.

"I fear that I have inconvenienced you dreadfully," she said. "You are just come home to find yourself encumbered with an injured servant and a fugitive. I need to be away . . . for both our sakes, my lord."

"Curiously put," he mused. "Are you not comfortable here, my lady?"

"I am . . . too comfortable here, my lord. I wish to be on my way . . . before . . ."

"Before what, *mitt kostbart?*" His voice had mellowed to a sultry rumble that gripped her most private regions in a fist of achy fire. The man could arouse with a word. She was no match for such a seducer. The cordial had loosened her tongue and she'd spoken her heart. How could she take it back, when what she wanted most was to be in those strong, comforting arms again?

"I simply wish not to become . . . too comfortable, my lord," she said, avoiding his eyes.

"It is my experience that one can never be too comfortable when one is in the company of friends."

"I still must be on my way," she returned, "as soon as Maud is able. I should like to have an audience with Anne-Lise when it is convenient to assess her progress. I sat with Maud myself most of the morning. The swelling has subsided, though the bruise is still angry-looking. I expect that will remain awhile, but what concerns me is her listlessness. She sleeps much of the time—too much, to my thinking. I have known her since a child, my lord, and you may take me at my word that she is definitely not herself."

"First thing in the morning, you will consult with Anne-Lise in regard to your maid, of course," he said. "The poor girl cushioned your fall, my lady, and took a dreadful tumble. It is only natural that her healing will take time. She is improving—that I have seen for myself—and we must be grateful for it. She will be up and about in no time. Then, once she has regained her strength enough to serve you, I will see you to Plymouth personally. If you still wish to go there."

"Thank you, my lord, but I wouldn't think of imposing upon you further. I am well able to pay for a hired coach."

"Ahhh, yes, of course. But would that be wise, considering—to call attention to yourself in that way? Hired coaches can be traced. I fear that the cordial has foxed you, my lady. When the time comes, I shall see you safely to wherever it is you wish to go, but not tonight." He surged to his feet, took the empty cordial glass from her, and raised her up alongside him, his hand in hers. "We have talked long enough," he said. "It would be a pity to waste that cordial, hmm? Let Ulla minister to you . . . and sleep, *mitt kostbart*. There will be plenty of time for such decisions later."

Klaus raised her hand to his lips and kissed it gently,

caressing the soft flesh of her palm underneath with his fingers in the process. In spite of herself, a gentle murmur escaped her throat at the caress. It shot her through with sensations so foreign—so mystifying—they had to be forbidden. Her hand stiffened in his. He was awakening her to delights she had never imagined, and though she didn't understand what was happening to her, she wanted it to go on forever.

He raised his lips but did not release her hand, and met her gaze with eyes so dilated in the candlelight that she could not see their seawater blue shimmer. They were dark and mysterious now, and if she let herself, she would be lost in their obsidian shadows.

"Good night, my lord," she said, reclaiming her hand at last.

Klaus sketched a heel-clicking bow after his inimitable fashion. "Pleasant dreams . . . my lady."

# Chapter Six

"Where are we going?" Becca murmured. Klaus was leading her by the hand. She glanced down at her feet. They were bare. "My slippers!" she said.

"You shan't need them, *mitt kostbart*," he murmured. "Shhh, now! Come, we do not want to wake the others, hmm?"

What a strange dream. She barely felt her feet touch the floor as he led her down the spiral staircase and out through the rear entrance of the cottage toward the forest. The grass was cool and damp with the evening dew beneath her toes. A ground-creeping mist was forming. Looking down, Becca noticed that their feet were nearly hidden in it. Groping their ankles, it seemed to caress them as they followed the path deeper in. Oddly, it didn't appear anywhere else in the forest.

Klaus wasn't naked this time. Only his feet were bare. Had her sense of propriety clothed him for this nocturnal adventure? Evidently so, but he might as well have been naked. His black satin pantaloons picked out every corded muscle in his legs, buttocks, and thighs, and his Egyptian cotton shirt, open at the throat and divested of his usual impeccably tied neckcloth, gave a glimpse of the soft mat of hair like burnished bronze that lay beneath.

He had not given her time to collect her wrapper. The flowing voile nightdress, skimming her shoulders, was hardly proper attire for a walk in the moonlight with a gentleman—unless one did so in one's dreams, of course. The moonbeams shone right through. And despite the cool mist swirling about her bare feet, she was not cold; the night was steamy and still.

They walked in a land enchanted. Woodland creatures roamed the forest floor yet made no sound. It was as if a thousand eyes were watching—from the trees, from the mist, from the curious bobbing lights dancing all around them just out of reach. They walked on in silence, and when they reached the waterfall, Klaus turned Becca toward him.

"Welcome to my world, *mitt kostbart*," he said. "Is there any music more beautiful in all creation than that which the waterfall makes?"

Becca inclined her ear to the sound. Indeed, it did seem like voices singing. She stared at the silvery ribbon of shimmer cascading over moss-covered rocks to the river below, at the wraithlike clouds of gossamer spindrift rising from it, dancing on the moonbeams. All at once Klaus's essence overwhelmed her, his distinctive male scent mixed with the clean fragrance of sea grass, of sweet cress, of the waterfall itself. A soft sigh escaped her throat as she drank her fill of him.

"I am going to kiss you, *mitt kostbart*," he murmured against her hair.

Becca gazed into his eyes, dilated black in the darkness, shimmering now with glints of phosphorescence, as if creatures that dwelled in the sea lived there, darting this way and that in the moonlight. His lips drew nearer—lowering, hovering, tantalizing—

until she could bear no more before they took hers in a tender kiss that drained her senses. Becca moaned at their touch and leaned into the kiss as he deepened it, gliding his skilled tongue between her teeth, teasing hers with it until her heart began to race and pound and echo in her ears. Unprepared for such an intimacy, she stiffened as though she'd been stung but could not bring herself to break the spell. He tasted her deeply, drawing her closer in the strong, sinewy arms she so longed to feel about her in her waking hours. Now, in the safety of the dream, there were no restrictions. Propriety held no sway over her here. She could abandon herself to her desires, to the awakening of her body to the forbidden sensations his embrace had set loose upon her.

Skilled fingers caressed her face, slid along her arched throat to her shoulders. Becca stood stock still as those deft fingers inched her nightdress down until he had bared her breasts to the mist that bound them there to the wood—bound them to the fall of moonlit water rushing into the river, frosting the night with gossamer sheen.

How tall he was, looming over her. How handsome he appeared, like an ancient god of myth risen from the mist, the moon-glow gleaming off the silvery streak in his hair. How like the waterfall itself that silvery wave seemed, standing out in bold relief against the rest.

His hooded gaze devoured her as he cupped first one breast and then the other, his thumbs grazing her nipples, bringing them erect. Groaning, he swooped down and took one in his mouth—sucking, nipping, circling it with his tongue until she cried out with pleasure.

Crushing her against his bruising hardness, he groaned again, and Becca gasped as he seized her hand and drove it down against the bulge of his sex, grown tight against his trouser seam. She gasped again as it responded to her touch. His searching mouth found her lips and swallowed the sound, mingled now with his own guttural groan.

All at once her hand was touching hot, veined flesh, not black satin, and her heart leapt. Pulsating ripples of achy heat were pumping through her very core. Lost in the wonder of him, in the heat of a passion unknown to her—in the magic of the breathless, sultry night—she tried to fight her way out of the dream. If it *was* a dream. It seemed so real. Her whole being was on fire for him.

All at once his voice sounded far away, as though unseen hands had wrenched them apart. She reached toward the place where he had been, but her hands closed upon air instead of throbbing flesh and taut muscle. The light failed. Where had the moon gone? Where had the arms gone that had held her so tenderly—so desperately? All that remained was his scent threading through her nostrils, surrounding her, filling her. It ghosted through her like a flesh-tearing wind, though there wasn't a breath of breeze in the forest. Then, in the distance, riding the imaginary zephyr, his deep, mellow voice echoed on the edge of consciousness.

"Sleep, *mitt kostbart*," he murmured. "The dream is done . . . for now."

Klaus staggered down the spiral staircase and reeled out through the back door of the cottage, leaving it flung wide behind him. Lady Rebecca Gildersleeve was back safe in her bed, none the worse for wear, no thanks to him. Hating himself for what he'd done and nearly done, he stumbled along the path in the wood, loosing a primeval moan that woke the sleeping birds and gave them flight. Every creature in his path fled his approach. Even the bobbing lights deserted him then, as he strode through the tall grass at the edge of the path and sank to his knees on the brink of the waterfall, pounding his fists on the moss-covered rocks until they came away slimed green, scuffed, and bleeding. His rigid shoulders heaved with dry, wracking sobs, and it wasn't until a gentle hand touched his shoulder, that he raised his head and stared through the mist of tears toward Henrik standing over him.

"Come away, your highness," the elder said. "Enough mischief has been done for one night."

"I've told you not to address me thus!" Klaus thundered.

"Who is to hear us in this place?"

"It matters not. Do it here and you will slip and do it in company."

"The urges are strong tonight," the elder observed. "It is always so when the moon is full and time is short. You know that, my lord. What were you playing at here? What were you trying to prove?"

"That I am master of my urges."

"And . . . have you done?"

"That should be fairly obvious," Klaus snapped, staring at the elder through the unshed tears in his narrowed eyes. "But not soon enough. The cordial I gave her . . . She thought she was dreaming, Henrik. That is what I meant her to think. I wanted to show her our world . . . gently. I was not prepared for her response to my advances. I thought she would keep me at a distance. She snatches her hand away when I try to offer a courtesy kiss ordinarily. She never would have allowed such . . . liberties in a conscious state. She is a lady."

"I warned you of the consequences of dreams. She evidently resonates to your feelings, or has begun to, at least in her subconscious mind. What else could you expect? You have awakened her to life. It is always thus with a female's first awakening—even in the world of mortals. What more perfect a subject could you possibly hope to find? I do not see the difficulty."

"You do not walk in my shoes, Henrik! She is an innocent—above reproach."

"And ripe for conquest, just as the others have been," the elder said. "Ideal for your purpose; you cannot deny it. Why will you not take her and have done, as it has always been with the *Fossegrim* since time out of mind? You cannot convince me that you do not want her—not after this."

"It is because I want her that I cannot take her, Henrik. It is because I ache to live inside her that I must not. This test is not for her. It is for *me*."

"And what comes next? You cannot mean to tell her who—*what*—you really are. That you exist between the parallel worlds of mortal man and the fey? That you must live within range of a waterfall—*your waterfall*, the one you have claimed as your own. That you must go to it daily to draw your strength or whither and die, and each mating season—each generation—take a mortal woman in that special place sacred to your kind. Will you also tell her that if she is the favored one, she will conceive a son from that mating and raise him alone, never to see you again? That when he is grown, he, too, will be driven to seek out his own waterfall, and do as you, his father and his prince, have done to keep your race alive?"

"If I do, I will not tell her in that cold and clinical manner, Henrik."

"You are not the only one in the history of our people who has done what you are contemplating. One case in particular too close to home comes to mind, and you know all too well the consequences of that occasion. The gods will hardly countenance the father *and* the son turned renegade. The tragedy of your father's untimely end as the result of his defection alone should be enough to deter you."

"You have no idea what I am contemplating."

Henrik raised his hand and backed up a pace. "No, I do not!" he said. "And do not tell me! I would rather not know. There is one thing, though, that curiosity bids me ask. What makes this mortal female so unlike the others?"

"I do not know, but it has never happened before. When the time came for me to continue the species, it was done as a matter of necessity, with no more emotion than any bodily function. There was no heart in it."

"*Heart*, is it?" the elder spat in disgust. "You have lived too long among these mortals. If only you would confine your visits here to once each generation to fulfill your obligation like the others. . . . But, no! You spend more time here in the physical world than you do in the astral, where you belong."

Klaus surged to his feet and staggered toward the waterfall. There was solace waiting for him there. He had always been able to go to it for comfort, just as a child goes to its mother's breast. It was a ritual as old as time, a rite as old as the fjords that spawned the elders who came before him. He would let it embrace him until the moonless darkness before dawn called him back to what the mortals called "the real world." So was the way of the *Fossegrim*.

"Perhaps, old friend," he said, disappearing behind the ribbon of shimmering water, "it is not that I have lived too long among them, but simply that I have lived too long."

Becca yawned and stretched awake at first light. Klaus's scent was all around her. Then she remembered the dream. It stole across her memory, triggering a conflicted wave of delight and remorse so soul-shattering that she hid her face in the down pillow as if to escape it. There was something shockingly real about the dreams she'd had since entering Lindegren Hall. This last had left her weak and trembling, longing to feel those lips—tasting, probing—and those strong arms clasping her fast in a smothering embrace again.

She reached beneath her pillow and drew out the sprig of rosemary. It smelled of the wood, of the strange ingredients in the cordial . . . and of him. She tucked it back in place again, and ran her hands down the length of her body, where his hands had roamed—over her breasts and belly and thighs. All at once a cold chill like a ghostly wind overspread her skin with gooseflesh, and she vaulted upright in the bed. If it had only been a dream, why did her belly and the mound beneath ache from the bruising pressure of his aroused manhood leaning heavily against her?

Hot blood surged to her temples and her heart began to pound. How could a dream bruise her? She swung her feet over the side of the bed. No. There was no mistaking it. The soreness was real. All else was suspect.

Ulla entered, and helped her dress for breakfast. More than once she saw the young maid cast a sidelong glance in her direction, no doubt monitoring the color of her cheeks. Becca didn't need to consult the mirror; they were on fire. But she would not hide in her chamber any longer. She would go down to breakfast and view *his* color after the supposed *dream*—but not before she'd given her own body time to return to some semblance of normalcy.

"How does my abigail fare this morning?" she asked, sitting at the vanity for the maid to arrange her hair.

"Well enough ta complain, m'lady," said Ulla. "She's on the mend, there's no doubt. Anne-Lise is goin' ta let her up outta the bed for a bit this afternoon."

"Good!" said Becca. "I will sit with her then. I wish a

word with Anne-Lise before I go down to the breakfast room. Will you summon her, please?"

The maid tugged the bell cord, and the housekeeper appeared on the threshold as if she had been waiting outside the chamber door. The way the servants at Lindegren Hall kept appearing and disappearing was jarring, to say the least, but welcome in this instance, since Becca was anxious to go down to breakfast and face Klaus before her courage flagged.

"I wish to know of my abigail's progress," she said as the housekeeper sketched a curtsy.

"The master told me ta expect your inquiry last evening," Anne-Lise said, "and I'm pleased ta say that she's comin' on right fine, m'lady."

"That is excellent news!" said Becca. "How soon will she be fit for travel?"

"Oh, that I can't say, m'lady. She's only just gettin' outta bed today for a bit. It's goin' ta depend upon how well she does gettin' up and about. The master is most particular about her bein' fit ta serve you proper before he gives me leave ta pronounce her well."

"Before *he* gives *you* leave?" Becca said. "So it is the master's decision, not yours—*her nurse*—when my maid is fit enough that I may leave Lindegren Hall and continue my journey?" Hot blood surged to her temples, from anger now, and after she'd worked so hard to fade the blush from her cheeks, too. That was unfortunate. Count Klaus Lindegren would just have to suffer her with a face like a lobster. "Well, we shall just see about that!"

"Oh, no, m'lady," Anne-Lise defended. "The master has only your welfare at heart . . . and your abigail's. His word is law in this house in all things. Is that not how it is among your . . . I mean, in English nobles' homes?"

"Here is 'how it is,' " said Becca. Shoving Ulla's hands away as the maid attempted to add ribbons to her hair, she surged to her feet. "Enough, thank you, Ulla," she said in an aside to the girl. "I shall go as I am. Unadorned." Then, to the housekeeper: "There will be no more tinctures. Maud is not accustomed to them, and she evidently does not tolerate them well. They are making her listless and weak. Nature is the best healer. *I* will decide when she is fit for travel, not you or your master. She is my responsibility—not yours, and certainly not your master's. Now, if you will excuse me, I will go and tell him the same!"

Turning her back on Anne-Lise's curtsy and Ulla's stifled gasp, Becca marched along the corridor and pattered down the spiral staircase as though her feet had wings.

Klaus was filling his plate at the sideboard when she skittered to a halt on the threshold. He turned, the plate suspended, and beamed a smile in her direction.

"Good morning, my lady," he said. "I trust you slept well?"

"No, my lord, I did not sleep well," Becca snapped. "And I did not wake well, either."

"I am truly sorry to hear that," he said, frowning. "I had hoped—"

"What had you 'hoped,' my lord? That you might keep me prisoner here indefinitely? I have just come from an interview with Anne-Lise—"

"And she told you this?" he interrupted. Strolling to the table, he set down his plate of coddled eggs, baked tomatoes, sausage, and caraway cheese biscuits, but remained standing.

"She did not have to, my lord. I have eyes in my head. Maud improves yet grows weaker. Her eyes are vacant and glazed. The stars alone know what she sees with them. She cannot stay awake long enough to see much. Any fool could see that she is being drugged. I want the herbal tinctures stopped at once! I have told

Anne-Lise as much, and now I have told you, since she tells me it is *you* not she who will decide when I may leave Lindegren Hall."

"Will you not sit and break your fast with me?" said Klaus in that pearly-smooth tone that had always melted her. Not so this time.

"I have no appetite at the moment, my lord. Well? Will you not explain yourself?"

"If you will not join me, will you at least sit so that I may? My food grows cold."

Becca bristled, and sank like a stone in a chair at the opposite end of the table.

"Thank you, my lady," he said, taking his seat with a flourish. "I would really prefer that you join me. It will be rude of me to eat in front of you. At least let Olav pour your coffee, hmm? If we must quarrel, do let us be civilized about it."

Until that moment, Becca hadn't even been aware that Olav was in the room—or had he been in the room a moment ago? She studied him skeptically. Another mysterious appearance?

Klaus signaled the footman, and he filled her cup. The audacity of the man! How was it that he always managed to charm her so thoroughly? Was he a sorcerer, this strange Swedish count whose servants addressed him as royalty?

"You are not a prisoner here," he said, taking up his fork. "I simply do as my conscience dictates. I mean to be certain that you are in good hands before I turn you out in a world where you are most certainly to face danger at the hands of men who would do you harm. I would be remiss as a host and as a gentleman to do otherwise."

"And the tincture?"

He sighed and set his fork down—with painstaking control, thought Becca, looking on. He didn't need to say a word, though she knew he would, and her heart sank. She'd been hoping that her suspicions were unfounded. Evidently not.

"You are quite right," he said. "I instructed Anne-Lise to dose your maid, and to keep her dosed until she was sufficiently recovered. She was in pain, my lady. I will not permit any living creature to suffer pain in my presence when it can be avoided. Nothing harmful was given her, only mild herbs that would allow her to rest so that her body could recover naturally. My . . . people are masters of the healing arts. Their skill with herbals is second to none. What you do not know is that the dosage has been lessened steadily, else she would not be getting out of bed this afternoon. And I have already instructed Anne-Lise to discontinue the dose altogether." He gestured toward her cup. "Your coffee is getting cold," he said.

"I want to leave, my lord," said Becca. "I want to leave now. Something . . . untoward is going on here. If you are the gentleman you pretend to be, you will not oppose me, sir."

Klaus stiffened. "You wound me, my lady," he said.

The tragic look of him drove her eyes away. There was something so genuine in it that she was almost ashamed she'd taken him to task so severely—almost . . . but not quite. She hadn't forgotten the *dream*, though she tried not to think of that then, grateful that this new press had put it in the shade for the moment.

"Your father will have reached Plymouth by now, and learned that you did not arrive there," he went on. "We both know he will be coming back, leaving no stone unturned, as you say, along the way in search of you. I told you that I will see you to wherever it is you wish to go when you are ready to leave. Do you really suppose it would be wise for us to be abroad, traveling along the same highway he will surely take returning?

Would it be prudent for me to be caught transporting you after denying your presence in this house? Such an inevitable discovery would surely lead to a confrontation—a duel, perhaps? I abhor violence and would be hard-put to justify such a thing with an old man. Would it not be wiser for you to remain here until all danger of such as that were past, and your maid recovered enough to minister to you properly once we part company? Be reasonable, *mitt kostbart*."

How was it that the man could make the most bizarre circumstance seem perfectly natural? He had a talent for it, and she was no match for him in any regard, she was learning. On the surface, he was right, of course, but her every instinct cried out against remaining. This enigmatic man had undermined her reason and crept into her heart. Dared she stay and let him jeopardize her very soul?

"What would you say if I were to insist that you have your stableman hitch up your carriage at once?" she asked.

He shrugged. "I would give the command."

There was a long silence.

"Is that what you truly want, *mitt kostbart*? Do you trust me so little? Have I ever done anything to cause you harm?"

Becca dropped her head in her hands. "I . . . I do not know," she moaned.

Klaus surged to his feet and skirted the table. Raising her up also, he took her in his arms. In spite of herself, Becca did not resist. Those strong arms holding her against his hard-muscled chest were her most cherished secret fantasy.

This was no dream. The sun was beaming through the leaded panes, casting rainbows on the wall, on the white linen tablecloth. The glare was dizzying. His clean scent threaded through her nostrils at close range. It was like a drug, draining her senses, drawing her closer. No man should have such power over a woman.

"Will you trust me with your precious life just a little longer, *mitt kostbart?*" he murmured against her hair.

His voice was husky with desire, drawing her closer still. How she wanted to trust him. How she wanted to believe him. His heart was hammering against her breast through the peach muslin frock. All at once something else throbbed lower down, leaning against the soreness left behind by the ghost of another arousal. If this was not a dream, how could *that* have been?

Pushing Klaus away with both hands pressed firmly against his chest, Becca uttered a strangled moan and fled the breakfast room.

# Chapter Seven

"My lady, wait!" Klaus called, bolting after her. She had nearly reached the staircase when he spun her around to face him. Her hazel eyes brimming with tears brought a mist of tears to his own. He could not think beyond the fact that he had put them there. "We need to settle this," he murmured, steering her inside the salon across the way.

It was obvious that she wasn't convinced that what had occurred between them in the night was a dream. Somehow he had to remedy that if they were to go forward. Cursing himself for the weakness of the flesh, for the power of the mating madness that had let him go too far, he eased her down on the chaise and sat beside her.

If he had been in his natural state last night, it would have been far worse, especially considering her response to his advances. The fey followed no code of ethics—no stilted protocols, no rigid proprieties or sensibilities, when it came to mating. Their code was among themselves, and it was carnal, erotic, and sensual beyond the experience of mortal man.

Both incarnations were doing battle for supremacy in him now, and only one thing was certain: He could not let her go, not now, knowing she returned his feelings. Not ever, now that he had faced his own.

"I had what I thought was a dream last night, my lord," she said. "I need to know if it truly *was* a dream, because if it was not, I have disgraced myself, and you, sir, are no gentleman!"

"The rosemary under your pillow," Klaus said, aiming for nonchalance—praying that he was better at it than she. "It has been known to bring quite scandalous dreams, *mitt kostbart*. That is, of course, its purpose. Who knows what . . . alchemy was afoot last night? I am most flattered that you evidently dreamed of me, no matter in what context, but if my alter ego overstepped his bounds, I must apologize. Perhaps I should have placed a sprig beneath my own pillow. I slept quite soundly last night, my slumber quite devoid of . . . dreams."

How charming she was when she blushed. The glow was not confined to her face. It spread down over her throat and décolletage, calling attention to the soft, round swell of her perfect breasts. It was all he could do to keep from reaching for that sweet flesh. He cursed the mating madness that had hold of his loins like hot pincers. He shifted position, gritted his teeth, and tried to ignore the sweat beading on his brow, and the *pain*. It was no use; his sex was on fire for her. How he longed to take her in his arms again, but this was not the time for that. Fighting the urges with gritted teeth and controlled breathing, he took her hand in his instead.

"Would you care to tell me about this dream?" he said.

"*No!*" she cried. "I want to leave, my lord. *I* shall decide when Maud is fit for travel. Not you. Not Anne-Lise."

"Just so, *mitt kostbart*," he soothed. "I shall leave it entirely up to you." It was a risk, but what else was he to do? "Sit with her this afternoon. If you feel that she is ready to leave, I will see you to the coast post-haste, as promised."

"No more tinctures?"

"No—none."

"And no more cordials for me, my lord."

He raised his hands in defeat. "Nothing stronger than sherry wine. You have my word."

She was silent apace.

"My lord . . . did you walk in the wood last evening?" she asked at last.

He hesitated. "I walk in the wood every evening," he said. "I like to . . . how do you say . . . commune with nature. It relaxes me, and reminds me of the homeland that I miss so dreadfully. But most of all, I enjoy my solitude there. I am a very . . . private person, my lady."

"I . . . did not . . . walk there with you . . . ?"

"That must have been some dream, *mitt kostbart*."

She blushed again, and his heart skipped a beat. How lovely she was, with the apples of her cheeks aflame, with the sunlight striking her strawberry-blond curls. How perfectly formed she was. He had seen what lay beneath the soft muslin frock. He had tasted her charms, and been beguiled by her innocent abandon to his caresses. He mustn't think of that now or it would happen all over again, but the primal, Other-worldly urges were calling him now. Time was growing short. The full moon would soon wane. Before it waxed full again, he must decide. Scarcely two fortnights and he must mate and fulfill his destiny . . . again, or be cast out in disgrace, shunned by his kind, condemned to live and possibly die as a mortal man, as the Tribunal dictated. It mattered not that he was the prince. There was no such thing as primogeniture among the *Fossegrim*. There would always be another ready to take his place, with the elders' blessing. He had but a month to win her heart and her trust if he were to claim her as a mortal man. No more than a blink in the jaundiced eye of time, if he were to take her as Prince of the *Fossegrim*. He had to keep her here until he decided. That meant undoing what, in the heat of passion, he had done in her supposed dream. All at once, inspiration struck.

"I know," he said, discovery lifting his baritone. "I shall show you! You have a—how shall I say—a fascination for the wood, no? The servants have said it."

"My lord?"

"You are intrigued by the forest, and the waterfall that lives there. Perhaps you would like to see first-hand what it is that I love so. I should like to show you. Perhaps you would walk with me there, once you have visited your maid. At the twilight hour—before dark, of course," he hastened to add. "It is most beautiful then, when the sunset strikes the falls. It is not safe for you to go below alone, I'm afraid. The spindrift and the mist make the approach slippery. I myself have mis-stepped on those moss-covered rocks. And then there is your father. If anyone is keeping you prisoner here, it is he. You daren't be seen outside in daylight, while he is abroad hunting you. But at twilight, sheltered among the trees, you would be safe . . . with me."

"I . . . I do not know, my lord," she hedged.

"I merely wish to show you the reality of this place, *mitt kostbart*, so that you might put your dream in its proper place, and see things as they truly are. There is a fine line between reality and dreams. I would not have whatever vision it was that tampered with your slumber spoil this beautiful place for you, to say nothing of spoiling me in your eyes. Do say yes, hmm?"

Again there was silence.

"You do not trust me," he said, answering his own

question. "You will never know how this pains me, my lady, to be chastised for the actions of a phantom in your dreams."

"How do you know my *phantom* needs chastising unless you are, indeed, he?" she snapped.

"There is no mystery to it. Your flaming cheeks attest to that, *mitt kostbart*. If it is a chaperone you desire, I shall call Ulla from her chores to accompany us. Would that suit? You must forgive my ignorance of all the protocols. As I have said before, such things are not so rigidly enforced in my . . . homeland. If I err, it is because I am not yet familiar with all the rules. There are so many, after all."

"That won't be necessary," said Becca.

"Does that mean that you do not wish me to engage Ulla . . . or that you will not stroll with me tonight?"

"I am just as anxious to put my dream to rest as you are, my lord," said Becca. "More so, I think."

"But you are still afraid," he knew.

"Yes," she murmured. "But not of you, my lord."

Becca wanted to say, *I'm not afraid of you, my lord, I'm afraid of myself*, but she didn't. She left him for the rest of the morning to wrestle with the wisdom of accepting his invitation.

Anne-Lise and Ulla helped Maud into the wing chair in her bedchamber, and nuncheon trays were brought for the abigail, and for Becca as well. Julienne soup, hot little rolls à la Duchesse, poached pears, and custard. Maud ate like a bird, needing Becca's help to manage her soup. She only nibbled at a roll, and cried off on the pears and custard altogether. Becca scarcely ate anything herself. She had lost her appetite. Klaus was right: Maud was in no condition to travel. There was no question that she was on the mend; the swelling on her brow was gone now, and the bruise was fading. It was the lethargy that troubled Becca. Perhaps now that the herbal draughts were to cease, the maid would regain her strength. She had to; so much depended upon it. If they remained at Lindegren Hall much longer, she wouldn't be able to leave it . . . to leave him.

At first she'd thought it was because he was so dashing, and the first man who had paid her any attention. It would stand to reason that a lady's first infatuation would render her birdwitted. But while that might have been the case at the start, her regard for Count Klaus Lindegren went much deeper now. The physical and obvious aside, some enigmatic facet in the man had touched her heart. Perhaps it was the air of mystery about him, or the glimmer of sadness she'd seen in his haunting seawater-colored eyes. What she most admired was his acute sense of honor and gentility, despite denying any understanding of the ways of the English aristocracy. What refinement English gentlemen possessed was learned—spoon-fed them—in the nursery. What Klaus Lindegren possessed seemed inherent. There was no pretense in the man, as she'd seen in so many of the coxcombs and dandies of her father's acquaintance. Refinement came to Klaus as easily as drawing breath. It was simply who he was, and she felt safe with him . . . at least, she had until the dream.

Still, the very air of mystery that drew her like a moth to the flame kept her at a distance. She had no experience with worldly men. That frightened her. She knew she was no match for his prowess; but like the moth, she could not help herself from venturing too close to a fire that would consume her.

Klaus called for her at twilight. She'd spent half the afternoon deciding what to wear for their outing. Finally, she had settled upon a high-waisted sprigged muslin frock, with dainty puffed sleeves and a modest décolletage that allowed for comfort while preserving decorum. She would not take a wrap, since the evening promised to be just as sweltering as the day had been. The costume suited for dinner as well, since that would occur after their walk.

He offered his arm, and she took it as they walked along the path. A pearly mist was rising from the forest floor. Weaving in and out among the ground-creeping vines, it seemed to pick and choose which plants to shroud and which to reject. The roar of the waterfall beckoned as they approached. Tinted red in the low-sliding sun, the sight took Becca's breath away, and she gasped.

"Did I not tell you it was beautiful?" said Klaus, covering the hand looped through his arm with his own. It was warm and strong, the long tapered fingers caressing as he spoke. "Waterfalls are sacred in my homeland," he went on. "The Swedes regard them as hallowed places, each possessed of its own spirit guardian. Come. Sit with me, and I will tell you a tale the elders tell."

He led her to a fallen log, stripped off his coat, and laid it down for her to sit upon, then sank down in the tall grass alongside and leaned his elbow on the log, gazing up at her. Why were his eyes so blue? Bluer than any she had ever seen. And the look in them! That gaze of his was nothing less than an intimate embrace. His eyes mirrored the smile on his lips, and waves of a thrill like the cascading fall itself broke over her soul. The man had the power to mesmerize with a look alone, and to ravage with a smile.

"Is it to be a true story or a fable, my lord?" she asked.

"I shall let you decide. The spirit guardians I spoke of are called the *Fossegrim,* male entities of the fey who live in the falls, and protect them. When time began, they were much smaller than human men, but as time drew on and their race began to dwindle, the gods granted them stature, that they might mate with human females, and thus perpetuate their line. The fey have always coveted the world of mortal man, you see, in much the same way as your lower classes envy the aristocracy."

Becca considered it, but made no reply.

"With stature came the power to transcend the worlds," he went on, "and once each generation, during the mating season, the *Fossegrim* crosses over from the Otherworld to inhabit his earthly waterfall, there to lure a mortal maiden and seduce her. Though he may live apart just as a mortal lives, he cannot stray far from his waterfall. From it, he draws his strength. He has one month to accomplish his mission, to fulfill his destiny, or forever remain in the mortal world, unable to return to the astral realm. Failure dooms him to live and die as a mortal dies. All privilege comes at a price."

Fascinated, Becca hung on his every word. She had not heard this fable before, and his delivery was so impassioned that the woodland creatures had crept close along the forest curtain, as if they were just as enthralled with the tale as she.

"And if the lady resists him?" she queried.

"The lure of the *Fossegrim* driven by mating lust is irresistible, *mitt kostbart*," he said. "The mortal female goes to him eagerly, and from their mating she conceives a son, who bears all resemblance to a mortal male until he is grown. When he reaches manhood he, too, gains the power to travel between worlds, as his father before him. He is *Fossegrim*, immortal, destined to seek out his own waterfall in the world of humans and, like his father before him, fulfill his destiny and perpetuate his race."

"And what of his mother, and the creature that sired him?" asked Becca. Did Klaus flinch? It seemed so. He evidently took his legends seriously. Perhaps she shouldn't have called the hero of his tale a *creature*. "Does he remain with her to raise their child?"

"No," said Klaus, through a tremor. "Once they have mated, he returns to the Otherworld—the astral, the world of the fey that exists on a parallel plane with this mortal realm . . . never to see her again."

"Are all your Swedish fables so sad, my lord?" said Becca. "A woman's heart is nothing to toy with. Your countrymen are possessed of a flair for the melodramatic, I think . . . or is it a total disregard for womankind that prompts such stories? I have heard it said that Swedes have been known to be quite . . . aggressive with their women."

Klaus didn't reply. He surged to his feet and brushed the loose grass spears from his breeches. "So you have decided," he said. Reaching for her hand, he raised her to her feet and took back his coat, folding it over his arm.

"My lord?"

"When we began, I said you should be the one to decide if my tale were fable or truth," he said. "You evidently have decided."

"Of course. What else but fable could it be? You told it well, however, my lord, with such passion in the delivery that, were I not possessed of a logical mind, you would surely have convinced me."

He smiled, looping her arm through his again. "A logical mind can be a . . . handicap, *mitt kostbart*," he said. "It limits one's imagination, and one's spirit. Think of the mind that once created such a tale. *Limitless*."

"My mother and my governess used to read me fairy tales when I was still in leading strings," Becca mused. "They were grand fun, but, of course, I knew they couldn't be real—not *really* real, you understand. Though there were times . . ."

"Yes?" he prompted. He seemed almost anxious, hanging on her every word.

"There were times when I wished they could be . . .

you know? Enchanted lands, fairies with gossamer wings dancing in fairy rings beneath the moon." She laughed. "Once, my governess fashioned me a pair of wings from milliner's wire and netting scraps. She pinned them to my frock and turned me loose in the garden to frolic among the butterflies. I always wondered if they really were butterflies flitting from flower to flower, or if I did indeed dance amongst the fairies?"

"Enchanting," Klaus murmured.

"Why did you tell me your tale, my lord?" Becca asked.

He shrugged. "To put you at your ease . . . and to give you a taste of my culture. Have you enjoyed our little walk in the wood this evening? Have I chased away your phantom—put him in his place?"

"Y-yes, my lord." She dared not tell him that he'd only made the phantom stronger, and risk remaining longer in that all-too-familiar setting with him.

"Excellent!" he said. "Now that I have shared a bit of my homeland with you, I would like you to experience a part of it firsthand." Reaching into his waistcoat pocket, he produced a small conch shell, pearly white on the outside, blushing pink on the inside. It fit in the palm of his hand. "Hold it thus," he said, placing it over her ear. She took a step back from him as the cold shell touched her. "Nooo," he murmured. "Do not fear it . . . *listen*. Do you hear? The roar of the North Sea . . . the sea of my homeland. I brought it with me from the shores of Sweden so I would always have a connection to the land I love—even in exile. Here, take it, hold it yourself. It was made to fit that delicate ear. See how perfectly it rests against it?"

Fascinated, Becca listened to what, indeed, sounded like the sighing of a great ocean. She smiled. And it did fit her ear. It was a long moment before she handed it back to him.

"No!" he said. "It is for you, *mitt kostbart*—a token to

remember me by when you . . . leave me to continue your journey. When you hold it thus and listen to the sighing of the ocean, you will think kindly of me, a humble count from a far-off land who came to your rescue in your time of need, and smile a little . . . just as you do now, yes?"

"Oh, but I couldn't take this," Becca protested. "How will you have the North Sea to comfort you if I do?" She shook her head, setting her curls atremble, and held it out to him, albeit reluctantly. "No . . . I couldn't."

Klaus took her hand in his and folded her fingers around the shell. "I have others, *mitt kostbart,*" he murmured, smiling softly down at her. Were those tears glistening in his seawater eyes? "I chose this one for you because I knew it was a perfect fit for that shell-like ear of yours, and it must fit snugly for you to hear the sound at its most powerful because of its size. Please take it. This is my home now, and I will take great comfort in the fact that this little seashell will forever bind us . . . It will be as if we are together, even when we are apart. Do this for me, hmm? I do not want you to forget me."

"It isn't likely that I will ever forget you, my lord," she said demurely, unable to meet his eyes then, for the strange look in them. A bold statement, but true. How could she ever forget him?

Slipping her hand through the slit in the side of her frock, she took out the little pocket suspended on a ribbon attached to her bodice underneath and tucked the little conch shell safely inside.

"Good!" he said, leading her back along the path the way they'd come. "Now we must return to the cottage. The light is fading, and Cook will be cross if we are late for dinner, hmm? She so rarely gets to prepare for company."

"Thank you, my lord," Becca murmured. "You are

too kind." The dream seemed far away now that they'd left the waterfall behind. And yet . . .

"It is my pleasure," Klaus replied. "But now I must ask for your promise that you will not ever come here alone. It simply is not safe."

Becca laughed. "Why?" she chided. "Are you afraid I will meet one of your *Fossegrim?*"

"One never knows, *mitt kostbart,*" he murmured. "One never knows."

# Chapter Eight

"So now what, my lord?" Henrik asked, helping Klaus change into his black tailcoat for dinner. His blue afternoon coat would have sufficed had it not suffered tree sap stains from the fallen log in the wood.

"Do not rush me. These thing take time," Klaus said, shrugging the coat on.

"Time, my lord, is something you can ill afford to squander. What is the press? You desire her, she evidently desires you. I do not see the difficulty. You could have done before the sun rises and leave her for her father to collect, while we quit this inhospitable realm. It isn't as though she will come to harm. He has already arranged a husband for her. She will not be left to raise the offspring alone as so many of the others have had to do, if that is what worries you. The way seems clear. Why do you hesitate?"

Klaus spun to face him. "I do not think that I can leave her," he snapped. He could scarcely stand being parted from her for an hour. Permanent separation was incomprehensible to him, now that he had held her in his arms, suckled at those perfect breasts, tasted the honey of her lips, her skin. "She has crept inside me, Henrik. I can *feel* her inside as if she is a part of me, moving when I move, breathing when I breathe, waiting underneath my skin, arousing me, tormenting me. How can I leave her and bear *that* for all eternity?"

"The longer you wait, the more difficult it will be."

"It is already too difficult. My desire for this woman is greater than my desire to procreate."

"Ah!" the elder cried, throwing his arms in the air. "Have you forgotten that I am responsible for you? Have you no care for my chastisement if I fail you?"

"You have options, Henrik."

"I am too old for *options*, my lord. I have grown too accustomed to immortality. Living eternally, with no fear of death, earning my place with the higher forms beyond the Golden Bower in my old age appeals to me tremendously."

"Immortality can be . . . overrated, old friend."

"So, you have decided. Well, then, there is nothing to be done but wait for the moon to wax full again and—"

"I have not decided, Henrik," Klaus interrupted. "There is still one more option, or had you forgotten?"

"But surely not a *serious* one. . . ."

"I am inclined to agree, but should not all options be exhausted in a decision of this magnitude?"

"I suppose, though I cannot imagine her allowing you to hand her over into our world for a glimpse of what she would be facing, much less facing it in earnest. And what if you did manage to persuade her to stay there with you? Do you imagine that she would be willing to sit idly by each mating season while you cross over and impregnate another to fulfill your obligation? You dream! It will never happen. My lord, these are *mortals*! They view the fey as fantasy, actors on a stage—players in a storybook designed to amuse children. Congeniality between the species was snuffed out eons ago, when they betrayed us. These petty skirmishes that mortals engage in here that they call *wars* are of no more consequence than a raindrop in the ocean compared to the Great War between man and fey. She may be willing enough to adapt; mortals have short memories, and tend to file away what seems improbable to them under the guise of legends. But we record the ancestral memories within, as you well know. We have total recall since time out of mind, which is why so many among us continue to plague the mortals so relentlessly. In view of that, do you really see her welcomed in the Otherworld? Have you become so obtuse in your pursuit of *love?*"

"I know it must be tested," said Klaus.

"And how do you propose to do that, pray? You cannot simply take her hand and cross her over. You have tried to prepare her with your tale, and she still hasn't the capacity to part legend from truth—despite your passionate oration."

"You were spying upon us, Henrik?"

"I am trying to *help* you. We, all of us, spy. We must. It is part of our legacy. And we are well equipped. Hah! Did you not enter m'lady's chamber on her first night in residence and gaze down upon her as she slept? Do not lecture me for spying. Now! She will not have the tincture again, and I cannot see her going willingly into a realm that she clearly does not believe exists. Tell me how you plan to show her our world."

"She will not have the tincture, 'tis true, but you are forgetting the fey wine. *That* she will drink if I drink it with her and it is poured from the same decanter. It will have no effect on me, but it is the means of parting the veil that our kind has always used to bring mortals over. You are getting old, Henrik. You will be passing through the Golden Bower before you know it, old friend. I cannot believe you have forgotten fey wine."

"I haven't forgotten, my lord," said the elder, his

words riding a sigh. "I was hoping you wouldn't resort to it. Once she's drunk it, her recall could be cruel . . . and permanent. Would it not be better to let her forget?"

"I am just selfish enough to want her to remember me. If I cannot have her, I will have that."

"My heart goes out to you, my lord," said the elder. "*Love!*" he spat in disgust. "Our version of the emotion is kinder, I'm thinking, being mental and not so monogamous, not this . . . this savage, all-consuming blight that seizes the mind and tears the heart to shreds. It is . . . uncivilized. Is it worth it, when all is said and done?"

"It is all that you say of it," said Klaus. "And yet . . . it is, I think, the one thing I cannot live without any longer, this side of the veil or the other."

Becca scarcely touched the oysters au gratin, and Olav was about to serve the squab. It wasn't the food; everything was delicious. She had no appetite. Across the table, Klaus relished his meal with gusto. Why couldn't she relax and do likewise? Except for the nagging possibility of her father's return, everything seemed as it should be. Klaus had gone out of his way to put her mind at ease. Still, she couldn't help feeling that there was something untoward afoot under the surface of things.

"Is the fare not to your liking, my lady?" Klaus asked, his fork suspended. "You have hardly touched a morsel."

"The food is excellent. I know I am not doing it justice. I'm sorry, my lord. I have no appetite."

"Something is . . . troubling you?"

"Much is troubling me," Becca said. "But there is nothing to be done about it."

"Have you assessed the situation with your abigail?"

"I have, my lord."

"And what did you find?"

"She is unfit for travel, and I *must* away before Father returns. That is at the root of things, my lord. Please do not take offense. You have been very kind, and I am most appreciative, but my entire future hangs in the balance here."

"It would be best that you do remain until your father has come and gone, my lady. To leave now would be to risk riding right into him returning. Surely you know that. On the other hand, we do not even know that he will pass this way again, not having found you here earlier. When your maid is ready to travel, enough time will have passed that meeting your father will no longer be likely in any case. I know you are impatient, but it is for the best, this . . . unfortunate delay—for you *and* for your maid. Meanwhile, you must have faith in me to deal with your father if he should return. Trust me, *mitt kostbart*, I have only your best interests at heart."

"Forgive me, but I wish you would not address me thus. It is an intimacy that I have not granted." She had allowed it previously, thinking there was no harm. She would soon be gone, and the endearment warmed her heart. Truth be told, she still secretly welcomed the thrill that raced through her innermost regions each time he spoke those mysterious words in that seductive accent. But now that leaving was no longer imminent, and considering that she had accepted his gift of the shell, the last thing she wanted was to encourage him when clearly nothing could exist between them.

"What? 'My precious' offends you? It is no more an intimacy than 'my dear,' or 'dear lady.' The formality of your protocols is stifling, and altogether tiresome." He set his fork aside and frowned, his posture deflated. "I may not call you by name. *Lady Rebecca* takes far too long to say, especially when I believe *Becca* is your preference and that is the way I think of you. And *my lady* is too general an address, considering that the circumstance of our acquaintance was nothing short of intimate in itself. When one saves a lady's life, some leniency should be granted. That I speak it in my own tongue and not in yours is meant to put you at your ease, while allowing me an opportunity to be myself, to say what I mean—not what your *ton* dictates. Your society is . . . dishonest—in its speech and in its thinking. We Swedes are not so rigid as you English."

"Very well, when you put it that way . . . I suppose it is allowed," said Becca wearily. There was no use belaboring the issue. She couldn't win. The endearment rolled off his tongue as easily as breathing. He was going to address her thus anyway, no matter what she said. She might as well give in, as long as he knew her reason for doing so. "It is just that I do not wish to encourage you by allowing familiarities that may be in some way misleading," she said.

He smiled. "Oh, I need no encouragement, *mitt kostbart*," he said. "You are a precious creature whose charm and grace have quite bewitched me."

Becca's heart began to race. The compliment was gracious and polite, but the throaty baritone rumble that delivered it smoldered. She did not know where to direct her eyes. The oysters on her plate were the safest choice, and she began to move them about with her fork.

"But I know my place," he said, as though he read her thoughts. The man *was* a sorcerer. "So! While you remain my guest, you must take what I say and what I do as respectful expressions of my admiration . . . the admiration of a bungling foreigner who must express himself truthfully but would rather sever his tongue than bring offense."

Becca nodded in reply. How curious, that he'd realized she preferred the shortened version of her name from the one and only time it had slipped out: when she'd introduced herself. Bungling, indeed! In his bungling, he was more correct than any among the *ton* in all their scrupulous capability. She had never met a man so unpretentious. He was honest to a fault, and yet she couldn't help but feel that there was something hidden beneath the surface that contradicted all the rest.

The remainder of the meal was had in silence. Neither spoke until Olav cleared the table and set out the jellies and creams, the apple rum cobbler, and the dessert wine. At sight of the decanter, Becca cried off, placing her hand over her glass as the footman was set to pour.

"Thank you, no," she demurred. "I am not fond of . . . spirits. They do not sit well with me. I will just have a bit of the cream."

Klaus inclined his head, his face a study in disappointment. "Ahhh, *mitt kostbart*," he said. "Not to drink with your host? You wound me again." He nodded for Olav to fill his glass from the decanter. "This is no tincture. It is the last of the May wine brought from my homeland, reserved for the most privileged of guests at Lindegren Hall. Now that it has been uncorked, it must be drunk or it will spoil. Please do not say that I have wasted it. Just a sip? It is the finest you will ever taste." He raised his glass. "There is nothing to fear. Am I not drinking it?"

Becca watched him taste the wine. Olav was standing over her, the decanter at the ready. It was against her better judgment after the tincture, but a sip couldn't hurt . . . just to keep peace at the table. He looked so forlorn. She nodded toward the footman, and he poured her glass, then returned to his place at the sideboard.

Becca stared at the wine in her glass. It had a rosy hue. Shimmering in the candle glow, it brought to mind the waterfall, tinted a similar shade in the earlier low-sliding sun. She reached for it and raised it to her lips. Its welcoming bouquet wafted toward her before she took a sip. It had a nut-sweet taste that tingled as it glided over her tongue. In spite of herself, she uttered a soft moan of approval.

"You see?" said Klaus through a swallow from his own glass. "Does it not delight the palate?"

"It is quite good, my lord," Becca agreed.

Klaus signaled Olav to refill his glass. Becca let him refill hers as well, but only halfway. The cordial glasses were very small. What harm could it do? Klaus seemed content now that she had drunk it, though his gaze remained riveted. She didn't have to force herself to empty her glass. It had a pleasant floral undertaste, and she frowned trying to place it but could not.

"Primrose," he said.

"My lord?"

"Aside from the obvious fruit—lingonberry, to be precise—what you taste is primrose."

"I have never heard of primroses in wine."

"In Sweden it is quite common," said Klaus. "Primrose imparts a piquant flavor that balances the sweetness of the fruit. It is made by the holy ones, from a very old and guarded recipe."

Becca cleared away the thickness in her throat. A strange warmth rose inside her. His voice seemed to be coming from the bottom of a deep well as he went on speaking about winemaking in Sweden. It had an echo about it that made the words overlap.

". . . and mulled wine is a favorite winter treat," he was saying. "Brambleberry wine is infused with citrus peel, cinnamon, and cloves. It is served in tankards shaped like horns, and heated with a red-hot poker before it's drunk. Then we have what is called grog— a strong black ale. The recipe for that goes back to Viking times, and is not for the faint of heart."

"Well, I am certainly glad that you have not brought any of that along for me to sample," said Becca. "I fear what little I have just drunk of this has foxed me . . . or very nearly. Forgive me, my lord, but I am at the least a trifle disguised. I think it is time that I retire before I disgrace myself."

Klaus got to his feet with a sinuous motion, as fluid as the waterfall in the wood, and went to her side. Becca let him take her hand and raise her to her feet. He slipped his arm around her waist when she swayed. Something was wrong with her vision. She could only see directly ahead, as though she were looking into a tiny tunnel.

"Lean upon me, *mitt kostbart*," said Klaus. "Look at me. Yes . . . that is right . . . good. The wine has made you giddy, 'tis true. Shhhh, it is all right . . . I will see you safely to your chamber. . . ."

He said more in that strange, hypnotic meter he had spoken in when he rescued her from the chaise. How soothing his voice was, as he moved her toward the spiral staircase. Gradually the tunnel widened, though her view inside was anything but clear. Becca raised her foot to ascend the stairs, but there were no stairs. There was no hall. Mist the color of sorrow had replaced it—as gray as the dawn, and as soft as down. Then, as quickly as it had come, it dissipated, and her eyes flashed in all directions. Where had the cottage gone?

# Chapter Nine

A ground-creeping mist ghosted over the land. Above it, the air was charged with a rainbow of sugary frost, like colored dust motes drifting all about. They hampered Becca's view, but oh, how beautiful they were, all a-glitter in the sunlight. But wait . . . why was the sun shining? It was well past dark. Wasn't it?

Klaus was with her, hidden in the mist. Someone else was there, too, someone whose voice was unfamiliar to her. They were speaking, but they sounded so far away, and they made no sense.

"How are you going to explain this?" said the unfamiliar voice. "She is already questioning the hour."

How did he know that? She hadn't spoken. Could this person read her thoughts?

"You know as well as I that time does not exist in the astral plane," Klaus responded, in that strange, echoing voice. "Much can be accomplished here in a blink of time's mortal eye, Henrik."

"I hope you know what you're doing, your highness."

His valet? Though they hadn't met, she'd heard his name spoken. What was his valet doing here? Where was this place? Someone was leading her. There was a hand on her elbow, guiding her along, yet there was no one there.

"Stay on the path, *mitt kostbart,*" Klaus said.

How could she stay on the path? She could not see the path for the mist, for the sugary prisms of rainbow glitter all about her, like curious living things come near to appraise her.

"Soon the mist will fade and you will see clearly," Klaus murmured, his voice still a far-off echo, despite the fact that he was right beside her. He *could* read her mind. "You are a visitor here . . . under my protection. No harm will come to you as long as you do just as I say."

"Where are we, my lord?" she asked. "Am I dreaming . . . again?"

"You are in my world, and it is no dream, though it may seem so to your mortal mind. Patience, *mitt kostbart.* Soon all will be made clear to you."

"Perhaps you should say the spell of forgetfulness, your highness," said Henrik, "while there is still time."

"Time does not exist, remember, old friend? Leave that for now. We will know if needs must."

All at once the mist parted like a curtain, revealing a lush and verdant land burgeoning with wildflowers in every imaginable hue, some she had never seen before. *And the fragrance!* The air, still speckled with rainbow glitter, was warm and sweet with it. Thistle seeds and milkpod silk floated on the breeze, spiraling down all around her like gently falling snow. They, too, seemed alive, as if they had a purpose and chose their direction.

Birds sang unseen in the trees, and there was laughter, soft and sweet, like the tinkling of far-off bells. It seemed to be coming from the uppermost branches.

"Bah! This is no test, your highness," Henrik said.

"The dryads welcome every entity with a giggle—even the satyrs."

"You are as impatient as she!" Klaus snapped. "There is a progression. This must be done but once, and gradually. The mortal mind cannot comprehend the astral world, Henrik. Force this and the experiment is all for naught."

They had left the mist behind now, and the path was visible. It wasn't a path at all, not in the usual sense, trodden down dirt or spread with stones. It was a dark swath of gently used grass sidling through fields in a lighter shade of green—a shade so bright and pure, Becca had never seen the like. Though dry underfoot, it shone with the sparkle of dew.

The dryads' musical laughter had grown distant. Becca glanced behind, toward the trees that had sheltered them, but they, too, had faded into the mist left behind. How could that be? They'd hardly taken three steps. And why couldn't she see Klaus? His hand still cupped her elbow and his voice still murmured reassuring phrases in her ear, but she could not see him. Where his body should be was naught but thin air!

They passed through gardens, one more glorious than the next, and mazes, led by what appeared to be dragonflies, mating in flight. Other winged insects all around them seemed engaged in mating rituals as well.

"The Great Rite," said Klaus, as if in answer to her mental query. "The mating of the male and female species is ongoing here, just as it is with the *Fossegrim*. It is a never-ending pulse that drives all astral creatures to seek out their mates in a manner unknown to mortal man in its intensity . . . *and in its pleasures.*"

The last was murmured seductively, and Becca didn't answer. It was beyond jarring that he could read her thoughts here. She had no doubt that her cheeks were as red as the roses that hemmed the path.

"Look closer," Klaus urged.

It was rude to stare, but Becca did just that. Taking a closer look at the winged creatures flitting about in amorous pairs, she gasped. These were not insects at all, but tiny beings with human-like faces, though there were subtle differences that set them apart.

His laughter told her all too clearly that he had read her thoughts again. She quickened her step, and his hand gave her elbow a little squeeze, reminding her that he still walked by her side. Why couldn't she *see* him? Hot blood surged to her temples. The heat in her cheeks narrowed her eyes. He laughed again: that heart-stopping, sensuous baritone rumble that echoed in her very soul. Was he mocking her? It didn't matter. She was enchanted. That she was in a dangerous place meant nothing. Klaus was with her, and while her rational mind flagged danger, her heart was filled with trust, and, God help her, love for him. How strange that she could recognize that emotion here in this magical place—admit to it here in his realm but not in her own mortal world. What sorcery was this? What was happening to her?

All at once a forest loomed before them, a wood so dense and dark it robbed the light of day, though the dancing rainbow motes still spangled the eerie green darkness. Gray-green eyes, rheumy and cold, gaped from the branches, and a monotonous murmur sifted through the trees. This was not a pleasant sound like that of the dryads. It was malevolent, and Becca picked up her pace again, anxious to be away from whatever these creatures were.

"Bear up, *mitt kostbart*," said Klaus. "These will not harm you."

"Hah!" Henrik cut in. He hadn't spoken in so long, Becca had thought him vanished. "And what if she were to venture here unescorted, your highness? You dream!"

"I wish you would refrain from addressing me

thus!" Klaus snapped. His voice was like gravel. The sound of it silenced the watchers, to Becca's great relief.

"It would be dangerous to call you less than that in this place," Henrik returned. "These owe you no allegiance."

"But they do bow to a higher power. Be still! You will frighten her."

"Me? You are the one who designed this mad ramble. Do not speak to me of frightening."

The forest, as thick as a primeval jungle, seemed to stretch on forever before it opened into a thicket where woodland creatures romped and frolicked and gamboled. How strange that she hadn't noticed their absence from the land until now. Apparently, the animals didn't much care for the watchers, either. The land here was dressed in autumnal hues, ablaze with red and purple and gold. Unseen creatures' voices sang again, their melody lifted on the breeze. Great oaks laden with acorns dipped branches to the ground. Tiny creatures rode upon them, like children upon ponies, and the air was infused with the heady scent of mulch and autumn berries ripening on the vine. It was a busy place, and the watchers here bore no malice while moving among them. Some were very beautiful, bowing as they passed, while others were shy, hiding behind tree trunks and stiles, in caves and cairns and barrows.

Soon the autumnal glades began to crunch with frost underfoot. Oddly, though snow fell all around them and ice frosted bare branches, Becca was not cold.

"You are but a visitor here, *mitt kostbart*," Klaus explained, answering her thoughts again, "nothing more than an illusion, a shadow on these lands. As long as you do not stray from the path, your comfort is assured."

Becca didn't answer. She hadn't since the journey

began. Why should she, when he needed no spoken words to answer her thoughts?

The mist returned as mysteriously as it had dissipated, and with it came a familiar sight—the dancing balls of light bobbing about all around them. Becca gasped. How glorious they were at close range, though they still frolicked just out of reach, the rainbow dust spangling the air in their nimbus. The mist seemed to buoy them, just as it had when she'd watched Klaus walk naked on the path in the moonlight. She gasped again, and his hand tightened, caressing her elbow.

Klaus hesitated. "You English call them Will-o'-the Wisps," he said. "Take care, lest they lead you astray. Many mortals have left the safety of the path in pursuit of them, only to find that they soon have lost their way. You shan't catch them. These have eluded mortal man since time out of mind. They are pure illusion, *mitt kostbart*, fairy glamour whose only purpose is to entice and mislead . . . unless, of course, they guard astral royalty."

Becca did feel a pull to follow the creatures, but his firm hold upon her elbow detained her. The urge was so strong that she failed to see the water world ahead. It wasn't until she stood on the brink of a frost-painted pool that it came into view. A towering waterfall cascading into it fractured the frozen surface. Beyond the rocky bank that enclosed it, there was a grove of pine trees, their long arms sweeping the frost-covered ground. It was not as dense as the other forest. Glimpses of the sea could be seen through the trees, its high-curling combers and rainbow-charged spindrift blowing in a wind that made no sound. And in the distance, what appeared to be a group of islands came into view, visible through a thick, drifting fog.

"My world, *mitt kostbart*," Klaus murmured. "The realm of the *Fossegrim*." His hot breath puffing against her ear sent shivers of pleasure along her spine. He was so close, yet she still could not see him, nor could she see Henrik, whose grousing from time to time proved his presence as well.

They began to stroll around the pond. Frost on the fallen leaves crunched underfoot. It was a pleasant sound that lulled Becca into such a relaxed state that she failed to see the troop of female creatures that had risen from the water until they surrounded her. These had no wings and before her eyes grew taller than the other creatures she had met along the way—almost the height of humans. Sirens, water sprites! Their long flowing hair, the color of seawater, was entwined with ropes of sea grass. Their tresses and the mist were all that cloaked their nakedness. A low murmur of discordant sound leaked from them as they grew to her height and began closing the circle, nudging Becca toward the edge of the path. It was a menacing rumble, despite Klaus's voice raised against them, clearly warning in an unfamiliar tongue. He spoke in his native Swedish now, and while she could not understand a word, the water sprites' wailing lament told her all too well that an argument was in progress.

"Now will you end this, your highness?" Henrik barked. "You must! Before harm is done!"

Klaus didn't reply. His hand had left her elbow. She missed its strength, its comfort. She still couldn't see him, but the sprites seemed to be able to, as they circled closer and closer. They were yelling now, at the air where she imagined his tall, handsome form to be from the sound of his voice. Their shrill cries hurt her ears so severely that she covered them to shut out the misshapen sound.

Judging from the way they lunged and darted about her, she presumed Klaus to be in front of her now, fending off an attack, but there were so many. How was it she could see them and not Klaus? Where was the path? Had she strayed from it without his hand to guide her?

All at once one sprite broke through the invisible circle and struck her, knocking her to the ground. How beautiful she was, her eyes like green fire, her hair fanned out on a wind Becca couldn't feel. Tiny hands slapped her face and pulled at her short-cropped curls. Though the sprite seemed almost transparent, she had substance enough to wound, and Becca fought with all her strength against the attack, her own hands grasping the sprite's seaweed-tangled hair.

"*Your highness!*" Henrik bellowed.

All at once, a swish of air passed in front of her face, as though a hand had swept past, and then . . .

"Lean upon me, *mitt kostbart*," said Klaus. "Look at me. Yes, that is right . . . good. The wine has made you giddy. Shhhh, it is all right. I will see you safely to your chamber."

He'd said that just a moment before . . . hadn't he? Oh, why did her head ache so? Why had she drunk that wine?

He led her away from his dining table and out into the shadowy corridor toward the spiral staircase. Becca leaned upon him. How strong he was, how his clean, masculine scent filled her senses.

"I think I just had another strange dream," she mused. "But how could I have? I am wide awake."

Klaus laughed. "I believe in truth you cannot handle strong spirits," he said. "It is best that you have found it out now . . . here with me. I think you ought to take care in future, and abstain in company you do not trust. Someone less honorable could have taken unfair advantage of you. What was this dream about?"

They had started to ascend the stairs, and Becca stopped halfway up. "I . . . I'm not altogether certain," she said, "except that it began pleasantly enough, and then ended . . . somewhat frighteningly, as nightmares so often do."

"You remember nothing more?"

"Only bits and fragments . . . in brief flashes. I was in such a beautiful place, like what we imagine heaven to be. Ohhhhh . . . if only my head didn't ache so. The wine is still with me, my lord, though my head seems clearer . . . or would be, but for the pain."

"I am sorry for the pain, *mitt kostbart*. I could have Anne-Lise prepare a remedy—"

"*No!* No more remedies, my lord . . . and no more wine. It still clouds my thoughts."

"Of course. Is there nothing more that you remember of the dream? I ask only because sometimes speaking of it will chase the memory of unpleasant visions."

"I was . . . struggling, I think . . . with a beautiful sea creature. You were in the dream as well, my lord, but I couldn't see you, or understand your speech much of the time. It was passing strange . . . especially since I saw these things while I was awake. I *was* awake, wasn't I? I didn't nod off at the table and disgrace myself . . . did I?"

They had resumed their progress on the stairs and had nearly reached the third-floor landing. He didn't speak, while handing her up onto the platform.

"My precious lady," he said at last, "you could not disgrace yourself even if you tried." They had arrived at her apartments, and he opened her sitting room door. "Ulla is waiting to ready you for bed," he went on. "Sleep is what's wanted. We shall talk of your . . . dream again tomorrow."

"Y-yes. Tomorrow. Oh! No, I should look in upon Maud first."

"She is surely asleep. You would not want to disturb her at this hour. Go now, and rest, while the wine is still with you. We will visit her together in the morning." Becca's hands were fisted at her sides. He reached for one and raised it to his lips—how gentle they were as he kissed it. His warm breath puffing against her moist skin was vaguely familiar. A soft moan escaped him before he returned the hand to her, bowed, and backed into the shadows of the hallway, his riveting eyes never leaving her face. "Good night, *mitt kostbart*," he said, his voice sounding along the hall as though it were coming from the bottom of a deep dark well. That, too, seemed familiar.

Becca shook her head in a vain attempt to loosen the cobwebs still remaining from the wine, but when she opened the hand still fisted to grasp the doorknob, she froze stock-still on the threshold. Stuck to her moist palm were several strings of sea grass, entwined with a few long strands of what appeared to be . . . hair the color of bright seawater.

Gooseflesh snaked its way down her spine, crippling Becca for a moment in the doorway. She glanced behind. The sitting room was vacant. Ulla was nowhere in sight, and she stepped back into the hall. Klaus had nearly reached the landing and, keeping to the shadows, she closed the door without a sound and followed him.

# Chapter Ten

"Well, I hope you're satisfied," said Henrik, helping Klaus into his dressing gown in his second-floor chamber. "You knew there would be jealousy among the sprites. I pity you upon your next visit to the astral realm, *my lord*," he mocked.

"Silence!" Klaus thundered. "I will deal with the sprites. They have no right to be jealous. What occurs in the Otherworld has no bearing upon what occurs in this one."

"Well, evidently they think differently. Could that possibly be because they are your handmaidens and you have flaunted an outsider in their faces?"

"They take themselves too seriously."

"Ahhh!" said Henrik, bowing dramatically. "And what of you, my lord? Could it possibly be that you do not take them—or yourself—seriously enough?"

"I will take the sprites to task, Henrik," Klaus said, pacing before the empty hearth. "Now, enough! We have solved the issue of whether or not Lady Rebecca Gildersleeve could exist in my realm. That was our mission, and now we know it could never be—not even if she were willing."

"Will she remember?"

"I do not know. I do not think so, though she does have some memory, albeit slight."

"You said the spell too late. I warned you! I told you to say it at the onset."

"Yes, well, I did not. I am not perfect, Henrik. I am not even human. I am Prince of the *Fossegrim*, as you so often remind me—astral royalty, a figurehead, a mentor presiding over all the lower forms of *Fossegrim* alone, with no more authority over the Otherworld entire than the poor mad king has over this realm! Spells are not my expertise. How can you expect me to know what is right or wrong when dealing with these mortals? The more I walk among them, the less I understand."

"I cannot, whilst you are infected with mortal love, which is why I must take you to task. A *Fossegrim* ought have no truck with love. It is uncivilized. What message are you sending to the lower forms? I shudder to wonder. You have not weighed the consequences of what you are planning."

"I only wish I knew what I was planning, old friend," said Klaus. Flopping into the wing chair at the edge of the carpet, he dropped his head in his hands. "I only know that I do not wish to live without her, in this world or the other. As cruel as love is, I would rather suffer the pain of it than wander through time without. One knows when he has met his soulmate. That knowledge comes quicker with our kind than it does with mortals, especially those of us who have lived so long among them. She has bewitched me, Henrik, and now that I have tasted her, I want no other."

"Take her then, and have done!" cried the elder.

"What stops you? You cannot have it both ways. Give over this foolish love prattle. It is as fleeting as the will-o'-the-wisp. Take her, I say, and fulfill your destiny."

Becca staggered back from the doorway. Klaus and Henrik went on speaking inside, but she had heard enough—more than her mind could take in. Still groggy, she wasn't aware until that moment that she still clutched the sea grass. It slipped from her fingers as she turned back down the corridor toward the spiral staircase, barely able to put one foot in front of the other.

It wasn't the wine that foxed her now. Her head was reeling with the stark realization that none of the strange episodes she had been experiencing since she entered Lindegren Hall were dreams. That meant she had allowed Klaus's intimate embrace. She had savored his kiss upon her lips—upon her breasts, half naked in the moonlight! And then there was the beautiful sprite she had wrestled with on the frost-clad forest floor. She'd brought back proof positive of her existence: a handful of sea grass, and hair the color of the sea itself. Was she one of Klaus's astral lovers? Nothing short of that would have prompted such fury.

The tale he'd told her of the *Fossegrim* was evidently *true*. But how could it be? These were creatures of myth. But it was. He'd said it with his own lips: *Prince of the Fossegrim*—that was what he had called himself. That meant he had chosen her to be his mate . . . to bear his child . . . a *Fossegrim* child, a son he would leave her to raise alone. Madness!

Tears blurred her vision so severely, she almost stumbled on the stairs. Everything that she had always looked upon as imaginary had suddenly become real, and she was cast in the midst of it. The worst of it was, she could no longer deny her feelings for Klaus. She had brought that back with her as well.

Perhaps it was his Otherworldly mystique that drew her so totally, enchanted her so completely from the moment they had met. But whatever had bewitched her, she longed to be in his arms, longed to savor his kiss, ached for the soft murmur of his deep, sensuous voice reverberating through her to her very core. How safe she had felt under his protection. Now she was terrified. He meant to seduce her and leave her with child. How dared he call such a thing *love?*

There was only one thing to do. She had to leave now, before she saw him again, before he had a chance to persuade her to stay, before her heart and body betrayed her again. He would never let her go if he knew her mind. But how could she just up and leave? What of Maud, hardly fit for travel? Well, she would simply have to be. Now, tonight.

Still dizzy from the wine, Becca climbed to the third-floor landing with the help of the banister and went to her chamber. Ulla was waiting, just as she expected, and she dismissed the nonplussed girl. She said she wanted to read awhile, and look in on Maud before retiring; she would dress herself for bed, she'd done it before.

Whether the girl believed her or not, Becca couldn't tell. It struck her then, with a crippling chill, that all the servants in the house might be astral creatures as well. That certainly would explain the way they kept appearing and disappearing at the oddest moments. It would also explain why his *cottage* had accommodations for them, when no English cottage she knew of boasted servants' quarters. Of course, Klaus would surround himself with his own kind. She shook herself the way a dog shakes off water, in a desperate attempt to shed the thoughts that had nearly convinced her that she'd gone mad. How could any of this be? Yet it was. She wasn't dreaming now. She was wide awake. She pinched herself just to be sure.

Becca ran through the foyer and entered her bedchamber, only to pull up short before the bed. The counterpane was strewn with blood-red rose petals. Their fragrance filled the air. She fingered them absently, a soft gasp escaping her. Was this to be the mating bed? Tears welled in her eyes, and she sprang toward the wardrobe, tugged out her small travel bag, and tossed it on the bed. It wouldn't hold much; several frocks and a few unmentionables were all she could cram into it, but that couldn't be helped. She couldn't take more than she could carry. The rest would have to stay.

Warm as the night was, she tossed her pelisse about her shoulders rather than leave it behind and stepped out into the hall. She couldn't access Maud's suite through the dressing room with Ulla camped there, and she tiptoed along until she'd reached the maid's bedchamber, a close eye upon the shadows. The hallway was deserted. Maud was fast asleep, as Becca knew she would be at that hour. She hated to wake her, but there was nothing for it. They had to leave Lindegren Hall now, tonight. She shook the abigail gently. After a moment, Maud stirred. When her eyes came open, a cry escaped her lips, and Becca covered her mouth with a quick hand.

"Shhhh!" she whispered. "We have to leave—at once, Maud. We are in danger here. I'll . . . explain, but there isn't time now. We must away while the rest are asleep. Do you think you can walk?"

"I . . . I do not understand, my lady," said Maud, struggling to a sitting position. "What danger? They have been so kind. . . ."

"They are not what they seem. Please! There is no time to explain. You will just have to trust me." She snatched Maud's frock from the wardrobe. "Here, I shall help you dress," she said. "Lindegren Hall is on the post route. We have only to walk a short distance—

away from here, to the south, and rest unseen in the wood by the side of the highway until a stage or mail coach comes by. One will surely pass before morning, and we will be safe and away to Plymouth, just as we originally planned."

Maud groaned, and Becca helped her slip the black twill frock on over her nightshift.

"We shall have to leave the rest of your things behind," said Becca. "No matter, I will replace them. I've left everything of mine but what is in this bag here. Can you stand on your own?"

The maid nodded, and stiffly got to her feet. She swayed, and Becca steadied her. "I am so sorry, Maud," she said. "You will be fine once I get you out of here; I'm certain of it. Unless I miss my guess, the tinctures they have been giving you have made you thus. Have you drunk any recently? I insisted that they stop dosing you."

"N-not today, my lady . . . but why would they do such a thing?"

"To keep me here!" said Becca. "I'll explain later." She grabbed the thin wrapper the maid had arrived in from the wardrobe and flung it about her shoulders. "Here, do as I have done," she said. "I know it is too warm a night for a wrap, but it is either wear it or leave it behind, and if the weather turns stormy again, you will be glad of it. Now, lean on me and be still. We are not out of this yet!"

Together, they crept down the stairs, acutely aware of every creak of the old wood. Maud was clearly not up to what lay ahead, but she made no complaint. It wasn't until they had left the house that Becca drew an easy breath. And even at that, fearing pursuit, her glance was cast behind more often than it was upon the road ahead.

It wouldn't be long before Klaus discovered her missing. Recalling the rose petals strewn over her counterpane, that could have already happened. He would come after her; there was no question. As soon as they rounded the bend in the path, she steered Maud toward the forest curtain and eased her down on a fallen log just inside a stand of tall saplings. The young trees gave them shelter, while affording a clear view of the road through their sparse branches in the light of the waning moon. Only then did she realize how severely she had taxed her maid. Maud's breath was coming short, and all color had drained from her face. She looked like a ghost in the darkness.

"Oh, Maud, I am so sorry for this," Becca said. "You really aren't up to it, are you?"

"The . . . night air has . . . quite revived me . . . I think."

Becca doubted that, observing the abigail with dismay. Was she really doing the right thing? Her head said yes, but her heart said no. She shrugged those thoughts off. She could no longer trust her heart. If it still beat a little faster at the thought of Klaus after such a colossal deception, and knowing his plan, she could no longer trust herself to his society. How would she ever explain it all to Maud? The maid would surely think her a Bedlamite.

But Maud didn't press for an explanation then. She looked haggard and worn. The mere sight of her tugged at Becca's conscience, the urgency of the situation notwithstanding.

She forced a smile. "So now our roles are reversed," she said, her voice lifted. "I shall serve you until you are able to resume your duties."

Maud offered a cheerless smile in return but said no more while they waited by the roadside in the darkness.

An hour passed. It seemed like two. Becca's thudding heart ticked off each second like a metronome. There wasn't a sound in the forest, though now and then she caught sight of a glimmer of reflected moonlight in the eye of a curious woodland creature come to observe them. Maud, who had been drifting in and out of sleep slumped there, had begun to nod off in earnest when the sound of a carriage crunching on gravel brought Becca to her feet.

"Come, Maud," she said. "A coach!"

She helped the abigail to stand, snatched up the travel bag, and led her out of the wood and onto the grassy shoulder. Straining her eyes toward the north, she craned her neck for some sign of the coach but saw nothing, though she heard it clearly, carrying toward them at a rapid pace.

"No, my lady!" the maid cried. "It's comin' from the other way!"

Becca spun around in time to see the coach tooling around a bend in the road to the south. The carriage lamps cast an eerie glow about it as it bore down upon them. Tugging on Maud's arm, Becca steered her back toward the forest, but not in time. They had been seen. The coach had nearly come abreast of them when the thunderous *rat-a-tat-tat* of a walking stick on the roof inside ran Becca through like cannon-fire. A gruff voice barked commands, and the driver pulled the groaning equipage to such an abrupt halt that it nearly met the same fate as the chaise had done.

The horses reared, defying the driver to keep control. In the midst of the struggle, the coach door flew open and a portly little flame-haired man, his temples frosted with gray, leaped through without setting down the steps.

"Rebecca Gildersleeve!" he thundered. "Stand where you are!"

"Oh, my lady!" Maud cried, sagging against her. "He's goin' ta skin us for fair!"

"Don't worry," Becca returned, "just say as I do— and not a word unless he addresses you directly. We must not implicate the count!"

Cedric Gildersleeve had reached them. He seized Becca by the arm. "You've come to no good, so I see," he said. "Where is your carriage?"

"Th-there was an accident . . . it went into the gorge," said Becca. "Do take care! Maud has been injured!"

"Hmmm," her father grunted. "That's what she gets for forgetting who pays her wages."

"There is no fault in Maud, Father," Becca defended, jabbing the maid in the side with her elbow when she opened her mouth to speak. "It is my fault. I persuaded her to accompany me."

"Get into the carriage—both of you. I will sort the truth of this out once I have you home, where you belong."

There was nothing for it but to do as he said. It was well past midnight, and all hope of escape to Plymouth was gone. She turned the maid toward the carriage.

"Come, Maud," she said. "There's nothing to be done . . . tonight." She turned hard eyes upon her father. "This does not mean I will marry that odious gambler you mean to shackle me to," she snapped.

"You will do as I say. Now get into this carriage!"

Becca handed Maud into the coach and climbed in after her, while her father tossed her travel bag up to the coachman. The worst of it was that they would pass right by Lindegren Hall heading north. She cast a sidelong glance in Maud's direction, trying to convey a message to the maid to keep silent and ignore the cottage when they passed it by. Her fear was that her father might take a notion to stop there, to inform Klaus that he had found her. Or worse yet, that he might seek hospitality for the night, since it was so late. Maud seemed not to notice, staring absently out of the window.

Something hard struck Becca's leg as she shifted position when the coach struck a rut, drawing her hand to her pocket. The little conch shell! She had nearly forgotten. Tears welled in her eyes as she fondled it through the muslin. The coach rounded another bend, and the sound of the waterfall set her heart racing. It was visible through the trees, lit in the glow of the low-sliding moon. But it shouldn't be! The cottage should be in front of it, blocking the view from the road. Where was the cottage? She blinked to clear her misty vision, but her eyes hadn't deceived her. She and Maud gasped in unison. Lindegren Hall was gone!

# Chapter Eleven

"Now what are we to do, your highness?" said Henrik. "Do we mean to stay cloaked indefinitely? Time may not exist in the astral realm, but it does exist here, and it is running out!"

Seated on the edge of the Grecian couch in his sitting room, where he was closeted with the elder, Klaus pounded his knee with his fist, rustling the seaweed he gripped in it, and glowered.

"And do not carp at how you are addressed!" Henrik said, answering the look. "I see that coming. Save your breath. There are no mortals here now, thank the gods!"

"You do not have to remind me!" Klaus barked at him, hurling the seaweed at his feet. Though it hadn't taken long to make the discovery, he'd found Becca missing too late. Quitting his chamber and finding the seaweed she'd dropped outside his door, he'd scaled the stairs two at a stride and gone straight to her chamber. One look at the undisturbed counterpane on her bed, still strewn with the rose petals he'd sprinkled there, told the tale. And her father had her before he could intervene. She was gone, her abigail with her, and he'd barely had time to hide the cottage from mortal view before they passed it heading north. How could he have been so careless?

"Well?" asked the elder, staring down, arms-akimbo.

"I shall go after her, of course," Klaus said.

"We haven't time for that!"

"She evidently overheard our conversation," said Klaus. He surged to his feet and gave the seaweed a vicious kick with the toe of his turned-down boot. "That there is a bleed-over. She evidently got hold of it when the damnable siren attacked her, brought it back with her, and realized she was not dreaming."

"That is unfortunate. You must let her go."

"I cannot. She is frightened, Henrik. I will not have her fear me! I want only to love her."

Henrik threw his arms into the air. "Madness!" he cried. "You do not even know where her home is, or if there is a waterfall near it. You cannot force her to return. She must come to you willingly."

"Her father's estate is at Boscastle," said Klaus. "And there is a waterfall. A fine one; I have heard of it—"

"Ahhh! But is it inhabited?"

"If it is, I will deal with it. I am the *prince!*"

"That still does not address the all-important question of her returning with you willingly."

"She is an innocent, and I have awakened her to life, Henrik. She feels as I do—I know it. But she is frightened, and why wouldn't she be? I never should have taken her into the astral. You were right about that. It was madness to imagine she could—or even would—live there with me. It is my fault that she is so frightened now, and I would give my eyes to allay her fears."

"Take care what you volunteer to forfeit. You may be prince, but there are those who rank above you. It would do you well to remember your father's folly and give this madness over, before you meet the same fate he did. You have already angered the gods—the great god Syl himself, I'll wager. Your father did not have his wits about him when he defected, either."

"Enough! I am not my father."

"He never did adjust to the transition," the elder went on over Klaus's bluster. "He was vulnerable, and ill-equipped to help your mother in her time of need without his astral powers. When she was set upon by brigands, he foolishly thought to take them on single-handed, which he could have done easily had he still possessed his gifts. She died for his ineptitude, for his bad judgment—"

"I have heard all this before," Klaus interrupted.

"And you will hear it again if needs must," said the elder. "Your father's failure had repercussions in this world and the other. Bereft, he suffered through his human life without her and died alone—a broken man—well before his mortal time would have put him in his grave. Which was when I took you under my protection, in time to groom you for your astral heritage, ungrateful whelp! Some say he died of heartbreak. Is that what you want for your lady—for yourself? Have you learned nothing from his mistake?"

"Leave my father to his rest, Henrik," said Klaus unequivocally. "I am a different entity than he. And as for the gods, there is nothing they can do to me that would be worse than losing Becca." A strange thrill crippled him at the sound of her name upon his lips. It was the first time he had spoken it familiarly aloud. All the tactile experience of her body broke over his senses as the intimacy of the sound reverberated through him, and tears moistened his eyes. He had to have her—he *had to*. Once she realized what he was prepared to give up for love of her . . .

Again the elder waved his arms about and bowed

dramatically. "I have wasted my breath again, eh?" he said. "You are obsessed with this woman. So! Let me see if I have all this correctly. You mean to dash off to Boscastle, evict another of your peers from his waterfall if needs must, storm the castle, and carry off the fair maiden—all before another moon is full. Is that all, then, your highness?"

How was it that the elder could always manage to make something perfectly simple seem utterly ridiculous? There was no doubt that Henrik had a talent for that, and there was no denying that he'd had sufficient practice as Klaus's protector. But he wasn't going to have his hour to gloat over this. As to the moon and time—benighted time!—that no longer mattered.

"No, not quite all," Klaus said, fixing what he hoped to be a look of smug satisfaction on his face. "You are coming with me. Now, then! Go and have Sven ready the brougham—the one with my device on the door, just in case I need to prove myself. We leave within the hour."

"I know it sounds preposterous, but that is how it is," said Becca. She was closeted with Maud in the confines of her chamber at Gildersleeve Grange, her sprawling gated home on the coast, a place she'd thought never to see again. "Do not look at me like that! Every word is true. I do not pretend to understand any of it, but it happened, and I had to leave while I still possessed the strength to resist him."

"It sounds like a tale for the nursery, it does," said Maud. "What was in that wine he gave you?"

"Did you or did you not see what I saw when we passed the place where Lindegren Hall should have been?"

"Oh, now, my lady it all looked so different at night. I . . . I . . ."

"Cottages do not disappear, Maud. They do not

vanish into thin air! We walked out of that front door
and down the highway no more than five minutes distance and then rode back again in the coach. That
house was gone! If it weren't, and we'd miscalculated
somehow, we would have seen it farther on."

"I dunno, my lady. I was so groggy—"

"Well, I was not—and that's another thing!" Becca
cried. "Your head is clear now, is it not? The minute I
got you out of that house, you made a remarkable re-
covery, didn't you?" She sank down upon the bed,
her head in her hands. "The awful thing is, he has
bewitched me, Maud. I shall die if I never see him
again. . . ."

Just then Cora the chambermaid entered with Becca's
travel bag. She set it on the floor at the foot of the bed,
curtsied, and left them. Maud lifted the case onto the
counterpane and opened it. She snaked out two of the
hastily folded frocks and gasped. Becca's head came
up in answer to the sound.

"What's this, then?" said the abigail, letting a handful of rose petals sift through her fingers.

Becca moaned and burst into tears.

Klaus and Henrik reached the coaching inn at Boscastle the following midnight, and Klaus discovered,
much to his chagrin, that it wasn't nearly close enough
to the local waterfall for his needs. However, after in-
structing Henrik to extract what information he could
regarding the whereabouts of the Gildersleeve estate,
Klaus left him to arrange for their accommodations
and made his way there. He had to, if he was to keep
up the strength that gave him both mortal and otherworldly substance. It would be so until the matter was
settled and he'd gone before the tribunal, if it came to
that, to seal his fate in the mortal realm. One condition
had no bearing upon the other, however; failure of a
*Fossegrim* to visit a waterfall in a timely fashion meant

sure and certain death in both realms. Water was as integral to his life as breathing air was to a mortal man.

The falls—a magnificent one-hundred-twenty-foot cascade from the dark green mass of Pentargon cliff—was nearly a third of a mile from Boscastle. Thank the gods it was unoccupied. Klaus was in no humor for a death struggle over property rights. He'd been away from his waterfall too long and his strength was flagging, which had no bearing upon his physical stamina but rather on his mortal visibility. No more than a shadow, he reached it on horseback, having caused more than one raised eyebrow at the inn when he insisted a horse be saddled and left so soon after arriving at the witching hour. The last thing he wanted was to make himself conspicuous, but it couldn't be helped.

He tethered his mount to a young sapling and started down the narrow, serpentine footpath that formed a gradual drop to the cliff. He needed no directions; his senses were like a sponge. Scent and sound alone drew him to the left, where presently the falls appeared in the waning moonlight. Klaus couldn't help but form a grim parallel between himself and that moon, for they both were fading. The moon, however, would rally as it always did. His fate offered no such guarantee.

Shedding his clothes, he plunged into the water, a groan of pleasure welling up from deep within him. Will-o'-the-wisps danced on the surface, skimming the undulating flow like playful children. Would he feel the pull of the falls if he renounced his heritage? He couldn't imagine not needing to go to it for solace . . . for comfort. There was so little of that left in either realm for him now.

Time was of the essence. He plunged deeper as he gained strength and finally crossed over into the Otherworld, where time meant nothing, where he could remain until he'd come back to himself without a second lost when he crossed over again. Siren sprites flocked to him there the moment he appeared, ready to service him, their undulating bodies pressed close, stroking, caressing. They had always been a comfort, but no longer. Not even Illia, the beautiful vixen who had battled poor, unsuspecting Becca—especially not Illia. Klaus banished the rest with a gesture and took her to task.

"Did you think that your actions would not have consequences?" he hissed close in her pointed ear. Water droplets like diamonds glistened in her hair. She smelled of sweet cress and ambergris—intoxicating and arousing no longer. She had overreached herself.

"Ye have never crossed a mortal over before," she snapped. "She is not welcome! She knows that now. Ye belong to me. It has always been so."

"I belong to no one, Illia," said Klaus, "No one but myself. And she is welcome wherever I am." Holding her at arm's distance, he removed her hand from his sex. "No!" he said. "I am much displeased. You may tell the others the same. Your time is past."

"Oh?" she snapped, tossing her seawater-green mane. Long and luxuriant, it reached below her buttocks and veiled her supple breasts. She was without blemish and eons old, though she seemed no more than twenty mortal years. She had always been his favorite . . . until now. She had always been able to pleasure him . . . until now. She had always been able to twist him around her little finger . . . until now. "The elders know what ye are about," she went on, jutting her chin at him. "Ye are not exempt from consequences, *your highness.*"

"I suppose that I have you to thank for that?"

"Ye have yourself to thank for it!" she flung at him. "Bringing a mortal female into the astral! Ye have upset the balance. Ye have tainted the memory of our ancestors, polluted sacred ground with the presence of their murderer!"

"She has not murdered anyone."

"Her kind has," Illia hissed, her green eyes ablaze. "In the Great War, when they drove us out—banished us to the astral. We are not all as privileged as ye are, Prince of the *Fossegrim*, allowed to span the bridge between both worlds and take the best of both. The rest of us are trapped here, else we venture among them cloaked. We cannot walk the earth and take our pleasures with mortal men as ye do with mortal women. I *hate* ye!" she cried, pummeling his well-muscled chest with both her tiny fists.

Klaus arrested them in one hand. "Enough!" he said. "You make it easy for me to face the tribunal. If I ever had a doubt—"

"I know your game, and hers!" Illia said, trying without success to free her wrists from his grip. "Well, let me tell ye, your highness, I know ye are here because *she* is here. Ye must come to this place. Ye are bound to it now—ye need it to live. She has no such need, but she will come, and when she does, I will be waiting for her. So! If ye know what is good for ye, my high and mighty waterlord, ye will see she stays away!"

Spinning like a whirlwind, the siren spiraled down and disappeared in the vortex of her rage, so powerful it caught Klaus unaware. He was not yet restored. Caught off balance on the edge of the whirlpool she'd created, it whipped him around and deflected him out of the astral realm and back into Boscastle falls with a mighty splash. Will-o'-the-wisps scattered every which way. He actually heard their squeaky cries as the wake and foam and spray dispersed them. That hadn't happened in awhile. Klaus couldn't recall when he'd last heard the usually silent creatures' voices. He emerged thrashing and flailing in a waterspout as if the Otherworld had spat him out.

Pounding the water with white-knuckled fists, Klaus

loosed a string of expletives, the byproduct of his mortal incarnation, and dove beneath the surface. It was some time before he emerged again, collected his clothes, and made his way back to his horse, tethered as he'd left it. But the animal wasn't alone. Henrik was waiting alongside.

At the sight of him, Klaus threw wild arms into the air, spooking the horse. It reared and complained, forefeet flailing a ghostly mist that had risen from the water. It was all the elder could do to bring the animal's feet back to earth, and Henrik dosed him with an ireful stare.

"So!" he said. "The purification has revived you too much . . . or not enough?"

"Do not start!" Klaus warned. "You know very well how I am *revived*, old one. Wipe off that look! You ought not even be here . . . spying. Or have you come to gloat?"

The elder's quicksilver eyes flashed in the moonlight. "She bested you!" he said. Was that a *smile*?

"That little vixen puts the rest of the sirens to shame," Klaus grumbled. "Do not dare make mock of me! You have no right. You are no *Fossegrim*. She caught me off guard."

"She is jealous."

"*She is over.*"

"You think so, do you? Well, I wouldn't count on that, your highness. Since time out of mind, the female—mortal or fey—has outwitted the male of her species, and jealousy is older than the oceans."

Klaus glowered. "I am not outwitted. I had not reached my most powerful, and I was . . . unprepared."

"Hah! What did you expect, after taking your lady among her rivals, hmm?"

"She has no rivals."

"Tell that to Illia."

"I want no more truck with Illia. Now, enough! Did you do as I asked? Have you news for me?"

The elder nodded. "Gildersleeve Grange, the place you seek, is just beyond the falls, a gated estate on the coast. My lady arrived this morning safe and sound."

"You are certain?"

The elder nodded. "Her father brought a sheaf of missives to be posted to the inn this morning. He insisted that they be dispatched at once—invitations to a masked ball at which my lady's betrothal will be announced Saturday next."

"Good!"

"*Good*, your highness? How can such a thing be *good*? The falls have waterlogged your brain."

"What better way for me to gain entrance to her home, hmm? One more costumed guest will not be noticed."

The elder made a strangled sound. "And how will you be attired, pray?"

"Why, as myself, Henrik. What else?"

# Chapter Twelve

Becca was beside herself. Only three more days until the elaborate masque her father had arranged to announce her betrothal. There was talk of a special license. Sir Percival Smedley was impatient.

She wouldn't be the first young lady to be sold in marriage to settle a gambling debt—such things were common enough—but by the stars, Becca would not number among such feckless and insipid creatures. She'd run once; she would run again—and keep on running if needs must. It mattered not where. She would wait. She would bide her time and gain her father's trust and then, when the moment was right, when he relaxed his guard, she would steal away. She would not settle for a loveless marriage with a spindly-legged toady twice her age. Not when she had been in the arms of a man who truly cherished her, who had brought her to life, who had awakened her to pleasures of the flesh she didn't even know existed. No! What was she thinking? she admonished herself. By his own admission, Klaus Lindegren wasn't even *human!*

Becca threw herself across her bed. She would not

cry again. She had never been a watering pot until now, and she wasn't about to make a habit of it. She needed her wits about her if she were to form a plan and escape her father's selfish and degrading arrangement for her future. Whatever that plan was, it had to be a better one than her last misadventure. Oh, why had she urged the coachman on? Why had she insisted he drive through that storm? She wished she'd never set eyes upon Klaus Lindegren. Then, on the other hand . . .

"What now, my lady?" said Maud. Sailing in from the dressing room with Becca's ball costume over her arm, she pulled up short beside the bed, clicking her tongue and shaking her head. "You'll want ta try this on for fit," she continued. "We've been working on it all the day long, while you've been sulkin' up here. The masque will be upon us in a trice."

Nothing could chase away the threatening tears, as well as anger. Casting the maid a withering stare, Becca vaulted upright. Whatever her plan turned out to be, Maud, she decided, wouldn't be part of it. The ungrateful twit hadn't been herself since they'd returned to Gildersleeve Grange. Maud didn't believe what had happened, but Becca couldn't fault her for that; she hardly believed what had occurred herself. It was the abigail's total acceptance of her betrothal to the odious Sir Percival Smedley that rankled so. Didn't the foolish woman realize Becca despised the gudgeon? Could she not see how devastating was the prospect of marriage to the man?

The masque. That deuced masque! The Devil take it. And how was Becca to be attired? As a Grecian goddess, draped in pongee silk, one shoulder daringly bared, with a diadem of gilded grapes on her head and a mask of grape leaves, likewise gilded, covering most of her face. She certainly hadn't chosen such a rig. That was her father's doing.

"I don't care about the costume!" she snapped. "I don't care about the masque, do you hear? *I do not care!*"

"There's nothing for it, my lady," said Maud. "You'll just have ta do as the master says. We were wrong ta leave the Grange. We should have known it was madness—*I* should have known. I never should have given in ta ya."

Becca bit her lower lip rather than say what was on the tip of her tongue—that the abigail needn't worry about being party to a next adventure; she would embark upon that alone. It wouldn't do to let that slip, however. Maude Ammen was too loyal to her father, and after the outcome of her last attempt at escape, Becca dared not risk it.

"If you breathe one word . . . !"

"I ain't about to, my lady. Who would believe me? They'd think I was daft. *Fos . . . Fosse . . . grum*, was it? They'd fling me straight inta Bedlam. You conjured yourself some fine visions drinkin' them herbal draughts that Anne-Lise person brewed up."

"You aren't to mention that, or the count. He tried to help me, Maud. I would not want him to suffer for it at Father's hands."

"I said I wouldn't, didn't I?" said Maud. She sucked in her breath with a start. "I think I see what's afoot here," she went on, enlightenment lifting her voice an octave. "He's took your fancy, the count! Oh, my lady! As shabby as Sir Percival is, he's your own kind, not some exiled foreign ne'er-do-well. The stars alone know what he's done to get himself booted outta his own country. We're fortunate not ta have been murdered in our beds."

Becca wasn't about to belabor the point. She'd learned what she wanted to know. Her secret was safe . . . for now. What might come later was another matter. She was on her own.

"Well, if ya won't try this on," Maud complained, waving the costume, "I'll just have ta guess at the seams, and it'll hang on ya like a flour sack. I wash my hands o' it."

"Good!" Becca snapped, flicking the silk pongee. "I hope that it does. As it is now, it's . . . it's *indecent!*"

"Are ya goin' downstairs in that old frock, then?" the maid asked. "It's all wrinkled, and your betrothed is comin' ta dinner."

Again, Becca bit her lip. "No," she forced out. It wouldn't do to give herself away now—not when the seed of an idea had begun to germinate. "You may dress me for dinner. The blue muslin, I think. The one with the scalloped overskirt."

Neither woman spoke as Maud readied her to go downstairs. The abigail bobbed about, arranging the frock, humming and fussing as she threaded the blue grosgrain ribbons that matched through Becca's hair. The excitement of the masque and the wedding festivities to come had quite taken the woman beyond the beyond. What with the urgency of the accident, and Maud in such a subdued state recovering, Becca had forgotten how enamored the maid had always been of all matters that concerned her betters. Maud took such things to heart, as if they were happening to her. Becca had duped the abigail with a mere smile, the girl was so anxious to retreat into her fantasies. Now if she could just dupe her father and Sir Percival as easily . . .

They assembled in the drawing room for sherry before dinner. Sir Percival and her father had already arrived there when Becca entered. Their boisterous voices, raised in raucous banter echoing through the empty halls of Gildersleeve Grange set her teeth on edge. How common they sounded. How common everyone sounded after Klaus.

No! She had promised herself she wouldn't think of him. Fact or fantasy, all that was over. *He* was over. Unwinding her present coil was what mattered, and she needed all her wits to be equal to the task.

Sir Percival looped her arm through his and led her into the dining hall. He scarcely reached her height, a squat, rotund little man of middle age who reeked of strong spirits and body odor. It was as if he'd dribbled whiskey upon himself and slept in his togs until the liquor ripened with the sweat. He threatened to make her retch. His spindly legs were bowed and would have benefited from padding, as the less adequately endowed gentlemen were wont to do. His hair, which had once been a nondescript shade of brown, was peppered now with gray, its thinness emphasized by the elaborate a là Brutus hairstyle held in place with gobs of pomade that stank on an unwashed head. His prattle was for the most part gammon—meaningless gambler's jargon, directed at her father. It was clear that they could hardly wait until their next wager, which was in her favor. While they were concentrating upon that, they wouldn't be concentrating too closely upon her.

Becca grimaced in spite of herself as the footmen presented the courses. The mere thought of food in such unsavory company had her stomach in knots. Sir Percival set his chicken skin fan aside and attacked the fare with gusto. Becca managed the julienne soup, but the whole steamed salmon, served with lobster cakes and cucumbers béchamel, was quite another matter. Now and then, Sir Percival took up his fan against the oppressive heat and wagged it relentlessly, spreading his foul essence. That combined with the aroma of the pungent fish wafting off the platter was beyond bearing. Becca resisted the urge to snatch the ridiculous fan from his hand and break it in two. Remembering the crisis, however, she took another tack.

"Just a little for me, Smithers," she said to the footman who was serving. Then, to Sir Percival sweetly: "Sir, if you please . . . the wind you make is disturbing my coiffure, and it does no good. Please, I beg you, desist awhile."

"Oh! Of course, my dear," Smedley returned, slapping the fan back down on the table as though it were afire. It came to rest a little too close to his wineglass, and some wine splashed over onto it. Judging from the other stains decorating the taut chicken skin, it wasn't hard to imagine how they got there. The man was insufferable.

Tears welled up inside her, closing her throat around the morsel of salmon she'd forced down. How could her father do such a thing to her? How could he condemn her to marriage with such a one, and over a gambling debt? *His only daughter! His only child!* There was nothing redeemable in the man—in either of them, for that matter. She loved her father dearly, but she could neither countenance nor forgive him for this.

"So, you've come to your senses, girl," her father said, answering his own question. "Sir Percival leaves for London Monday for the special license. We announce at the masque, and the wedding takes place the moment he returns. Right here at St. Symphorian's—a splendid affair at the height of the season, eh, Smedley?"

His mouth full, Sir Percival nodded vigorously.

"That soon?" Becca cried, her fork suspended. "I am not prepared! My trousseau—I . . . I must at least go to London to choose my gown. Surely Sir Percival can muster enough patience to allow for that? And then there are the parties, the fetes, Almack's. Am I not allowed the amenities other debutantes enjoy before their betrothals?" Anything to stall for time. "And why St. Symphorian's? Why a dilapidated Norman relic? Why not one of the fine churches in London?"

Her father waved her off with a gesture. "I haven't the blunt for all that taradiddle. Parties and fetes, harrumph! Money thrown away, if you ask me. I've settled enough upon you, my girl. And the vicar at St.

Symphorian's will be glad of any token. Not so your toplofty London vicars. Why, they'd rob me blind, the mealy-mouthed grubbers."

"Ah!" she said. "I had forgotten that we wouldn't be having this at all but for what you have *settled* upon me, Father."

The words were a mistake, she realized, the minute they were out. They brought his hard stare upon her from the carver's chair. She wasn't sorry she'd spoken, though. Enough was enough. She was what she was, after all; an independent—no milk-and-water-miss to be brought to her knees and made to pay for the vile deeds of others. That was why she'd run away in the first place. Granted, independence in women of her class was not something that had gained widespread acceptance. Neither was it encouraged. She did, therefore, need to be more mindful of her attitude, else she be found out. That would take some doing, across the table from two such unscrupulous individuals as these, who cunningly thought to shape her future. She had to keep in mind that no matter what they said or did, she knew something they did not. She would never be the wife of Sir Percival Smedley. Never, ever. She would carry out her original plan and shut herself up in a convent, if needs must, first.

"Still willful and unbending, I see," said her father, laying his fork aside. A blustery nasal sigh bowed his posture. "I spoke too soon earlier, but no matter. That will change soon enough, daughter. Now then, there will be no trip to London for your trousseau. Your gown and whatever fripperies you require you may purchase in Truro. I shall accompany you and your abigail there while Sir Percival journeys to Town for the license. I will not squander good blunt after bad having you off to teas and parties and fetes—no voucher from those harpies at Almack's so that you may flit around the ballroom floor like a horse on the block at

Tattersall's. To what purpose? You have bagged your bridegroom. There is no need to bait a trap already sprung—not with my coin. I am no Golden Ball Hughes. And now, I think you will leave the table, but before you do, you have been rude to your betrothed. You owe him an apology."

Becca tossed her serviette in the middle of her plate of salmon, splattering the sauce, and surged to her feet. Her father's intractable eyes were riveted on hers. Sir Percival's rheumy, half-foxed gaze was fixed upon his cucumbers béchamel. She gave both men a passing glance before addressing her father.

"Sir Percival would think me disingenuous were I to pretend that this forced union were in any way desired by me. You cannot make of it what it is not, Father, for all that you will try in order to assuage your conscience." She turned cold eyes upon Sir Percival. "While we are on the subject of my *betrothed* here," she added, "it might behoove you to teach him the ways of a proper toilette. He stinks, sir! He reeks of filth and sweat and urine from head to toe, not to mention the spirits he's spilled more than drunk. He offends! It is no hardship being sent from the table, Father. It is a *mercy!*"

Leaving them both with their jaws sagging, Becca spun on her heel and stalked from the dining hall. She would have run screaming into the night if the doors were not barred against it. Instead, she dragged herself up the staircase and locked herself inside her chamber.

The waning moon winking through her terrace doors caught her eye, and she opened them and stepped outside on the little balcony that overlooked the garden. On nights such as this, when conditions were just right, the clean water scent of Boscastle Falls drifted close on the evening mist. Becca took a deep breath to cleanse the stench of Sir Percival Smedley, and another scent wafted close—Klaus's scent. Where had he gone? Where had Lindegren Hall gone? She couldn't have dreamed it. There were times when she almost wished she had, because of the intimacies they'd shared . . . but she had not. His voice was in her head—*mitt kostbart*—that strange foreign endearment delivered in a baritone rumble that sent shivers through her soul. What she wouldn't give to hear him speak it just once more.

Yes, his essence was in her nostrils. But the warmth of his strong arms around her was gone. If what he'd told her was the truth, she had done what had to be done. She had spared herself a life of loneliness and misery, because she would have yielded to his prowess, succumbed to the promise of ecstasy in those arms she now fantasized around her. She would not have been able to resist. Her instincts were correct. She'd done the right thing in leaving Lindegren Hall. But she hadn't really left him. He was still with her. She could feel him, smell him, taste him. She'd carried the little conch shell with her ever since he'd given it to her. Reaching for it now, she slipped it from her pocket and raised it to her ear. Like magic, the sighing ocean echoed from inside—*his* ocean. She could almost see it in her mind: majestic fjords, high-curling breakers crashing on the Swedish shore. Her lower lip began to tremble. Tears welled in her eyes. She blinked them back relentlessly. If she'd done the right thing, why couldn't she forget him, and why did her heart hurt so?

# *Chapter Thirteen*

The night of the masked ball came too soon to suit Becca. The guests began arriving at dusk. Before full dark, the drive and the lane to the stables were littered with carriages of every size and description. Broughams and landaus, coupes and phaetons, high- and low-perched carriages of distinction—open and closed—lined the well-manicured grounds.

The lavish Grand Ballroom was decked out in festoons and garlands of flowers from the garden. The scent and sight reminded Becca of the breathtaking flowers she'd viewed in the astral realm. Why did everything remind her of Klaus?

Despite her refusal to model her costume for alterations, it fit like a glove. Literally. All eyes were upon her as she moved among the guests in Grecian glory, her head draped in a flowing scarf of matching silk, with only one thought in mind: escape. If things went as planned, before the night was out she would be safe and away from Gildersleeve Grange—this time, forever.

By midnight, when the betrothal was to be announced, the guests would be in their altitudes. The gentlemen among them were already mildly foxed, their conversation a constant buzz of anticipation of private games to commence once the announcement was made. It was a house party, after all. Most of the guests would be staying the weekend. These, however, would be her father's gambling associates, hardly the *haute ton*. They were for the most part parvenues possessed of "new money," as the ladies delicately put it, usually ill-gotten gains. Such monies were often obtained in the gambling hells, through crafty investments or blatant extortions. But these men were all anxious to court the company of any plump enough in the pockets to assure them of more blunt at the gaming tables.

Their wives and daughters, brought along for show, would remain closeted with the chaperones who had come to take charge of the younger girls after hours, while the men pursued other sports, such as shooting, boxing, and all manner of mindless male competitions, ultimately leading back to the private salon, and the cards and dice and endless rounds of wine and Blue Ruin that fueled their passion for the almighty games of chance. Becca had suffered through many such weekends at Gildersleeve Grange. This was the last. The gates were unlocked to accommodate the endless parade of coaches. If things went as planned, she would slip away when the opportunity presented itself, with no one the wiser. If all went well, she wouldn't be missed until morning. By then, she would be long gone, alone.

Becca picked out Sir Percival early on. Dressed as a nabob, he cut a ridiculous figure among the domino-clad populace where flowing, hooded capes and elaborate bird masks seemed the attire of choice. Few men were decked out in genuine costume. It wasn't a serious masque, after all, nothing more than a thinly veiled excuse to gamble. Not so where the women were concerned, however. Everyone from milkmaids to neoclassical queens of the Nile lined the fringes of the ballroom, for the most part standing idle and ignored. They jigged about in place to the rhythm of the low-country dances, to the new French quadrilles, and to lively gallops, their fans fluttering in a vain attempt to stir a breeze in the hot, crowded ballroom. Few of their male counterparts whisked them out on the dance floor. The men stood huddled in groups, their hooded heads together, their glasses lifted, clinking musically, as they planned their strategies for the gaming to come.

Across the corridor, the dining hall was overflowing with food. Hot and cold viands were laid out upon the sideboards and dining table, awaiting the guests, who would straggle in throughout the evening and avail themselves of the fare. Two footmen decked out in gold and crimson livery presided, keeping the food in good supply and the punch bowls, as big as washtubs, filled with rum punch, ratafia, and claret cup: something for everyone's taste. Servants lurked everywhere, hoping for a glimpse of the costumes, of the dancing, and the splendid decorations that had brought the Grange to life. Maud was among them, as Becca knew she would be. With a close eye upon her abigail, she moved among the guests awaiting the right moment to slip away and disappear.

Thank the stars Sir Percival was not a dancer. The mere thought of being so close to the man turned Becca's stomach. Mercifully, he kept his distance, casting her sheepish glances now and again. Had her tirade in the dining hall humbled him? He'd seemed embarrassed at the time, and had kept his distance since. Soon, he and her father would be occupied with the gaming, and she would be free.

The orchestra had struck up a scandalous *valse du*

*temps,* very new, very French, and very shocking, but
something everyone was anxious to try. Becca supposed the musicians had chosen the piece to stimulate
more interest in dancing, since the entire gathering
had separated into male and female camps, and their
efforts thus far had been wasted. Several pairs ven-
tured forth, then several more, but Becca was not
among them. Marveling at how few of the guests she
recognized, she crept back toward one of the convenient alcoves curtained with potted palms and ferns
and aspidistras perching upon pedestals.

Only a few of the local gentry—a doctor, and the
Earl of Sustenbury and his wife—were familiar to her;
the others she surmised to be gambling associates of
her father's. On the whole, the costumes fooled no
one. The wearers were easily recognized behind their
finery and feather masks. Disguises simply gave the
guests the freedom to behave in an unconventional
manner, often bordering upon something less than
proper. These affairs did have a way of going beyond
the pale.

Gentlemen in their cups, or well on their way there,
often took bold liberties: a hand prowling too close to a
lady's décolletage, or settling familiarly on a provocative bottom, a stolen kiss, a risqué phrase whispered in
an inclined ear. Masked balls were notorious for en-
couraging all manner of lewd behavior. Considering
her father's preoccupation and the lack of a mature
hostess, who might have kept such occurrences to a
minimum, this ball was no exception, despite the aus-
picious occasion it marked.

How like ostriches they all seemed, hiding behind
their masks, as though no one could see what they
were about. The women were no better, twittering behind their fans, signaling to the gentlemen. Left hand
flutter, "Come hither." Right hand flutter, "You are too
bold." Closed fan tapping the face, "I love you." Still

fan open in the right hand, "I am married." Still fan open in the left hand, "I love another"—all the hidden meanings. How ridiculous it seemed.

Becca had nearly reached the alcove when strong hands whirled her into stronger arms. All at once she found herself gliding over the ballroom floor in the embrace of a tall, domino-clad gentleman wearing a mask of silvery spangles fitted like scales. She gasped. The costume he wore beneath the flowing hooded cape shone like silver, also. It was sheer and skintight— so fine in texture, the way the candlelight struck it he seemed naked. Her heart tumbled in her breast.

"I have missed you, *mitt kostbart*," he murmured, in that seductive baritone rumble that set her on fire.

"Wh-what are you doing here? H-how have you come here?" Becca breathed. She clung to him as he whirled her about, for then she had need of support. "You cannot stay . . . My father! He will see you! He will *know* you!"

"He cannot see me and he will not know me. This moment does not exist. Look around you. It is as it was when I took you into the astral."

"No! I shan't go back there! I *won't!*" Panic at the thought almost rendered her senseless.

"Shhh, my Becca . . . my love . . . not *there*, but away from here . . . just for a little. You will not be missed, and you will not be harmed. Do you trust me, *mitt kostbart?*"

"*No!*" she cried. How could he even ask? She glanced about. She had shouted, yet no one seemed to notice. What sorcery was this?

He inclined his head, and his quicksilver eyes shone through the eyeholes in the spangled mask, shimmering in the candle glow. Tears glistened there. They evoked her own. He looked so dreadfully sad, like a wounded animal.

"Of course you do not," he said, answering his own

question. "It was too much to hope for . . . though I foolishly did hope. You would never have left me if you did. But we must not part as we have done. Will you give me one last chance to prove myself worthy of your trust . . . so that if we must part, at least we do so as friends?"

"No," she said. "I mean . . . yes . . . oh, I don't know what I mean!"

"Close your eyes and hold fast to me," he whispered.

His hot, moist breath against her ear sent shivers of unbridled pleasure racing along her spine, fiery waves of sweet sensation gripping her belly and thighs. Across the way, her father and Sir Percival had attached themselves to a group of gentlemen heading for the dining hall. They were gone in a blink. They hadn't even seen her. The waltz was coming to an end, and the heat of Klaus's hand at her waist through the pongee silk called her back to meet his hooded gaze.

"Now, my Becca," he murmured. "It must be now. . . ."

Becca could not meet those eyes. She could not bear the look in them, nor think beyond the fact that she was the cause of it. Just as he bade her, she held him tight with all her strength and shut her eyes. When she opened them again, they were standing in the midst of Boscastle Falls, cloaked in the sugary-fine spindrift rising all around them. It had soaked the thin pongee silk of her costume. She glanced down, and her heart leapt. The wet fabric clinging to her body had become transparent. She might as well have been naked.

In spite of herself, she stiffened in his arms, those wonderful strong arms she had so longed to hold her. They were holding her now, and she should pull away—but she couldn't. She should run for her life, but she couldn't do that either. It was as if her feet had become rooted in the mist, just as his were. Invisible. They betrayed her. The magnetism between them was riveting. The pull was more than she could resist. He was all she wanted—all she ever would want. Those arms were crushing her fast to his hard, muscled chest, to the pulsating pressure of his sex leaning heavily against her, and she wanted it to go on forever.

"Why did you run from me?" Klaus murmured against her hair. He tilted her face up to meet his gaze. The spangled mask was gone. So were the great flowing domino and the skintight silvery, costume that made him appear naked. He *was* naked! Only the mist stood between them then, groping their bodies like living things in the moonlight. "You were listening at the door, weren't you? What was said that sent you out of my house, where you were safe, in the dead of night, right into the arms of your father—the last place you wanted to be, *mitt kostbart?*"

"The tale you told me of the *Fossegrim* . . . it was true, wasn't it? I heard you say it! You meant to . . . to take my virtue and leave me with child. With *your* child, never to see you again. And in the same breath, you speak of love? Who are you—*what* are you—that you could do such a thing? No! Do not be so quick to answer, *your highness*. I will not give you my virtue, and I will not let you take it, either! When I give myself it will be for love of a man I will spend the rest of my life with, whose children I will bear, and whose life will be one with my own."

"I cannot take your virtue, *mitt kostbart*," said Klaus, searching her face. "Remember? You must give it freely in order to fulfill that destiny. You did not listen long enough to what was said behind that closed door or you would have heard more of love."

"Love is not enough."

"You do love me, my Becca. I know you do . . ." he murmured. "I knew it before you did, and it unfolded like a perfect rose when I took you into the astral. I read your thoughts there. It was worth the journey to the Otherworld for that alone."

"But I do not trust you, or your kind. You are deceivers! You say one thing and mean another. You pretend one thing when you are something else entirely. You have managed to convince me that the astral realm is real, but the creatures that dwell there are cruel deceivers who mean humans harm. That part of legend is truth entire. I have witnessed it firsthand—that she-creature. She would have killed me if she could!"

"Oh, yes, quite so. You strayed from the path. And who saved you?"

Becca scowled, her eyes flashing. "Y-you did," she said in a small voice.

"Were you harmed?"

"No, just shaken."

"No, and you will never be harmed in my keeping. But I see that I must earn your trust, *mitt kostbart*, before I tell you what is in my heart—what you would know if you hadn't run from me and taken my heart with you . . . ripped it out of me as if you'd gouged it from my body with a cleaver."

"Your highness—"

"Say my name, Becca. Please?"

"Your highness, I—"

He shook her gently. "*Say it.* No idiotic protocol applies here in this place. We are not bound by the dictates of society here, only by nature and the gods. Speak my name, my Becca. Just once."

"Take me back, Klaus," Becca murmured, "if that even is your name. If you love me, as you say you do . . . I beg you, take me back."

"To what? To *him*—to your *betrothed?* I saw the coxcomb—an aging coxcomb, come to that. You would rather suffer a union with such a one than let me love you?"

"I will never suffer that. But I cannot stay with you either. I cannot."

"Still, you do not trust me."

"No, Klaus. I do not trust myself."

Those eyes! Those mesmerizing, ice-blue quicksilver eyes were boring into her. His hand on her cheek was like balm as he tilted up her head to meet his hooded gaze again. How gently he handled her, as if she were made of the finest porcelain, and likely to break. His breathing had become rapid, his hot breath sweet against her skin. When he spoke, her heart leapt. Though his voice was no more than a whisper, it crackled with desire, sending shivers along her spine, reverberating through her trembling body. She moaned in spite of herself. She was helpless against the power of his passion.

"You need not trust yourself if you can trust me, Becca. Let me prove it. . . ."

The mating urge was stronger than it had ever been. It would be thus until the moon waxed full again. For all his fine words, Klaus was not all that certain he could resist. He had never been in love before. Making matters worse, he was fading. He had been away from the falls too long. The energy he'd used transporting Becca there had weakened everything but his libido. It was always heightened with exhaustion. This test was not only to prove something to Becca, it was for himself as well. Everything depended upon his being equal to it. The water would revive him, but was that really wise? He was ravenous with want of her.

Her skin was like rose petals beneath his fingers as he slid them along her arched throat and over her shoulders. It was no use. He couldn't prevent them from touching. It was as if they had a will of their own. Catching the drape that held the Grecian gown in place, he inched it down in a painstakingly lingering motion that wrenched a breathless gasp from Becca's throat.

"Don't!" she murmured, though she made no other protest. It was as if she were frozen in place, gazing up into his eyes, her own dilated with desire, sparkling like black diamonds in the moonlight. He'd seen them once, black diamonds . . . in another lifetime. But these! These were far more precious—far rarer, more mysterious. They shone only for him.

His thumbnail grazed her nipple as he exposed her breasts. Again she gasped, as the taut tip hardened and grew tall beneath his fingertips. His own breath caught at the dimpled feel of it tightening against his skin. He could not dissuade his fingers from caressing that perfect breast now, from cupping its trembling, silken fullness.

His manhood leapt erect, and he could bear no more. One motion cast off the gown. It disappeared in the mist about her slender ankles, and she stood naked before him, but for the long rectangular scarf draped about her head and fluttering in the breeze. She was perfectly formed—every quivering inch that she so desperately tried to hide from his hungry eyes gleamed like Parian marble. Her arms flew every which way at once in a bold attempt to conceal her charms. She could not. He would not let her. Capturing her tiny hands in his, he raised them to his lips, and she shuddered as he slid his warm tongue along the tender flesh on the insides of her wrists—first one and then the other, feeling the pulse beat—savoring the rhythm of the blood pumping wildly through her veins. She was his for the taking, on the verge of surrender.

"Let me . . . look at you," he panted, sliding his familiar gaze the length of her from the fine cap of sunset-gold ringlets that crowned her to the likewise fiery wisps of down curling between her thighs. Her gaze was riveted to his sex, and it leapt again, as if she'd touched it, for that look alone was a caress. He groaned, pulling her against him, nestling his anxious member in that downy thatch he ached to part and enter. How perfectly they fit together—like two pieces of a puzzle. She was the missing part of him. That was what frightened him so. It threatened his immortality. No female creature—human or fey—had ever done that before. *And from the very first.* Was she a sorceress, a witch? It didn't matter. Nothing did, except that she must be his, no matter the cost. "You are . . . exquisite," he murmured against her ear.

She was ready, ripe for conquest. Her slender arms were around him, pulling him closer to the warm, moist promise of fulfillment beyond imagining. All was as it should be. There was no protest. She had come willingly into his arms. They stood where it must happen, with the falls spinning yards of gossamer mist about them, rooting them to the riverbed— to their destiny. His sex was bursting, aching, ready to explode. He took it in his hand and guided it between her legs until it rested upon her hardened bud, and he held his breath.

The cosmic pull was unbearable, like the pull of the moon upon water, powerful enough to turn the tides. It rocked his very soul. His head spun dizzily. Ancestral voices whispered to him, urging him on. They had never had to coax him before. Becca groaned at the pressure of his sex leaning heavily against her, and he feared his bones would melt. He swallowed her groan with a hungry mouth. Another and another resonated through his body as she crowded eagerly into his embrace. He kissed her deeply, tasting the warm, honey sweetness of her mouth, of her silken skin. He suckled at her breasts, a heartbeat away from mating with this exquisite creature who had set loose a firestorm in his quaking loins. The pain was excruciating—beyond bearing. Why, when the way was clear for him to fulfill his obligation, did he hesitate?

Klaus ground his teeth and raised his eyes to the heavens. They smarted with unshed tears of anguish and pain that blurred his vision. Gray clouds raced before the moon. It looked wounded in its waning, as if a chunk had been bitten out. Soon it would be moon dark then slowly it would wax full again, and his time would be at an end. Now, it winked down through the passing clouds as if to capture his attention. Where had the sudden wind come from? It lifted the scarf still clinging to Becca's head and carried it away. Strong gusts ruffled his own hair, and he narrowed his gaze upon the breathtaking beauty in his arms. She seemed not to notice in her rapture. The spell had worked. The gods help him—*Syl* help him . . . she was his!

His breath was coming short, and his heart hammered so fiercely against his ribs that he was certain it would burst from his breast. The voices in his head grew louder, buzzing around in his brain like a swarm of angry bees. The sound was rife with threats and righteous indignation. The elders were angry. Becca was ripe for the plucking. Why did he hesitate? What was he waiting for? Their shouts filtered through his brain in a surly rumble. He would pay for this. He would go before the tribunal if he failed.

Her breasts were flattened against him, the nipples buried in his chest hair. Their hardened nubs shot him through with excruciating ecstasy. Her tiny hand reached for the shaft of his sex pressed against her. How soft her fingers were. How delicate and fine. Her touch was like the kiss of a butterfly's wing. It was enough. His manhood heaved with the contractions he'd fought so valiantly to hold back, and he groaned and put her from him just in time. The wind had brought her headscarf back. It was as if the elements would torment him with it, spreading her scent, blocking his view of her. Seizing it in a white-knuckled fist, he took the fabric back from the wind. His body convulsed, and he melted into the astral with a bestial howl that echoed, amplified by the fall of rainbow-bright water glistening in the moonlight.

## *Chapter Fourteen*

Becca's whole body throbbed like a pulse. She was standing in the middle of the ballroom at Gildersleeve Grange. Her father was leading Sir Percival and a group of domino-clad men toward the dining hall, just as he had been before the dream began. It had to have been a dream. She never would have done those things, permitted such liberties otherwise. Was she having nightmares in her waking hours now? Just so! But it had seemed so real.

She glanced down at her Grecian costume. It was dry. She groped her head. Where had her scarf gone? She glanced about. It was nowhere to be seen. Klaus had said the moment didn't exist. Had she imagined him? Whether she had or she hadn't, the throbbing in her body was real enough. So was the terrible pounding of her heart, as though she'd nearly run herself to death.

It was said that lovers possessed the power to meet in their dreams. Is that what had just occurred? Had she conjured him out of a secret wish to be in those dynamic arms? No . . . she couldn't have imagined the shocking intimacies they'd shared. She had no knowledge of such things. How could she have? Aside from Klaus, no man had ever touched her lips, much less disrobed her. And exploring her body with his hands, with his lips, and causing such scandalous sensations at her very core. . . . Hot blood rushed to her temples, and she thrilled afresh, remembering. Her cheeks were on fire.

She was losing her mind. She had to be. The *Fossegrim* was *myth*. But if that were so, why did her thrumming sex feel thick and swollen, wanting release from the brink of ecstasy to which he'd led her? Why was his scent still in her nostrils, as sweet and fresh as the sea—as the waterfall itself?

Becca backed toward the alcove and the convenient potted plant she'd been heading for when the dream began. She glanced around the room. No one noticed her. Maud was nowhere in sight, and her father had disappeared into the hallway, no doubt gorging himself upon the endless viands and dainties and spirits in the dining hall across the way. She shook herself the way a dog sheds water, as if to rid herself of the shocking thoughts of Klaus Lindegren. There was no time for him now. This was the perfect moment to carry out her plan, to steal out unobserved. The few men who remained in the ballroom were too foxed to dance. The women had given over their ridiculous jigging and were now engrossed in idle conversation instead. Meanwhile, the orchestra played on, dance after dance, in a vain attempt to coax someone out on the ballroom floor.

Becca crept along the fringes, pretending she was headed for the dining hall. No one detained her. No one even noticed. She drew an easy breath. She would steal away and never return. Her father could sort out his debt with Sir Percival how he would. It mattered not. She would have no part in it. Tonight she would be

free. Free of a marriage she could not bear. Free of her
father's pitiable weakness that had driven him to such
lengths and nearly ruined her life . . . and free of Klaus,
the phantom lover of her dreams. But . . . not yet. There
was something she must do first, just to be sure.

She had already packed her traveling bag. All that
remained was to fetch her hooded cloak. It was still far
too warm for such a wrap, but she could hardly go
about scantily costumed as a Grecian goddess, and
there wasn't time to change. She had nearly reached
the staircase, when a hand on her arm arrested her.

"And where might you be goin', my lady?" said a
voice that ran her through and stopped her in her
tracks.

It was Maud. What she wouldn't give for some of
Anne-Lise's herbal potion now!

"To my rooms . . . to relieve myself, if you must
know," said Becca, thinking on her feet, hoping the excuse would gain her some measure of privacy.

"You'd best hurry, then," said the abigail. " 'Tis
nearly midnight. They'll be makin' the announcement
soon. The men are rarin' ta have a go at the gamin'."

"I shan't be long," Becca replied.

"I know it. I'm comin' with ya ta make sure. You're
all flushed from the heat. Ya need a bit o' talc on them
cheeks. It's your big moment. Ya don't want ta look all
red in the face."

"As you wish, Maud," Becca begrudged loftily, "but
then you may retire. I shan't need you again tonight.
This flimsy gown poses no difficulties. I shall ready
myself for bed."

The abigail pulled a face. It was plain she wanted to
remain until the last of the guests had staggered up to
their rooms, to soak up every drop of ambience that
she could never hope to experience otherwise. Well,
that wasn't to be. Becca could hardly escape while
Maud was watching her like a hawk.

Perhaps this was a better plan. Once the announcement was made, the men would be about their gambling, closeted in one of the gaming rooms until dawn, and the women would retire. It would be easier to slip out unnoticed. Becca almost smiled, treading up the stairs, a close eye upon Maud trailing after her, the maid's pinched face like a thunderhead.

"What?" she reproached the abigail. "Once the announcement is made and our engagement is official, I will take an interview alone with my betrothed. I am allowed; am I not? It is permitted that we sit and talk unchaperoned for a bit. Would you watch that, too? I've seen you spying upon your betters, Maud, as though you would live vicariously through them. It is reprehensible. You need to remember your place. Now, enough! Dust me with talc if you must, but then retire. I do not wish to see you gawking at the guests downstairs again tonight. You needn't guard me any longer. Am I plain?"

"Y-yes, my lady," Maud grumbled. "You've had a change o' heart, then? I thought, well . . . you wasn't agreeable before. That's why we left so sudden, and—"

"That is my prerogative," Becca interrupted, "and none of your affair. Suffice it to say that I have decided to make the best of a bad situation in deference to my father's wishes and have done. Now, come along if you're coming. Don't dawdle. You were the one concerned about the time."

At the stroke of twelve, liveried footmen carried trays of glasses filled with French champagne into the Grand Ballroom, each glass adorned with a fresh raspberry. A net stretched across the vaulted ceiling was undone, releasing a shower of rose petals as Cedric Gildersleeve announced his daughter's betrothal to Sir Percival Smedley. At sight of the petals drifting down, Becca's heart sank. They reminded her of the ones

Klaus had strewn over her bed on her last night at Lindegren Hall. She bit her lip, fighting back sorrow.

Maud was nowhere in sight. Becca was glad of that, since she had no true intention of having a moment alone with her blithering, half-castaway fool of a fiancé. There wouldn't have been much danger of that in any case. The minute the champagne was drunk, Sir Percival disappeared with the others to the gaming room, and Becca blended in with the ladies as they retired to their respective chambers. It worked like a charm. Too well, thought Becca. Tossing her cloak about her shoulders, she dragged the traveling bag out from under her bed. As she started toward the door, something shiny and catching glints from the candle branch on the bedside table caught her eye: the conch shell, its pearly patina seeming to beckon to her. Taking a pocket from the drawer in her chiffonier, she slipped the shell into it and tied the ribbon inside the bodice of her gown. She couldn't bear to leave the shell behind; it was all she had of him, and tears misted her eyes as she tiptoed down the backstairs, and out into the blustery night.

The air was too sultry to cool the fever in her face and in her blood. The heavy cloak made matters worse. The grooms and stablehands were fast asleep in the haymow when she reached the stables. It was just as well. She knew how to saddle a horse and set about it as quietly as possible, though she needn't have bothered. The stable floor, littered with a dozen empty bottles that once held wine, whiskey, and gin—her father's best Blue Ruin, at that—attested to the condition of those sorry men—one yet a boy. The horse was saddled in a trice, Becca's travel bag tied on securely behind, and she was on her way without a backward glance.

She would leave the horse at the coaching inn and hire a chaise, just as she had done before. Only this time she would have a reasonable head start, and she would succeed. By morning she would have put enough distance between herself and Gildersleeve Grange to elude pursuit, thanks to her father's gambling obsession. But first there was something she must do. Boscastle Falls were on the way, only a short distance through the wood from the lane she'd taken— a secluded lane, not one well-traveled. She'd chosen not to take the main route, just in case. She didn't know why, but she had to see the waterfall one last time . . . to prove Klaus's appearing at the masque, and everything following, had been a figment of her imagination. What she would do if it proved otherwise hadn't occurred to her. That was too embarrassing to think about.

Still clutching Becca's scarf, Klaus knelt at the edge of the river in the Otherworld, beating the pebble-crusted bottom with both clenched fists, scattering water in all directions. It was a moment before he saw Illia standing over him, her tiny fists braced on her shapely hips. Her demeanor bristled with smug satisfaction. A mocking water sprite was the last thing he needed, especially not *this* sprite, who thought she owned him. She snatched the pongee silk scarf out of his hand and draped it about her neck and shoulders, preening before her distorted reflection in the water.

"So! Ye have failed," she trumpeted, tripping this way and that as she adjusted the silk so as not to hide her perfect breasts.

"Be gone, petulant child," Klaus growled. "And take that off! You look ridiculous in it."

"And I suppose *she* did not? What manner of dress is this, then? There's scarce enough of the stuff to make a shift, and ye can almost see right through it. The fabric is fine, though," she conceded, rubbing the silk against her face.

Klaus made a grab for it. "Give it here!" he demanded, but she was too quick for him, whirling out of his reach.

"Oh, no!" she said. "I think I shall just keep this. It's only fair, don't ye think, since she has kept a hank of my hair?" She flicked her sea grass–plaited tresses with a rigid finger.

"Have it as you will. Just be gone and leave me in peace."

"To lick your wounds?"

"I have no wounds, but you surely will if you do not let me be!"

The sprite's demeanor changed and she sauntered closer, flaunting her nakedness. There had been times when the sight of her so had aroused him. The astral being a sensual plane, mating was as natural a function as breathing air, and often as frequent among the different species. Unabashed public coupling was common. There was no such thing as modesty among the fey. Illia had been his favorite. Looking at her now, he wondered how he could ever have embraced her. The slender, shapely figure she displayed—literally brandished in his face—aroused him no longer. Nothing could after Becca. *Ye gods! She has ruined me—even for my own kind,* he realized, with not a little panic.

"I would have ye *wound me* with your . . . weapon— even now, come fresh from your milk-and-water maiden, with her dew still fresh upon you," Illia purred, circling him. Each undulating motion was a seduction, from her jiggling breasts to the way she spread her legs when she moved. "What? Ye think I cannot smell her on your body? Yes, I would have ye even thus. Would she, if the situation were reversed? I think not, your highness. She would not touch ye if ye went to her with *my* juices still upon ye. She'd claw yer eyes out."

"You can be sure that we shall never put that to the

test," Klaus snapped. "Besides, we have not mated, she and I. And even if we had—"

"No, I know not," Illia flashed. "Because then ye would see her no more, and ye cannot do that, can ye? Ye cannot bear to leave her! Ye do yer father's sin. He could not leave yer mother, and they begat *ye*, more human than fey—a half-breed—with just enough of the *Fossegrim* in your tainted blood to keep ye bound to the astral as well, and give ye immortality."

"Enough!"

"No! I will keep silent no longer. Puffed up in your humanity, ye look down upon us! Ye mock us! Ye *betray* us! Ye take from both worlds and give to neither, Klaus Lindegren, and ye will come to the same sad end yer father did. Ye will wither and die alone, with yer woman, and yer seed will die with ye. So spend it where ye will. The world of mortal man is not so free with its pleasures as we of the astral are. Ye will see, my high and mighty prince, when her stiff morality keeps ye at your distance. When ye grow sore for wanting, ye will think of Illia and her willing ways, but then it will be too late!"

She snarled the last, and struck him in the face with the tail of Becca's scarf. Klaus vaulted to his feet and made another grab for it, but Illia spun out of reach again, taunting him with it from the rim of the falls above. Her harsh laughter rivaled the roar of the waterfall. It used to sound like bells tinkling. Now it sounded brittle, grating to his ears, like the rasp of breaking glass.

"I am still prince here yet awhile," he shouted. "You would do well to remember that."

"Here, yes . . . for a little while. But *there* ye are nothing, Klaus Lindegren. Nothing! Ye will see."

She was gone in a blink, vanished behind the tall curtain of water and mist, Becca's pongee silk scarf with her.

Klaus spiraled down on his haunches and pounded the river again. "Gods, ye fickle *gods!*" he roared. The curse sounded back from the falls, from the rocks, from the very night around him. The surrounding trees seemed to gasp at the outburst, but he paid them no mind. "Syl on his throne! No peace in this world— no peace in the other . . . !" he railed.

"And whose fault is that?" said an all-too-familiar voice close in his ear. "Do you really think angering the gods with blasphemy atop the rest will help your situation, your highness?"

Klaus's shuttered eyes came wide open. He glanced about. There was no one there. Loosing a string of blasphemies in Swedish, he screwed his eyes shut again and plunged headlong into the river. When he emerged again, he rose from the diaphanous mist of Boscastle Falls exactly as he'd left it, to face Henrik, waiting in his most reproachful foot-tapping attitude— arms folded across his chest—on the riverbank.

"She's right, you know," the elder said, "and I tire of playing the lowly valet. It is demeaning and degrading. I never should have consented to it. I am a venerable elder—a demigod, which you conveniently tend to forget. You might as well remain among these. You have fraternized so long with humans, you have become as one!"

"Because, I *am* one, at least by half, owing to my mother's lineage, which is something that *you* conveniently tend to forget, old one. That rankles the elders and the gods—and you, by god! I have no doubt. But what really catapults the lot of you into alt is that I was conceived *before* my father was cast out. He had fulfilled his obligation with my conception and *still* he chose to abdicate—to stay with my mother, and with me. That is what the astral hierarchy cannot countenance! He took a chance, caught them off guard. It shan't happen again. They are ready for me. I shan't be so fortunate. No matter all the years I have striven to prove myself; all that is wasted. I now stand upon the same threshold my father did, and what I do is crueler. I will not give them their token child. I will have my Becca as a mortal man. They will be cheated, and I will suffer for that. So be it! Let me be, Henrik!"

"Let you be—to waste your seed in the river, with a naked willing mortal female in your arms? What is this fine babbling now? Have you gone addle-witted?"

Klaus heaved a sigh. He wasn't even going to ask him how he knew. He stomped out of the water, snatched his domino up from the moss along the bank, and flung it about his shoulders with careless hands.

The elder made a rough gesture toward the heavens. "Do you see that moon up there?" he said. "We are running out of time, and I have wasted more of it than I care to measure helping you make reparation for your father's iniquity. You have much to atone for in his stead. No rebellion is without consequence. As the humans say, 'The sins of the fathers are visited upon the children.' You see? I do not fault the mortals in all things. I give credit where credit is due. I also mete out justice where that is due. You have an obligation to set things right."

"I am not the last of my kind, Henrik."

"No, not the last, but *the best!*" the elder retorted. Why did he argue with Henrik? He couldn't win. "You must set the example for the others," the elder went on. "Have you no idea of the damage your father's selfishness has done to the astral? Have you no inkling of the tear his leaving has rent in the cosmos? And now you mean to tear it *again?* And, as you say, more cruelly? The fabric is too fragile to stand a second rent. You will be outcast. You will lose your right of passage between the worlds. No waterfall will welcome you. You will condemn yourself to the agony of a mortal death. Is she worth your immortality, this human chit?

Is she worth your passage to the Otherworld? Think carefully, your highness. Does she feel as you do? I think not. She lusts, as you lust! She is bewitched by fairy glamour and you are bewitched by fleshly desire! Think! Did she believe your tale? No! She does not even acknowledge that you exist, my fine, blind water-lord. Take her now, I say, or take another, and have done with mortal fantasies! Carry on as you are and I wash my hands of you. As things stand, you court the tribunal. So be it!"

"Right now I court a clean, dry bed," said Klaus, turning the elder toward the lane, "and time to plan my next encounter with her. She thinks it was a dream—that all of our intimate encounters were dreams, come to that. It has been beneficial that she thought so in the past, but no longer. Somehow I must show her that her dreams are real. After tonight, it is plain that it is time."

"Madness!" cried Henrik, throwing wild arms into the air. "You have not heard one word I've said!"

"I've heard," Klaus said succinctly. "But I do not agree. You're wrong, you know . . . about what she feels. Oh, I will own that she probably does not know it yet, but she does love me, Henrik. You may have observed, but you did not hold her in your arms."

All at once, an epiphany:

"By the gods, perhaps that is it!" he ranted on. "It is the love that has bewitched me, and my father before me. There is no fault in you that you cannot see it. How could you? There is no love as the mortals know it in the astral—only lust—mindless, perfunctory lust. But the sweet madness of love . . . that and that alone is what has bewitched me, old friend. And yes, it is well worth the price of immortality."

# *Chapter Fifteen*

Becca approached the falls with caution. It was just as she'd seen it in the dream, like a place enchanted, ethereal and dazzling in the moonlight. The water tumbled over the rocks in a thunderous rush of impenetrable sound, giving way to great gauzy clouds on the breast of the water. The river sang as it rushed by, dispersing the tullelike mist as it carried south around the bend and disappeared among the overhanging foliage.

She slid from the gelding's back and tethered him to a young sapling. There, in the center, was the place where she'd stood with Klaus, where he'd held her, where his prowess and passion had almost taken her virtue . . . or would have done, if it weren't a dream.

The wind that had risen, ceased. The air was hot and still, and she pushed the hood back from her face. There was no need of it here, not until she set out on the lane again, in case she met with someone who might recognize her.

She dared not linger long. She wasn't even certain why she'd come, not consciously . . . until she saw it: a splotch of white cloth clinging to a patch of green raspberry canes a few yards upriver. Her heart leapt and sank all in one motion. The cold, crippling fingers of a crawling chill parted her hair and slithered down her back like a lazy snake, rooting her to the spot. It couldn't be. But it *was*. There was the oblong head scarf of pongee silk that completed her costume, fluttering in a gentle breeze that had suddenly risen. The very one she'd missed when she returned to the masque.

Returned! It wasn't a dream, but that meant . . . Frantically, she reeled back in her mind to the exact moment she'd lost the scarf, praying for a logical explanation. But she hadn't lost it. Klaus had taken it. He'd gripped it in his fist and disappeared. Then in a blink she was back at the Grange, just as she had been before he'd whisked her off that ballroom floor. This was why she'd had to come, to see if it had bled over into the astral with him, or if he had left it behind. Not until that moment did she realize it: Her mind was fogged with love and lust and *him*.

Becca glanced in all directions, half-expecting Klaus to materialize out of the mist, but he did not. She was alone, with the ghost of him moving against her, holding her, caressing her, bringing her to the brink of an ecstasy beyond her wildest dreams. She had fallen in love with him. Not just the physical Klaus Lindegren, but the mysterious Otherworldly Klaus that she feared as much as loved, because she didn't fully understand him. The qualities that attracted her were rooted in that mystery, however. No other gentleman she'd ever met possessed them. It was true that she hadn't met many, only those who came and went to gamble with her father, but those she had met seemed shallow and flat by comparison. They had no depth, no layers to peel away, each to reveal another gem facet more brilliant than the last. How could a woman not love a man who worshipped her? Bereft of even her father's affection since her mother's death, and longing for love, how could she not respond to the tender attentiveness, to the gallantry that could spit in death's face to save another from its grasp? There in that haunted place, she could no longer deny what she had known almost from the first—that she had met her soulmate, and she'd had to fold a pleat in time and space to do it.

That, however, did not excuse the fact that he meant to fulfill his destiny in her and leave her with child, never to see her again. He could have done that in the dream that wasn't a dream, in that blink of time's eye that he'd made stand still. But he hadn't. He'd stopped just short of the mating that would have fulfilled him. He'd asked that she trust him. What was it he'd said? *You need not trust yourself if you can trust me, Becca. Let me prove it.* Then time stood still. What did it mean—that her fears were unfounded? That his love for her was greater than the instinct in his Otherworldly psyche that drove him in some mad, lascivious frenzy to answer the mating call? He *did* love her, even if he didn't fully realize it yet. There was no mistaking that, and he had resisted the mating call. But if he hadn't, would she have been able? Dared she trust herself in his presence again to find out? As much as she longed to live in those arms forever, the answer to that was a resounding *no.* She needed to put as much distance between herself and Klaus Lindegren as was humanly possible. Besides, if everything he'd told her were true by some mad happenstance, to defy his destiny would cast him out of the Otherworld for all time. If that were the case, she would not—could not—rob him of his immortality. The thought of such as that burdening her conscience was more than she could bear.

Time stood still again now, but differently. How much passed before she could put one foot in front of the other and move toward the scarf, she couldn't tell.

Fluttering in the hot night air, it seemed to beckon, and she stumbled toward it as if in a daze, until she'd come close enough to reach out toward it. Just as she did, a stronger gust lifted it, bellied the silk, and carried it off toward the falls.

Becca raced in pursuit, not even knowing why, except that she must reclaim it. It was all she had left of him. Something he'd touched. All she ever would have. Teased by the wind, it danced overhead at the edge of the river. She kicked off her Moroccan leather slippers in anticipation of having to step into the water to retrieve it and wriggled out of her cape. It was too heavy. It would drag her down, and she cast it aside on the riverbank. An odd dance ensued at the river's edge as she darted to and fro, jumping into the air in a vain attempt to grasp the elusive silk, but still it eluded her. There was nothing for it: She waded into the water, almost losing her balance to the current. There was no one to embrace her this time. No strong arms to steady her. Oh, how she longed for his arms, and yet she feared them now, or rather feared herself in them. Worse still, she was embarrassed. She had indulged her fantasy, thinking it a dream, and . . .

No! She wouldn't—couldn't—think about that now. It was too much to take in, even though he had told her all of it. Her mind simply would not grasp the connotations presented. One thing and one thing only occupied her then—retrieving that scarf. It was her only link to him—her only proof, because without it, she would never be able to make herself believe. As long as she had it, she would never be able to forget the reason she had to let him go. She needed it as a reminder of what was at stake if she were to give in to temptation in a moment of weakness.

She stepped deeper in. The water was nearly waist-high now. The scarf billowed like a ship's sail above her head, but she dared not jump up to reach it for fear

of losing her footing and being carried away by the
river. She didn't have to. All at once, the scarf dropped
down and covered her head. The trailing ends wound
themselves around her throat and tugged. The sheer
silk was pulled taut over her face, but through it an image took shape: the sea-green form of a woman, with
long flowing hair threaded through with slender plaits
of sea grass. Water droplets glistened in it like diamonds in the light of the low-sliding moon.

Becca opened her mouth to scream, but she could
not. Her gasping sucked the silk into her mouth and
cut off her air. She tugged at the twist that circled her
throat to no avail. It only grew tighter. Something was
driving her down into the water. The last thing she
heard before she sank beneath the surface was the
sound of a woman's wicked laughter.

All doubt of the astral plane's existence melted away
as Becca slipped beneath the breast of the river. She
had crossed the boundaries of the physical world and
entered the distortion just outside, where time passed
at the discretion of the astral gods. She recognized the
heady, evocative scent of the air from her last visit.
Then, she had taken it for a dream, but no longer. The
distinct freshness of water, and the scent of the plants
and herbs that grew in it, wafted through her nostrils.
Mysterious. Intoxicating. It smelled of ancient secrets,
scents remembered from another lifetime—strange
and yet familiar—and of *him*. But Klaus had not crossed
her over this time, and there was no rainbow mist to
guide her way, only blackness. The pongee silk scarf
that had lured her bound her eyes now, and her hands
were restrained with slender threads of something
strong, like vines that leaked a milky sap and smelled
of the earth. Though she could move her wrists about
in the slippery stuff, she could not work them free.

The ground beneath her was hard and unyielding.

When she squirmed about, her hands grazed it. Rock! Was this a cave? Whatever it was, there was an echo when she cried out, and no light seeped through her blindfold. It was dark as coal tar pitch.

"Ye cannot break free," said a female voice dripping venom, "and he will never find ye here. But I am not unfeeling. There is wine to quench your thirst, and if ye behave there will be food as well." The last was spoken in a softer tone, but Becca did not trust it. She gave a lurch when the cold marble goblet touched her lips and turned her head aside. Wracking her brain, she tried to call back every scrap of lore she'd learned in the nursery about the creatures of the astral plane. How much of it was actually true? She had no way of knowing. Only hours ago, no one could have convinced her that the Otherworld even existed. But now . . .

One thing that stood out in her mind was that one must never accept food or drink from the fey. Judging from the sprite's reaction to her refusal, she was glad she'd remembered, though her throat was parched and she longed to quench her thirst. To do so would enslave her in the astral. How cruel was Providence. Had she been granted her childhood dream to frolic among the fairies in the land of the fey only to discover that her wish had been granted but her dream had turned into a nightmare? She would be trapped there, never to return to the physical world again . . . if the tales were true.

"Who are you?" she demanded. "And why are you doing this? I have no quarrel with you."

"No quarrel, eh?" the sprite snapped. "He is mine, and he will always be mine. Without ye to turn his head from his duty to his race, to the elders—to the *gods*—he will be mine again. He will forget, just as he has forgotten all the others, and return to me."

"And how do you plan to keep me hidden here in his own domain, of all places—right under his nose?

You have not thought this through. He will find me, and no one will suffer for this but you!"

"Ahhhh, but ye are not in his domain, my lady, far from it, and he will never find ye. Ye will never find your way back, either, without a guide, and no one in this place will have truck with ye. Ye may as well drink the wine. It is foolish to abstain, and of no consequence. Ye are captured either way."

Again Becca turned her head aside and screwed her lips shut against the cold cup. Another thing she recalled was to never trust the word of an astral creature.

The sprite shrieked and thrashed about, spilling the contents of the goblet on Becca's Grecian gown. It chilled her, seeping through the already damp silk, and Becca shuddered. She was on her own in this inhospitable place, and at an acute disadvantage against this creature. She needed to know more if she would outwit her captor and escape. But where would she go if she did? The creature was right: She would never find her way back without a guide.

"You haven't answered my question," she hedged. "Who *are* you?"

The sprite made no reply.

"Take off the blindfold that I might see you for myself. I am not comfortable conversing with shadows."

"Your comfort means naught to me," the sprite shot back. "Take care, else what *comfort* I have graciously spared ye be rescinded."

"Oh, well then, if you are that afraid—"

"Illia fears nothing!" the sprite shrilled. "Least of all the milk-and-water likes of ye." Her voice echoed, grating on the silence. Gooseflesh crimped Becca's scalp and riddled her body with chills at the sound. At least now she knew the creature's name, but was it the sprite's *real* name? It was said that all entities that dwelled in the Otherworld had secret names—true names, known only to themselves and the gods who had awarded them, along with their protective spirit totems. To know such a name, and to address a creature thus, would break the hold it had upon one. What could that name be? What could Klaus's be, for that matter? Oddly, Becca dismissed the latter thought out of hand, chilled at the realization that she didn't want to be set free from the enigmatic Klaus Lindegren. Ever. Illia, however, was quite another matter. She had already outwitted the sprite once. Please God, she could do so again.

"That being the case, why keep me blindfolded?" she asked.

The sprite was silent.

"Is your power so weak that you cannot look me in the eye, then?"

There was a tug at the knot in the scarf, and then it was ripped away. It was a moment before Becca could see clearly. The blindfold had been tied so tightly, her long eyelashes were tangled, and her vision was fuzzy until she blinked the condition away.

"Satisfied?" Illia snapped.

"Somewhat," said Becca. She glanced about the perimeter. A cave, indeed, at the end of what seemed like a tunnel lined with stalactites and stalagmites, like teeth poised to bite along the narrow ledge that parted a cavernous abyss. Dripping water echoed, amplified by the vaulted ceiling of the place. The slimy deposits glistened in an illusive light source that took Becca a moment to identify—will-o'the-wisps, bobbing about just out of view. The light they gave off came clear before their spherical shapes appeared. But their presence was short-lived. A shriek from Illia dispersed them, and fireflies were all that remained. Flitting to and fro, the insects were more of a distraction than a help, and Becca longed to free her hands and swat them away as they buzzed about her face.

Yes. This was the creature that had attacked her earlier. She was certain. It was a fistful of Illia's lustrous sea green hair that she had brought back into the physical world—proof positive that the astral existed, though then she'd still had doubts. Not so any longer. This was no dream. Becca had stumbled onto a phenomenon known only to a privileged few. She was beginning to regret the fact that she numbered among them.

"You cannot mean to keep me bound here indefinitely," Becca said to the sprite. "You shall have to loose my tethers eventually unless you mean to murder me, and quite frankly I cannot believe you are so foolish. The body of a mortal isn't something all that easy to hide. And I cannot believe that all who dwell here are of a like mind with you."

"Ye shall be hidden well enough if I toss ye into that chasm," said the sprite.

"True, but if that was your intent, I think you would have done so by now. If you were going to, that is. Why haven't you?"

The sprite fell silent again. Becca took heart: This was a good sign. Illia had captured her, but she wasn't sure what to do next.

"I shall not do murder," Illia purred, as though struck with inspiration, dashing Becca's hopes. "There is no need. I shall simply keep ye here confined just so, until my lord's time in the mortal plane is up. When the moon waxes full again, he will either have fulfilled his destiny in the belly of another or been driven back in disgrace to face the tribunal." She shrugged. "They will chastise him, but he is too powerful to banish. Either way, he will forget ye, but he will never forget me."

"You forget there is another alternative," Becca reminded her.

"Hah! I think not," said the sprite, confident at first. After a moment, a frown spoiled her face. "What other alternative? Speak it!" she demanded.

"That he decides to remain in the physical plane."

"Not without ye, he won't."

"Ahhh, but if he doesn't know my whereabouts and is convinced that he will find me there—"

"*Silence!* Be still! Ye mean to confuse me. He will return, I say, when time grows short, whether he has mated with your kind or not. I know him better than ye."

"You evidently do not know him as well as you think, Illia," Becca crowed, "but I shall let you find that out on your own."

"Silence, I say!" the sprite screeched. Her voice was like a wind roaring through the tunnel. It set Becca's teeth on edge. "It is decided! Ye remain until his time among your kind is done. Ye will be offered food and drink. The bonds on your hands will be loosened and ye will be leg-shackled, so that ye can take nourishment. Wipe off that look! The tethers are what ye mortals call *enchanted;* they cannot be broken. If ye do not partake of nourishment, the consequences are upon your head." She stooped and snatched the silk scarf up from the floor of the cave. Taking great pains to flaunt her perfect body, she draped it around her neck and fluffed out her hair. It reached to her buttocks in a cloud of seaweed-plaited splendor, and she obviously took great pride in it. She was exquisite. "Now, enough!" she concluded. "Ye will live to rue the day your modesty prevented him from spending his seed in ye so that he could return to me! Ye had best pray to your God that your *other alternative* does not occur, for if it does, ye will not ever see the sun rise on your world again."

# Chapter Sixteen

Klaus cared not a whit that a house party was in progress at Gildersleeve Grange; it worked to his advantage. Who could object to an acquaintance dropping by to inquire of the baron if he had found his daughter? Why, it would almost be a foregone conclusion that there would be such a visit. At least he was hoping so as he quit his carriage in the circular drive before the sun had cleared the tree line.

He addressed the brass doorknocker with authority—two rapid strikes—and stood back, taking his measure and adjusting his lapels. He dusted off his buckskins and polished the toes of his turned-down boots on the heels behind. Adjusting his low-crowned hat, he offset the wide brim at a casual angle, as befitting a gentleman on a leisurely jaunt in the country and waited. Just one glimpse of Becca—no matter her attitude toward him—would put his mind at ease. She had a propensity for flight. He needed reassurance that she hadn't gone that route again. That need was so great, he had forgone his early morning visit to Boscastle Falls. He was already beginning to regret it.

It seemed an eternity before a liveried footman opened the door. Klaus didn't need to enter to have his hopes dashed. The uproar spilled right past him and flooded the drive with a keening din that startled the horses the instant the old wood parted from the jamb.

"Count Klaus Lindegren," he announced, his voice raised over the racket, "come to pay my respects to the baron. I see that I have arrived at a bad time, but perhaps I might be of service . . ."

The footman hesitated, glancing behind toward a crowd that had gathered in the Great Hall. Klaus craned his neck, trying to assess the situation. Women were milling about in distress, Maud among them, wringing her hands and wailing. When their gazes met, her cries grew louder. Becca was nowhere to be seen, and Klaus could taste his fear, a cold, metallic taste, like blood—salty and thick, building at the back of his palate. It was a human condition. There was no fear in the astral realm, at least not this kind. Things were much easier when heart and loins were disjoined.

"Who is that there, Foster?" the baron barked, lumbering toward Klaus in the open doorway. He reeled like a man in his cups, the haggard look of him evidence of a sleepless night. He wore no coat or waistcoat, and his breeches were liquor-stained and wrinkled. Another man of middle age, likewise rumpled, came trailing after: Becca's infamous betrothed. It was easy to deduce that they had come fresh from a night of gambling and elbow bending. Anger set Klaus's blood racing. This did not bode well.

"C-Cou . . . Count . . ." the footman stammered.

"Count Klaus Lindegren, at your service, my lord," Klaus spoke up, with a heel-clicking bow, sparing the flustered footman the embarrassment of an awkward introduction, since the man had evidently forgotten his name in the rumpus. "You visited my estate on Bodimn Moor a fortnight ago."

"Ah!" the baron said, seizing Klaus's arm. "Come in, come in, old chap. Forgive the turmoil here. You might be of assistance."

"Your servant, sir," said Klaus, jogging along in tow.

Parting the milling crowd, the baron led him to the study. When they reached it, a firm hand planted in the middle of the chest of the man following halted him on the threshold, and the baron whisked Klaus inside, slamming the study door in the nonplussed man's face.

"Sit, sir!" said the baron, indicating a rolled-arm lounge. He strode to the liquor cabinet. "A brandy?" he queried, exhibiting the decanter.

"Thank you, no, my lord," said Klaus. "I do not imbibe at such an early hour—it hinders the digestion."

"Hmm," the baron grunted, filling his glass. "Then I hope you will excuse me," he said. "Digestion be damned! I need the fortification."

"I seem to have arrived at a most unfortunate moment," said Klaus. "I took a notion for a jaunt to the coast and thought to stop and inquire of your lost daughter, sir. When last we met, you were most distressed, searching for her. Did you ever find her?"

The baron tossed back his brandy and poured another. "She was found and now is lost again," he said, "which is the reason for the brouhaha in this house this morning."

"Lost again?" Klaus said. "How, lost?" Gooseflesh drew his scalp back suddenly, and his jaw muscles began to tick. He'd surmised as much, but hearing his fears confirmed had stricken him.

"Well, sir, I found the foolish chit walking the post road not far from your cottage with her abigail in the dead of night on my way back from Plymouth. At least I thought it was nearby your place, though for the life of me I couldn't find it afterward, or I would have stopped to ease your mind after my rather . . . abrupt intrusion. I am not entirely devoid of manners." He waved the thought off with a gesture and began to pace, brandy in hand. "My daughter, sir, is a wild, rebellious twit who has no respect for her father. Last evening, we had a grand engagement ball here to commemorate her betrothal to Sir Percival Smedley, the gentleman I left rather abruptly upon the doorstep just now. The announcement was made at midnight, then the gentlemen in our party retired to the gaming room and the ladies to their chambers—all but Rebecca, who has fled *again*."

"I am sorry, my lord," said Klaus. "What prompted her on this occasion?"

"The same thing that prompted her on the last. She is too shortsighted to see the benefit of a union with a man of Smedley's stamp. I wash my hands of her! That's why I'd given consent for the marriage. However, I will have her back before she does herself a mischief, to clear my conscience in the matter. Then, as soon as the special license is procured, I am well out of the whole unfortunate business."

It was easy enough to read between the lines. Rather than trust herself to him, or face marriage with Sir Percival, Becca had struck out, this time on her own. Klaus had to find her.

"I am at your disposal, sir, in whatever capacity, but if she is not inclined to wed the man, I do not see how—"

"She has no choice!" Gildersleeve interrupted. "She is promised. There is nothing for it. It is all arranged. We mean to organize a search. Will you join us, sir?"

"Of course, my lord."

"Capital! She's taken a gelding from the stables. My groom went 'round to the coaching inn at first light to inquire, but she never reached the inn. We assumed she would hire a coach, you see, as she did the last time. I cannot believe she would be foolish enough to ride the whole distance to whatever hind side of beyond she's headed for—if she even knows herself. She gets it from her sainted mother, you know, this rebellious independence. Well, Smedley can have a go at taming that. I've had no luck curing her of it—or my poor wife, either, while she lived, come to that. Now, in my day—"

"What time was she last seen?" Klaus interrupted. The brandy was addressing him now, and time was of the essence.

"That's just it, sir—she wasn't seen. Her abigail was the last person to converse with her. The other lady guests took no notice when she retired."

"Have you questioned the abigail?"

"Can't get an intelligible word out of the gel, sir. She weeps and wails incessantly, but not a clear syllable, much less a sentence, will she speak."

"With your permission, Gildersleeve, I am quite adept at . . . putting people at their ease. A trait learned and cultivated in my native Sweden. If you will allow, I should like to try my hand with the gel . . . privately, if that would be agreeable. My methods lend themselves best without the distraction of an audience."

"Most irregular, I daresay."

"Yes, but necessary with such a one as she, I'm thinking. She is a simple gel. You are her employer, sir. She evidently fears reprisal for having let her charge escape, as it were. Your presence would only alarm her, and gain us nothing. Not to say that my method offers guarantees, you understand. These things are delicate and subjective at best, but certainly worth a try with so much at stake, no?"

Worth a try, indeed—absolutely vital! How much had Becca confided in the maid? He hadn't missed the way the abigail's blubbering increased the minute he entered the Grange. He had to get to her before she told all, and before the baron learned that he'd harbored his daughter.

"What you say makes sense, Lindegren, but let us have done in haste. The trail grows cold, sir, and her bridegroom grows impatient."

Klaus had no doubt. Such gambling men set great store in their wagers. Gildersleeve would not be off the hook until the debt was satisfied and Becca was Smedley's. There was no time to lose, and then there was his need to visit the falls. Klaus had already been away from them too long. It wouldn't do to fade to a thin transparency before their very eyes.

Gildersleeve strode to the door and quit the study, leaving it ajar. The discordant rumble still prevailed without, echoing along the parquetry, and Klaus began to pace the length of the Persian carpet before the vacant hearth. It wasn't long before a puling whimper bloomed into a crescendo of wailing in the hall outside, and Gildersleeve's bark rose over it.

"You'll get in there and do as you're told, my girl!" the baron charged, "or face the consequences. I'm at the end of my tether this morning. Do not put me to the test!"

With that, the study door opened, and Gildersleeve handed Maud over the threshold none too gently. Letting her go with a shove, he nodded in Klaus's direction and shut the door with a bang.

Klaus steeled himself. Maud began creeping around the perimeter of the room, her eyes—wide as an owl's—riveted to his. Inching along, she groped the furniture against the wall as she bumped into it, and his posture collapsed watching her.

"Please," he said, raising his hands in a gesture meant to allay her distress, "you have naught to fear from me. I am come to help find your lady, but I need your help, Maud. There is no time for hysterics."

"My lady said you was a . . . a . . ."

"Yes, I'm sure I can imagine what she said. She spoke it to me as well. It was the wine. It gave her dreams, and she imagined . . . things. I never should have told her the folktales of my people on top of that wine. Some ladies do not have the fortitude for strong spirits. I only meant to share some of my heritage with her. Believe me, I regret it, because it drove her away from my keeping, where she was safe, and brought her back to the last place she wanted to be—and now, to this!"

The maid stopped her progress around the room. She stood staring at him warily. She was not convinced. He had to ensure her silence, and quickly—before she left the study, or face more than he'd bargained for at the hands of her master.

"Maud, sit with me and talk—only that. This will not do. We must work together to find your lady." He extended his hand, gesturing toward a stiff-backed Chippendale chair against the wall. It seemed prudent to let her stay at her comfortable distance, far enough away from the study door to avoid eavesdroppers. "There, that is better," he breathed in relief as she sank into the chair. Easing down on the edge of a horsehair lounge across the way, he heaved a sigh, relaxing the muscles that had cramped between his shoulder blades. "Now then," he said, "regardless of what you think of me, I have only your lady's welfare in mind. How could you imagine I would mean her harm? Did I not save both your lives? Would I have done that if I had evil intent? No. The baron does not know you were at my cottage, Maud. Your lady did not wish him to, and I honored her wishes when he came searching for her there while you were indisposed. It is vital that he does not learn that I deceived him. If he should find me out, I will not be able to help her. Do you understand?"

There was a painfully long hesitation before the abigail sketched a nod.

"Good!" said Klaus. "Now then, I need you to tell me when you saw her last."

"I . . . she sent me from the ball right after midnight," Maud wailed. "She said hateful things . . . that I was oglin' my betters . . ."

"That is of no consequence—only that which will help me find her need concern us now. Go on, then. Did you do as she bade you?"

Maud nodded. "I did, sir," she said. "I took myself off ta bed and good riddance! She had no call ta rail at me that way. No call!" She began to weep again.

"Shhh, now," Klaus soothed. "Do you not see? She wasn't railing at you . . . not really. She wanted to escape this betrothal and she needed no witnesses to that escape. She could not do that under your watchful eye, now, could she?"

A glimmer of enlightenment flashed in the abigail's gaze.

"Hmm?" Klaus prompted.

"Sh-she said I could retire . . . that she wouldn't need me ta ready her for bed, and I went off, that sure I was that she'd ring for me the minute she come up. But she didn't. Or at any rate, I didn't hear her if she did. I must've fallen asleep. The next thing I knew it was mornin', and the house was in an uproar. She was gone, and nobody knew where. That's all I know—I swear it!"

"All right, now, shhh," he soothed. "There is no time for tears. We are going to leave this room. I must know before we do . . . will you betray me? Think carefully, Maud. Your lady's life may well depend upon your answer."

Maud was silent apace. Long enough for Klaus to realize he had to play his final card.

"Do you want what is best for your lady, Maud?" he murmured.

The abigail nodded.

"Good. She does not love this Sir Percival Smedley. I love her, and I believe that she loves me. If that is so, would you condemn her to a life of sorrow shackled to another? You are not that cruel, Maud Ammen. If I must prove myself, then give me the chance to do so. It is all I ask. If I should fail, you may expose me to your master how you will. You have nothing to lose, and we both have much to gain." He rose to his feet and crossed the room, offering his hand. Maud took it, her head bent low. "Will you keep my secret?"

She nodded.

They had nearly reached the door when a quick knock upon it announced Gildersleeve as he threw it wide, extracting a shrill exclamation from Maud.

"I can spare no more time for trivialities, Lindegren," the baron said. "The horses are saddled. The gentlemen are mounted in the drive. The search must commence. Has the silly chit anything to say besides that infernal blubbering?"

Maud cringed at his bluster, and Klaus gave her arm a reassuring squeeze. "It is all right, Maud," he said. "Run on now, and be about your duties. All will be well." It was presumptuous of him to give the abigail a command in her master's house, and it earned him a withering look from the baron, but that couldn't be helped.

"Forgive the bold liberty, Gildersleeve," he said, "but the maid is in distress, and I have just quieted her. I thought it best to send her off before the wailing resumed. She has told me what we need to know. Your daughter left the Grange sometime shortly after midnight, after dismissing her. There is no fault in the gel. She was doing as her mistress bade. You are quite right; we must set out at once."

"You will come with us?"

"Yes," said Klaus, "if you will be good enough to

lend a mount. I can cover much more ground astride than in my carriage."

"Yes, yes—of course, sir," the baron said, waving him off with an impatient gesture.

"Do not wait for me," Klaus said, striding along the hall, his boot heels sounding back hollow from the parquetry. "Enough time has been lost already. We should not all go off in the same direction, in any case. Have no fear. I will . . . catch up."

# Chapter Seventeen

Instinct drove Klaus straight to Boscastle Falls. Though it was too much to hope for, and highly unlikely, he prayed that Becca might have passed by the falls in search of him. All odds were against it, of course. She was fleeing him as much as Smedley. Even if she did leave by way of the falls, too much time had passed for finding her there to be logical. But logic played no part in what motivated Klaus. Nothing mattered but that he find her.

The others had taken another direction. They were nowhere in sight when he left the road and turned down the winding lane that led to the falls. The horse tethered in the raspberry canes came into view the minute he rounded the bend, and he leaped off his mount and spanned the distance, calling Becca's name like a man possessed. The sound echoed back in his ears, amplified by the mist rising from the water. Bouncing back from rock to rock, it rivaled the thunder of the rushing cascade spilling down from the ledges above. Again and again he called, but there was no answer.

Klaus raked his hair back from a furrowed brow and heaved a sigh. She would have heard him if she were near. But where could she have gone? Was she hiding from him? Did she fear him that much? He was loath to believe it, though he could certainly see how she might. She was an innocent, and he had brought her to the brink of yielding to a passion unknown to her. She thought she was dreaming, or she never would have let him take such liberties. There, in that primeval setting, he cursed his heritage—cursed the pull of the mating frenzy that had nearly betrayed him and let him take her virtue there in that very river.

He glanced at the horse. Maybe it wasn't her mount. He almost convinced himself, despite the fact that the animal answered the call of his own mount not far distant as if they knew each other. And why wouldn't they, if they'd come from the same stables? His confidence began to flag. He reached the horse in two great strides and took down the traveling bag tied behind the saddle. His hands were shaking as he loosened the latch and rummaged inside. He groaned as his fingers closed around a familiar sprigged muslin frock, and he snapped it shut again. He would know that frock anywhere. But where was she?

He stared at the swirling water rushing past, at the lacy foam riding the surface clear to the bend in the river. Another fear gripped him, drawing his scalp taut for the second time in the space of an hour. Could she have been swept away? Could she even swim? He slapped his forehead with the heel of his hand and cursed himself for not knowing. She had never seemed afraid of the water, but that proved nothing. He'd always had hold of her, *and she'd thought she was dreaming!* Then he saw her mantle lying crumpled at the edge of the water. Snatching it up, he held it to his nose and breathed her in. A guttural groan escaped his throat and he tossed it down again.

Wasting no time to strip down to bare skin, Klaus pulled off his boots, tore off his coat and waistcoat, and plunged into the river. Instinct moved him again now. He ruled the water. He would know if she had drowned in it. The thought was too terrible to credit, though he had to credit it. Back and forth he swam, diving beneath the surface, riding the creaming foam downriver and back toward the falls again. It was there that he picked up her scent in almost the same spot he'd transported her to and from the masked ball. Could her fragrance still be lingering, or was it more recent? He plunged beneath the water again. Her essence was stronger there, and he loosed a guttural growl and spiraled into the astral realm.

Illia was sunning herself on a rock at the edge of the river, playing with Becca's silk scarf, when he surfaced. She leaped to her feet at the sight of him, adjusting the silk about her neck and shoulders as he plowed toward her through the water. If ever two eyes were steeped in guilt, he faced them now. They were snapping with fright. Was that due to his sudden appearance, or was there something more sinister afoot? He'd known the water sprite far too long not to suspect the latter. By the look of things, she would have bolted like a deer in the wood if he hadn't caught her unaware.

"Ye startled me!" she gushed, keeping him at his distance with quick footwork. "What do ye here, like *that?*" She gestured to his wet shirt and breeches, sliding her familiar gaze the length of him. "H-has something untoward occurred?"

"I need not answer to you for my comings and goings," he snapped. "But since you would provoke me, I am keeping an eye upon you."

She sauntered nearer. "Have ye come to your senses, then?" she purred. "I knew ye would, your highness."

"Come no closer!" he warned. "Our time is over."

"Our time will never be over."

He made a lunge for her and seized the scarf. "I told you to take this off!" he said, tugging against her grip upon it. "Your defiance used to stimulate me. Now it only angers me. You have brought the consequences down upon your own head, Illia. Now give that here!"

One final wrench won it for him. Again Becca's scent filled his nostrils. Sweet herbs and wildflowers bound with her own distinctive fragrance overwhelmed him. It was all around him, far too strong to be explained away as bleed-over residue on the scarf. *She has just passed through here!* He was certain of it. Her scent alone aroused him, threading through his nostrils, setting his loins afire. Every pore, every nerve ending had become sensitive to her sweet essence. It was agony being so close and not being able to touch her, to hold her, to feel her soft, eager flesh in his arms. *Where could she be?*

"What have you done with her?" he demanded. Throwing the scarf down, he lunged for the sprite only to close his hands around empty air. Illia's mocking laughter echoed after her, trailing off into the waterfall noise.

Klaus loosed a mighty roar. Where she had gone he could not follow—no man could follow. Not even the elders could disturb the handmaidens of the sea in their domain, only the gods. It was forbidden. The islands that edged the astral waters were sacrosanct. They lived in the drifting mist that wreathed the fringes of the Otherworld Sea. Cloaked from view by the silvery fog that never lifted, they were for the most part invisible. Mermen were the only males permitted, and they were not allowed to leave the astral archipelago. No other male creature—astral or mortal—had ever even seen the islands, or the mysterious caves upon them, where the water elementals dwelled. Some had tried. The fools had never been seen or heard from again. Speculation had it that they were devoured by the cannibalistic kelpies that lived in astral waters. Fact or fantasy, such tales were enough to keep astral youngsters at their distance.

Here was true mystery and danger—even for the prince of the *Fossegrim*, limited to the confines of his waterfall. The isles were linked to the parallel physical plane to such mortal isles as the illusive Avalon, to Anglesea, Gresholm, the Isle of the Blest, and the Isle of Man. Here lived such infamous creatures as the Nixen and the devious water women, who cunningly disguised themselves as seaweed, or the lazy, swaying plants that lived on the river bottom and the ocean floor. Here lived all manner of merpeople, including the dreaded Cornish kelpies called *Sjofn*, sinister carnivores, always at the ready to devour the mermaids' human catch, lured from their ill-fated ships. Ruling over the rest were the siren Lorelei, the sisterhood of water sprites, over which Illia held sway. *Illia!* How could he ever have formed an alliance with such a treacherous creature? All that now seemed as though it had happened to someone else.

Little by little, Klaus realized with bone-chilling clarity, he was losing his astral connection. Time was, he would have anticipated the sprite's plan instinctively and seized her sea-green flesh instead of air. Then, in his domain, he could have commanded her. Now, his instincts were growing sharper in the physical plane and fading in the astral, where he so desperately needed them. *"You cannot have it both ways."* Henrik's words bombarded him like cannon-fire. No, he could not, and he had become resigned. He *had*. Hadn't he?

Klaus shook himself like a wet dog and slicked the damp hair back from his brow. First things first. He stooped to retrieve the silk scarf and jammed it into his pocket. He had to find Becca. What had he brought her to? If he could not venture to the astral archipelago, he must find someone who could, and enlist the help of whomever that might be to find her. There was no time to lose—no telling what she faced at the mercy of the vindictive sprite.

As if they'd read his mind, the Will-o'-the-Wisps appeared, bobbing about like faithful dogs, just out of reach. Neither male nor female, the bouncing fairy lights were denied no access in the astral world. They were too elusive to catch and harmed no one, though they possessed the power to lure any who would follow them into the unknown. Humans thought them to be cavorting fairies, or lights from fairy revels. Some thought them to be wandering souls of the departed, and that to see them was an omen of one's own death. All sorts of outlandish beliefs surrounded the ethereal bobbing lights, but Klaus knew them for what they really were—the *Irrbloss*, as they were called by the Swedes—protectors of the astral realm. Playful creatures possessed of the innocent curiosity of children and the steadfastness of the faithful dogs they emulated. He bowed to them. But before he could speak, a familiar voice at his back spun him around to face a crowd emerging from the mist. Henrik was at the forefront.

"You were warned," the elder said sadly, his gray head cocked in a sorrowful attitude. "Now you must come."

"I cannot until I have found her!" Klaus argued.

"You have no choice," the elder said, punctuating his words with a thump of his ritual staff on the ground. Cold chills spiraled down Klaus's spine. He hadn't seen the elder wield that staff in eons, and never had it been raised toward him.

Another pushed forward. Older, and bearded, he wore ancestral robes and carried a scepter crowned with a scrying ball. This was the Inquisitor General.

His eyes blazed with green fire. When he spoke, not a creature stirred in the wood or in the water, and no sound save the roar of the falls competed with his voice.

"Your brethren have fulfilled their commitment, one and all," he said. "Yet you, their prince—their fine example—have not. You needn't defend yourself. We know your mind—"

"Then you know more than I do!" Klaus blurted.

"*Silence!*" the inquisitor thundered. "You are your father's son to a fault! Insolent! Disrespectful! Will you accept his fate as easily as you put on his mantle, young lord? No! Do not be so quick to speak, for if you do, you seal the fates of all the satellites that surround you—Henrik's, the girl's, and we, your lords and protectors. Can you really do without us now?" He swept his robed arm wide. "All this will be denied you. You will have no access to it evermore. You will grow old, as the mortals grow old. You will die, as the mortals die, withered and brittle to the bone, moldering in the earth of the physical plane. Time will have meaning then. It will exist, and yours will be short, as all mortals' time is short, and then you are naught but a memory in the wind. *Pay attention!* Moon dark is almost past. Take the girl or find another, and fulfill your obligation while there is still time. Turn away from the mortal realm and have done! Or suffer the consequences."

"I cannot just leave her at the mercy of the sirens," Klaus argued.

"If she is with the sirens, she is lost to you anyway. There is no help for her, save in their mercy they give it. You know the way of it, young lord."

"Then if she is lost it is my fault, and I must redeem her. Do what you will with me, but spare her your wrath."

"We do naught to you, young lord. What happens

now is your doing, not ours. And we can neither spare nor condemn her. We have not trespassed in her world. She has trespassed in ours."

"She was lured here by one of our own!" Klaus defended. "There is no fault in her. She did not come willingly. I am certain of it."

The inquisitor shrugged. "That is of no consequence. She is beyond our reach, but you are not. You must decide! And it must be now, so that we may decide your fate."

"There is nothing to decide. It is plain that Illia means to force me to return. By keeping Becca prisoner here, she means to ensure it. I will not reward her treachery. When she sees that I will not bend to her will, that I will remain in the mortal realm regardless, there will no longer be a need to keep Becca prisoner. She will let her go. The others will demand it! They are jealous of mortal females and will not brook one come among them for long. I gladly accept my father's fate. Believe me, I have lost my appetite for immortality."

"Oh, no, young lord, that is not how it is to be. The matter is taken out of your hands. That is the decree of this tribunal. You are not competent to make your own decisions while you are addled by the witchery of mortal love. You will not repeat your father's sin! We will not allow it. Have it your way and the race of *Fossegrim* will soon disappear from the astral. You have a sennight to fulfill your obligation to perpetuate it or we will petition the gods to give us your ancestral name and make an end of you. Once known and spoken, that name will banish you from both worlds, my fine young waterlord. You will be stricken from the sacred scrolls. You will disappear and exist no more. For whoever holds that name holds power over you. There is only one way to forestall what is put in motion today. You must fulfill your destiny or we must

make an example of you to deter others from following in your footsteps. Once you mate and return to
your own kind, the lady will be released unharmed. If
I were you, I would go and be about it."

"You are a part of this . . . this abduction!" Klaus
thundered, "You are in league with the sprites—all of
you! Henrik . . . ?"

"We have had no hand in Lady Rebecca's capture,
your highness," the elder responded. "We do not stoop
to such measures, but it has forced this action. Now,
enough! Get you back to the mortal realm while you
can still explain your absence. There are other maidens
ripe for mating at Gildersleeve Grange, but they will
not remain there for long."

" 'Explain my absence,' Henrik?" said Klaus. "Have
you forgotten the time warp? I shan't even have been
missed."

The Inquisitor General brandished his scepter. "Time
has not stood still in the physical plane while you have
been absent today, young lord," he said. "That favor
has been rescinded on this occasion as a foretaste of
your inevitable chastisement, and now the searchers
have begun searching for *you!* The gods have spoken.
You do not make these mysteries occur; *they* do. What
the gods have given, the gods can take away. It would
do you well to remember that."

Klaus barely had time to command the *Irrbloss* before
he crossed back over. The enigmatic Will-o'-the wisps
drifted off and disappeared, giving Henrik a wide
berth as he led Klaus away. It was a mental communi-
cation in the Swedish tongue, encrypted to confuse astral eavesdroppers who also were familiar with mind
language. Only *Fossegrim,* who were Norse in origin,
Henrik and the *Irrbloss,* who were bilingual, and Klaus's
house servants, who had served him in his homeland

and followed him in his exile, spoke the Swedish tongue, although Illia had picked up bits and pieces of the language over time. Much to his relief, Klaus had not lost his mental powers. That meant he still had command over the dreams of others. He would need that skill, and quickly, if he were to save Becca.

"You were warned," the elder said again, as they emerged at Boscastle Falls. "There was naught that I could do. Your recklessness has brought this about."

"Oh?" Klaus snapped. "And what of Illia's treachery? That you allow without reprisal? This you permit with no threats of extracting *her* name from the gods?" All at once, enlightenment struck, as though a window had been flung open in his brain. Of course! Why hadn't he thought of it before? "Well, let me tell you, old one," he went on, his voice lifted with renewed conviction, "I will have Becca back, and I will violate the astral archipelago to do it if needs must, so you had best come off that lofty fence of yours. It is too high and thin to straddle for an elder such as you. You are either on my side or theirs. Think carefully. And now, be gone! I want no more truck with you until you decide, and not even then if you do not decide rightly—in my favor."

Turning his back on the elder, Klaus collected his cast-off boots and stalked downriver to where his horse had strayed. Mounting, he rode back to the raspberry canes, where he loosened the tether on Becca's mount and led it off through the wood to the thicket on the other side. There he left it, close enough to the lane to be found. Then, doubling back, he walked his own horse toward the falls again.

No, there was no sign of her. It was too much to hope for, though he did hope. There was no sign of Henrik, either. He was on his own against the elders and the gods, all for the love of a mortal woman. He hadn't lied: Immortality meant nothing to him without Becca to share it. He would gladly exchange it for one mortal lifetime in her arms. With that thought to drive him, he gouged his horse with heavy heels, rode off at a gallop, and reached Gildersleeve Grange in time for nuncheon to set the rest of his plan in motion.

# *Chapter Eighteen*

Becca had lost track of time. It was impossible to tell day from night in the confines of the siren's cave. Since time didn't exist in the astral realm, she had no idea how much had passed in the physical plane since her abduction. Being human, without the favor of the astral gods, time wouldn't have stood still for her, especially since to them she was the cause of Klaus being sanctioned. She would certainly have been missed by now, at any rate. There would be a search, but they would never find her here. They would find her mount tethered beside the waterfall, however, and when they saw no sign of her, they would assume she had drowned. The connotations of that were not to be borne. They would call off the search and she would be lost forever. She barely let the thought cross her mind. It was too terrible.

Becca turned her face to the wall of the cave and screwed her eyes shut tight against the threatening tears. She would not—could not—give way to them. Everything depended upon her keeping a level head if she were to outwit the jealous sprite.

Though her wrists were still bound, the tethers, made of some sort of stiff, unyielding vines, had been loosened, and they were tied in front so she could eat and drink. Food was laid out on a large leaf nearby, an assortment of fragrant greens tossed with fresh berries, and little savory cakes that appeared to have been made of whole grains clotted together with honey. Alongside, there stood a flagon of mead or wine, Becca couldn't tell, and she wasn't about to taste it to be sure. She meant what she'd said; she would not touch the food of the astral creatures. But as the day wore on, her resolve began to diminish. She could do without food, but her throat was so dry, and her thirst so great, she had to quench it. More than once she reached toward the flagon, seduced by the ambery liquid. Fireflies buzzed about it, showing her its crystal clarity, picking out the golden glints that seemed to beckon to her through the glass. Finally, she could stand no more, and she grabbed the flask and drank. It was just as delicious as it looked, like the May wine Klaus had given her before her first visit to the astral realm, nut-sweet and honey-smooth. She gulped it greedily.

She grew dizzy the instant she'd drunk it. She had forgotten how strong spirits affected her. There was nothing for it; it was done. If she slept, so be it. Working the conch shell free of her pocket, she held it to her ear. The magical roar of the sea echoed mysteriously— *his* sea—resonating through her body. Curling on her side on the pallet of rushes beneath her, she shut her misted eyes to the undulating whorls and pinpoints of white light that starred her vision. Finally, she drifted off, lulled by the haunting ocean music in her ear and the distant echo of real waves lapping at the shore outside. The combined sounds crashed over her like the waves themselves. Though she hadn't seen it, she'd suspected the sea was near by the salty tang in the air. It filled her nostrils and lingered on her lips. The sound came and went like a pulse beat at times, but it wasn't consistent, suggesting that it could only be heard when the seas were running high. Where was she? In her May wine daze, she was too spent to care.

All at once a familiar voice rose over the rest. It was Klaus's voice; Becca would recognize that seductive baritone anywhere. His accent alone was a caress. She moaned at the sound of it. Frantically, she tried to open her eyes, but they wouldn't budge. This *was* a dream. She'd had many like it, when she'd fought to open her eyes to no avail. What was he saying? Why couldn't she hear what he was saying? It sounded so urgent. . . .

Klaus stood under the cascade of Boscastle Falls, reaching out to Becca with his mind. His body ramrod-rigid under the flow, he shut his eyes and sank into deep meditation. He had done it before, and she had responded, but it hadn't been vital then. It was now. Her life could well depend upon it.

Again and again he tried, but it was no use. He couldn't concentrate. He couldn't block out all the other urgencies banging about in his brain. The waterfall had always been able to do that for him, which was why he'd chosen this lonely, sacred place to attempt to reach her. Boscastle Falls provided an umbilical chord that linked the physical falls to the falls in the Otherworld. It formed a bridge between the parallel worlds, just as any waterfall he had claimed or borrowed would have done. The sensual, pulsating flow of the living water was a conductor of energy between the two realms, just as all waterfalls had been since time out of mind. Had it shunned him? Had it shut him out now, when he needed it most? Was this another cruel chastisement?

He had lost favor with the elders. Had he lost favor with the gods they served? His father had. He had given up everything for love. He had fallen from grace, but he had *loved* and been loved. He hadn't been content to settle for the mindless functions of his obligation to the rest. Only now did Klaus understand what his father must have suffered in his decision to exile himself to the physical world.

Every muscle in his body had grown as hard as the rocks above, every sinew stretched to its limit of strain. Baron Gildersleeve had called off the search for the night. They would resume at dawn, but there wasn't much hope, now that her mount had been found wandering aimlessly over the moor so close to the river, its ribbons dragging in the mire. Everyone was certain Becca had drowned.

The worst of it was Maud. She was inconsolable. Klaus had tried to reassure her, but he dared not say too much too soon. He dared not risk her betraying him, either. That was a very real danger. He could see it in her accusing eyes. Everything he'd said to put her mind at ease was wiped away when her lady's mount was led back riderless. It was chillingly plain that the abigail suspected he'd had a hand in her disappearance. She needed reassurance, but Becca needed the key to her liberation while it was still possible. That would lay the maid's fears to rest. If only he could effect it in a timely fashion. *Time.* Oh, how he wished that this were taking place in the astral, where time didn't exist!

Raking his wet hair back with both his hands, as if the motion would keep his brain from bursting, Klaus began repeating his mantra again. He had to reach her, but that wasn't enough. She had to answer him.

Becca opened her eyes to blackness. The fireflies had fled. The roar of the sea had diminished to a distant murmur again. To her dismay, the conch shell had rolled out of her hand and lay just out of reach. The only sound was the constant hollow splat of moisture dripping down the stalactites to whatever dark well of water lay at the bottom of the cavern. That wasn't what woke her. That sound was much too hushed to have aroused her from a stuporous sleep. Her eyelids drooped shut. It must have been part of the dream.

All at once it came again, stronger this time. That voice—*his voice*—calling her name, whispering that strange foreign endearment that bound her to him completely.

"I cannot come for you, *mitt kostbart*," he murmured. How close he sounded. She could almost feel his warm breath upon her ear. It shot her through with shivers of delight and ignited strange stirrings at her very core. "You are in a place forbidden to the men of my race—to all men, astral and mortal alike. The portal is closed to transportation. If I were to attempt to penetrate the barrier or gain entrance through the astral oceans, I would risk my life both in your world and in mine. The gods forbid it. If I were to fail, without me you would surely be lost forever."

Becca didn't answer. It was only a dream.

"You must return to me," the phantom voice continued. "I want you for my own . . . for my wife . . . in your world, *mitt kostbart* . . . never to be parted. . . ."

Tears welled in Becca's closed eyes. This was her most secret fantasy come creeping in the night to haunt her—to torment her. Oh, if it were only true! But no, he wanted to ravish her and leave her with child, so he could return to the exquisite, fiery-eyed creature that had captured her.

"I will not touch you except thus . . . in your dreams . . . until it can be so," he said, as if he'd read her thoughts.

Becca groaned. His closeness was palpable. It was as though his hands were upon her, stroking her through the thin silk she wore. His warmth took the chill of the damp away and raised the fever in her blood. She tried to open her eyes, but they were locked shut again and would not move. Her heart began to pound until it echoed in her ears, drowning out the hollow sound of dripping water and the plaintive sighing of the distant sea. Her sex thrummed with waves of searing fire, as his hand—so hot, so urgent—stroked her there through the gown.

Becca writhed under the touch of that phantom hand as it inched the costume up and delved beneath—seeking—searching—bringing her to the brink of excruciating ecstasy. She lay very still, scarcely breathing now. To do so would bring the stars alone knew what wonderful, terrible sensation to loins already swollen and aching in anticipation of she knew not what.

All at once, the dark behind her closed eyes turned a golden hue, then blazed to auburn flame as her body became feverish. Still, she could not open her eyes. It didn't matter. If she did, the dream would end. He would be gone, and she would be alone again in the dank, dark cave.

Her breath caught as the phantom hand slid higher, cupping her breast. The fingers seemed to tremble as he slipped the silk down past her shoulder and sought the naked flesh beneath. Both hands fondled her now, baring her breasts, coaxing the nipples to life. Soft, involuntary moans escaped her throat as his lips tugged at the buds until they hardened against his warm, skilled tongue. Oh, how he fed upon them, in wild abandon, like a starving beggar at a king's banquet. The feeding frenzy, though desperate, was not savage, but rather overwhelmed by a tender urgency that drew her to him totally. The undulating rhythm of that hungry mouth—sucking, nipping—tugged so deeply at her core that it was as though he sought to drain the very essence from her soul.

"It is but a dream, my Becca," he murmured, answering her thoughts again, his hot breath puffing against the swell of her breast. "It is only fairy glamour, naught but illusion. You need neither fear it nor try to understand. I am here in spirit only . . . the dream but a foretaste of what will be when we are one. . . ."

His full weight was suddenly upon her. He was moving against her—slow, voluptuous revolutions—his thick sex heavy upon her belly, its bruising hardness pushing against her. He found her lips, and his moan filled her throat, reverberating through her body like a ravaging wind. Becca tried to fling her arms around him—to clasp him fast to her quivering body—but they wouldn't move. She arched herself against him, against the anxious hardness bearing down upon her, setting loose a firestorm of riveting convulsions that left her weak and trembling, her breath coming in short, ragged spurts as the floodgates burst.

"Just a dream, *mitt kostbart,*" the phantom heaving against her panted in her ear. "But you will remember, just as you remembered all the other dreams. You are mine, my Becca. I have awakened you to secrets of the flesh beyond your wildest dreams . . . and now you are mine."

She lay cocooned in the tender rapture of his embrace for a time, content to be in the arms she longed so to hold her. Then, all at once, his weight was lifted. Again, she tried to reach out to him, but she could neither move, speak, nor see.

"Come back to me," he murmured. His voice had grown distant, and she strained to hear it. "My time grows short . . . in my world . . . and in yours. It must be soon or we are lost to each other for all eternity, *mitt kostbart.* I can give you the power to return . . . but you must be the one to use it, my Becca. Here I am but spirit, naught but a shadow in the mind. The siren has a name known to no other save the gods and me. Speak it to her and she is yours to command. Her astral name is *Maj;* it means 'pearl of the sea.' Once, it suited her, for she is very beautiful, a true treasure of the depths. But no more. A pearl is formed inside the shell of a mollusk. A bit of sand lodged there irritates it, and so the creature secretes nacre that coats the sand particle. Little by little, the many coats of nacre form a pearl of great price. Illia is no more that pearl, but the grain of sand that irritates. Say '*Maj,* I command thee, release me,' and she must obey. Say it just so. Then follow the *Irrbloss*—the Will-o'-the wisps. It is safe to do so now. I have commanded them, and they will lead you back to me. They will lead you home. Do you hear me, my Becca? If you hear me, you must answer. You must agree or all this is for naught. . . ."

She thought she did, but his voice sounded so far away now, like a whisper at the very back of her mind. She strained to hear it more clearly, but it only grew more distant.

All at once, like the rush of a whirlwind, she heard her name as though it came from an echo chamber and she bolted upright, her eyes flung wide to the darkness.

"*Klaus?*" she cried. But her words rang back in her ears from the walls of the cave—from the ceiling— ringing from the jaws of the stalactites and stalagmites, and faded away to a memory.

Klaus emerged from the waterfall weary to the bone, every inch of his body still tingling from the astral exercise that had drained him. It was a mind projection, but the effect it had upon his physical body was staggering. There was no rejuvenation from the waterfall this time. He had spent his energies reaching out to Becca. She had heard him, felt his presence. He was certain of it. She had answered him at the last, but did she understand what she must do to free herself? There was no way to tell. Time alone would reveal it.

Oh, how he hated mortal time. How much had passed since he came to the falls? It had to be hours since he'd stolen away from the Grange. He studied the heavens. Judging the position of the moon, it was well into the wee hours. The gentlemen would still be gaming. He growled in disgust. Not even his daughter's disappearance—her presumed *death*—could keep Gildersleeve and Becca's betrothed from the gaming tables. No doubt they were still at it. It was a sickness with these weak-minded mortals.

He half-expected to find Henrik lurking in wait as he plowed out of the churning froth and spindrift mist. But no, he was alone, unsure of whether to take the elder's absence as a good sign or as an omen that his longtime protector had turned against him. Still, it was a lonely homecoming. *Homecoming?* Was this home? Could he adjust to the physical realm of mortals? He had existed in both planes for so long a time, it seemed second nature to him to walk among humans, to eat and drink with them and be a part of their society. He had long aspired to it; he knew that now. That was inbred. He was an astral love child born and reared in the physical plane, though equally endowed with the pull of the Otherworld, having been conceived before his father was outcast—a half-breed, just as all *Fossegrim* were half-breeds. How he detested his heritage. How he longed to be whole. It had never mattered in which incarnation until now. Now, there was no choice. He could give up either in a heartbeat, but not Becca. Where she was, he would be also.

He dressed and collected his horse. There was no need to wait beside the falls. If Becca did as he bade her, she would come to him in due course. He cast a thoughtful glance behind him. Though he desperately needed to replenish the astral energy he'd used up while wrapping his mind around her, he dared not linger any longer. He would have to return to the falls at another opportunity for that. By the time he reached the Grange it would be nearly first light. The object was to sneak back in as he'd sneaked out, with no one the wiser. First on his agenda would be to reassure Maud. He hadn't liked the look in her eyes when the search had turned up nothing but fear that Becca had drowned. With that in mind, he turned his mount toward Gildersleeve Grange and rode off through the misty darkness before dawn.

The house was ablaze with light when Klaus emerged from the copse at the edge of the moor. It did not bode well for sneaking back in unseen if the whole house was awake. Nevertheless, he left his mount with the groom in the stables and made his way around the back to the service entrance, where he'd stuffed the lock with a bit of parchment to keep it from snapping shut. It was just as he'd left it. The servants' quarters were in darkness, and he plucked out the parchment, slipped inside, and started along the corridor toward the stairs.

The rooms he'd been assigned to were on the second floor, and he'd nearly reached the landing when a gathering emerged from the shadows under the stairwell and surrounded him. Guests and servants en masse backed him against the wall. A sinister rumble rose from the group as Gildersleeve parted the crowd, his coarse bark preceding him.

"Seize him!" the baron thundered.

"What is the meaning of this?" Klaus demanded, as several of the footmen grabbed his arms. The press of bodies close around him reeking of liquor and sweat was suffocating in the hot, still air. "Is this the way you treat a guest in your house, who has just come from searching for your daughter, sir?"

"You, sir, are no gentleman," Gildersleeve roared. "You are a liar and a fraud. There's no use denying it. I've had it all from my daughter's abigail, how you hid

Rebecca's presence from me when I called, when I came—a distraught father, begging for news of her— how you mean to seduce her. For all I know, you've done so already! Where have you got her? Speak up, or by heaven—"

"I know no more about her whereabouts than you do, Gildersleeve," Klaus defended himself. "If you would but give me a chance to explain . . ." He could easily escape—cross over into the astral, vanish before their very eyes. What a stir that would cause! He still had the power, but it wouldn't last long unless he returned to the waterfall soon. No, he dared not cross over. He was of no use to Becca in the astral now. It was here that he needed to await her return. It was here that he needed to stay to prevent her from slipping through his fingers again.

Maud's wailing from the sidelines ran him through like a sword. It was just as he'd feared. The foolish chit had betrayed him. It couldn't have happened at a worse time.

"Where is my daughter?" Gildersleeve persisted, brandishing Becca's pongee silk scarf. "This was found in your rooms, sir. It looks to have been dragged through the mire. What have you done with her?"

"If you would let us speak privately," Klaus said, straining against the footmen who tethered him.

Smedley stepped forward, glove in hand. "Perhaps you would speak with this!" he snarled, flinging the glove in Klaus's face. "She is *my* betrothed, sir! You will answer to me for this outrage on the dueling ground. I demand satisfaction!"

"Your servant, sir," said Klaus through clenched teeth. The glove stung, whipping moisture into his eyes. Maud shrieked again, drawing his gaze toward the landing, where she stood clutching the newel post. There was terror in her eyes, riveted to his. "Now see what you've done," he snapped at her. "I do hope you are satisfied, because now she may be lost to us all."

"Silence, I say!" Gildersleeve bellowed. "Enough! Take him below and chain him in the wine cellar. By heaven, I'll have the truth of it from him privately, if he wishes."

"I've just called him out!" Sir Percival protested. "Let me have at him."

"Aye, in due time, Smedley," the baron said. "There'll be enough of him left for you when I've done." He turned to the footmen. "Well, you lot, are you deaf? What are you waiting for? Get him below!"

# Chapter Nineteen

Becca awoke to the roar of the sea. The sound was deafening, filling the cave with ear-splitting noise. She forced her eyes open to see a pearly haze. The bobbing lights had returned. They seemed to beckon from the distance, playing about the jaws of the stalactites and stalagmites, as if they dared the fanglike deposits to clamp shut upon them. How like mischievous children they were. She almost smiled. *Irrbloss*, Klaus had called them in the dream. *The dream!* How could she possibly know that if he hadn't spoken it to her? She had never heard that name before.

She would not question his powers. Somehow, he had come to her. He had reached out to her with his spirit. He had embraced her with his mind, caressed her with his psyche, and given her the means of her escape. She wracked her brain trying to remember—trying to hear again the words he'd spoken. But his voice was fading at the last, and she had been so transported by his ardor that she hadn't really been paying attention. She knew it was only a dream.

Becca dropped her head in her hands and tried to

concentrate. It began with the letter *M*, she was certain of that. Was it Mae . . . Meve . . . Moll, perhaps? Why couldn't she remember?

She wasn't given time to wonder. All at once the *Irrbloss* were gone—dispersed as Illia entered. The noise they made—a squeaking sound—suggested pain, as if they had been slapped, or kicked. How odd. The curious Will-o'-the-wisps had never made a sound before— at least not one she had ever heard—and they had always kept their distance, just out of reach. Illia had evidently caught them by surprise. Judging from the sour expression on the sprite's face, Becca wouldn't put such meanness past her.

Illia sauntered close carrying a lantern filled with fireflies, her sea-green eyes flashing, her sensuous lips pursed in a pout that in no way diminished their sensuality. The sprite slapped the lantern down in a niche in the cave wall and faced Becca arms-akimbo. Becca noticed at once that she wasn't wearing the scarf.

"Ye haven't touched your food," Illia observed, wagging an accusing finger. It was hooked like a talon. "Unborn grains are a chore to gather, and the bees do not take kindly to their honey going to waste."

"You eat it, then!" Becca snapped. "I have no liking for *unborn grains.*"

The siren shrugged, setting her perfect breasts atremble. "Starve yourself as ye please. Ye'll come 'round once your belly roils for want of nourishment."

"He won't take it kindly when he learns what you have done," Becca said. Why couldn't she remember the name Klaus had spoken? "Can you be such a fool as to imagine he will not seek reprisal once he finds out?"

"He already knows." Illia laughed. She had an odd habit of playing with her hair. She seemed to be trying to count the strands as she tripped to and fro. "I am still here, am I not?" she said. "And I will be here, *with him,* long after your time is done, earthling."

"Then what harm to let me go? Are you that unsure of him—of yourself—that you would risk his wrath keeping me here against my will?"

Again the sprite shrugged. "He has no power over me here. In this place, I am the Lorelei. I rule the astral isles; my handmaidens—*his* handmaidens—with me. He cannot venture here, but we can go to him, and we do, to serve and pleasure him. It will always be so."

"It will not!" Becca cried, her whole body delivering the words. Anger brought recall. Her mind reeled back to the dream, to Klaus's voice. *Maj, it was Maj!* She would stake her life upon it, and indeed that was just what it seemed she was doing. She read her demise in the vindictive sprite's cold glare, and crippling chills trickled down her spine.

Just out of reach, the conch shell glimmered in the glow of the fireflies, capturing Illia's attention. Swooping down, the sprite snatched it from the floor of the cave and turned it to and fro in her tiny hands.

"What have we here?" she said, lifting it to her ear. She gave a start. "*He* gave ye this!"

Becca strained against her tethers, snatching at the shell, but Illia whirled out of her reach. "Give that to me!" she demanded, panicked at the thought of losing it to the vindictive siren.

"Aye, he gave it ye!" the sprite crowed. "Well, 'tis mine now!"

Illia began circling Becca, strutting and preening. Becca did not take her eyes from the sprite, who stalked closer and closer with each revolution. All at once, the sprite probed for something hidden in her flowing sea-green hair. The object, set there like a comb, flashed in the soft light of the firefly lantern. The fireflies caught Becca's attention, flitting and buzzing about inside, their wings and bodies tapping against the lantern glass as if they were trying to escape.

Becca's eyes oscillated between the lantern and the sprite advancing. In the feeble light, she caught a glimpse of something shiny in the sprite's hand—the long, slim shell of a razor clam, honed to a deadly edge. As sharp as any blade, it gleamed as the sprite drew it from her seaweed-plaited mane, and lunged, taking aim at her throat.

The vines that shackled Becca's legs were too short to put much distance between them. There was nothing at hand to fend off the attack except the half-full flagon of May wine. In a flash, she hurled it, hitting Illia squarely in the chest, and jumped to her feet, praying that Klaus hadn't deceived her—that at least that part of the dream had been real.

"Maj! I command thee, release me!" she shrilled.

For one terrible moment everything stood still. Not even the fireflies moved in the lantern. Then Illia began to shake, her buttock-length hair fanned out around her as if a mighty wind had risen; yet there was no wind. An ear-splitting screech spilled from her throat. It shook the cave and burst the lantern, freeing the fireflies. They fled in all directions—dispersed by the siren shrieks—to disappear through the jaws of the stalactites and stalagmites, which collapsed and tumbled into the abyss, shards flying in all directions.

The rocky cave wall began to crumble, as the deadly shrieks grew louder. The awful sound reverberated through Becca's body, riveting her to the spot. Such heart-stopping wails were known to lure ships in and drive them down beneath the waves. To dash them to splinters upon the reefs and shoals, with all hands lost to the deep, fodder for the creatures that dwelled there.

Illia began to spin like a whirlwind, her arms above her head. Becca held her breath. The sprite was no more than a blur, and she plunged the razor-sharp shell straight for her . . . severing the vines that bound her wrists. Then, loosing one last, heart-stopping shriek, she flung the conch shell down and disappeared in a blinding swirl of debris whipped up from the floor of the cave.

A great fissure split the ground in two. Dancing to and fro as the cavern shook and began to break apart, Becca snatched the razor clamshell up from the undulating ground and severed her leg shackles with it. Loose rocks rained down all around. The ground swayed as she scooped up the conch shell half buried in the rubble and, clutching it like a lifeline, tried to follow the narrow ledge to freedom in the darkness. The echo of Illia's siren song lived after her as the cave began to collapse in upon itself and break apart with a deafening roar. Then there was silence—cool and dark and deathly still.

"You must believe me when I say that I do not know your daughter's whereabouts, Gildersleeve," Klaus insisted. He was bound with ropes in the wine cellar at Gildersleeve Grange, the baron standing over him, working a wicked-looking horsewhip in white-knuckled fists. That they were alone was little consolation. The man was foxed on Blue Ruin, and enraged. Klaus would have welcomed witnesses.

"You're a liar!" the baron thundered.

"I will admit that I deceived you," Klaus conceded. "And for the necessity of that, I am truly sorry, but it could not be helped. The carriage your daughter and her abigail were traveling in overturned beside the gorge on the moor. I pulled them to safety just before it toppled over into the river, and offered them the hospitality of my home while the maid recovered. Your daughter, sir, begged me not to betray her presence when you came seeking her. She is opposed to this preposterous marriage you have forced upon her to settle your gambling debt. What sort of man—"

The handle of Gildersleeve's whip across Klaus's mouth cut off the rest.

"That's none of your concern," the baron said. "Maud told me how you drugged her—*drugged* her! Did you drug my daughter as well? You must have done, to get her to turn on her own father!"

Klaus spat the blood from his lips. "I had no hand in that," he said thickly around the swelling. "Your daughter turned against you long before she ever made my acquaintance, Gildersleeve. I would not harm one hair upon her head. She begged for my help and I gave it. If the situation were reversed, you would have done the same. She has shown you her mind. She has run again, and this time I was not there to protect her. If harm has come to her, it is your doing, not mine. You do not deserve such a daughter."

The baron began to pace the length of the wine racks. He had a ragged gait. No doubt the gin had had its way with him. Klaus could only hope that when he sobered, he would see reason. Now there didn't seem to be much hope of that, and time was of the essence. *Damn and blast mortal time!* It was the ruin of both worlds. If he did not return to Boscastle Falls soon, his mortal incarnation would diminish and ultimately fade away before their very eyes. That thought offered an element of fiendish satisfaction. He couldn't help but feel that it would serve them right to see first-hand what Maud had doubtless blubbered while telling her tale. If it weren't for Becca, it would almost be worth it.

Wondering what was happening in the astral realm had all but driven him mad. Illia was an entity not to be trifled with, and she was no fool. He had given Becca the means of her release from astral captivity without having to storm the siren's bastions and risk both their lives. If only she were brave enough to use it. If only she did not dismiss their meeting of the minds as a mere nocturnal fantasy. Not knowing was sheer torture. Nothing Cedric Gildersleeve could do to him in that dank wine cellar would rival that. He had made his choice, and he was on his own. Betraying the siren had sealed his fate in the astral realm. What would happen if the physical world rejected him as well was too terrible to contemplate.

The baron stopped pacing and wheeled to face him. The man looked a shambles. His bleary bloodshot eyes were glaring, his faded red hair fanned out like a misshapen halo in the candlelight, his liquor-stained clothes clinging to his portly form in careless disarray. The look in his eyes was deadly.

"Maud spins a preposterous yarn," he said. "To hear her tell, you aren't even *human*. She's spouting some gammon about a waterfall, and a world parallel to this one. The gel is addled in the beanbox to be sure, but what would make her tell such a tale? There has to be some seed of truth in such an accusation. No yarn is spun without one. Explain!"

Klaus swallowed. What was one more lie? Even if he told the truth, the baron would never believe him. That Maud credited it gave him pause for thought. He should have anticipated this. The Cornish were notoriously superstitious.

"Mayhap another dose of this will loosen your tongue!" the baron said, brandishing the whip in his face. "If not, there's tar and feathers in the stables—that, by god, is what you rightly deserve."

"I cannot presume to get inside the head of a bird-witted ninnyhammer," Klaus said, in his most convincing voice. "I told some folktales of my native Sweden about a waterfall to your daughter, evidently within Maud's hearing, and the silly goose has made fact of fantasy. There is a fine waterfall on my estate, which is what inspired me. Look here, none of this is important. I want your daughter's return just as much as you do, sir. She has quite stolen my heart, and I mean to offer for her."

"Hah! Bold as brass, you foreign chaps, eh? Cut a dash in your dandy togs, with your fancy speech and wily ways, seducing young ladies, taking their virtue—"

"I have taken no one's virtue, Gildersleeve."

"Well, let me tell you, Lindegren, you've a better chance of seeing hell freeze solid than you have of marrying my daughter, sir! She is already *betrothed*, and if she is found, she will marry Sir Percival Smedley. I have given my word."

"Your *vowel*, you mean!" Klaus snapped. It earned him another blow from the whip handle, which split his lip. Retaliation could be swift and deadly and permanent, if he were of a mind to dole it out. *This is her father*, he reminded himself. Gritting his teeth, he met the baron's gelid eyes. "This will not have her back," he forced through clenched teeth. "I have just come from conducting a search of my own. I was not ready to quit, you see, when you did to hurry back to your gaming tables. I can be of assistance to you, but I cannot do that shackled here. Loose my bonds and let me help you find her—let me prove my innocence. That, or haul me before the magistrate and have done. If you were not in your altitudes, you would see that what you do is against the law! If you were not so blind with gaming madness—so steeped in your own selfishness—you would also see that I am by far the better prospect for Becca. Smedley cannot match my title, or my fortune. You would stand to gain much in an alliance with me. What can you possibly expect to gain from an alliance with him, except more debt—more vowels that you cannot honor? Hah! He is evidently a better gambler than you. You'll be plucked clean in no time."

"Eh?" the baron grunted. "What use is your Swedish fortune to me?"

"My *Swedish fortune* has long since been converted into English pounds. I have been cleverer with my investments than you can boast of yours, sir."

The baron snatched a wine bottle from a nearby rack, drew the cork, and upended it while he gave thought. He'd downed nearly half its contents before he opened his mouth to speak, but a hollow pounding on the locked cellar door turned him toward it instead.

"What's the hold-up, Gildersleeve?" Smedley barked from the other side. "Let me in there! I'll have it out of him!"

"I'll deal with this!" the baron returned. "If you're needed, you'll be summoned." A surly, drunken rumble replied to that, and the baron turned back to Klaus. "You heard that," he said. "Even if I were to let you go, he won't cry off. You'll still have to face him on the dueling field."

"I'm looking forward to it!" Klaus returned. "With him out of the way, she will no longer be betrothed."

The baron made no reply. Staring down, whip in hand, he studied Klaus for a painfully long moment, then reeled off toward the wine cellar door and left without a word.

Klaus sagged against the supports of the wine barrel that he was shackled to and drew a ragged breath. Making matters worse, the stand it rested upon was made of iron—the bane of all astral creatures. It seared him like a firebrand, and he twisted aside, inching as far away from the deadly metal as he could in the circumstances. Precious little was accomplished, since his fetters were snugged up to it, and he cursed the air blue. The blasted stuff would drain what little strength he had left if the baron didn't return in a timely fashion and set him free.

Had he gotten through to the gudgeon? Only time would tell. But he had no time. He was not at his most powerful to attempt a duel in the physical plane, nor would he be until the moon waxed full again and he renounced his astral heritage. Then the waterfall would no longer command him. He would lose all ties to the astral realm and, for all intent and purposes, become human. Half-human already, his mortal self would supplant his astral self. He would be denied the Otherworld and all its pleasures. How much of its magic would bleed over with him was as yet undetermined. That would depend upon his prowess, and upon the generosity of the gods, who had never to his knowledge been prone to leniency toward renegades. None of this, however, could occur but through the elders, or before his mating time was up, and he had failed to fulfill his destiny. Only then could he renounce his heritage and give up his astral immortality.

There would be a reckoning—an ostracizing ceremony. He would be humiliated, shamed before all and cast out in disgrace, his name stricken from the sacred ancestral scrolls, just as his father before him. It didn't matter. None of it mattered. That he would spend the rest of his days with Becca was all that did. Pushed to the back of his mind was the Inquisitor General's cryptic alternative to his plan: that the elders would petition the gods to reveal his astral name, and use it to snuff out his existence in both realms. He would not dwell upon that now, however.

He flexed stiff jaw muscles and winced as the split in his lip cracked open again. Purging his psyche of all thoughts save reaching Becca with his mind, he shut his eyes and repeated the mantra. Again and again, he hummed the all but silent incantation, but he saw nothing, heard nothing but the sloshing of the wine inside the barrel he sat slumped against.

# Chapter Twenty

The candle had burned down to a nub and the wine cellar was in darkness when Klaus emerged from his trance without reaching Becca. The nauseating stench of stale wine, mildew, and dust rose in his nostrils. His head ached and his split lip was sore and distended. He had no idea how much time had passed, but it had to be a substantial amount. His energy was flagging. He was still the astral creature who needed the nourishment of his life-giving waterfall. It was time, or very soon all would know the truth of Maud Ammen's hysterical babblings; he would simply disappear before their very eyes. That couldn't happen now, not when he was so close, when he'd gone to such lengths to keep his true identity secret.

Klaus was contemplating the consequences of that when the rasp of a key in the wine cellar lock turned his head toward the door in anticipation. A sudden burst of candlelight flooded the room. After being so long in the dark, it made his eyes smart, and he narrowed them as the baron swaggered close, wielding a heavy silver candle branch.

"Just how much of a *gain* are we talking about, if I were to form an alliance with you?" Gildersleeve asked, thrusting the candelabra into Klaus's face. Hot wax from the tilted candles dripped on Klaus's sleeve, and he screwed his lips tight in disgust at the baron's words.

"Let me understand you, sir," he said. "When last we spoke you were set to tar and feather me. Why this sudden change of heart?"

The baron gave a crisp nod. "There's some truth in what you said," he replied. "You are in a better position to provide for my daughter. And since, as you say, she is so opposed to the match with Smedley . . . well, the thought occurred to me, it's just common sense that I try to make the best possible arrangement for my daughter. If we are speaking about a considerable sum here that you're prepared to settle on her, why . . . Are you following me, Lindegren?"

Klaus was following him all too clearly. He had forced his lips so tight to hold back a spate of expletives—in English and Swedish—that they had begun to bleed again. *Syl, almighty!* If ever he'd had reservations about saving Becca from such a father, they existed no longer. He knew that Becca was alive, but Gildersleeve did not. That the man could stand there and broker her future regardless was more then he could bear. It was beyond the beyond, and for the first time since the baron had bound him there, he was glad of his tethers.

"Should we not be seeking her safe return before we quibble over blunt, sir?" he said. "I should think that would take priority here."

"Yes, yes, of course, but, by your leave, let me explain myself—"

"Please do," Klaus growled.

"Yes, you see . . . I'm thinking, if what you propose is a greater sum than what I owe Smedley, I might be able to satisfy the wager and have done. That is, if there would be enough left over afterward to assure me a fresh start, sir. This unfortunate business has all but rolled me up as it is, you see."

"What? You mean to risk it at the gaming tables?" Klaus was incredulous.

"Well, eh . . . not necessarily, but we are both gentlemen, and you must appreciate the necessity of a practical solution here. It wouldn't do for me to hand Rebecca over to you if I were left without a feather to fly with. That simply wouldn't be a wise business venture—not considering that handing her over to Smedley would cancel the debt entire. I think you see my position here."

"Yes, I do," said Klaus, straining against his tethers. *Syl on his throne!* He could scarcely believe his ears. "And what if he bests me in the duel?" he grunted, wrestling with the ropes. "What will you do then?"

The baron shrugged. "Then I would be forced to honor the bet and hand my daughter over to Smedley as arranged, wouldn't I—but we do not know that he will best you, do we? Drunken men do not tend to shoot straight, as it were. If you take my meaning."

"I see," said Klaus, chilled to the bone. "You mean to ensure my safety, then. Let us leave that awhile. You are securing your position against all odds is what it amounts to. Correct me if I am mistaken." Conversing with the man in gambler's terms was the best tack, though the words tasted of bile on his lips.

"Just so!" Gildersleeve gushed. "You have it exactly!"

"Well, then, what are the terms of your wager?"

" 'Tis . . . a thousand pounds altogether I'm into him for."

Klaus had no doubt in his mind that it was considerably less, but money was no object, and he nodded. To free Becca from such an arrangement was worth ten times the sum. Besides, he did not feel duty bound to honor any sort of arrangement with Cecil Gilder-sleeve. Being free to help Becca was his only obligation, and his only motive in discussing the matter at all.

"I knew you were a reasonable man," said the baron. Slapping the candle branch down on the floor, he began fumbling with the ropes binding Klaus's wrists. "You've been foolish here," he observed. "You've rubbed the skin clean off."

Klaus soothed the abrasions as the ropes fell away. "You have the terms in writing, I presume?" he said.

The baron nodded, helping him to his feet. "I have, sir."

"Who holds the vowels?" said Klaus.

"Smedley, of course," the baron returned.

"Then you needs must get them back!" Klaus charged.

"H-how can I do that?"

"I am sure I do not know, sir. That is your coil to unwind. As you pointed out, the man's a chronic elbow-bender. Use your imagination. I make no bargain without the written vowels in hand."

"But . . . if I had the vowels . . . I wouldn't need to bargain with *either* of you!" the baron said, discovery in his voice.

Klaus narrowed cold eyes and dosed him with a withering glance down the bridge of his uptilted nose. "Ahhh," he said, "but what would you gain—except a daughter that you have made all too plain you will be glad to see off your hands again. What would you profit, sir?"

"Yes, I see," the baron contemplated. "I do need compensation, don't I?"

"We have a bargain, then," said Klaus.

"Yes . . . after the duel."

"In case I am killed?" Klaus laughed outright, opening the cut on his lip wider. His rage was such that he scarcely noticed, or tasted the salty, metallic leakage of blood oozing from it. "You are even less of a gambler than I've credited you for, if such a thing could be possible, Gildersleeve," he said. "No wonder you are in such a predicament. No matter. Stand aside! You have wasted enough precious time already."

They hadn't taken two steps when the door the baron had left ajar came open and Smedley stepped inside.

"Not so fast, Gildersleeve," he said. "Where does he think he's going?"

"Have you been eavesdropping, Smedley?" the baron asked. He'd gone as white as the candlewax.

"No, but by the looks of this, I should have been. Why is he loose of his tethers?"

"H-he has convinced me that he is of more use to us free than bound," the baron replied.

"Have you attics to let, man? He may have duped you, but I'm no clunch. He's got her hidden somewhere. Let him go and we'll never see either one of them again!"

"When I need your advice, Smedley, I'll ask for it. This is my house, and Rebecca is my daughter—"

"Not for long. Let us not forget that she is my betrothed!"

"Then you should be the one concerned for her welfare. What are you doing skulking about down here?"

"Looking for you! The sun is up. We're resuming the search."

"Then let us be about it."

"Ohhh, no," said Smedley, planting a rough hand squarely in the center of Klaus's chest. "He shan't leave my sight until we settle our differences on the dueling ground. I do not trust this slippery Swede any farther than a hair's breadth of distance. Perhaps we should settle that first. Name your weapon, sir!"

Gildersleeve began to fidget. Smedley was stone

cold sober. If the situation weren't so grave, Klaus would have burst into laughter. The baron obviously wanted time to fox his opponent on Blue Ruin before the duel in anticipation of what he stood to profit if Smedley were to lose. At that moment, a gun was the last thing Klaus needed in his hand. He would have been hard-pressed to decide which one to aim at.

"Pistols," he said succinctly.

Smedley nodded.

"Later!" Gildersleeve put in, his voice quavering in falsetto. "My poor daughter could be lying injured in the mire out on that moor. There will be plenty of time to arrange the duel after we've exhausted all avenues in the search."

"Then I go with him," Smedley said. "He doesn't leave my sight until I've had satisfaction!"

This was the last thing Klaus wanted. He couldn't return to Boscastle Falls with Smedley in tow, and there wasn't a minute to waste. "We shall all go off together," he said. He turned cold eyes upon Smedley. "I am a gentleman, sir," he said. "You will have your satisfaction, I assure you, and *I* will have the satisfaction of telling Becca that you placed taking a shot at me above having her back safely. Now then, gentlemen, shall we commence?"

It was a play for time. There would have to be a change of plans. There was no possibility of reaching Boscastle Falls alone so closely watched by Smedley. The elders' chastisement revoking his ability to make time stand still was only supposed to be a temporary one. Praying that the sanction had been lifted, and that he still had enough energy to disappear into the astral and rejuvenate there with time suspended, he joined the others waiting mounted in the circular drive and set out with Smedley alongside.

The blink of an eye was all the time Klaus needed to cross over. The trick was to do it at a moment when he wasn't in Smedley's sights, which was next to impossible the way the hawk-eyed gudgeon kept him in view. It was not the safest plan. Even if the sanction had been lifted, he had no idea of the welcome he would receive in the astral—from the elders or the sirens, and from one siren sprite in particular, who was bound to be laying in wait to dole out retribution for his betrayal. And then there was Becca, who should have returned by now if she had heard him.

To Klaus's relief, it wasn't difficult to convince Smedley to resume the search at Boscastle Falls, since that was where Becca's mount had been found. There were several turns along the lane where two could not ride abreast. He was hoping to urge Smedley on ahead through one of these, so that he could cross over into the astral unseen. The first two attempts failed, and Klaus was forced to go first through the narrow passages. The third was nearly impassable. The bramble bushes that edged it encroached upon the path and threatened the horses—Klaus's horse especially. When it reared too close to Smedley's mount, the animal plunged ahead, all but unseating him. But dealing with the urgency of that claimed Smedley's concentration long enough for Klaus to cross over. If all went well, when he crossed back, it would be just as it had when he'd whisked Becca from the masked ball: as though no time had passed in the physical world at all. If not . . . well, the tar and feathers loomed larger with each passing moment.

Klaus emerged a stone's throw from the waterfall, stripped down, and dove in under the pulsating flow. No, he would not miss this when he had no more need of the waterfall to give him life. He no longer enjoyed it as he used to. It had become a mundane function. There was no pleasure in it anymore. This was the way—the *curse*, as he viewed it now—of the *Fossegrim*. Come the full moon, he would be mortal, just as his father was mortal after his fall—for that is what it was, a fall from grace. And the way the fey viewed abdication: Once embarked upon, there was no turning back. Once he renounced his astral heritage, all would forever be turned against him.

While he stood beneath the roaring flow, arms raised above his head to the thundering cascade, the one thought he'd suppressed came back to haunt him: What would he do if Becca rejected him now, when he'd given sway to his mortal self? What would he do if he couldn't find her—if she had succumbed to Illia's treachery or dismissed his instructions as naught but a dream? What would he do if she didn't want him? It was too terrible to contemplate, and he chased the thought by diving under the water in a vain attempt to drown it, but it would not be quelled. Neither world meant anything to him without Becca. He had to find her.

A fine sheeting mist was gathering about the river when Klaus emerged from the flow. A string of elders trudging through it along the riverbank passed him by as if he didn't exist, though they saw him well enough. He heaved a sorrowful sigh, watching them disappear into the fog. He was already shunned. He'd expected it. The tribunal had made its position plain. It would have pained him more if Henrik were among these. But the healer-cum-valet was conspicuous in his absence. What could it mean? Henrik had always been close at hand—always nearby when needed—immersed in his role as surrogate father. What would the beloved elder do when Klaus renounced his astral connection? Would he leave him, or forsake his own immortality and remain in the physical plane? Klaus couldn't imagine life without the man.

He had reached his full power now—rejuvenated by the life-giving waterfall. In this state, no human male could match his strength. No woman could resist his prowess. Such was the legacy of the *Fossegrim*. He was fortunate that as prince of his race, he could live apart from the falls for short intervals as long as he visited daily. The lower forms were restricted to their waterfalls, never to venture beyond the banks of their chosen river. In his youth, he had often fantasized about what it would be like to live without such a restriction. He had envied his father for breaking with the tradition. Suddenly, he was faced with the same decision, and the fantasies were real. Yes, his mortality was working in him. He hadn't thought about these things in eons.

Shaking the thoughts away, he tried again to reach Becca with his mind, in hopes that rejuvenation would give him the power to break through as it had before. But no, there was only silence. An eerie stillness had come over the land. Even the voice of the waterfall was reduced to a murmur. Not a creature, not a being welcomed him. They were there; he sensed their presence. The tiny winged creatures of land, water, and air that always crowded around him in awe and adoration welcomed him no more. It was a very clever demonstration. And if this was how they shunned him, what of Becca? They would certainly shun her also— or worse, for to them, she was the cause of his fall from grace. The fingers of a chill walked down his spine. Becca was alone, lost in the astral archipelago, with only the faithful *Irrbloss* to lead her back.

All at once a familiar spate of keening laughter echoed all around him, riding the breast of the water like a skipping stone. *Illia!* Klaus's heart leapt and his narrowed eyes glanced in all directions, but he saw nothing. Raking his wet hair back, he strained to hear, and it came again, closer now.

"She is free," the voice said, close in his ear, "but ye will never be, your highness. Ye have meddled with a sacred trust ordained by *Syl* himself, betraying me! What ye have won is not without consequence."

Something ghosted past him then, grazing his face— something gossamer fine, though it stung. He knew its ambergris fragrance well, that length of the siren's sea-green hair.

Again, he spun, searching the mist for her, but she was nowhere to be seen. Then something seized his sex cruelly, and he swatted at the hand that gripped it like a vise, but there was nothing there.

*"Syl on his throne!"* he seethed, spinning like a blind man.

A mischievous giggle rippled his scalp with goose-flesh. "He hears ye no longer," the siren tittered close in his ear. Her cold, moist breath puffed against his face. "Ye shall have to call upon the God of mortals for your salvation now."

"Come out where I can see you!" Klaus thundered, protecting his manhood with one hand, groping the fog with the other. "What have you done with her?"

"I have *done* what she commanded me to do—what ye told her to command me to do, your highness," she said, her voice and bone-chilling laughter fading to an echo. "What happens now is on your head. Ye will live to rue the day ye spoke my astral name to your whore! Just as I rue the day I told it ye. This is only the beginning. . . ."

## Chapter Twenty-one

Becca stumbled out of the cave as it collapsed in upon itself. The *Irrbloss* led the way. How like precocious children they were, bobbing along, always out of reach, as if engaged in a game where they alone knew the rules. Though she longed to embrace them, she respected their distance. Klaus said they would lead her back to him. In that terrible moment, when her whole world seemed to be caving in, she would have welcomed his strong arms around her regardless of his motive.

Everything was steeped in mist. It was nearly impossible to see where the land ended and the water began. Straining her eyes in all directions, she determined that she was on an island. It was one of many, spread out all around her in a becalmed sea, their veiled heads poking eerily through the fog. So this was where the sound of breakers crashing on the shore had come from. There wasn't a breath of a breeze blowing now, and she prayed it would remain so until she'd reached the mainland. She had never been fond of storms at sea. Living at Gildersleeve Grange on the coast, she had seen many.

The *Irrbloss* did not seem concerned, dancing on ahead. Klaus trusted them, and so would she. She had no choice. Though she strained her ears until her head ached, she did not hear Klaus's voice again. Had she ever really heard it? Or had the longing for him in her soul conjured that deep, sensuous baritone murmur she so longed to hear whisper *"mitt kostbart?"* It could have been a curse and still it would have seduced her the way he spoke it. He possessed the power to bewitch her heart. Had he ever spoken to Illia in that way? He must have done. No wonder she was ready to do black murder to keep him. It was only a little pang of jealousy, but jealousy nonetheless. She shrugged it off. There was no time for that now. Though, if Illia were to suddenly materialize before her, she would be moved to scratch the siren's sea-green eyes out.

All at once a boat appeared, veiled in the mist at the edge of the water. The *Irrbloss* hovered over it, and when she climbed inside and took up the oars, they skittered away and fanned out wide, keeping their distance. One of the bobbing balls of light seemed to be leading her, and she rowed in its direction, the water lapping softly at the little boat as it glided over the ripples—she could not see its surface for the mist. She was in their hands completely, wondering why they seemed prepared for battle in such a calm setting.

She wasn't left long to puzzle over it. The little boat had scarcely left the shore when webbed hands reached out toward her from the water—mercreatures, stroking her arms, tugging at her gown, groping her familiarly. Becca screamed. These were male, and there was no mistaking their intent. She rowed harder, but they followed, rocking the boat, trying to tip it over. She drew in the oars and began fighting them off with one, pounding the webbed hands blow after blow. For the second time she heard the voice of the *Irrbloss*. This time, it resembled a growl, and it chilled her to the marrow.

Becca began to row again with all her strength. The mercreatures followed, gaining on the boat. All at once, the *Irrbloss* began to close in, spinning in a circle, faster and faster, creating a vortex in the satiny water. Becca screamed again. Voicing their complaints in discordant unison, the mercreatures dispersed in all directions as the little boat plunged bow downward into the whirlpool—Will-o'-the-whisps and all. . . .

It emerged in the frothy, undulant flow of the waterfall Klaus had shown her on her first visit to the astral—the very site where Illia had attacked her. Glancing about, Becca expected the vindictive sprite to materialize out of thin air, but except for the *Irrbloss*, she was alone . . . or so she thought. Upon closer scrutiny, she noticed throngs of winged creatures of various shapes and sizes hovering like dragonflies on the breast of the water, watching from the trees, collecting in silent clusters on the riverbank. Staring at her in silence.

Chills riddled her from head to toe. She shuddered. This was not how they had appeared on her first visit. Then, they had seemed curious at the least, and welcoming at best. Their mute observation now did not bode well.

One by one, others came. These were older male creatures that were not winged—humanlike, but smaller in stature. The elders? More and more gathered, staring as the rest stared. As impractical as it was, Becca stood in the rocking boat and cupped her hands around her mouth.

"Please, sirs, will you help me home?" she called, blinking back tears. Home. Where was home for her? This strange, inhospitable place was Klaus's home. It struck her suddenly that there was no love here. It was a sensual, lascivious place, to be sure, where creatures cavorted naked and mated publicly with no compunction at all, but their coupling was detached. The beasts in the wild showed more emotion. Is this how Klaus had lived? It must have been; he was one of them . . . and yet, he seemed so passionate. Again she called out: "Please, I beg you. Show me the way."

None replied. En masse, they turned and walked away, elders and creatures alike melting into the mist as if they hadn't heard. They had, of course, and their silence spoke volumes. There would be no help for her here.

Becca stood in the rocking boat, watching them disappear. She'd had her fill of the astral realm. It wasn't the sweetly magical land she'd once supposed it to be. It was cold and hostile, devoid of compassion, unwelcoming to wayfarers—to captives in its midst who had no wish to be there. She had heard that creatures of the Otherworld could be cruel and dangerous. Evidently, that was true. One had tried to murder her, and the rest had left her to her own devices for her journey home. Only the faithful *Irrbloss* remained. Strange, misunderstood entities they were, feared by mankind as harbingers of death and ill fortune, while the opposite was true.

The thought had barely crossed her mind when they began to spin around the little boat again. *No!* Becca had no time to resume her seat before another vortex churned up the water and pitched her over the side. The last thing she saw before slipping into the swirls were the *Irrbloss* bouncing merrily away.

To his great relief, Klaus emerged in the physical plane as easily as he'd left it. *Praise Syl for lifted sanctions, and that time does not exist in the astral*, he thought. In the same breath, however, he cursed the elders' power to tamper. The more he became familiar with the world of mortals, the more he detested time. It was the one condition of life among humans that he doubted he would ever become accustomed to, made even more impossible with the elders' magic.

He prayed he would find Becca waiting at the falls, but she was not there when he reached it, and his heart sank. Together, he and Smedley searched both sides of the riverbank downstream for perilous miles, but there was no sign of her. His instincts told him that she hadn't drowned in the swift flowing current, but so much accursed *time* had passed since she'd disappeared, he was beginning to doubt. They returned by way of the wood and joined the others, but there was no sign of Becca anywhere, and the weary searchers plodded back to the Grange at dusk, borne down and dejected, their lathered mounts laboring.

The duel was to take place at first light on the moor. Gildersleeve took himself off to the gaming room in a blue funk the minute they returned, with Smedley in tow. It was plain, to Klaus's disgust, that the blunt the baron would have gained had they found Becca alive was the reason for his Friday-faced demeanor. Now, without Becca to bargain with, he didn't stand to gain a halfpenny—from either of them. Klaus could only imagine the man's panic over what he would placate Sir Percival with in case she was never recovered. That, no doubt, was the reason for his hasty retreat to the gaming room. He was evidently hoping to win back enough from Smedley to cancel the debt. It was a pleasant fiction; the man was as inept at the gaming tables as he was as a father.

Klaus wasn't remanded to the wine cellar this time. He was, however, confined to his rooms under guard. This amused him since now, at his most powerful, he could easily escape into the Otherworld if he was of a mind to. Half-mad with worry over Becca, he almost convinced himself to do just that: storm the astral archipelago, wreak havoc upon the sirens, have her back how he would, restrictions be damned! What more could they do to him, after all? He was already shunned, on the verge of being outcast, deserted by his elders and his gods. What more did he stand to lose? The answer to that came in the form of whispered words that chilled him from the inside out.

"Your Becca, and your very existence," Henrik murmured across his mind, just as if the elder stood in the room beside him. "You have already divested yourself of your immortality in your heart. Do not tamper with the sirens. You have lost favor in the astral. Your strength is here, *Syl* help you! Though I doubt he will. You have lost favor there as well. I pray, for your sake, that the God of humans is a more forgiving deity."

"Does this visit mean that you have not turned against me with the rest?" Klaus said to the elder in his mind.

"It means, your highness, that I will not desert you as the others have. But be warned: My help is short-lived. Do not squander it. And do not abuse your reinstated privileges. The sanctions have been lifted, but you are watched. It was the best I could do. Misuse your power now and not even I will be able to barter it back for you."

"You will leave me, then," said Klaus, answering his own question.

"I will remain . . . where I can do you the most good . . . until you need me no more," Henrik said haltingly, and spoke not another word.

Klaus paced the room like a caged animal. Why hadn't he asked the elder if Becca were safe? Henrik would have told him if she weren't . . . wouldn't he? If the man even knew. The more he thought about what might be happening to Becca at Illia's hands, the more Klaus roiled inside. *She should have returned by now— would have returned . . . if she were able.* Cold sweat beaded on his brow. He knew well the sprite's capabilities. He'd been at the center of her jealous rages many times before, but on those occasions there was no love to muddle the mind.

No! This was different. Henrik was wrong. The elder had never felt the all-consuming fires of love. How could he understand? How could he know that existence meant nothing without it?

Klaus gave it no more thought. He was gone in a heartbeat.

Becca emerged in the river beneath Boscastle Falls in the exact place where she had been abducted. Wading through the torrent, its lace-edged froth creaming around her, she reached the riverbank and collapsed on the moss. Almost at once, she felt a presence. Fearing another abduction—and why wouldn't she, after such cruel mishandling?—her eyes flicked in all directions.

"Who is it? Who's there?" she cried. "Klaus . . . is that you?"

"No, not Klaus," said a softer, older voice. "It is I, Henrik, the elder. I am come to help you."

Becca's giddy, scornful laughter skipped over the water, amplified by the falls.

"It is only natural that you should mistrust me, my lady," he replied.

"Why should you help me when the others would not? Where was your help when I needed it? How am I to trust you when you've been against me from the very start?"

"I will not lie to you, my lady," Henrik said. "I was opposed to your alignment with his lordship—I still am, because I fear he does not fully realize what he stands to lose. However, he loves you, and if you are what is best for him, his true heart's desire, I bow to that higher authority. We of the astral are not heartless, my lady, only suspicious of emotions we do not ourselves possess." He appeared then, and bowed from the waist. "I could not openly defy the Inquisitor General," he went on seamlessly. "His lordship knew it, and charged the *Irrbloss* with your keeping. Helping you now, I put myself at risk, but by doing so I also help him. The others have ostracised him on your account."

"Well, have no fear they have condemned me, also."

"I have his lordship's carriage," Henrik said. "I shall see you home. Much has happened since you left."

"And suppose I do not wish to return to the Grange?" said Becca haughtily.

"You must."

"I beg your pardon, Henrik?"

"You must return, my lady, if you hope to ever see him again."

"Where is he? What's happened? Why did he not come to help me in the first place?"

"He could not come without grave risk to you both. It is forbidden. No male creatures save the mermen are permitted to invade the sanctuary of the astral archipelago. The sirens rule the isles. It has been so since time out of mind, my lady."

"H-he came to me in my mind," Becca reflected, thinking out loud.

The elder nodded.

"Then it wasn't a dream!"

"It was . . . how can I put it so that you will understand? A meeting of the minds. What he could not do in the flesh, he did in spirit. It is one of his gifts. He shan't have it much longer."

"How is it that you have come now in his place? Surely he is not forbidden *here*? Why has he sent you instead?"

"No . . . not forbidden," said Henrik. "And he has not sent me. He does not even know I am here. He is . . . gone, my lady."

"Gone? Gone where?"

"Into the astral, looking for you."

"T-to that place where I was held captive—to those terrible isles?" Becca shrilled. "But you just said he could not go there. You said it is forbidden!"

Henrik nodded. "It is," he said. "He is on his own now. No male who has tried to invade the astral isles has ever returned from them. I tried to warn him, but he would not listen. He is drunk with love madness."

Becca scrambled to her feet and bolted toward the river. She didn't fear for his safety—she believed too much in his power—but that Illia would enslave him and that she would never see him again. In that terrible instant, she knew her heart and mind. She could not exist without him. Nor would she share him with the siren who had used her to lure him back.

Henrik seized her arm and spun her toward him, slowly shaking his head. "Where he has gone, you cannot follow," he said, his voice ringing in her ears, a hollow echo that chilled her to the marrow. "You cannot help him—neither of us can help him now."

# *Chapter Twenty-two*

Klaus emerged in the astral realm on the brink of twilight. All was still. A thousand eyes watched him from the gathering shadows, but none came forth to greet him as they had done in the past when he crossed over. It was forbidden to welcome an outcast. Klaus paid them no mind; he wasn't here to socialize.

Through a gap in the shoreline beyond, the forbidden isles rose from the evening mist as they always did at dusk. It was a phenomenon peculiar to both worlds that had beckoned and lured mortal and astral creatures since time began. The mysterious isles were the doom of sailors in the physical plane and the bane of curious fey. Convinced that he had nothing more to lose, Klaus made straight for the gentle ripples lapping at the shore and dove into the water.

As agile as any fish, he navigated the gentle swells. He didn't miss a stroke when clashing tremors on the ocean floor caused great upheavals, and tall, high-curling waves rose about him. A creature not so skilled in the water would have succumbed at this stage of the approach. For an instant he thought the wind had risen, from the sighing sound that echoed over the water, but there was no wind. It was the collective gasp of creatures on the shore behind him, watching his progress from safer ground.

He made no attempt at secrecy. He wanted Illia to confront him. Astral creatures could wreak havoc on mortals in the physical plane. They could torment and deceive, cause hair to snarl and toes to stub. They could steal objects—even children—and leave worthless trinkets and hideous changelings in their place, or nothing at all, as it suited their mood. In the astral, however, they were far more than mere pranksters. Here, they were deadly—especially to those mortals unfortunate enough to have strayed into their midst. All Klaus could think of was that Becca was in grave danger among them.

He plowed out of the surf and tramped up the beach on one of the larger isles, presuming that this was what Illia wanted him to do, from the way the mist parted, making his way clear. Sirens on the lesser isles and on the rocks that framed the archipelago on three sides sang their seductions: high-pitched, wailing strains of ethereal music, sung to lure unsuspecting mariners to their death on the reefs or to captivity among the sprites. Klaus was immune to their enticements. There was a time when he would have succumbed to their wiles, but no longer. Rage moved his heaving breast now, and dilated his hooded eyes, not passion. If this was the best Illia could do, he had naught to fear. Still, he proceeded with caution. He'd known her long enough to be wary. Once, she had been a loyal consort. Infected with jealousy, now she was a formidable enemy.

A dense forest of oak, rowan, and ash—all sacred to astral creatures—overspread the island. An eerie iridescent darkness prevailed on the cusp of night. Illia was near. Though Klaus couldn't see her, he felt her presence. A tramped-down ring of bent grass wreathed the wood. He could barely see it in the gathering dim, but he knew it for what it was: a trap. Once he stepped inside, he would be caught like a partridge in a snare, hers to command.

He blinked, and the ring of trampled grass was gone, and the last of the daylight with it. Had he imagined it? He dared not count upon it—especially not now, as the sprite's mocking laughter ripped through the trees like a whip. It stung him, riding a hot breath of wind that ruffled his wet hair, and narrowing his eyes, he probed the darkness for some sign of her. But there was none, only the laughter—that cold, triumphant laughter he knew so well. It chilled him to the bone, despite the sultry summer night.

"Where is she? What have you done with her?" Klaus demanded of the air around him, straining through the evening mist to see her familiar silhouette.

Another burst of laughter replied.

"If you have harmed one hair on her head—"

"What will ye do?" the cold voice interrupted. "Ye have no dominion here. *I* rule this place—these isles, your highness. No male has ever reached the archipelago alive, much less escaped from it—human or fey. Ye are here by the grace of *me* and mine."

Remembering his last invisible encounter with Illia, he protected his sex with a quick hand. "What do you hope to gain in this . . . entrapment?" he asked.

"Entrapment? This is no entrapment, your highness. It is *enslavement*. The price ye must pay for her freedom."

"What have you done with her?"

"I have set her free," said the disembodied voice. "I have already told ye that. I had no choice, and it is of no consequence, though ye will pay for that. Her part in this is done. Ye are outcast. The elders have shunned ye. It wants only for the moon to wax full again for your failure to end your passage to the physical plane forever. Neither realm will welcome ye then. Ye should thank me! But for me, when the moon rises round and bright again, ye will exist no more. Here in this haven none can touch ye, none save the gods, and I have their favor. Ye have much to thank me for. I have saved ye."

"Have you forgotten that I need the power of the waterfall to give me life? I see none anywhere about. You defeat your purpose, Illia."

There was a long silence. Klaus held his breath. If he dared believe her, Becca was safe. That was all that mattered.

"My purpose is to have ye back as we were," the sprite said at last. "We were happy once . . . until your fine lady meddled with your heart and head—until she bewitched ye! We could be so again. What can she give to ye that I cannot? How can she pleasure ye that I have not? Ye want what is forbidden. Ye whore after the unattainable. Once ye had her, ye would see how shallow this *love* of yours really is. Ye would see how fleeting her beauty—how short-lived your union. Ye would realize too late that ye had squandered your immortality, spent yourself in flesh and bone that decay and turn to dust." She materialized before him in all her voluptuous splendor, a shaft of pale, pearlescent moonlight gilding her naked skin as she sidled close. "She is an innocent—unskilled in the raptures of the flesh. I know your appetites. How could she hope to pleasure ye in her ineptitude? Forget her! She is *death*. Spend yourself in me and live. . . ."

Klaus stared down at the perfect creature gazing up at him, her shimmering eyes glazed with desire. It was as if the intimacies she'd spoken of that had occurred between them had happened to someone else; he had no recollection of them in his memory. His Otherworldly self had given way to the mortal man within in all but his dependence upon the waterfall for his existence. That had begun when he made the conscious decision to forsake his astral heritage. He had done that not even knowing if Becca would accept him— not even caring for the consequences if she did or didn't at the time. Somehow, he would convince her. Such was the power of love.

He would not deceive himself. Simply reaching the astral archipelago was no great feat. He'd been expected—guided! How far would Illia take it? That was the question. In this mystic place, her power was absolute. She had lured him like a spider in its web. Like the fly, he would not escape easily.

She flung her arms around his neck and drew him closer, their naked bodies touching. "I have forgotten nothing," she murmured. "There is a waterfall in the wood. It is a shallow one, though broad and strong. It feeds the tide pools on the far side of the isle. Come . . . I will show ye. We will bathe in it together. Give over thoughts of her. She does not even want you. She knew that ye would come, that ye would defy the restriction and come for her. Did she wait? No! She couldn't flee fast enough once ye gave her the means. . . ."

Klaus took hold of her upper arms and put her from him. "Even if what you say were true, I would have none of you," he said. "Your treachery has erased you from my mind. To me you no longer exist."

"That there says differently," she snapped, gesturing to his member.

"I am not dead, Illia," he responded. "You can claim no credit for arousing me. You know well the force of the mating ritual, the pull that drives a *Fossegrim* to fulfill his destiny. You have little to do with it. It is involuntary. That you would take advantage of it only drives me farther from you, little fool. I would sooner sever it from my body than relieve it in you."

The sting of the flat of her hand across his face caught him unaware. She raised the hand to strike again, but he captured both her wrists in one great fist and shook her.

"I have made my decision," he said. "Whether she chooses to accept my suit or not makes no difference. My astral life is over. *You* are over. You cannot enslave me here. I saw your trap when I arrived, and I avoided it. I shan't be caught that easily. I will take my chances returning in these waters, just as I have come. So, do your worst. Not all who dwell in the astral have forsaken me. I still command my allies, and you are not their equal—"

"*There*, perhaps," she snarled, gesturing toward the mainland barely visible in the moonlight through the mist. "Not here. None can help you here, fool. None save me!"

"I would have liked that we part as friends, not adversaries, Illia, but since you are not of a like mind, so be it."

He flung her arms away and turned to go, but her shrill voice ripped through the quiet. "Stop!" she cried. "Ye cannot leave. Ye are enslaved already. Ye were from the moment ye set foot on this isle. That trap was only one of many. Look!" she said, pointing to the shore. "Look behind ye, Prince of the *Fossegrim*. Tell me . . . what do ye see?"

Klaus spun in the direction of her rigid arm and pointing finger. His eyebrows rose, his body riddled with chills, his feet rooted to the spot. The ring of tamped down grass still stood between him and the forest. He hadn't crossed it, but behind there were more rings hidden in the mist, like ripples in a stream, that he had crossed over unaware.

Though it was useless to try, he bolted toward the shore only to be repelled, as though an invisible wall had risen up, preventing him. He was trapped.

"Ye might as well cross this last one," said Illia, preening alongside it, disturbing its flattened surface with her dainty toe. "Oh, that look! How did ye imagine the isles have captured intruders in the past, hmm? What? Do you think that fear of the consequences alone has kept men from our shores? Ye know little of the nature of the male creature, your highness, if ye suppose such to be true. Men—human and fey—are curious creatures, puffed up with imaginings of their own infallibility. Their bones edge our isles against the tides, like seashells gird the sandy beaches in the physical world. Are ye blind? Did ye not see them when ye came? This is how they got there, your highness. So! Ye have two choices. Ye will either stay, and live in this paradise that awaits ye, or your bones will join the others. The choice is yours. Either way, Klaus Lindegren, ye will never leave this isle." She reached out her hand. "Now then," she purred, "come and see the haven that awaits ye. Soon ye will forget—Illia will make ye forget—and then ye will be mine again."

# *Chapter Twenty-three*

Becca gazed out at the gathering twilight through her bedchamber window at Gildersleeve Grange. Overhead, the misshapen moon shone down, a grim reminder that soon it would be full and round, and Klaus would be lost to her forever.

She had dismissed Maud early, wanting no witnesses to what she was about to do, least of all the traitorous abigail who had betrayed Klaus and brought all this about. Her father posed no problem. He was closeted in the gaming room with several of his cronies. Sir Percival Smedley was not among them; the moment he set eyes on her, he'd rushed off to London for the special license. It was the perfect opportunity to succeed in her plan, and she would succeed, because this time she had the right sort of help to ensure it. Henrik had brought her here, but he had hardly left her unattended. When the moon was high, she would make her way to Boscastle Falls, where he would be waiting to take her where none save Klaus would find her.

But . . . what if he never came? It was a sennight

since he had disappeared, and time had not stood still. Her father was certain he'd fled to avoid the duel with Smedley. There was no redeeming him in Cedric Gildersleeve's eyes. The baron had grown sullen and morose, subject to black sulks and blue funks. In his cups, he would rant about how Klaus had duped him into letting him go by plying him with the promise of a greater settlement than Smedley could match. He'd been played for a fool, and when Klaus was found, if Smedley didn't kill him in the duel, they could bet their blunt that Baron Cedric Gildersleeve would!

It was all taradiddle, of course, the bluster just a means to save face before his gambling partners, and the least of Becca's worries. What haunted her more was the fear that she'd come to terms with her heart too late. Klaus had proved himself. He'd had more than one opportunity to succumb to the mating frenzy, and he had not. He was ready to forsake his immortality for her. Could there be any greater sacrifice a man could make for love? But now . . . was it really too late? Had she driven him back into Illia's arms, and lost him to the powers of that vindictive sprite's magic? Her heart was breaking.

Becca poked her head out into the hall. It was deserted. All was still. Once again, she snared her traveling bag out from under her bed. It had been packed for days, awaiting the ideal moment to make her escape. Henrik would come to the falls every night until she managed to steal away and join him there. In her heart of hearts, she hoped and prayed that it would be Klaus, not the elder, who met her there tonight. If it was, she would not be able to resist him. If only those arms could hold her again, she would never let him go, no matter the consequences.

Tears welled in her eyes. Up until now, she had made a valiant effort to keep them at bay. Still, despite her resolve, each time she let fear that she might never see him again creep into her thoughts, her eyes misted. If only she knew what was happening.

Becca tossed her hooded cloak about her shoulders, not against the steamy evening mist that had come as it always did at dusk in sultry summer, but for anonymity. She would walk to the falls. This time, she would not risk waking the stabler and alerting the household to her escape. It was a distance on foot, but her traveling bag was light. She had only packed the barest necessities. One last glance about the room and she stepped out into the hall and tiptoed toward the stairs.

The gentle creaking of old boards underfoot was the only sound. There wasn't a soul in sight, and she reached the double doors at the end of the Great Hall passageway and stepped out into the darkness. Hugging the tall, sculptured hedgerows that hemmed the circular drive, she crept along at a cautious pace until she'd left the courtyard behind and turned down the lane. Above, the waxing moon—a grim reminder of the urgency of her flight—shone down in all its misshapen splendor. *Are you friend or foe?* she wondered, studying its pockmarked surface. For while it lit her way, somehow it seemed to mock her. She was delving into mysteries she had no right to tamper with— secrets of a parallel universe no mortal had a right to know. Somehow, that didn't seem to matter. All that mattered was having Klaus back, never leaving him again. If only it wasn't too late.

The distance to the falls had never seemed so long, and she plodded along, keeping to the fringes of the wood, well out of view though there wasn't a soul in sight. Nevertheless, when she'd gone half the distance, a rustling sound behind raised her hackles. She stopped dead in her tracks, straining her ears, but the sound stopped also. Only the ragged thudding of her pounding heart broke the silence.

Becca moved on, and the sound came again. This time, she spun around in hopes of catching out whomever it was, but there was no one there. Wait! Did that clump of bracken move? She blinked to clear her vision and looked again, but there was nothing in the lane but shadows. Was her imagination playing tricks on her? Coming so recently from a cruel captivity, she wasn't brave enough to walk back and see. Perhaps it was the hermit her father tolerated on his land—a raggedy person, seldom seen, who wasn't above poaching game at night. He made his camp somewhere in this vicinity. Just what purpose he served had never been clear, except that he was expected to keep trespassers out, and frighten the ladies who came to house parties at the Grange, which was expected, and all in the spirit of fun.

Becca quickened her step and moved on. Several times as she progressed, the faint rustling sound turned her back, but nothing met her eyes. Finally, deciding that it was probably just some forest creature—a deer or a rabbit perhaps—she dismissed it from her mind, and made her way through the drifting mist to the falls.

The coach was waiting in the lane. Sven, the coachman, straightened from his slouch as she approached, and Henrik climbed out stiffly and took her traveling bag. He seemed borne down and older, if that were possible. The man was ageless to begin with.

"Have you come away clean?" he asked, handing her into the coach.

"I . . . I think so," she replied. "I did hear something earlier, but I suspect . . . *Oh!*"

A louder rustling turned her attention toward the lane behind, and a familiar figure emerged from the edge of the wood. It was Maud, huffing and panting as she skittered to a halt beside the carriage, tears streaming down her face.

"I . . . won't . . . let you go all on your own!" she wailed, dropping her valise. " 'Tis all my fault, what it's come ta, my lady. Ya can't go off unattended. My conscience would never stand it. There's no use arguin'! I'm goin' with ya."

Henrik's intense gaze settled on Becca, seeking her approval. This was the last thing she wanted. She heaved a mammoth sigh. She didn't want to take the abigail, but she dared not send her back. Oh, what to do! There was only one answer, and she pulled herself up ramrod-rigid in the coach, with all the presence of a queen to deliver it.

"You may come, Maud," she said. "Not because I want or need you, understand, but because I cannot trust you."

"Aw, now, my lady . . . !"

"Be still! You are right. Much of this is your fault, and I shudder to wonder what other disasters you might cause if I leave you behind now that you've found me out. Once you set foot inside this carriage, however, there will be no turning back."

"I know, my lady."

"Well, that is admirable, because *I* do not know where this decision will lead either one of us. Well? Get in if you're coming." She flung the carriage door open, and Maud scrambled inside. Meanwhile, Henrik passed the maid's valise up to Sven and climbed up on the seat beside him. A nod of his gray head set the coach in motion.

"Ya won't be sorry, my lady," said Maud, settling herself back against the squabs.

"I'm sorry already," Becca shot back. "That was you on the lane earlier, I presume?"

"Y-yes, my lady . . ."

"Well, you frightened me half to death! Why didn't you make your presence known?"

"I was afraid ya'd send me back, my lady."

"Hmm. Well, before 'tis done, you may well wish I had."

"Why, my lady? Where are we goin', then?"

"To Lindegren Hall," said Becca, ignoring the abigail's gasp. Then, giving the dark wooded lane zipping past the coach window her full and fierce attention, she said no more.

"This is the first place Father will look," Becca said dismally. She was seated on a rolled-arm lounge in the parlor at Lindegren Hall, where Henrik suggested they talk after breakfast. They'd arrived late the night before, by the conventional method—no astral tricks— but Becca was up at the crack of dawn notwithstanding.

Henrik smiled his patronizing smile. "That may well be," he said, "but he will never find you, my lady."

"How can you be so sure?"

"Come," he said, sweeping his arm wide.

Becca surged to her feet and followed him into the corridor, nonplussed, as he led her into the Great Hall and out through the front entrance onto the bluestone drive.

"Henrik, I fail to see—"

"Turn 'round, my lady," Henrik said, crooking his thumb toward the cottage behind.

Becca gave an exasperated grunt and spun toward the cottage with a toss of her curls, only to pull up short. Her jaw dropped and her eyes glanced in all directions. The cottage wasn't there!

"What?" she cried. "Where . . . where has it gone?"

"It was the most efficient way of showing you, my lady," said Henrik. "Forgive me if I've been too abrupt. I am far too weary with all this for bandying words about."

"*Abrupt?*" Her mind reeled back to the night when her father had found her on the road, when his coach had passed the place where the cottage should have been, though it had disappeared. She gasped, remembering how even Maud was taken aback by its absence.

"The Hall is cloaked from mortals' view," he said. "All things in time and space are but illusion, my lady. You father will seek, but he will not find you. You are safe here . . . 'til his highness . . . returns."

"Is Maud aware?"

"No, my lady, I've left that up to you. I know you do not want her here, but it may be best that she has come—for the reason you have already stated, and for your own piece of mind among us. You need one of your own kind for company now."

"Do you mean to say that Sven, Ulla, Anne-Lise, and the others are . . ." Though she'd suspected for some time that they were fey, it was still a shock to know for certain.

"Astral creatures," he concluded for her. "Yes, my lady. Oh, but you need have no fear. We are *his* creatures—that is to say, we serve him, and would give our lives for him . . . and for his lady. We have not brought you into danger, we have saved you from the union you abhor . . . for him. However, if you do not choose to stay, you are quite at liberty to leave at any time. You have been treated unkindly by one of our own. It is quite understandable that you would have . . . reservations when it comes to trusting us after such treatment. It is my intention to put your mind at ease."

"When we were here before, Anne-Lise drugged us!" Becca reminded him.

"You were not harmed, my lady."

"Not harmed, no, but that is not the sort of thing that fosters trust."

"I fully agree, and while I cannot change the fact

that it did occur, I can give you my word that it shan't happen again."

"Why did his highness give me that wine?" Becca asked, almost afraid of the answer, but while he was being so truthful . . .

Henrik hesitated. "Come. Walk with me," he said, sweeping his arm toward the falls. Becca's heart leapt. She had almost forgotten the falls where she'd first been alone with Klaus. Where he'd first held her, made love to her, in the dream that wasn't a dream. Cold chills puckered her scalp and crawled over her skin, as she let him lead her away from the invisible house.

"But . . . Maud," she murmured, glancing over her shoulder.

"You will not be missed," Henrik soothed. "Time does not exist inside the cottage. It will be as if you have never left it once we return. It lives in the astral, my lady. That it appears here, as I've said, is but illusion. Come."

For a time the only sound was the gravelly bluestone crunching underfoot, the silence so thick it was palpable, until Becca broke it.

"You aren't going to answer my question, are you, Henrik?" she said.

"It was fey wine that you drank. A magical distillation that allows those who partake of it access to the astral realm. His highness wanted to show you his world, my lady."

"Why?"

"He is drunk—not with wine—but with *love*. No! Do not speak. In order to explain, I must tell you something of the way of astral creatures. We do not . . . how shall I say . . . *experience* love in the same manner as humans. We of the astral realm mate fiercely and often . . . in ways that mortals would deem shocking—open and unabashed coupling of the flesh. You were witness to some of which I speak when you first visited the astral. We do take life partners and rear young, but while our sexual experience is . . . highly charged and sensual, we do not have the depth of feeling, the passion of the heart that you mortals know as love. Once one of us is infected with the malaise of such, he is lost to it. Once tasted, it is craved. The same was so of his highness's father. It was his ruin, which is why I have been so opposed to a union between you and his highness. Immortality is the greatest gift. It flies in the face of the gods to waste it."

"My God grants immortality as well," said Becca, "for those who believe. But differently. In the afterlife. In a separate place, much as the astral exists apart from the physical world."

Henrik thought on it. "I have heard that such is true. Let us pray to both our gods that his highness finds favor with Him, then. I fear that our gods have forsaken him."

Becca wasn't about to engage in a theological debate with the elder. She needed answers of a more immediate nature.

"You haven't answered my question, Henrik. Please go on. Why did he take me into the Otherworld?"

"As I have said, he is infected with love madness. He wants you for his life partner. At first, you were a candidate for fulfilling his destiny. I am certain he has told you that it is the nature of the *Fossegrim* to reproduce with a human female creature to perpetuate his race. It is not a decision, but rather an involuntary function of mind and body, over which he has precious little control, a condition of his existence that he must obey. Failure would cause him to be outcast from the astral for an undetermined time as punishment prescribed by the tribunal—possibly forever. Since his father was a renegade also, that is almost a certainty. He would be abandoned to fend for himself in the unwelcoming physical realm, among mortals as one of them. His choices were to have you and fulfill his destiny, which he rejected, to take you into the astral to dwell with him there, if you were willing—to remain just as you are now through all eternity—or to voluntarily renounce his astral heritage, give up his immortality, and remain in your world . . . to live and die with you, a mortal. The same choice his father made eons ago."

Becca stared, hanging upon his every word in rapt attention.

"When the siren sprites attacked you," Henrik went on, "his highness realized that you could never live in his world safely. Illia, their leader was his consort—"

"You say *was?*" she interrupted, seeking reassurance.

Henrik nodded. "Sirens are the handmaidens of the *Fossegrim*, and you have usurped her place."

"If as you say astral creatures have no capacity for physical love, how do you explain her behavior? She meant to claw my eyes out. And when she took me captive, she meant to *kill* me!"

"I never said we have no capacity for lust or jealousy, my lady. Illia considers his highness her mate—a plum catch, as you mortals say. She is proud and possessive, unwilling to allow a mere mortal to seduce him away. He is a coveted prize among the sprites. She is loath to lose face among her sisters, to bear their snickers, their ridicule. Sirens guard their possessions ferociously. Mark my words, there will be a firestorm in the astral over this."

"And yet, she would allow him to cohabit with a mortal female without consequence? I do not understand."

Henrik smiled. "Because it would be a mechanical mating, it would mean nothing, and afterward he would return to her. All quite acceptable, my lady. It simply is the way of things."

Becca shook her head. "I do not understand your ways," she said. They had reached the falls, and her gaze fell upon the sunlit water cascading into the river. "I could not bring myself to share him with another for any reason—mechanical or no. My heart is breaking as we speak, imagining him in that vile creature's arms."

Henrik fell silent apace. That he offered no words of reassurance put a damper on her hopes. Tears threatened again. He knew them both better than she. If he couldn't assuage her fears that Klaus was in the siren's arms right now . . .

"Where is he, Henrik?" she murmured, pleading.

"We both know the answer to that," he said. "He is out of our reach."

"Can he not use her astral name to free himself as I did?"

"No, my lady," he said. "She is his equal. That is why there was no danger in him knowing it, and evidently why she chose to share the knowledge with him—the ultimate bonding, if you will. She is no fool. He could not have used it against her. Only lesser creatures and greater mortals can wield that weapon."

"Is there nothing to be done, then?"

"There is . . . something, but we must wait."

"Wait? Wait for what? There is no time, Henrik. The moon will be full soon. By then she will have enslaved him."

"She has done that already, my lady. I shan't lie to you, but be of good cheer. All is not lost . . . yet."

"Can you not reach him with your mind the way he reached me? He does not know what is in my heart. He does not know how much I love him. Oh, please, will you try . . . ?"

"I have tried, my lady," the elder said, shaking his head. "I know your heart and your mind in the matter, even if he does not. Why is it, do you suppose, that I have brought you here to wait?"

"To wait for what?" cried Becca.

"Patience, my lady, we must wait for the moon to free him."

# Chapter Twenty-four

Klaus kept to the waterfall in the wood, only leaving it for brief intervals, gaining strength for what was to come. He bided his time, repelling Illia's advances. Though her song was like nothing he had ever heard, he thought of nothing but Becca, and of what he must do to free himself from captivity on the isle.

Though he wracked his brain for an answer, he could think of only one way to escape. He had to wait for the moon to wax full—to be cast out, to embrace his humanity. Only then, in human form, could he speak Illia's astral name and demand what she only could grant—his freedom. Only then, when they were no longer astral equals, when his power as a mortal man was greater than hers, could he hope to break her spell.

He would have no help from the elders, from the Inquisitor General, or from the creatures that had bowed before him through the ages. None in the astral could help him even if they wanted to. Were he to return there, it would mean his life—his very existence—just as the Inquisitor General had warned. The moment had to be precise. Illia had no inkling of what he was planning. If he were to make his move too soon and expose his strategy, somehow she would block it. Were he to wait too long, he would be cast onto the astral mainland, at the mercy of the elders and the tribunal. He watched the moon and waited, depending upon its pull to cue him as to the exact moment to speak her name and be flung back, like a fish too small to keep, into the physical world. It mattered not where. He would find Becca. If he had to search to the ends of the earth, he would find his soulmate and somehow convince her of his love.

It seemed the perfect plan until, on the brink of the full moon, dense cloud cover obscured his view and made precision doubtful if not impossible. Had Illia guessed his plan after all? Was this more fairy glamour—illusion conjured to thwart his escape?

There seemed no way out. Making matters worse, when Illia appeared at the edge of the shallow waterfall deep in the wood at twilight, he was on the brink of his mating frenzy. The pull of the moon—the very force that ruled the tides—ruled him now in one last struggle for his astral soul. He had never let it go this far—to the very edge of existence—*his* existence. It was painful beyond bearing to resist, more painful than he'd imagined. Fever raged inside him, boiling his blood, arousing him beyond all possibility. It was as if his loins had been cast in a lake of fire, as if hot daggers stabbed at his sex, thrusting deeper with each breath he drew. Without the moon, he would have to depend upon the pain to guide him now. It was a process much like the birth pangs of a woman in labor. At least, that was what he imagined. The result would be the same: an emergence, an awakening to life in another plane.

Illia stepped out of the eerie green fog with a sinuous grace. Klaus had just emerged from the water. Silvery droplets beaded upon his skin and ran in rivulets downward, and over the corded ridges of his well-muscled chest. Steam rose from his body in the still, hot air, clinging to his bronzed skin like an aura.

"How long will ye keep me waiting, your highness?" she asked, sauntering close.

"I've made you no promises, Illia," he said. "You cannot force my attentions."

She slid her eyes familiarly over his body. "It does not appear that there is much need of *forcing*," she tittered. "My task will be an easy one."

"You have but one task," he returned. "To let me go. Do it and we part amicably. Oppose me and there will be a reckoning."

"Ye are in no position to dictate conditions, your highness. No one save the gods have power here—the gods that have forsaken ye."

She drew close to him him in a catlike motion. "Ye do not have an alternative," she murmured. "Here ye are protected. Ye cannot be outcast when ye are outcast already. Here, ye may remain without fear of the tribunal, or the lure of the physical world denied ye. No one can touch ye lest the gods fling ye out, and ye will want for nothing." She took a step back and twirled slowly, flaunting her body. "What more could ye want?"

Klaus looked to the heavens. It must be time—it had to be time. There was no way to tell. Dense cloud cover still veiled the moon.

"Is this your doing?" he asked, nodding toward the sky. "Some siren trick played on the mind. Can you imagine that glamour could fool *me?* I do not only see with my eyes, Illia. I see with my senses. Take one away and the rest grow sharper. I do not need the moon to know when the time has come."

The siren shrieked, pounding her well-rounded thighs with her fists.

Distracted then, Klaus's eyes flashed toward the

river's edge, and his gaze fell upon a sight he had thought never to see again—the *Irrbloss*, bobbing playfully along the shore. He smiled. He'd forgotten that, being neither male nor female, they were the only creatures who could travel the archipelago. That was why he'd sent them to Becca. All at once, their impish cavorting took on a more serious feel. Their motion seemed frantic, and a smile lifted the corners of his lips as he watched them travel the riverbank.

Illia followed his gaze with eyes narrowed to slits. "Hideous creatures!" she shrilled. Stomping off after them, she raised her arms in the air, her tiny fists clenched. "Get out! Get away!" Gathering stones from the edge of the water, she began hurling them at the bobbing balls of light. "Be off, I say!"

"Leave them!" Klaus thundered. "They do no harm."

The creatures' gyrations grew more frantic, and suddenly Klaus knew their message, though he could no longer understand their astral voices. Had Henrik sent them? He could no longer reach the elder with his mind as he had always done. His mortal self was gaining strength. It had taken over. Was it time?

The *Irrbloss* managed to stay just out of reach of Illia's missiles, as was their nature, but she had the power to transport herself through space and air. It soon became a deadly contest, and she had nearly overtaken them, her strident shrieks at fever pitch, when Klaus's voice boomed through the otherwise still night—black as printer's ink without the moon, but for the fireflies.

"Maj! I command you to *set me free!*" he thundered.

Illia spun to face him and froze. All color seemed to leave her body. She appeared ghostlike in the darkness. A primeval screech spilled from her throat in wild, orgasmic spasms. Like a window shade descending, the dark clouds rolled back, exposing the moon, full and round and clear. Illia shrieked again, and flew at him. The last thing he felt was the final punishing spurts of blinding, searing pain that all but brought him to his knees. The last thing he saw was her perfect naked body hurtling toward him through space, before the impact and unconsciousness.

It wasn't long before a low moan woke him. Several moments later, Klaus realized it was coming from his own dry throat. He was alone, wet and naked, lying on a musty-smelling Persian carpet. The room was in darkness, except for the shaft of silvery moonlight striking him through the leaded panes of the window above. Dust motes danced along it, traveling up and down as if they had a purpose. They reminded him of the astral creatures—no bigger than gnats—that cavorted in the very air of the Otherworld. He followed the stream to its source, the full, round moon in a cloudless sky, and groaned again, remembering. Evidently the incantation had worked, and he'd come to earth in the worst of all possible places—the bedchamber at Gildersleeve Grange, from which he had departed.

Klaus rolled to his knees and shook himself like a dog. His head was reeling, but the pain . . . the awful pain was gone. Had it worked? Was he outcast from the astral plane? He surged to his feet in a bold attempt to cross back over just to be sure, but he could not. Twice—three times, he tried, each time to blink his eyes open again to the four walls of the musty bedchamber and the wan moonbeam at his feet. The astral was denied him. His mortality had overcome his astral self. It was what he had wanted after all—what he'd risked everything to attain. Why, then, was he still uneasy?

Nothing seemed as it should. His clothes were not where they'd fallen on the carpet when he'd shed them; they were neatly folded on a lounge across the way. Time had passed in the physical plane since he'd left it. He had committed the ultimate offense and, just as Henrik warned, time stood still for him no longer. His severance from the Otherworld and entrance into the realm of mortal man had cancelled that. He was running on a mortal clock now, and he had no idea how much time had passed in the physical world since he'd left it.

Klaus raked both hands through his hair, as if he hoped the motion would keep his brain from bursting. Would he ever get used to the concept of time? Outside, the moon was sinking low behind dark clouds on the horizon, and the sky had begun to lighten, threatening rain. His head ached from trying to plan his next course of action. One thing was certain: He could not stay here. He must away before anyone saw him. He reeled toward his clothes on the lounge—but not soon enough. Halfway there, the chamber door came open, and a chambermaid stood on the threshold, a bucket of water in one hand, a scrubbing brush in the other. Both hit the floor with a thud and a splash, rivaled only by her ear-splitting screams, and the sound of her ankle boots echoing a bold *rat-a-tat-tat* along the corridor outside as she fled.

Becca searched for Henrik all morning, but he was nowhere to be found in the rambling cottage. When nuncheon passed with still no sign of him, she decided to seek him at the waterfall, where he often went to meditate and, she suspected, to cross over into the astral realm.

Maud was occupied refurbishing what remained of her wardrobe, the worse for wear, having been crammed into her small traveling bag, and would be for some time. Becca had decided not to confide their situation to the abigail. Maud had betrayed her in the past; as sincere as she seemed at the present moment, Becca was not about to give her the opportunity to do so again. Who knew what she would do if she were to learn that their existence was but illusion in the grand Tudor cottage. She dared not risk that the foolish chit might beat a path straight back to Gildersleeve Grange, with the stars alone knew what tales. No, it was best to let her think that Klaus's kindly valet had brought them here to await his return so that they could be wed—a tale that would appeal to the simple maid's romantic soul.

The weather that had been so fair and still was unusual for Cornwall at the end of August. A change was due, and coming. The morning had dawned gray with fugitive mists haunting the hollows. They were chased by strong gusts by the time Becca pattered along the path in her freshly pressed sprigged muslin frock. Twice now, she'd taken her overskirt back from the wind. Soon storms would roll up the coast, bringing dark days and dirty weather, just as they always did on the cusp of autumn.

By the time she reached the waterfall, dark clouds had robbed the warmth from the sun, and turned the early afternoon a dismal shade of twilight gray. Henrik was standing on the brink of the falls. Wishing she'd worn her pelerine, Becca hugged herself against the wind, and began picking her way in his direction through the tall grass at the edge of the lane. A fine veil of sheeting mist rose around her, dampening her frock before she'd traveled half the distance. The starch Maud had so carefully applied to the fabric dissolved in a trice.

Henrik did not see her approaching. He seemed immersed in thought or prayer, standing mesmerized by the rushing water. He did not hear her, either; the deafening thunder of the waterfall amplified by the threatening storm prevented him. It wasn't until she rested a gentle hand upon his arm that he turned to face her. The somber look in his eyes nearly stopped her heart.

"Henrik?" she murmured. "Henrik, . . . what is it? You look as if you've seen a ghost."

"I have just come from the astral," he said. "It is . . . done, my lady. He has crossed over."

"Where? Where is he?" she asked, her eyes narrowed agasint the wind.

"Not here, my lady," said the elder. "Oh, how I wish . . . He has come through wherever the gods have flung him," he went on over her gasp. "And right now I expect he is having his first bitter taste of what it means to be a mortal, on his own, without benefit of his astral gifts to fall back upon for protection as he has always done in the past."

"Suppose he is at Gildersleeve Grange!" she cried. "I have to go to him!"

Henrik caught her wrist and turned her back. "We do not know that," he said. "Go there now and you expose yourself to all you have striven to escape. You would do more harm than good. You must let him work it out. It is what he wanted, after all, to be human, with all the faults and fallibilities of your accursed race . . . eh, no offense intended. Not even *I* can help him now . . . at least not yet. Not until the gods decide which gifts they will allow him to keep, if any. Wait now! A word of warning: Do not take heart hoping for much. I wouldn't count upon what your kind call miracles. I have managed to convince the others not to learn his astral name from the gods, but that is all I have won, and even that is tenuous and subject to revocation. You have no inkling of the tempest he has set loose in the Otherworld, my lady."

"But you do not understand," Becca persisted, resisting. "I need to go to him. I need to tell him my heart." She gasped. "*The duel!* I'd forgotten about the duel. Father and Smedley think he ran off to avoid it. He'll be killed, Henrik! He'll be killed, and it's all my fault!"

"Take ease, my lady. He is hardly inept with firearms. He has learned the use of many through the ages in his infernal fascination with his mortal side."

"I never should have left the Grange . . ."

"Come," Henrik said. "We must return to the cottage. There is naught to be done here, and there is danger."

"What danger? I thought you just said he crossed over."

"He has, my lady. The danger is not for him. He no longer has access to the astral realm. He can never return to it—ever. His life is here now, in the physical world, with you, and with all the pitfalls that await him as a mortal."

"I don't understand," Becca despaired.

"He knows well how to avoid Illia's wiles. The danger is for *you*, my lady. You are no longer safe near water—any water. The siren Illia is an entity to be reckoned with. She has sworn her vengeance upon you. If it takes your lifetime, she means to extract it. She has no power upon the land, but upon the water she can and will wreak havoc against you if you let her. You must heed my words, my lady. I shall not always be near to protect you. Do not come to these falls again—not ever. You will not find him here. He no longer needs the waterfall to give him life; all that is in the past. Do not frequent *any* waterfalls, and if you ever travel over water, carry this talisman. . . ." Reaching into his waistcoat pocket, he produced an amulet, a gemstone of great price, the color of a cresting wave backlit by the sun. It reminded her of Klaus's eyes. "Aquamarine has protected mariners from sirens' songs since time out of mind," he told her. "Few vessels leave port without one imbedded in the navigator's wheel, or affixed to the figurehead upon the prow. You will never, ever be safe upon—or in—the water again, lest it be your bathing tub. I am sorry." He handed it over as if it were something hot, and likely to burn him.

"I cannot take this," she said, gazing at its sparkle in the half-light. "The cost is much too dear. It is too great a treasure."

"It has no value for me, my lady. We of the astral put no price upon such baubles. Our treasures lie in that which Nature bestows upon us. While she gives us gems as well, they have no value save the aesthetic. It is mortal man who gives such trivialities a price."

Becca wondered how it was that he possessed such a stone, considering that it repelled creatures of his own kind.

"I am not a water elemental, my lady," he said, as if he'd read her thoughts. "My roots go deep into the land—into the wood. We elders take charge of those from all four corners of the astral, not necessarily from our own. It is better when not." He pointed at the stone in her hand. "That amulet has spared me the Lorelei's wrath on more than one occasion in my guardianship of his highness—Forgive me, it is *his lordship* now. It holds an enchantment. Guard it well."

Becca uttered a strangled gasp. "You read my thoughts?"

He nodded. "One of my gifts," he said. "It is how I know your heart, that it is pure. Elsewise we would not be having this conversation. My first obligation is to him. It will always be so, just as it was with his father before him."

"But if you can read my thoughts, why can't you read his and find out where he is? Oh Henrik, please!"

The elder hesitated. "I have tried," he said. "The channels must be open for me to do so. He could be sleeping, or too preoccupied for me to reach him. He is mortal now, remember."

"But *I* am mortal and you read mine," Becca persisted.

"Quite so. But not at a distance, my lady—you must

be near. He evidently is not in range of my gift as you are now."

"Is there nothing we can do?"

"There is nothing *you* can do, my lady," said the elder. "There is something that I can do."

"Oh, Henrik, I beg you do it, then!"

"All in due time, my lady. There are lessons to be learned here. He first must earn his land legs, as it were. Despite that he has lived among you, he is out of his element in more ways than one—he is a new creature, in a new dimension, faced with new and terrifying circumstances. Just as a child in leading strings must learn to cast off the tethers and walk upright on its own, so must he learn to walk among mortals as one of them. There is no one to help him with this. It is a rite of passage. He must evolve, and he alone can do it. But take heart! Wipe away those tears. There is great strength in him—strength enough to invade the astral archipelago and outwit the sirens—strength enough to defy his elders and his gods for love of you. He will stumble, and he will fall. This is how all creatures learn. This is how they grow. But he will adapt. What clouds his mind and slows his thinking is worry over you. That I can assuage. I will go in search of him, and in good and perfect time I will find him. But you must let me. Now, come. One of your dreadful flaws is on the make. If we hurry, we can avoid its rain."

Becca said no more. Henrik wasn't about to confide his plans. She wasn't even sure she wanted him to. She had to trust that whatever those plans were, he knew how to implement them. Right now, avoiding the storm was the first order of business. Tucking the aquamarine into her pocket with the conch shell, she let the elder lead her. They reached the cloaked cottage just as the first heavy raindrops fell.

# Chapter Twenty-five

Klaus had barely tugged his buckskins on when Gildersleeve, flanked by a troop of gentlemen houseguests and footmen, poured through his bedchamber door. Brandishing a formidable-looking walking stick with a silver wolf's head handle, the baron swaggered up to Klaus as the others fanned out wide in a ragged semicircle around him. This time they did not lay hands upon him. There was no danger that he might escape. His back was up against the tapestry-hung wall.

"Well, sir," Gildersleeve said, "and where have you been for a sennight in the altogether? More at issue, why have you returned? Are you simply a clodpole, or have you genuine attics to let?"

"I was searching for your daughter, sir," Klaus said steadily.

"In the buff, sir—afoot? Your carriage sits idle in my stables these past seven days and nights. Explain yourself!"

Klaus's mind was racing. What would they believe? What would he believe if he were they? His mind was a virtual blank.

"Well? Speak up, man! You were safe and away. What save madness possessed you to return?"

"We had a bargain, Gildersleeve," Klaus said with conviction. "I did not break it, or run from the duel. I am no coward, sir. As you say, my carriage sits in your stable, with my traveling bag and fresh togs in the boot these past seven days. One does not refresh oneself in the river clothed. If I were disposed toward backing down from a challenge—a thing I have never done, sir—would it not be reasonable to assume I would have fled *in* my carriage? Coaches do tend to travel faster than a man on foot." It sounded credible, and he was quite pleased with himself for thinking on his feet, but the baron's demeanor remained unchanged.

"How do you account for your comings and goings without being seen by the staff in this house?" Gildersleeve asked, his hand working his walking stick. "Are you the sorcerer Maud Ammen accuses, then? Or perhaps you have bribed some member of my staff?"

Klaus opened his mouth to speak, but a familiar voice from the threshold left him slack-jawed, as all eyes flashed toward the doorway.

"I can answer that to your satisfaction, I think," said Henrik, shuffling into the room. "I managed it all on my own just now without bribing—*or seeing*—anyone. Do not blame his lordship for your inability to post trustworthy sentries at your portals. Napoleon's army could have marched in below just now and not been noticed."

"Who, sir, are you?" said Gildersleeve with narrowed eyes. "I have seen you about . . ."

"I am Henrik, sir, his lordship's valet and traveling companion. I keep rooms at the coaching inn, where his lordship also lodged until you offered him your *hospitality*. A rented carriage has sufficed him in his search, since it was his intent and instruction to leave his own equipage here as insurance, as it were, to ease your mind that he had not fled were he delayed returning."

"We have covered half the countryside," Klaus put in, getting the drift of the elder's explanation. He was never so happy to see anyone in his entire eons-long life. "And I came and went but once—as easily as my valet here has just done."

"Ahhh, but you were locked in this room under guard," said the baron.

"I do not take kindly to being . . . confined," Klaus returned, with as much authority as he could muster before what amounted to another sort of tribunal. "Locks can be picked, Gildersleeve, and guards nod off. I was hoping to find your daughter straightaway, and return to reinstate our bargain with the prize found, but my leads took me farther afield than I'd planned, and bore no fruit."

"Hmm," the baron said warily, though he did seem to be giving it thought.

"Where is Smedley? Bring him on, and let us have done. Then, once that is settled, we can get on with our . . . arrangements. She will be found, sir. If she were dead, that would have occurred already. I would stake my life on it."

"Sir Percival has gone to London for the special license. He returns in two days time."

"Ah! Of course . . . the special license," said Klaus. "Very well, then, kindly allow my valet to minister to me in the meanwhile. You have none here that will do."

The baron gave it thought.

"Come, come, Gildersleeve, have you forgotten our terms?"

The baron drew a ragged breath and his posture slumped.

"Good, then!" said Klaus, responding to the gesture. "Now leave us, and if you would do something in the way of hospitality, have your footmen prepare my bath so that Henrik can assist me with a proper toilette. I've seven days of road dust to remove."

The baron hesitated. "Very well," he said at last. "But be warned: I have you in my eye, Lindegren. I have you in my eye."

"You are certain she is safe at the cottage?" Klaus asked Henrik. They were closeted in the dressing room adjoining the bedchamber. Klaus had bathed and changed into the dressing gown Henrik had had brought up from the carriage, along with the rest of the clothing he'd carried from the cottage. He was seated in a high-back wing chair, his long legs stretched out in front of him and crossed at the ankles, a brandy snifter in his hand.

"For the hundredth time, your high—my lord, *yes!* As safe as she can ever be. The lady has a penchant for risk-taking. She is no longer disposed toward escaping, if that is at the root of your inquiry. She is just as anxious to see you as you are to see her. That is what worries me. I knew exactly where you had crossed back over, and I had to lie to her—a thing I do not do well, I don't mind telling you. Had I not, wild horses would not have prevented her coming here straightaway. As it was, I had to physically restrain her when it crossed her mind that you might be at the Grange."

Klaus sighed and was silent for a time. Swirling the brandy in his glass, he pulled a face. "I have never been overly fond of this stuff," he complained. "Now I cannot abide it."

"You will become accustomed to it."

"Too many things . . ." Klaus mused.

"Are you having regrets, my lord?"

"Never!" he said. "It is just . . . I do not feel . . . I do not quite know who I am now, Henrik."

"You are who you always were," said the elder.

"Losing of your astral powers will take getting used to, but you will adapt, my lord."

"And what of you, old friend?" Klaus said. "I thought I'd lost you."

"I told you I would remain with you as long as you had need of me . . . where I could best serve you, my lord. That has not changed. I served you well enough here this morning, did I not? You hadn't a prayer, half-naked in this room up against that lot."

Klaus heaved a sigh and tossed back another swallow from the snifter around a grimace.

"You have lived among mortals long enough, my lord, to have acquired some of their quirks and protocols by association. These are a rougher—that is to say, a more roughly hewn society than we of the astral, with our more ethereal . . . more spiritual ways—like gems as yet uncut. It is because they do not recognize their gifts. They have them, they just do not know that they do. For all that they profess their spirituality, most have never communed with their spiritual selves. They haven't the capacity. This is where you have the edge, my lord. You are already in tune with yours in a way that they will never be—not even your Becca. Your father's astral blood still flows in your veins, remember. Mortality cannot take that away. Your senses are still charged with astral knowledge, and with what gifts the gods see fit to let you keep. In time . . . it will not be so with your offspring conceived after you became mortal. Your father was too impetuous, siring you on what these call 'the wrong side of the blanket,' though that faux pas has given you the best of both worlds . . . until now."

"Hah! I wouldn't count upon gifts of the gods, Henrik."

"They do not despise you, my lord. They are disappointed, and saddened that you forsook them like your father before you. Hah! What he did was kinder in their eyes. At least he fulfilled his destiny and perpetuated the race before defecting. I have just come from pleading your case before the Tribunal, from making burnt offerings to the gods, and they will not betray your astral name. I have had a sign. It was . . . exhausting, and no easier the second time around, I don't mind telling you."

"You have lost favor," Klaus knew.

"That is not important. I have placated the other elders and the Inquisitor General, but *nothing* will placate the sprites. They can no longer touch you, but they can—and will—harm your lady if she ventures near water. Illia has sworn vengeance, and you know her capabilities."

"I do now," said Klaus, his words riding a sigh.

"I have warned your lady, my lord, but she is headstrong and is possessed of a stubborn independence that defies reason. It will be up to you to enforce that edict, and you needs must do it quickly. Perhaps, coming from you . . ."

"My supposed *arrest* here—the duel—none of it troubles me. What does is being separated from her now, before she knows the way of things, before I can reassure her of our future . . . of my love. The longer you are gone from the cottage, the greater the risk that she might do something foolish. Perhaps I was hasty in demanding that you remain. Perhaps you ought to return to her at once and put her mind at ease."

The elder shook his head. "I can be at her side in the blink of an eye," he said. "I have not lost my gifts yet. Right now, you need me more than she. You have just crossed over, and you are forgetting something. . . ."

"What?"

"As an astral creature, you were not vulnerable to life-threatening circumstances. Speaking plain—you could suffer injury, but you could not die; your immortality prevented it. Not so now, my lord. Your immortality is forfeit. You are just as vulnerable to death as any other mortal. You have bought yourself that mortality, but at a price more dear than the earth, and there are no guarantees. You could live to a ripe old age or die day after tomorrow in that accursed duel. Smedley has no inkling that his betrothed has run off again, or that you have returned. The chucklehead believes he is coming home to nuptials. Until she is found you are suspect, and the duel is inevitable no matter the situation. You haven't a prayer that he will cry off. You need your wits about you now. Like the stuff or not, my lord, you had best let me refill that glass. We have much to discuss."

"Please, my lady, you'll wear the rug threadbare," Maud pleaded.

Becca was pacing the length of the Aubusson carpet in her bedchamber and had been most of the morning, clutching the conch shell as if it were a magic charm that would make Klaus materialize before her. Henrik should have returned by now—long before now. He could travel between worlds in a heartbeat. How long could it take an astral elder with supernatural powers to scour the Cornish moors? Something was wrong—terribly wrong. She could feel it. She *knew* it.

The dreary face of the day poking in at the window didn't help matters any. Rain tapped at the panes as if it begged admittance, and the wind howled and moaned about the pilasters outside. The flaw was a ripper, the house so damp from the flaying gusts that the hearths had been lit to chase the chill—*in August.*

Becca hadn't confided their situation to Maud. The superstitious chit was wary as it was, had betrayed her mistress with naught save suspicions for cause. The stars alone knew what she would do were she to learn that those suspicions were true. That she was living in limbo between the world she knew and the astral realm, attended by the fey. Madness! It was easier to let her think that Klaus had gone missing looking for her. That his valet, who knew his haunts, had gone in search of him with the news that Becca had been found and conveyed safely to his cottage. Just how long she would be able to keep up the pretense she had no idea. Hopefully, now that Klaus had become mortal, the abigail might never need know the truth.

"Henrik should have come back by now," she couldn't help admitting, thinking out loud. She stopped pacing and spun around to face the fretting maid. "Suppose Klaus has returned to the Grange," she cried. "The duel! Ye gods, the damned confounded duel . . ."

"Hush, my lady! I've never known ya to blaspheme before. 'Tisn't goin' to bring him any quicker. Look at you, you're all flushed. You're goin' ta make yourself sick. Why, you're fair done to a crow's thumb—just this side of a swoon, to be sure."

Becca couldn't tell her that she feared she'd unwittingly seduced Klaus from his own kind, that she was responsible for his giving up his immortality in the astral realm, possibly only to have it all end on the dueling ground. How would she ever live with herself? How could she bear to live at all if she were responsible for his death? The thought was too terrible to consider, and she threw herself across the bed and sobbed her heart dry.

There they were: the tears, at last. Maud's hovering only made matters worse. The distraught abigail fled the room and returned minutes later with Anne-Lise in tow. *Henrik was wrong*, Becca thought ruefully. It wasn't her own kind that she needed now. It was reassurance from Klaus's kind—those who knew him better than she—that would bear her up.

"Why won't ya let me fix ya a nice herbal draught to settle yer blue devils, m'lady?" the housekeeper said.

"Ohhhh, no," Becca responded. "No more herbal draughts!"

"Ya can come down and fix it yerself," Anne-Lise said flatly. "There's chamomile, or borage. In my opinion, the borage—it will quiet those heart palpitations and ease yer love sickness." She raised her tiny hands in response to Becca's black look. "All right, m'lady. Choose for yerself, but come . . . do. I'll put the kettle on."

Becca gave in, if only to be rid of Maud for a little while. Her fretting was making matters worse. Leaving the maid to sew new ribbon streamers on her bonnet, she followed the strange little housekeeper below to the kitchen.

She did not brew the herbal tea herself, though she did watch carefully as Anne-Lise steeped the chamomile blossoms in boiling water. When she asked to drink it there, at the old scarred kitchen table, and invited the housekeeper to join her, Anne-Lise dug in her heels.

"Oh, I couldn't, m'lady!" she breathed. "The master would skin me."

"Well, the master isn't here, and I wish to speak with you in private," Becca said, spooning a little honey into her cup.

"Well, in that case," said the housekeeper, casting a sideways glance, as if she expected Klaus to materialize before her eyes. *Oh, if only he would!* "But if he was ta come in . . ."

"I only wish," said Becca, while the woman sank down at the table, "—and if he does, I guarantee you my greeting will be such as to make him forget your breach of conduct, if he were even to notice. Now, tell me, Anne-Lise, are you afraid of the master? You always seem so . . . awkward in his presence."

"We all love the master," she replied. "We live ta serve him . . . and ta serve ya, m'lady. I know ya do not believe that, but it's true. If I have seemed awkward, it is only because I try too hard."

"Why did you drug us when we first came to the Hall?" It was a bold question, and the housekeeper bristled, but Becca needed to know.

"I . . . we did ya no harm, m'lady. We knew the master had a tendre for ya from the start. It wasn't like the other times . . . the other mating seasons. He needed time ta see if ya could feel the same, is all." She rose from the table and began to wring her apron. "I'm talkin' out of turn," she said. "No harm was meant to ya, and none was done—not really, except for givin' ya dreams now and again . . ."

"How many of those dreams *were* dreams, Anne-Lise?"

"Yer a bright lass. Ya know the answer to that, m'lady."

"I expect I do," Becca said on a sigh. "Please sit down. This is as difficult for me as it is for you—more so, because I do not know him as you do. But it isn't the master that I wish to discuss. Well, not directly. Please?" She gestured toward the chair the housekeeper had vacated.

Anne-Lise hesitated, then sank back down at the table, her spine broomstick-straight.

"That's better," Becca said. "Why hasn't Henrik returned? I know you can communicate with your minds. He is gone too long. I know something is wrong, and I shall go mad with worry unless you tell me. Nothing in your herbal stores will prevent it."

"He will come soon now."

"Why is he detained? Is it the master? It must be! Where has Henrik gone? What has detained him?"

"Ya mustn't excite yerself, m'lady. He is with the master. All will be well."

"But all is not well, is it? *Where are they?* He hasn't gone back into the astral?"

"N-no, m'lady. He cannot."

"The Grange, then? Tell me not Gildersleeve Grange."

Anne-Lise didn't answer. Pale to begin with, all color fled her face, and the housekeeper's eyes suddenly resembled an owl's.

On her feet now, Becca backed away from the table, upsetting her chamomile tea. It bled in a wide, ragged circle. Anne-Lise didn't seem to notice. Springing to her feet, she raised her hands, making wild circles in the air, but nothing intelligible came from her stuttering lips.

"Oh, my God! I feared it. I *knew* it. He will be killed!" Becca cried.

"No, m'lady, wait!" Anne-Lise said. "Ya can't go! There's a ragin' storm out there!"

But her words fell upon deaf ears. Becca had already fled.

# Chapter Twenty-six

"What do you mean, when the flaw is done?" Smedley barked. They were assembled in Klaus's sitting room at the Grange—Baron Gildersleeve, Henrik, Klaus, and the bedraggled Sir Percival, just returned from London. "The bloody flaw! Harumph! What care I for the bloody flaw! I'm soaked to the cods as it is, coming on from Town in this maelstrom. I say get him out on the moor right now and have done!"

"Your servant, sir," said Klaus, with a heel-clicking bow. The muscles along his jaw had begun to tick and his hands itched to clench into fists.

"N-now, let us not be hasty," Gildersleeve tittered. "There's hardly a need for that. The man's under guard, after all, and—"

"Hah! He was under guard before, as I recall, and got out just as if he were a wraith despite you lot. Now, if I'd been here—"

"Well, you weren't," said Gildersleeve, "and I do not relish mucking about in that morass out there whilst you two kill each other, and one of you lies stinking till the storm abates so we can bury you. We wait for fair weather!"

"He's got her hid somewhere! I knew it all along. Gildersleeve, if I find out that you are in on this, he won't be the only one in this room in need of a second!"

The baron's face clouded, and he sank deep in thought before speaking. "Everyone out!" he finally said. "Smedley, go dry off! You're half-sprung. I can smell the whiskey from here. Have another if needs must, and settle down. I'll speak with you directly . . . after I've had a word with the count." Taking Sir Percival by the arm, he steered him toward the door and pushed him through as the others filed past. "Go on, then," he said. Slamming the door shut, he turned back to Henrik. "You, too," he said. "Well? Don't stand there gaping. Take yourself off, man!"

Sketching a bow, Henrik repaired to the dressing room adjoining, a close eye upon Klaus as he backed through the door. Klaus noticed that he didn't close it all the way. Spying was second nature to the elder. For the first time in his life, he was glad of it.

"*Have* you got her stashed away somewhere, Lindegren?" the baron whispered excitedly the minute Henrik was out of sight. "Is that where you've been for a sennight, then—with Rebecca?"

Klaus's lips formed a tight line. Gildersleeve was as transparent as the glass in the shuddering windowpane. He didn't have a care that his daughter might have been compromised—robbed of her virtue. If Becca were alive, the gudgeon stood to gain from an alliance. He had no regard for her welfare, no concern for her safety. Settling his debt with Smedley was all that mattered—putting it behind him, and getting shot of a bothersome daughter so he could move on to the next wager. Klaus fumed.

"She is alive," he said through clenched teeth, "but I was not with her. I am a gentleman, sir. I told you the truth. I searched until I found her—only just. She has fled this marriage you force upon her once more, just as she did when we first met, and will do again if you persist."

"He was right. You have got her stashed away somewhere!"

"I have given her refuge, yes. I want her for my wife, Gildersleeve. But for this ridiculous duel, and your confounded stupidity, I would have settled your debt with Smedley long since, and your daughter and I would be married by now."

The baron's grin faded. "He won't cry off," he said. "There's no hope of that. The duel must be fought, but as I've said, the man's a notorious elbow bender. He's on the cut right now—you saw him. He'll be bosky in an hour. But for this blasted flaw . . ."

"I am a gentleman, sir! And an excellent shot. He need not be foxed for me to best him. I take that as an insult!"

"Yes, yes, whatever you will, but what say we have the duel now after all, and have done—the flaw be damned, sir! What harm to take advantage of the man's top-heavy condition *and* the dirty weather to narrow the odds in our favor, eh? Trust me, I have an instinct for such things. I'm a gambling man, Lindegren."

"How well I know it!" Klaus shot back, his arched brow and crimped lips a study in sarcasm.

"It isn't like we've deliberately got him foxed. He's done that all on his own, no thanks to us. We're in the clear, thank Divine Providence. Why not have a ride on the coattails of the Divine, eh?"

"Do not include me in that number, Gildersleeve. I have been challenged. That gives me the choice, and I say we wait. You may not have a care for your conscience, but I prefer to remain on good terms with mine. Regardless of whether you've fed him the rotgut or not, the man's at an acute disadvantage—storm or no storm—and I do not mean to start out in this manner!"

"Start out?" Gildersleeve queried.

Klaus cleared his voice. He'd been caught thinking out loud. "I . . . I was referring to the marriage," he recovered. "Deception in any form is hardly the way to start out married life."

"Hmm. It's your call. But I still say . . ."

"As soon as the storm lessens," said Klaus. "Meanwhile, Henrik will call upon Smedley's second. He will serve as mine, since I do not know your other gentlemen guests, and I trust Henrik implicitly."

"Harumph! Highly irregular. Now you insult me, Lindegren."

"Just so, we are even, but that is the way of it. Henrik will make certain that Smedley is sober beforehand. That is my main concern. I think that you will be diligent in that regard, however, because if he is even a trifle disguised, we will not go forward. If that man comes up against me foxed, or anything else untoward occurs on that dueling ground, you can forget our so-called bargain. You'll get no settlement from me."

"You're sure you're that good, eh?"

"I am better than good," Klaus boasted, and he was, with every weapon from the longbow to the battle ax, from spear to rapier, down through the ages. He'd had to be; and as to the pistol, he'd done a turn or two at Manton's Gallery. Such a weapon was a treat, after some of the others he'd had to master and wield through the centuries, when it was necessary that he walk among mortals.

"You'd better be," Gildersleeve growled, pushing past him.

Klaus stiffened as the door slammed shut, at the rasp of the key turning in the old lock. All his suite doors were kept locked, and had been since the astral flung him back in the middle of his bedchamber floor. Even Henrik was kept confined to the dressing room. If they only knew that in a blink the elder could escape their paltry prison. *It would almost be worth it, just to watch their bloody jaws drop,* Klaus thought with dark delight.

"Well done, my lord," Henrik said, stepping back over the threshold from the dressing room.

"You heard?" asked Klaus, pouring himself a brandy.

Henrik nodded, his expression indicating surprise that he would even ask such a question in these circumstances.

"I will not face Smedley while he is in his cups. Poor gudgeon. It's Gildersleeve I would like to meet out on that moor. The man should be horsewhipped."

"What sort of an arrangement is it that you have committed to, my lord?"

"Hah! Just wait and see, Henrik."

"My lord, if you fund that man, he will be living in your pocket like a piece of lint until he dies."

"You just leave Baron Gildersleeve to me," said Klaus, tossing back the contents of his snifter with a grimace. "I am hardly inept among mortal men . . . just feeling rather naked without my other self at the moment."

"That will pass," Henrik said through a sigh.

Klaus set the snifter down and looked him in the eye. "I have no right to ask it, but you know that I must. Do not leave me, old friend."

The elder hesitated, a sad smile creasing his wrinkled lips. "I will never leave you . . . in spirit, my lord," he said. "Do you recall my saying that I would be with you as long as you needed me, and where I could do you the most good?"

Klaus nodded. "You're going back."

"I am too long immortal to give it up now," said the

elder. "Unlike yourself, I relish immortality—even in this withered old state. You would have come to such a pass had you remained, one day. You will age quickly now—just as mortals age, a little with each year's passing until you . . . die. Forgive me, but the prospect of your eventual death disturbs me. It pains me that I will still remain to suffer it, when it should have come long centuries after I've passed through the Golden Bower of the gods and am retired till the end of time. I will miss your company there on that plateau of our existence." He wagged his head. "*Love,*" he ground out archly. "All for accursed love . . ."

"When will you leave me?" Klaus asked, almost afraid of the answer.

"I will never leave you, my lord, not in the absolute sense. I still have the power to transcend worlds, but where you need me most is in the astral now. You have a formidable enemy there, and elders who are still incensed at your leaving must be placated. Not to mention the gods, if you ever expect to have any of your gifts restored—at least your powers of mind and thought. Have you no idea how many 'mortal' men roam the earth in the physical plane with special gifts allowed them when they fell? Do you think you are the only astral creature who has fallen from grace? You will meet many, my lord. They roam the planet in great numbers. Why do you suppose the gods are so incensed?"

So wound in his own coil, Klaus had never thought about that.

"You are well able to deal with your mortal enemies," the elder went on. "Leave your astral ones to me, and keep your lady clear of water. There is only so much I can do against the sirens. Once the duel is fought and you are reunited with your bride, you will see me no more as you see me now . . . unless there is grave need. It is what must be."

"I will miss you, old friend," said Klaus.

"And I you, young son," said the elder. "Just as I miss your father before you. The gods were cruel when they denied us the mystery of mortal love but gave us the pain of mortal sorrow."

The flaw had spent itself by Tuesday, howling its last over the headlands before spinning out to sea. The wind finally held its breath, and dawn rose with drifting fog too dense to give way to the fine sheeting mist veiling the moor south of Boscastle.

Klaus was beside himself. He could bear to wait no longer. Henrik hadn't been able to leave to placate Becca without risking exposure. They were heavily guarded night and day. When he tugged the bell rope that morning, it was to announce that the duel would go forward the minute the sky lightened.

The moor was steeped in fog when they reached it, the stubborn rain still falling lightly. One Algernon Pembroke, a local squire, fair and rugged-looking in his mid-thirties, had volunteered to stand as Smedley's second. Reginald Somers, a doctor from the valley, was assigned to referee, and to tend the loser. Both were men picked from the baron's gambling cronies, men staying at the Grange for a week-long house party—hangers-on who all but lived at Gildersleeve's gaming tables. Neither was familiar.

Klaus stepped down from his carriage knee-deep in fog, stripped off his coat of superfine, and handed it to Henrik; he wore no waistcoat; he would shoot in his shirtsleeves for the best advantage. He hadn't taken two steps in his turned-down boots when the slick, saturated grass in need of scything undermined his balance and he slipped. Recovering his footing, he loosed a string of blue expletives. He would have to be more careful.

A folding table had been set up at the edge of the

clearing. A brace of pistols in a wooden case lined with burgundy baise was laid out under an umbrella, sheltered from the drizzle. Once the pistols were chosen, and loaded by the seconds, both returned to the duelists, while the referee paced off the distance, set the stakes, and barked the rules.

Klaus tested the pistol for balance. It was cold and rigid in his grip. He handled it with ease, and a fluid grace that took Smedley's notice across the way. Klaus exuded self-confidence, and why wouldn't he? He'd handled many pistols. His opponent, however, was shaking noticeably.

Henrik leaned close. "The man is quaking in his boots, my lord," he said. "Take care; frightened men are dangerous ones."

"How well I know it," Klaus returned. "He's sober, then?"

The elder nodded. "Quite, my lord," he said. "Which is why he's trembling so. Will you give him a chance to cry off?"

"Of course, but he will not."

"Have your gifts been restored that you would know that?" Henrik chided.

"Hardly. He fancies himself a gambler, just as Gildersleeve does. He is too proud to admit defeat. When his kind fights to the death, it usually *is* their death."

"Just remember, you are no longer immune to death, my lord. Remember, but do not fear. You have the best of both worlds in you. Listen to your spirit. Not all gifts are astral in nature."

There was wisdom in that somewhere, though Klaus wasted no time digging for it. He stood, his eyes narrowed as Henrik approached Smedley through the stubborn rain.

"His lordship wishes to offer you a chance to rescind your challenge," said the elder.

"Never!" Smedley vowed.

Klaus gave a dry grunt that drew the elder's eyes.

"Again, sir, will you withdraw?" Henrik offered.

"No sir, I am no coward." Though Smedley squared his posture, the pistol shuddered in his hand.

"So be it," Henrik said, wagging his head toward Klaus.

"Let the duel begin," Dr. Somers intoned.

Klaus and Smedley waded through the wet grass to the center stake and stood back to back.

"When you reach your marker, turn and cock your pistols," Dr. Somers charged. "But wait until I give the signal before you fire."

Out of the corner of his eye, Klaus caught sight of Gildersleeve alongside Smedley's second, his eyes flicking between the duellists as they paced off the distance. Klaus reached his marker and had just begun to turn when a shot rang out. It sounded like thunder, echoing in his ears, and it felt as though he'd been struck by lightning. Something lifted him into the air and spun him around. Was that Henrik who cried out?

The pistol in his grip discharged and spiraled out of his hand. It hit the ground before he did, and a sharp, tearing pain ripped through his chest . . . or was it his shoulder? Klaus couldn't be sure, lying doubled over in the wet grass, his shirt sodden with blood. Had he slipped again?

"Give me that pistol, you gudgeon!" Gildersleeve demanded of Pembroke, Smedley's thunderstruck second, staring slack-jawed at Smedley, who was running away. When Pembroke didn't reply, the baron ripped the weapon from his hands, aimed it, and fired.

Smedley froze in his tracks. His body clenched, convulsed, and he toppled over. The impact of his bulk hitting the earth reverberated through Klaus's body, as Klaus lay writhing in the smashed grass. He shuddered. It reminded him of the rings of flattened grass that had trapped him on the sirens' isle.

"There, then!" Gildersleeeve shouted. "That settles the benighted debt!"

Somebody groaned. It was a moment before Klaus realized that he had made the sound. Something cut off the light. It was the press of people bending over him.

Behind, there was some sort of commotion on the lane. Sven and Henrik had gone to address it. Klaus had never seen the elder move so fast. He wouldn't have thought it possible. It was all a dream, of course. Anything was possible in dreams. He would wake soon and finish the duel. . . .

"No, my lady, stay back!" Henrik cried.

What lady? Klaus saw no lady, only the scowling face of Dr. Somers hovering over him. He smelled of onions. He felt nothing but the man's fat fingers poking, probing. What was he saying? He couldn't make it out. *Don't do that! The pain! Bloody hell . . . the pain . . .*

"*Klaus!*"

Becca? Now he was certain it was a dream.

"You've killed him!" that beloved voice shrilled. "Stand aside! Let me pass!"

All at once her scent filled his nostrils, replacing the doctor's foul onion breath. He breathed her in deeply. The last thing he saw was her face descending. The last thing he felt was the petal softness of her lips upon his.

# Chapter Twenty-seven

"And that is the sort of man you intended to shackle me to for the rest of my days?" Becca said to her father, "A cowardly back-shooter—even as yourself!" They were seated in Klaus's sitting room, while the doctor worked to remove the pistol ball in the bedchamber adjoining.

"Well, it's over now. There's no point doing it to death, daughter."

"No point? Aside from the fact that you were set to sacrifice me, a man lies dead on the heath, another could well be dying at the hands of that cup-shot charlatan in there—all for a few measly pounds wagered. I'm surprised you haven't taken bets on Klaus's chances to survive. Or have you?"

"Mind your tongue!" her father snapped.

"And why this sudden concern for the count, might I ask? You were set to tar and feather him not so long ago."

"Where did that come from?"

"The servants, Father. You know the walls have ears

in this house. What did he offer you that has turned you 'round? Something, I think."

"Eh . . . well, there was some talk of a substantial settlement." He dismissed the thought with a gesture. "I didn't for a moment believe it. He meant to buy his freedom with the bribe."

"Of greater value than the vowels, I have no doubt. Hah! I'm surprised you haven't shot Smedley sooner."

"That's quite enough, daughter! You are not too old to fit across my knee!"

"Well, I *am* surprised," she flung at him, ignoring the threat, though she knew he meant every word. "I heard you out there on the moor, 'That settles the benighted debt,' I heard you! Oh, *Father!* Have you killed Sir Percival and brought Klaus low all for *the benighted debt?*"

"I killed Sir Percival because he back-shot the count and was fleeing the dueling ground."

"Where could he have gone on the open moor afoot in the rain? How far could he have gotten? You didn't need to shoot the man. Any one of the others could have run him to ground to face the consequences of what he'd done. But that wouldn't do, would it? No! If he had lived, you would have had to honor the wager. That would have meant losing whatever the count offered you. *You have done murder*, and you mean to bury it on the field of honor! Duels are outlawed to begin with. You shot a man in the back. There is nothing for it. There were witnesses. We shall have to have the Watch in, and they will take it straight to the magistrate, and you shall surely die on the gibbet. Father, what have you done?"

"Now, let's not be hasty, daughter," Gildersleeve said. His face had flushed as red as his hair, and he'd begun to fidget with his soiled cravat.

"You are a sick man, Father. Gambling is a sickness.

Sicknesses can be treated. Maybe a turn in one of the Wiltshire asyl—hospitals might be in order. Belle Vue . . . Fiddington, Kingsdown, perhaps. Several practice Dr. Mesmer's technique—"

"You would have me flung into the madhouse?"

"Better the madhouse than the gallows," Becca said. "And it shan't be up to me. The magistrate will decide."

"You would do that to your own father?"

Becca stared. "I did not bring this about, Father. You did. Can you honestly sit there and tell me you will give over the gambling madness?"

"My gambling is none of your affair, daughter. Hah! You've no right to complain. It's kept you in frocks and fine carriages, put the finest of fare—sweets and dainties fit for a queen—into that pretty mouth, by god!"

"Your gambling has ruined us, plain and simple. A game of cards or dice, a bet on the horses or dogs—even an occasional cockfight, though I abhor such cruelty—are one thing. But you, Father, you eat, sleep, and breathe gambling. You thrive upon it as the very air you take into your body. It must stop! I will never again be put in the position of becoming the stakes in one of your games of chance, and you have no more daughters to ante up."

"No one need know what occurred out there," the baron argued. "It happened on the dueling ground. How can we report it and not implicate the others—make them subject to arrest? You said yourself that dueling is illegal."

"You are absolutely certain that all in residence here will—even in their cups—stand behind you and hold their tongues? This lot of notorious elbow crookers? Oh, Father, how naïve you are." She made a wild gesture. "There's a body lying out there on that moor!"

The baron was about to speak when the bedchamber door came open and Dr. Somers lumbered through, a housemaid with him, her head bowed. The bundle of bloodied linens wrapped in the girl's apron had Becca's full attention. She gasped.

"He'll live," said the doctor. "The blighter caught him on the turn. If he'd drilled him head on, it would be quite another matter. He's lost a bit of blood, but he's a strong one, and he'll be up and about and doubtless up to more mischief again in no time."

Becca scarcely heard anything past the fact that Klaus would live. She flew through the door, all but upsetting Henrik at the bedside.

Klaus lay stripped to the waist beneath the counterpane, his shoulder thickly padded with bandage linen. Becca reached out, then retracted her hand. He looked like death itself.

"Is he really all right?" she begged the elder. "He looks so pale . . . so still. . . ."

"The laudanum, my lady," said Henrik. "It spared him much of the pain. He will come 'round soon now. All will be well. It isn't as bad as it looks. He was most fortunate."

"I will stay with him, tend him. . . ."

"My lady, look at yourself," said the elder. "You are soaked through. The flaw has turned the air cooler. I needn't tell you that the days soon will be drawing in. You need to go and change before you take pneumonia. I will see to him. Believe me, it will not be the first time I have done."

Only then did Becca feel the weight of her saturated cloak, or take notice that her feet were squishing in the Moroccan leather slippers. She brushed the damp tendrils of hair from her eyes and blinked back tears.

"I rode the distance," she said. "I knew there was something wrong when you didn't return."

"You've left your abigail behind?" Henrik said with a start.

"I had no choice."

"That was not wise. If she leaves the cottage . . ."

"I think we can count upon Anne-Lise and the others to prevent that," said Becca. "Believe me, Henrik, Maud is the least of my worries. Father has done murder out on that moor!"

"Leave that coil for others to unwind. Your future lies with his lordship."

"His lordship has made Father an offer for me. That is why Father shot Sir Percival out there."

"I know, my lady. You must not concern yourself with these matters. Leave them to us. Go and minister to yourself. As soon as his lordship is able, you will want to leave, and you shan't be able to do that if you've taken to your bed. He is safe in my charge, I promise you. Safer than you know."

Would the dreams never end? It was deep in the night, and Klaus was standing over her, fully dressed, his jacket thrown over his shoulder, bandaged beneath his shirt. Why was she dreaming of him like this? She started to ask him . . .

"Shhhh, *mitt kostbart*, you must wake," he murmured. "We must away now, while the others are closeted in the gaming salon."

"K-Klaus?" she breathed. "It *is* you! I thought I was dreaming. It's become so hard to tell when I am and when I'm not."

"Shhhh," he said. "There is no time for you to dress. The cloak you came in is too wet to wear. I have taken the liberty—" He nodded toward the wardrobe. "Slip on this pelisse and come. Sven and Henrik have the coach waiting."

"But your wound," she cried.

His quick, gentle hand covered her mouth. "Not a sound!" he said. "The devil take my wound. It is little more than a scratch. I have to get you out of here now, before we have it all over again."

Those words shot Becca through with spine-tingling chills. What could he mean? For a moment, she lay stock-still, searching his face in the thin gauze of moonlight spilling in at the window. How pale he was. It seemed as if all the blood had drained from him. His eyes, boring into her, were sparkling onyx. There was no trace of the seawater blue; that was hidden behind the dilated pupils.

Becca said no more. She scrambled out of bed and put on her slippers. He wrapped her in the pelisse with his good arm, and clasped her to his side, as if he feared to lose her, as they stepped out into the corridor.

"Not a word," he cautioned, leading her toward the landing. "I'll explain once we are safe and away."

"But your shoulder!" It was a whispered exclamation that lost nothing in the hushed delivery. "A scratch, indeed! You're *bleeding!* I can see it through your shirt."

"Anne-Lise will tend to it," he murmured. "None here have her skills." All at once, he stopped and turned her toward him, searching her face with those glazed eyes, as black as sin in the shadow-steeped corridor. "Are you through running from me, *mitt kostbart?*" he said. "I will help you either way, but I must know. Have I proved myself—proved my love at last? Will you be my lifemate, my Becca?"

"*Help me how?*" she puzzled. "I . . . I don't understand."

"There is danger for you here. I will spare you that regardless, you have my word as a gentleman, but I need to know if you will have me. My heart needs to know."

"Yes, oh *yes!*" she whispered against his hard-muscled chest.

All the tension seemed to drain from his body and he moaned, clasping her closer. "Then, come!" he said, grazing the tousled curls on her brow with his lips. They were hot and dry to the touch. "We say no more till I have you in that carriage. Henrik still has the power to cloak it, even if I do not."

He spoke the last as if to himself, and while she wasn't certain she understood his meaning, she did understand the urgency in the voice that delivered the words, and didn't speak again until he'd gotten her inside the waiting brougham and it was tooling down the drive.

Klaus was holding her so fiercely against him, his ragged heartbeat thrumming against her made her own heart race. She reached to stroke his face and he kissed her moist palm, holding it to his fever-parched lips, and moaned again. All the tension seemed to drain from him as if someone had opened a spigot, and she crowded closer against him, slipping her arm around his waist beneath his jacket. His body seemed drenched in fire.

"Now will you tell me what's happening?" she murmured.

"Are you able, or shall I, my lord?" said Henrik, drawing her eyes. Until that moment, Becca wasn't even aware of his presence across the way. She had eyes only for Klaus.

"I am all right," Klaus said on a sigh. "It is just that I am grateful to a God I do not even know for this moment, old friend." He drew a deep breath that wracked his whole body, meanwhile soothing Becca with his good arm wrapped around her shoulder, and spoke to her haltingly. "I asked Henrik if he wished to tell it, since it is he that we have to thank for this escape," he began. He gave a bitter laugh, and said in an aside to the elder, "I have so often berated you for spying. This time I cannot tell you how grateful I am for it." Then, to Becca: "I am sorry for this, because the baron is your father, *mitt kostbart*, and that is the only reason that I have not handled this . . . differently. To make short of it, Henrik's gifts are many, his instincts never failing. They led him to eavesdrop at the gaming salon door this evening. He overheard your father anteing you up again in a game of cards with Smedley's second, that young sot Pembroke."

Becca gasped. "But . . . *you* had arranged a settlement with Father! That was the reason he shot Sir Percival."

"Just so," said Klaus. "He never gave me a chance to make a definite offer. It pains me to say that your father is no gentleman, *mitt kostbart*. He evidently took me at my word, when I told him there would be no settlement if anything untoward occurred out on that moor. Or it could be that he just couldn't resist the temptation of yet another venture at the gaming table."

"He has precious little remaining to wager," said Becca. "He has frittered away all our unentailed lands— my mother's jewels, my jewels—everything."

"Well, there you have it."

"Not entirely," Henrik spoke up. "*His lordship* is a gentleman—so much so that he would spare you the truth entire. I, on the other hand, make no pretense at such a noble attribute, thank the gods. Your father's newest venture goes beyond the gaming table. Even if he were to win the wager, he means to see you wed to Pembroke. The squire is a parvenue. He made his fortune *privateering*—'smuggling' would be more accurate. He still dabbles, and he has assured the baron of an on-going share of the spoils if you and he were to align—a sweet consolation should he lose you in the game."

Becca gasped, and the elder went on quickly. "Your father, my lady, has a deep-rooted bias against . . . *for-*

*eigners,* as he puts it. The thought of mixing the blood was most repugnant to him. When Pembroke brought up the point that his lordship has formed a tendre for you and would most assuredly oppose him, wager or no, your father simply said that you are underage by one year, and he would never give his consent for you to wed an 'older exiled Swedish nobody.' Especially not one whose authenticity could not be shown but by great expense of time and blunt to prove the letters patent.

"When Pembroke persisted that his lordship mightn't be put off without a confrontation, your father suggested that there could always be another duel—one from which his lordship would not emerge so easily . . . or so intact. The thing that set my feet in motion, got his lordship out of a sickbed, and brought you to this carriage in the dead of this dreadful night, however, was Pembroke's reminder that there was a dead body to be taken into account. That and his veiled threat that if he won the wager, no one need ever know what occurred on the dueling ground . . . implying that if things did *not* go his way . . . Well, I needn't go on. I believe you have the gist of it. The wager is but a sham."

Tears welled in Becca's eyes. She would not waste them on such a situation, though her heart was breaking. To think that her father would stoop so low was more than she could bear. She had always known the dubious nature of his gaming partners. But this! She'd begun to fear that his obsession with gambling had finally driven him mad. *My God! Father is going to forfeit the game apurpose!* she realized with bone-chilling certainty. *Such stakes are too great for him to resist.*

"D-did Pembroke win?" she murmured, uncertain if she really wanted to hear the answer.

Henrik hesitated. "I . . . did not stay to find out," he said. "They were still playing when I went to rouse his lordship. My first thought was to get you both away while they were occupied—before the gaming ended, my lady. It was the ideal opportunity, his lordship's wound notwithstanding."

Henrik was a poor liar, Becca was certain. While his stoic demeanor might have fooled many, it did not fool her. She knew her father too well. She uttered a dry sob in spite of herself. The only saving grace was that they'd had time to set out with a good head start.

"What will we ever do?" she murmured. "He will come after me. You know he will, just as he did before. There is too much at stake this time—far more than there ever was with Smedley."

"Let him come," said Klaus, drawing her closer in the custody of his strong arm. "This carriage is cloaked to the mortal eye. So is the cottage. Once Anne-Lise has seen to this shoulder, we set out for Gretna Green. We do not need your father's consent to wed there, and once 'tis done, there is naught he can do."

"But . . . the coach will not be cloaked once we leave the cottage. Will it?" she asked.

"No, *mitt kostbart*," admitted Klaus. "Henrik's gifts cloak both now, but he will not be coming with us. His work is done in the physical plane. Once we leave the cottage, my Becca, we are on our own."

# Chapter Twenty-eight

Maud was overjoyed at their return to the cottage. She even seemed glad to see Klaus. How Anne-Lise and the others had managed to keep the abigail confined was a mystery Becca wasn't prepared to probe, though she had a sneaking suspicion that herbal draughts were at the bottom of it.

They arrived at dawn, and Anne-Lise took charge of Klaus at once, applying herbal poultices to the wound and dosing him with tinctures of balm and bilberry to keep the fever at bay. She filled his chamber with little pots of aromatic chamomile blossoms, which were kept lit like incense, perfuming the air. She insisted that inhaling the fragrant smoke would protect him. From what, exactly, Becca wasn't certain, nor was she brave enough to ask, looking in dismay at the housekeeper's tears, which hadn't ceased to flow since they entered the cottage.

Klaus might have lost his astral connection, but not his ability to benefit from astral healing methods. The following morning as the sun rose, after spending two mysterious hours closeted in his chamber with Henrik, he emerged ready to embark on the journey to Scotland. Anne-Lise, ever tearful, stood at the fore of the line of servants assembled in the Great Hall to bid them farewell. As he passed, she crammed a little cloth bag of fragrant herbs into Klaus's hand.

"For the good of all, your highness," she murmured. "Use them sparingly. You'll know when . . . and how. . . ."

This time, Klaus did not berate her for using his former title. His expression was an endearing one, for it was a farewell. Becca's eyes misted looking on. Though he hadn't said, it was clear he would never see any of them again.

He had the same look in his eyes when he handed her into the brougham waiting in the lane, with groom, driver, and postillions Sven had hired from the coaching inn on Bodmin Moor at the ready. Going post would have been preferred, but it wasn't an option since the post chaises only seated two, and they were three in number including Maud. Four horses pranced in place, post boys mounted on the leaders for speed. The groom was stationed on the dickey, the driver seated in the box up top, ramrod-rigid, his long-handled horsewhip furled.

Once they were settled, Klaus rapped the carriage roof with his walking stick to signal the driver. He didn't look toward the cottage as the horsewhip cracked and the carriage tooled northwest along the muddy track. Neither did Maud, seated with her back toward it in the chaise, which was no accident. Klaus had seated her there to obscure her view. Becca saw, however, and wasn't surprised that there was no sign of the cottage or Henrik or any of the others. A cold, gripping chill chased the blood from her face. They were on their own, indeed.

Klaus drew her closer when she shuddered. The warmth of his strong arm around her was a comfort. It was a long moment before she spoke, and not until

Maud began to nod off across the way. Even at that, she spoke in a hushed stage whisper.

"It will be a long journey," she said. "Father will know where we've gone. He will guess, and he will come after us."

"I have been patient with your father for your sake, *mitt kostbart*, but my patience is at an end. I need no astral magic to dispose of him if needs must, and I will . . . but only if needs must. I am not altogether convinced that madness is at the root of his appalling treatment of you. He is a heartless, self-serving, narrow-minded creature, with no regard for anything but his gaming appetites. That he was disposed toward anteing you up in a game of chance once was reprehensible enough, but *twice?* I do not mind telling you now that we are away, it took all Henrik's powers of persuasion to restrain me from giving the bounder exactly what he deserves and the devil take the hindmost! Still, he is your father—but you'd best be warned that the day may come that I no longer make allowances for that."

"Father has always been a gambling man," Becca said. "But since Mother died, it's all he thinks of. He is obsessed with it, and there are many like him, judging from what I've seen of his so-called friends since. They come and go like the shadows, night and day leering, besotted spongers, like flies in his web when he wins, which sadly isn't often. He has gone beyond the pale this time. It saddens me, but I cannot abide it, Klaus, and I will never go back to it again. Never, ever."

"You will never have to. You are mine now, *mitt kostbart*, my precious Becca, for as long as we both shall live."

"Are you sure?" she murmured against his chest, her eyes screwed tight as she steeled herself against some change of heart. "You have given up so much for me. I am so afraid—"

"Never fear," he interrupted. But she had feared his

hesitation; her heart leapt when he didn't even give her time to finish. A flood of warmth washed over her at the sultry sound of his deep baritone in her ear, at the puff of his warm breath against her skin. *"Never,"* he repeated, tilting up her chin with his finger until their eyes met—his hooded with desire, hers swimming in unshed tears. He kissed her eyelids softly, first one and then the other. "The decision was mine," he said. "I will never regret it. We speak of it no more. Ever. The mother who gave birth to me was mortal, *mitt kostbart*. My father did what I have done after I was conceived. He could not bear to leave her. I have known the best of both worlds. There are many like me roaming this planet, and many more will follow after me. You have stolen my heart. You possess it. It is no longer mine. It is yours, my Becca."

"But . . . you do not even know if . . . if . . ." She couldn't say it. She was thinking of his past—of Illia, and what two astral beings must have shared—and feeling so inadequate in all her innocence. Hot blood rushed to her temples. This was a fine time to be having this conversation. All at once she realized they hardly knew each other.

"Oh, my love," he murmured. "If only you know how foolish those fears are. I have had you waking and sleeping in my heart and mind from the first moment we met."

"And . . . in my dreams?"

"Those were no dreams, *mitt kostbart*," he said. There was laughter in his voice—soft, musical laughter as suggestive as a caress.

She gasped. Suspecting was one thing; hearing it from his own lips was something else entirely. "But I thought . . . and we nearly . . . I never would have . . ."

"I know you would not," he said. "And I did not let you carry your dream too far. But soon, my Becca, that dream will come true . . . for both of us."

\*   \*   \*

Klaus would have been more at ease if the distance from Cornwall to Scotland were shorter. He had opted for the fastest means of travel, over the mail coach route, with four horses pulling the brougham, and post boys to boot. Still, it would take four days at best, if they only made brief stopovers for changing horses and for the women to refresh themselves. At the worst, it could be a sennight before they reached Gretna Green, depending upon the weather, and if they took lodgings at inns for the night. Either way, they were at risk of unforeseen calamities that would slow their progress—bent wheels, flooded rivers, and lame horses. Nothing was entirely predictable when traveling the highways.

Klaus was counting upon leaving the storms behind once they left the coast. So far, as they neared the end of their second day on the highway, that had been the case. The weather was fine once they left Cornwall, the air sweet with the last breath of summer, the night sky asparkle with stars and lit by a full moon already waning. That moon no longer held sway over him, and though they'd passed several waterfalls along the way, he no longer felt their pull. That was the strangest part of the metamorphosis from *Fossegrim* to mortal. It wasn't that he missed it; he did not. He was in awe of his new independence. He was free, just as his father had been free to live and love and die a mortal man.

It was late when they reached the coaching inn at Bath. So far, but for changing horses, they hadn't stopped along the way. It was clear that Becca was exhausted. Klaus hated to wake her, sleeping soundly against his arm, her strawberry-gold curls bouncing against his waistcoat. How light she was, how pink and soft and perfect the flesh beneath that plum-colored traveling costume. It was emblazoned upon his memory. He did not need to see that exquisite body to feel its softness, to bask in its sweetness. He did not need to kiss those pouty lips or caress those delectable curves to become aroused. She had set fire to his blood. The urgent astral mating frenzy no longer ruled him. His passion was a mortal torture now, but no less urgent. He was what he was, a sensual creature no matter his incarnation, he was finding out.

Her sweet, warm breath against his hand as he caressed her cheek quickened his own breath. The innocent rise and fall of her breast against him, her evocative scent wafting toward his nostrils from her hair, her translucent skin, triggered a tight, coiled feeling deep inside that riddled his loins with achy heat. She was malleable in his hands. Her exquisite body crowding closer, stirring against him in perfect trust, gripped his loins like a fiery fist as the carriage rolled to a creaking halt in the mews. His sex leapt erect. This was worse than the *Fossegrim* mating frenzy. It demanded so much more—a lifetime of more. How did he deserve it? How did he deserve *her*?

Suppressing a throaty moan that rumbled up from depths he had never before plumbed, he grazed her brow with his lips. Across the way, Maud sat slumped against the tufted squabs, her awakening abrupt as the screeching carriage wheels and shouts of the groom and driver broke the silence. Once the groom set the step, Klaus exited the coach, helped Becca and Maud down, and settled them at a scarred wooden table in the corner of the common room that offered a sheltered view of the door, while he arranged for their lodgings for the night. He kept a close eye upon them as he paid for their rooms, and ordered tankards of ale and plates of venison stew. He was uneasy, wishing they hadn't needed to stop at all. He wouldn't worry Becca, but she was right: Gildersleeve would follow. That the baron hadn't overtaken them yet was a miracle, and a mystery Klaus would take as a gift from the

God he had yet to acquaint himself with on a personal level.

Lazy smoke from clay pipes and cheroots drifted toward the exposed beam ceiling. Blending with the sour stench of ale-soaked wood and the press of unwashed bodies milling about, the air was oppressive. Most of the patrons were occupied with their food and lively banter, but one gentleman caught Klaus's eye. He stood apart, puffing on a tavern pipe, one turned-down boot braced against the andiron at the vacant hearth, his tankard resting nearby on the mantel. Tall and slender, though well muscled, he was dressed in dark clothing, from breeches to waistcoat beneath a sweeping, caped greatcoat, dingy with road dust. This struck Klaus as odd, since the night was too mild for such heavy attire. The wide-brimmed slouch hat the man wore cast his features in shadow, made darker by a growth of careless stubble. All that notwithstanding, it was the man's eyes that caught and held Klaus's attention. They were trained upon Becca and Maud.

"Ya need a surgeon fer that lame wing, do ya, gov-'nor?" the innkeeper said, calling Klaus's attention back to the chore at hand.

He took the offered change from the transaction and tipped the man.

"Thank ye!" the innkeeper said, his eyes wide, as his hand clamped shut like a steel trap on the coins in his dingy palm.

"Thank you, no," said Klaus. "It has been tended." Truth be told, he'd nearly forgotten about his shoulder wound. Anne-Lise's doctoring had done wonders. Aside from mild soreness and an occasional sharp reminder that he'd been under the surgeon's knife, he scarcely noticed. If he were any judge, by morning he would be able to get both arms into his tight-fitting frock coat.

He inclined his head toward the man beside the hearth. "Regular customer is he?" he asked, low-voiced.

" 'Im? Not in 'ere he ain't, gov'nor. Never set eyes on 'im before. What's it to ya?"

Klaus shrugged. "Nothing . . . yet," he said, "except that his manners seem lacking. Someone should have told him it is impolite to stare."

The innkeeper squinted toward the man, following his gaze to Becca and Maud, who were conversing in the corner unaware. "Oh, now, ya can't be bringin' a pretty bird like that into a place such as this without drawin' a man's eye, gov'nor."

"Hmm," Klaus growled, assessing the situation.

"Ya ain't goin' ta start no trouble in 'ere, are ya now?" the innkeeper said.

"No," Klaus returned, "but do not let this *lame wing* deceive you. If trouble does start, you can bet your blunt I'll finish it."

The man wasn't watching him; Becca and Maud still had his full attention. Sliding out of his coat altogether, Klaus looped it over the crook of his injured arm and sidled through the crowd to the corner table. He took a seat between the women with his back to the wall, where he could observe who came and went without being obvious, and monitor the movements of the darkly clad man by the hearth, who had turned his attention to his tankard. Maybe it was his imagination. Perhaps the innkeeper was right; with such a lovely treat for the eyes as Becca come into the common room, who wouldn't stare?

The barmaid set down their tankards, slopping ale suds onto the table, and lumbered off for their fare. As soon as she was out of earshot, Klaus leaned across the table and said, "I have secured our rooms. Yours and Maud's adjoin. I am assured that they are well appointed, though in such places one never knows. Mine is directly across the hall—well within earshot should there be need."

Becca frowned. "Is something wrong?" she said. "You look . . . troubled."

Klaus silenced her with a meaningful glance, while the barmaid slapped down her tray, and set out their plates of stew. The less these people knew, the better.

"I will rest easier once we've taken to the highway again," he said. "There's a man standing over by the hearth—No! Do not look. Do not make it obvious, just a casual glance. Do you know him?"

"Who?" said Becca, nonplussed.

Klaus did look then, but the man was gone. His tankard remained behind on the mantel, the candles picking out the wet rings it had left on the scarred wood. He searched every corner of the room with a sweeping gaze, but there was no sign. Perhaps it had been his imagination after all. At any rate, he wouldn't worry the ladies with his suspicions. His posture relaxed, and all three ate their stew. It was greasy and a bit salty for his taste, spiced to disguise meat that was less than choice, but Becca and Maud didn't seem to notice. They were hungry after their journey, and Klaus was too preoccupied to care.

The minute they finished, he led them upstairs, where he saw Maud safely inside Becca's suite to prepare her charge's toilette and set out her nightshift. When Becca started to follow, he whisked her into his room across the hall and drew her into his arms.

"A kiss good night out of that woman's view," he said. Holding her was all that mattered then. The imminent pursuit, the threat of danger—both human and astral—his wrenching rite of passage, all paled before the prize—his Becca, clinging to him, warm and fragrant in his arms. She was all that mattered, all that ever would matter. It was to be no mere good-night kiss, this. He knew it the moment he swept her over the threshold. She knew it, too; he could see it in her gaze. He could feel it, as the invisible tethers of silken fire that joined them tightened. This time there would be no end short of consummation.

For the space of a heartbeat he stared down into her shuttered hazel eyes, sparkling in the light of a single candle on the nightstand. Her lips parted, and he was undone. Swooping down with a groan, he took her in a hungry, smothering kiss that drained his senses. All passions under heaven lived in that kiss, in that volatile embrace. His arousal rose between them, pushing heavily against her, soft flesh yielding to its pressure beneath her traveling costume. How perfectly they fit together, like two halves of a whole. How could he let her go without tasting her passions, without making them one with his own?

All at once her arms were around him, holding him, her tiny hands fisted in the back of his burgundy brocade waistcoat as she leaned into the thick bulk of his hardness. A groan that seemed to bubble up from his very soul leaked from him, mingling with hers as he tasted her deeply—drank in her honey sweetness, like one dying of thirst in the desert.

He reached with trembling hands and opened her spencer, then her muslin waist and underwaist beneath, spreading them wide. Sliding his lips along the curve of her arched throat, he sought her breast, and the tawny nipple grown hard in anticipation of his kiss. Becca's caught breath echoed in his ears. She laced her fingers through his hair. His sex throbbed against her as she held his head to her breast while he suckled at first one perfect tip and then the other. All at once, he groaned again and took her face in his hands, searching her eyes deeply beyond their candlelit shimmer to the dark depths of arousal swimming beneath.

"This is no dream, *mitt kostbart,*" he murmured. His

heart was racing, thudding against his ribs, his breath coming short, his turgid member bursting.

"I-I know," she murmured, meeting his gaze.

Klaus dropped his head down against her shoulder, his brow covered with sweat. He could feel the blood racing through her body under the skin—pumping, singing, on fire for him. He gathered her against him, lifting her feet off the ground, and spun her in his arms.

"Your shoulder!" Becca cried.

"The devil take it!" he responded, his voice sounding in his ears like the crackle of breaking glass. "There is no fairy glamour here now, no *waterlord* . . . only a man—a mortal man who loves you."

What he had begun would not be slaked unless his anxious life lived inside her, and he stripped the layers away until she stood naked before him, just as she had in the waterfall with diaphanous clouds of rainbow-spangled spindrift showering her. She was no less breathtaking bathed in flickering candlelight now. Feasting his eyes upon her, he stripped off his boots and tore at his clothes like a madman, casting them down with careless hands, while her hands slid the length of him, exploring his hard-muscled chest, gliding along his torso, over his narrow waist and corded thighs. When her delicate fingers neared the thick, curved shaft of his sex, it leapt again in anticipation of her touch, and he scooped her up in his arms and carried her to the bed. In that heart-stopping moment, if she were ever to touch him there . . .

He could feel the gentle tremors that shocked her as they lay skin to skin atop the counterpane. She was shuddering—not from cold, but in anticipation of their joining. He could see it in her hooded eyes, he could feel it in her caress. He saw the glimmer of apprehension in those misted eyes, but he saw something else there also—raw passion beyond imagining.

He heard it in her rapid breathing, felt it in the tiny hands that drew him closer still, that felt so cool against the fever in his skin. He had awakened her to pleasures of the flesh long ago. Now she opened herself to those pleasures, to *him*, like the petals of a flower drenched in the dew of its first awakening. She was his for the taking.

He murmured her name against her mouth as his lips took hers in a flurry of kisses. "Are you certain?" he panted. "It is not too late to—"

Her ravenous kiss was her response as she laced her fingers in his hair again until they fisted and she arched herself against him.

Groaning, Klaus spread her legs and fondled the hard, dewy bud of her sex—gently at first, until she writhed against the pressure of his fingers, arching her body, reaching for him in total abandon. Thick and hard, his veined sex responded, hot and moist against her thigh, and he spread her legs and eased himself between them.

Once before he had nestled his anxious member in that soft mound of red-gold hair; he had touched her sex to sex and found the strength to pull away. Not so this time. His heart hammering against hers, he looked deep into her eyes, dilated with arousal.

"There will be . . . pain . . . just this first time . . ." he murmured, short of breath. "It cannot be helped, *mitt kostbart.*"

Becca leaked a soft response and nodded, pulling him closer still as his fingers wildly stroked her sex, then penetrated her in one swift thrust. She made no outcry, just a quick intake of breath—a brief hesitation in the undulation of her hips as she rubbed herself against the fingers that entered her.

Then, like lightning, Klaus rolled off the bed and in one motion stood and lifted her onto his member. Leaning her against the tapestry-hung wall, he plunged into her until he could go no farther, his deep guttural groan thrumming through his body, resonating with hers. Gripping the soft flesh of her buttocks, he nudged her legs around his waist, and she flung her arms around his neck as he moved inside her—quick, hot, shuddering thrusts in mindless abandon, as she clung to him matching his rhythm, taking him deeper, drenching him in her silken wetness, milking him as he filled her.

It was a different kind of frenzy that commanded him now, unlike any he'd ever felt. The swift, frantic coupling took his breath away and nearly stopped his heart, and the warm flood of his seed rushed inside her, riding the orgasmic waves of her own release. She was his.

Dazed, her breath coming rapid and shallow, Becca dropped her head upon his moist shoulder and gasped, "Your wound! You're *bleeding!*"

"Shhhh," he murmured. "It is nothing. Anne-Lise's herbs will mend it." Lifting her, he eased her down and carried her back to the bed, where he laid her on the counterpane. Splashing water from the pitcher into the porcelain basin on the dry sink, he moistened a towel. Sinking down beside her, he gently rested it against her sex, stroking gently.

Becca released a breathless moan of pleasure, and he gathered her into his arms, crushing her close. "You are mine, *mitt kostbart*"" he crooned close in her ear. "At last, you are mine."

"You have given up so much," she said. There were tears in her voice, but not in her eyes, and he gathered her closer still.

"And gained paradise," he said. "Until death do us part."

"Do not speak of death!" she cried, clinging to him so tightly, his sex again leapt to life. "You could not die before, but now . . ."

"Shhh," he soothed, "No god is that unkind." Thinking of his father then, cold chills puckered his scalp. He beat those thoughts back. He was *not* his father. He lay in the arms of his Becca, absorbed in the power of a passion that was stronger than death. It had to be.

It was a long moment before he stood and drew her up beside him, taking her in his arms. "I long to lie here with you until dawn, but we dare not," he said. "Your abigail will be worried. She is an inquisitive sort, and we must not give her food for on-dits, hmm? Come. I will help you dress and see you to your room. Tomorrow we continue upon a course to sanctify the marriage we have consummated here, my love. Nothing must hinder that."

Scarcely able to tear himself away from her, he helped her dress and dressed himself. The hall was vacant when he led her to her room. He would have bet against it. He half-expected the nosy abigail to come tumbling over the threshold when he opened the door. Ushering her into the room, he spun Becca toward him, cupping her face in his hand.

"When I leave this room, you must lock your door, *mitt kostbart*," he said. "I am but a heartbeat away. If anything untoward occurs, you have only to cry out and I will come to you."

"You are troubled," Becca murmured, snuggling closer, her arms wrapped around him.

Her closeness was torture. Already he wanted her again. His need to live in that perfect, eager body overwhelmed him. So *this* was mortal love. The astral mating frenzy paled before it. He toyed with the idea of staying there in the room with her, but that would be dangerous in his present state, with the maid but a few steps away in the adjoining chamber.

And she was right; he was troubled. Perhaps the man in the common room had been nothing. Perhaps he was just a wayfarer like the rest, admiring Becca's unique beauty in a room filled with rough-cut, half-castaway travelers. But whatever the case, his presence meant danger. He served as a grim reminder that the race was not yet run. It was a long way to Scotland, and while Klaus didn't want to alarm her, he had to be certain Becca would not inadvertently put herself in harm's way.

"I do not want to take chances," he said against her hair, soothing her. "I want you to stay here in this room until I come for you in the morning. Do not open the door to anyone else—no matter what they tell you—only to me. Will you give me your promise?"

Becca nodded. "I wish we could just drive on," she said absently.

"No more than I, but we cannot. It is too long a journey, and you are exhausted. If the weather holds and no unforeseen difficulties arise, we should reach the border in three days' time . . . even if we must stray from the coach road. We may do that in any case. We do not know what we face ahead. We may not get another chance to stop. Pursuers might not find us so easily if we choose a less-traveled route. But such roads can be dangerous, because of the riffraff—thatchgallows and brigands lying in wait in lonely places—and we may not be able to stop and rest. We must take advantage of the opportunity while we can."

He tilted up her head and looked her in the eyes. Everything he had ever longed for lived in them. Her trust warmed him. Her beauty thrilled him. The innocent seduction in her gaze threatened to melt his bones—and his resolve. Unable to resist those dewy lips, he took them, tasting her deeply. But the kiss was short-lived. He dared not prolong the agony of that sweet ecstasy.

He put her from him with a groan. "Get some sleep, my Becca," he murmured around a tremor. "Morning comes quickly, and we leave at first light."

"Wait," she said, as he started to pull away, her tiny hand on his arm. "May I ask you something?"

"Anything," he responded.

"I can understand the others," she began, "but how is it that Henrik could not make the journey with us? I have Maud, but you have no one to serve you now."

Klaus hesitated. How much should he tell her? How much would she understand? He almost laughed at that. Hadn't she seen firsthand the mysteries of the astral realm? Had she not been held captive there, and escaped a cruel adversary from a race unknown to her, by her bravery and sheer wits alone? Still, he didn't want to frighten her, and when he spoke, he skirted the issue.

"Henrik did serve me, my love, but he was never my servant," he said. "He is too far above me. I can no longer enter the astral realm. You know that, *mitt kostbart*. But it can still reach out to me . . . to *us*, in dangerous ways. Did Henrik not tell you that being in or crossing over water will forever hold danger for you?" She nodded, and he went on quickly before she could speak. "It is true. Henrik can do more in the Otherworld for us than he can in this one. He has gone, but he is with us still in spirit, as he always will be. One day I shall explain, but not tonight. Now, you must sleep, and dream of the day soon coming when no doors or walls will part us."

Maud stepped in from her adjoining chamber as Becca locked the door. Waiting outside, Klaus whispered his good night through the old, scarred wood at the sound of the key rasping in the lock. She heard his footfalls recede and his own door click shut across the hall, and turned to the maid.

"Lock yours as well," she said, as Maud approached to help her undress.

"I know . . . I did . . . I . . . I heard, my lady," the abigail stammered. "I was afeared when you didn't come back directly. I was just fixin' ta come after ya."

Becca had no doubt of it. How much had she heard eavesdropping just now? *Probably all*, Becca thought ruefully. Who knew but that she had tiptoed across the hall and listened at Klaus's door as well. The girl was hopelessly flawed, but she was all there was, and Becca needed her now regardless. She wouldn't scold her. What did it matter? What the maid didn't understand was best left unaddressed. She would never believe it, in any case. Besides, now that Klaus had embraced mortality, there was no reason for her to ever know the truth. Still, Maud needed to be put in her place. She needed to know what she'd done had not gone without notice.

"It is all well and good that you have locked your door, Maud," Becca said frostily, "but if I catch you out eavesdropping again it will be the worse for you. We have discussed this before, and I do not intend to discuss it again. Am I plain?"

"Y-yes, my lady," the maid said, taking up the night-shift she'd set out earlier.

"Good," said Becca. "Now then, you heard what his lordship said. Morning comes quickly. Leave that and take yourself off to bed. We are up at first light."

"But don't ya want me ta help ya undress, my lady?"

"I will tend to myself. Well? Run on, then. I am not pleased with you at the moment, Maud. I will not have you privy to personal matters and intimate conversations. You had best take stock. Now, leave me."

Maud hesitated a moment, then sketched a curtsy and floated off to her chamber, closing the door between with a gentle click.

Becca drew a ragged breath and went to the window. The view was of the mews, and a blacksmith's shop below, reminding her that soon she would stand with Klaus in another such establishment at their wedding. Overhead the vacant moon shone down upon the dingy, dilapidated building, picking out the fire burning in its open hearth, the blacksmith's tools immersed there glowing blood red. Was it an omen of good or ill? She drew the drapes with a shudder. The action reminded her of the drapes at her bedchamber window at Lindegren Hall, the drapes that should have remained drawn—*would* have remained drawn if she hadn't defied the maid Ulla and begun this odyssey. That simple gesture had changed her life forever.

She could still see Klaus strolling naked through the mist to his waterfall, the bobbing balls of glowing light she now knew were the *Irrbloss* cavorting about him like playful children. Tears misted her eyes, and she swallowed a lump that suddenly constricted her throat. Once, those Will-o'-the-wisps had saved her life. Would she never see them again?

Becca breathed a sigh and slumped forward, turning away from the musty drapes. What was wrong with her? Why was she waxing nostalgic now, come so soon from his intimate embrace? Perhaps it was a twinge of guilt tweaking her conscience. He'd given up so much for her. Had she lived up to his expectations? Could she ever hope to be equal to his prowess— to eons of sensual experience instinctive to a race that embodied unbridled passion? Could she ever hope to satisfy his needs in her unskilled innocence without pretending, as she always had when in his arms, that it was a dream? Hot blood sped to her cheeks, thrummed at her temples, as she thrilled, reliving the intimacies they had just shared. Sliding her hands over her belly, she recalled how perfectly he had loved her, how shockingly she had responded to passions she never dreamed existed. But still . . . oh, still, the nagging doubts . . .

Becca shook those thoughts free just as she had so

many times before when they crept close in the night, in the deep, dark solitude of her soul. It was becoming harder and harder to dispel them now that he had made the sacrifice, now that there was no turning back, now that the fantasy—the delicious dream—had become a reality. Pondering that exhausted her, and she sank down upon the bed—"just for a moment. Then I will undress," she told herself, but she was soon fast asleep, the excruciating ecstasy of his sex inside her no more than a ghost of the pain he'd warned of while haunting her dreams.

Sometime later, when a sound at the door woke her with a start, she blinked awake, disoriented. What time was it? Surely it couldn't be morning so soon. No light was leaking through the draperies to disprove her point, and she sat bolt upright, rubbing the sleep from her eyes. Yes! She scrambled off the bed and pattered toward the door. She hadn't imagined it—a rasping sound . . .

"Klaus?" she said. "Is it morning already?"

# Chapter Twenty-nine

"It is I, Becca," Klaus whispered against her door. "The coach is waiting. It is time." He rapped again, gently but firmly. "There's barely time to break our fast before we leave. We must away before the sun rises." He had just come from the hostlers in the mews. Wanting to be certain all was in readiness before waking her, he'd left that to the last. He was beginning to regret it.

He knocked yet again, with more authority. When still no answer came, he reached for the knob, hesitated, then turned it. A crippling panic froze him for a moment when, to his surprise, the door came open with a painfully loud creak. He flung it wide to an empty room.

In the flickering shaft of light issuing from the wall sconce in the hall, he saw that the bed hadn't been slept in, though the counterpane showed the imprint of Becca's body, where she'd evidently fallen asleep atop the bed instead of in it. Her little traveling bag was nowhere in sight.

He streaked through the room, calling at the top of

his voice. No answer came. He burst into Maud's chamber, but that was vacant also. His hands were shaking as he lit the candle branch. The minute the candles blazed, his heart sank. Maud's bed had been slept in. By the look of the disarray, it appeared that she'd been dragged from it by force. The counterpane was spilling over onto the floor, and her open traveling bag and clothes were strewn about the threadbare carpet.

He slapped the candle branch down on the chiffonier and raked back his hair ruthlessly, his eyes wild and flashing. Beads of sweat had broken out on his brow, and cold chills gripped him. She was gone! But where?

Wasting no more time, he raced back into the hall, down the narrow stairs, and burst into the common room, turning the heads of the few travelers awaiting the arrival of the morning mail coach. Becca and Maud were not among them, and he reached the bleary-eyed innkeeper filling tankards beside the ale barrels in two ragged strides and seized him by his shirtfront, all but lifting him off the floor.

"The ladies I arrived with last evening," he snarled into the man's face, "where have they gone? Answer me, man!"

One of the tankards in the inkeeper's hand hit the floor with a clang, the spilled brew splattering Klaus's polished and turned-down boots and bleeding over the dingy boards in a wide circle. The ale in the other flew every which way, flinging suds, staining the innkeeper's apron and decorating Klaus's white shirt and brocade waistcoat. On the verge of running mad, Klaus scarcely noticed the dull ache in his shoulder from the exertion. He shook the man with little regard for the flesh he'd caught beneath the shirt.

"Speak!"

The innkeeper sputtered, dropped the other tankard,

and gripped both of Klaus's wrists with pinching fingers. "I . . . they . . . it was 'bout an hour or so ago," he stammered. "I dunno exactly. 'Twas a busy night, and I ain't even been ta bed yet. . . ."

"*Where . . . did . . . they . . . go?*" Klaus demanded, buffeting the man until he wobbled like a rag poppet.

"T-two men took 'em out," said the innkeeper. "It didn't look like anythin' untoward was afoot, though they took off quick, like."

"What men? What did they look like? Where did they go?"

"Hold off, gov'nor, yer . . . chokin' me ta . . . death. How . . . can I tell ya if ya choke . . . the livin' breath outta me?"

"I'll do worse if you do not speak up," Klaus threatened.

Everyone was staring. The patrons had stopped eating and drinking. All eyes were upon him and the terrified innkeeper whom he shook again.

"One of 'em was short and stocky-built—the older one. He had red hair, he did, mixed with gray. I never seen him in 'ere before. The other I did, though—we both did. He was in 'ere last night—"

"The man dressed in black?" said Klaus. "The man I questioned you about?"

The innkeeper nodded. "That's 'im all right . . ."

"And you just let them take the ladies off—just like that? You cup-shot gudgeon! Are you addled?" He jerked his head toward the ale barrels. "How much of that there have you drunk?" he said. "They came in here with *me!*"

"Oh, aye, they did, but birds'll be birds, gov'nor. They come and they go, and not always with the gents they come in with. It aint nothing ta me. A man can get hisself kilt stepping in where he ain't got no business."

"But I inquired about that fellow last night. I suspected something then. How could you just let them go off with him after that? You should have come and told me—warned me!"

"Like I said, this is a coaching station, gov'nor. We get all kinds in 'ere. I don't mix inta other folks' private business. It ain't healthy. Ya should have kept a leash on them birds if ya wanted 'em for yerself. That ain't up ta me. Now, lemme go!"

Klaus held him fast. "Where did they go? Which way? How?" he said.

"How am I supposed ta know that? Take it up with the hostlers, or the station master. Now, lemme go!"

Klaus flung him aside, crashed through the common room door—coattails flying—and stalked straight back to the mews. The station master had just dismissed a post chaise, and was entering its departure time in the ledger, when he burst in and seized the man's arm, upsetting the inkwell.

"A lady and her maid left about an hour ago with two men," he said, ignoring the man's wide-flung eyes flicking between his face and the hand on his arm and ink-stained shirtsleeve. "One man was older—stout and red-haired. The other was tall and slim, dressed all in black, wearing a caped greatcoat and a slouch hat. Which way did they go?"

"Unhand me, sir!" the station master said, wrenching himself free. "What is that to you?"

"The lady is my betrothed, and those men have abducted her!" said Klaus, raking his disheveled hair.

The man eyed him skeptically. "You say," he said. "For all I know, you could be the one up to foul play. You're no Englishman."

"No, I am not," Klaus said, his jaw muscles ticking. "I am Count Klaus Lindegren of Sweden, and we are wasting time—my device is on the carriage I came in. Those men have abducted my bride and her abigail. By what means do they travel? I need to know which direction they have taken. Quickly, man!" He had come up against such mistrust of foreigners many times before and taken it in stride, even in the case of Baron Gildersleeve. Not so now. He was raving like a man possessed. *Benighted time again!* It was working against him. Would he ever get used to it? Things were so much simpler when time stood still.

The station master hesitated, studying him closely. "There were three men in that party, my lord," he finally said.

"*Three* men?"

The station master nodded. "A regular coxcomb, about your age, I'd wager . . . maybe a tad younger. Cut a dash, all got up in silk and superfine. Sandy hair, face all angles and planes. Not the sort you'd call handsome by any means, but the kind what gets noticed, if you take my meaning."

"Pembroke," Klaus said under his breath.

"My lord?"

"Never mind," Klaus snapped. "Which way did they go?"

"They took the post road north."

"On the mail coach—the stage? Come, come, *which*, man? They couldn't have gone post, a party of five!"

"They left in the carriage they come in. I changed the team myself, the hostlers are put to it tonight—two men inside with the ladies, the third in the box with the driver."

"The one with the caped greatcoat," Klaus said, answering his own question.

"Just so."

"Did they say where they were going—anything? Think, man! My betrothed's life may well depend upon it."

"I don't make it a practice of eavesdropping on the patrons," the man said. "But now that you mention it, there was some mention made of a wedding."

Klaus felt the blood drain from his face. Reaching

out to Henrik with his mind, he prayed the elder would hear him and guide him. But there was only silence. It was as if his brain were paralyzed. No. He was on his own without a moment to lose.

"How long ago did they leave?' he said. "I need to know exactly."

"They've got about two hours head start, if that's what you're asking. Will you be wanting your brougham rigged up?"

Klaus shook his head. "No, no time," he said. I'll never catch them by carriage. Saddle me a horse—the fastest horse you have in this godforsaken place. And do it quickly. There's not a moment to lose."

Maud hadn't stopped bawling since they left the coaching inn. The constant caterwauling had Becca at the end of her tether. She could scarcely think for the din, and she had to now. It was imperative. Somehow she had to get away from her father—from Algernon Pembroke and his smuggling crony, Jack Andrews—before they reached Gretna Green.

"Shut that damn bird up!" Andrews shouted from his seat in the box above. Even with the windows closed, his thunder sliced through Becca's nerves like a hot knife through butter. This was a dangerous man—one to be reckoned with. It was he who had stepped over the threshold of her room at the inn when she was expecting Klaus. She would never forget the oily, stale tobacco smell of his great paw clamped over her mouth, or the force behind the arm that shook her off her feet, demanding her silence if she wanted Klaus to see the sunrise that morning.

She had almost felt relief when they met her father at the bottom of the stairs and Andrews handed her over before going back for Maud. But that was short-lived. Not only did her father mean to prevent her marrying Klaus, he intended to see her wed to Pembroke, just as Henrik had warned. His potential gain in such an alliance was too great to resist. The man was truly mad. He was salivating over the prospect of an ongoing share in the young squire's smuggling cache. The lure of contraband, of goods of untold worth to be turned into blunt to risk at the gambling tables, had foxed him as totally as any spirits could have. He was a gambler, after all. The odds were all in his favor . . . and then there was that business about the body. . . .

Becca had overheard him say that Klaus was expendable. That he would surely die in a confrontation—three against one—come so soon after surgery from the duel. Her father had already killed once; it would be easier the second time. Becca couldn't let that happen—not when it was in her power to prevent it. Instead, she made no protest. Somehow, she would wait for her chance and slip away. Only one thing was certain: She would never marry Algernon Pembroke.

It was stifling, shut up in the coach with no air save that which was tainted with the ripened odor of unwashed men and stale cheroot smoke. The closeness threatened to make her retch.

"Maud, be still!" she snapped at the maid, through the handkerchief she'd pressed to her nose against the unpleasantness. "You are only making matters worse!"

But the maid wailed on.

Across the way, her father and Pembroke sat staring. Her father's face was stern, the squire's spread with smug satisfaction and a leering, bemused half-smile.

"You may as well let us out of this coach, Father," she said. "I will never marry that . . . that person!"

"You're underage and you'll do as your told, daughter," said the baron. "You've been nothing but trouble since your mother died. You've proved you cannot govern yourself, traipsing over the countryside like a Gypsy. 'Tis time you earned your worth. Pembroke here will see you want for nothing. It's an excellent match, my girl, even if you are too dense to see it. He'll keep you like a queen. Why, you'd think I was leg-shackling you to the Devil himself, instead of a fine gentleman of means."

Becca wanted to shout: *He's a rake and a loathsome pirate!* But she didn't. She wanted to fly across the span between and claw the leering thing's eyes out. But she dared not. Too much depended upon her remaining calm, upon biding her time until the right moment. When that time came, she thought ruefully, Maud was on her own.

"Shut that cow *up*, I said!" Andrews barked again, this time thumping his foot above so hard that loose dust sifted down from the tufted cloth on the carriage roof. "If you can't, I will! I'll pitch her right out on the heath in a trice if that racket don't stop. I ain't goin' all the way nonstop to Scotland with *that!*"

Becca elbowed Maud in the side. "Be still!" she whispered. "He means what he says, and there's none here to prevent him."

The abigail's wails died to whimpers, but nothing would stop them altogether. She was simply too frightened.

Becca turned a pleading gaze upon her father. "It will be days before we reach the border," she pointed out. "You cannot mean to drive straight through. We shall have to stop sometime for food . . . and we shall need to refresh ourselves."

"Hrumph!" the baron blurted. "And give the count time to catch up, eh? That's exactly how we caught up to you. You'd like that, would you? No, I think not, daughter. You'd best give it more thought. I've been damn generous letting him off, after the way he deceived me—hid you from me. I almost let him charm me into forgetting that. I say *almost*. It's his fault Smedley's dead, not mine. If he'd stayed away, minded his own affairs, we wouldn't be having all this here now."

"No, Father. Every bit of this is your fault, not Klaus's. I shudder to think what Mother would do if she knew what you're about. Who knows but that she does?"

"Enough!" the baron thundered. "Not another word." The outburst caused Becca to jump in spite of herself, and wrenched a fresh outcry from Maud. "And you!" he went on, his hard stare trained upon the abigail, "you stop that puling this instant or I'll help him pitch you out on the heath myself. I've not forgotten that you've run off with Rebecca twice. I'd take care if I were you, Maud Ammen. You stand to lose your situation, and you shan't find another so soon without references.

"Now then," he continued, slapping his knee, "as far as food is concerned, I've seen to that. I had the innkeeper pack plenty to last until we've put enough distance between ourselves and Lindegren to chance stopping again. And as to refreshing yourselves, there will be streams along the way, and plenty of bracken and gorse to squat behind, since you force me to be crude. But you will do so under guard. Now, enough! You might as well accept this. I've had my fill of trekking over marsh and moor after you, my girl. There is nothing for it. I have given my word. This marriage is arranged."

Becca said no more. It was no use attempting to reason with a madman. That was how she viewed her father now. That image—as terrible as it was—was kinder to her sensibilities than admitting what he really was: a gambling-obsessed, cold-blooded murderer. Her own father! But there it was. She'd seen what he was capable of with her own eyes. Well, he might be able to drag her to the anvil, but he would never be able to force the consent to wed Pembroke from her to finalize the marriage. That was all it took at an anvil wedding, that the parties declare their wish to be wed before witnesses. Even if he got her there, he would never have those words from her lips. She was already wed to Count Klaus Lindegren in her heart, and in her soul.

The others ate at intervals. Even Maud nibbled at a cold meat pasty, but not Becca. The thought of taking food in that foul-smelling atmosphere closed her throat over her stomach's rumblings. They had left the mail coach route in favor of a more secluded road far off the beaten path. Her father and Pembroke dozed now and again, taking turns until late in the day when, somewhere along the Welsh border, they entered a dense, dark forest.

It must have been the soothing scent of pine in the air that managed to seep in through the closed windows that dragged both men's eyelids down. There hadn't been a sound from Andrews now that Maud had quieted, though Becca knew he wasn't sleeping up top. She pictured him just as he was when they set out, his long legs spread beneath the greatcoat, a formidable-looking long-barrel flintlock pistol at the ready, resting upon his knee. He couldn't overhear at his distance above the clatter and jingle of the tack and the thunder of the horses' hooves if they spoke in hushed murmurs, but the two dozing opposite could, and she leaned close to Maud and whispered in her ear.

"Maud, you are in no danger," she said. "This is only about me. You must not provoke anger—especially in the one outside. That man is dangerous."

"He come at me," said Maud. "He grabbed me and yanked me up outta my bed when I was sleepin'—wouldn't even let me get my things. He rummaged through my bag, snatched out my mantle, and tossed it over me, said if I breathed a sound it would be my last."

"I know. He said the same to me," Becca soothed. "When I saw Father, I thought it would be all right, that he would never let me come to harm at the hands of such a creature. I realized what was happening, and I thought I could talk him 'round. . I have always been able to handle Father . . . But no longer. That is why I ran in the first place. Gambling has possessed him, Maud. It is like a sickness. He isn't the man he was when Mother was alive. Surely you can see it?"

"What are we goin' ta do, my lady?"

"I don't know," said Becca. "And I can't puzzle it out while you are whining and sobbing with every breath. You must desist. While I'm worrying about you, and what your disturbances will cause, I cannot concentrate on what needs must. There may come a time when your tears will be necessary to draw their attention. If you're bawling all the time, those tears will have no effect."

"You're not goin' to give in and marry him, then?" Maud said, nodding toward Pembroke, slumped across the way.

"Of course not. But I need your help. Sooner or later we will have to stop and change horses. These poor beasts cannot run all the way to Scotland. They will drop. When that time comes, you need to be prepared for anything. If I tell you to cry, bawl your head off! But not unless I tell you to. Now, get some sleep while you can. The stars alone know when we'll dare chance it again."

# Chapter Thirty

Becca could almost reach out and touch him. Her eyes were shut tight. They wouldn't open. But if they did, and she reached out her hand, he would be there, her beloved Klaus. She would rush into his arms. They would wrap around her, those strong comforting arms she so longed to hold her, and the nightmare would fade away. But this was only a dream. The nightmare was real. So very real! Her heart had never felt so heavy. Her own flesh and blood had betrayed her.

It was no more than a brief catnap. She snatched them whenever she could. She was exhausted. Her body still ached inside and out from her brief yet fierce lovemaking with Klaus, but oh, what a delicious ache! She could still feel him moving inside her—feel herself responding to the rhythm of his thrusts. The memory set her cheeks afire.

They had only stopped twice to change horses since they set out. The team was lathered and laboring. Again and again, the coachman's whip snapped through the still air. Becca started each time he cracked it. That was what had woken her just now.

Pembroke and Andrews changed places every so often, but her father never left the carriage. As strange as it seemed, considering his vile plans for her, she felt safer with him there than she would have if the squire and his smuggling partner were seated across the way. Sadly, it wasn't because she supposed her father had a jot of compassion for her, but rather because he stood to gain greatly from the alliance she represented. She did not fear for her life at his hands, only for her future.

How did they mean to accomplish their ends? By what method did they plan to force her union with Pembroke—an opiate, perhaps. Something slipped into her food or drink? They must know she would never agree willingly. It was too early to worry over that, however. They had sacrificed speed when they opted for the rougher terrain of roads less traveled. Three days had passed since they'd set out and they hadn't even gone half the distance. It would be a sennight at least from start to finish before they reached the border, and her stamina was flagging. She longed to stretch out full-length upon a real bed and rest her head upon eiderdown, instead of the stiff, tufted squabs or Maud's bony shoulder.

They hadn't stopped once at an inn except to change horses. On those occasions she and Maud had remained inside the coach, where no one could get a good look at them. They were not even let out to refresh themselves or relieve their bladders; that was done in secluded spots along the road. Food and drink that wasn't too perishable—usually bread, cheese, fruit, and ale—was purchased to eat along the way.

Becca was unfamiliar with the area they traveled through. She had never been east of London or north of Bath, but she knew the geography of her country well enough from her girlhood studies to surmise that they'd opted for the westernmost approach to the border, one that would take them into Scotland closest to the first coaching station on the other side, at Gretna Green. That would mean instead of taking a Midlands route, they would pass through the fells and the Lake District, west of the main highways north. These aspects were strikingly beautiful by all accounts, but harsh and rugged terrain. While eating their evening meal, just to be certain her calculations were correct, Becca decided to sound her father out on the subject.

"Where are we exactly?" she said, a close eye on Pembroke, who hung upon her every word, though he'd uttered precious few himself the whole journey. His familiar gaze lanced through her each time she met those steely, hooded eyes. The look in them made her shudder. "I have never seen such trees," she went on. "We have none so tall and fine as these in Cornwall."

"The prevailing winds prohibit growth," said the baron, around a mouthful of his meat pasty. Crumbs collected in the stubble on his chin. He made no move to brush them away. "Cornwall is a place apart, with a climate unique in England," he went on. "The wind is constant on the coast. The trees bend their backs to it."

"But . . . surely we are near the coast here, too?" Becca persisted.

"Why do you ask, daughter? Are you planning another escape? You'd best give it over, Rebecca. You shan't get away this time. Not with three of us to rein you in. When this journey ends, your future is resolved . . . and mine . . . is secured."

"Actually, I was trying to recall my nursery geography lessons," Becca said as nonchalantly as she could manage. "It is quite a challenge; all that was so long ago. I remember how Mother and I and that first governess . . . what was her name? Etta, yes, Etta used to air dream over the maps in my books, picking out all the places we would one day love to visit. Mother always wanted to see—"

"Enough about your mother!" he interrupted. "You know I do not like to raise the dead. You're a clever little chit; you're up to something. I can see it in those eyes of yours. You're as transparent as that coach window there."

Becca shrugged. "I'm merely trying to make the best of all this," she said on a sigh, avoiding Maud's quizzical glance. "If we are—heading for the fells, that is— it's one of those places. You know? One of the places we dreamed about back then. Mother especially longed to—"

"I told you I do not wish to discuss your mother!" her father snapped. "Let's have an end to it."

"Leave her be, Gildersleeve," Pembroke put in around a guttural chuckle. His voice was like boots crunching gravel. "Better this than black sulks and the dismals, eh?"

The baron dosed him with a withering glance. "She knows what is and isn't acceptable conversation, Pembroke," he said. "She's having us on. We do not discuss her mother."

Aha! She *had* found a sore spot. If she could only attack his conscience, she might at the very least cause a distraction.

"I just wish Mother could be here to see them, is all," she said. "The fells, that is."

"Enough, I say! There's nothing to see save hills that think they're mountains, and a tree is a tree no matter where it grows."

"Just think! Why, we might even catch a glimpse of Samuel Coleridge or William Wordsworth. They come from the lakes. Mother so loved their poetry."

"Poetry?" her father spat out in disgust. "More dreaming! Bah! Women's blather." He wound the window down just far enough to toss away his half-eaten pasty and rolled it up again. "There! Are you finally satisfied? You've spoiled my supper. Now, enough!"

The brief whiff of sweet air distinctive to the higher elevations revived Becca momentarily. She drank it in greedily and said no more. She had her answer. Just what she would do with the information she wasn't certain, but if she did manage to break free, at least she would know generally where she was. If there was only some way to get word to Klaus, some way to leave him a message . . .

Fantasizing now over that, she closed her eyes and drifted off to sleep.

Klaus scarcely noticed the ache in his shoulder. He rode like a madman until he practically dropped out of the saddle for want of sleep before stopping to rest. The maddening thing was, he had no idea which route they'd taken. Only that they were traveling north. Considering that Pembroke was with them, it was reasonable to assume they were headed for Gretna Green. He couldn't imagine them trying to force a marriage anywhere in England, considering the restrictions involved, and they would hardly take time to arrange for a special license.

After inquiring at all the coaching inns on the main route north with no results, Klaus had come to the conclusion that they must have strayed off the beaten path to avoid pursuit. Though he veered off course as well, his chances of finding them were bleak. More important than overtaking them now was reaching the border before they did, and he drove himself and the animal beneath him relentlessly to that end. He had to find her before it was too late.

Dawn broke dreary, though less humid, in the higher elevation. The farther north he traveled, the cooler the air became. He'd driven his mount until the poor horse was nearly lame, forcing him to stop at a coaching inn just north of Shrewsbury to hire another. He was fast becoming aware of the restrictions the physical plane imposed upon him. Were this happening in the astral realm, he would have all manner of magic at his disposal—clever tricks and fairy glamour to fox and confuse. He would possess the power of projection, of cloaking, and of harnessing time to his advantage—of pleating it, folding it, peeling away its many layers like those of an onion. He would be able to call upon the creatures of the Otherworld to lend their aid; all that was denied him now. He was on his own, dependent upon his wits, his strength, and a strange God, whom he wasn't too proud to call upon as he limped his horse into the coaching station as first light broke over the tree line.

"I am looking for a party that might have passed this way heading north," he said to the station master, while the hostler readied him a fresh mount in the mews. "Three men and two women, in a private carriage."

The station master scratched his head as if to awaken his brain. "There was one come through here last night 'round the supper hour," he said. "It was a fine barouche with a team of four. Didn't stay but long enough to change horses before they lit right out again, like the Devil hisself was after 'em."

"The lady and her maid—did you see them clearly? Were they . . . all right?"

The man looked at him strangely. "Well, now, I dunno," he said. "I never seen 'em clear. They never got out of the carriage. The men that was with 'em did all the arrangin'—"

"A short, stocky, older man, ruddy complexion, a dandy, and a tall man dressed all in black?" Klaus urged.

The station master nodded. "The older gent didn't get out of the carriage either, just hollered commands at the other two. One went in after victuals to take along, while the other settled up with me."

"Did they say where they were going?"

"No, gov'nor, can't say that they did. They were in one devil of a hurry, though—wouldn't even let the ladies out to freshen up. Took off all out straight, they did."

"Which way?"

"North. 'Peared ta me they were headed for the border. I've seen enough coaches come through here to know a wedding party when I see one. Unless I miss my guess, they're runnin' from someone."

"That would be me," said Klaus.

The station master's eyes popped open wide. "*You?*"

"Me," Klaus said succinctly. "The lady in that carriage is my betrothed. She has been abducted against her will. Think, man! Is there anything—anything at all that you overheard—anything that will help me find them . . . no matter how trivial it seems?"

The station master's jaw fell slack. "N-no, gov'nor, " he said. "Wait! There was one peculiar thing . . ." He opened a drawer in his desk and snaked out a lace edged linen handkerchief. A scrollwork *R* was embroidered in one corner. "This come flyin' out of the coach window as they drove off. Like one of 'em tossed it apurpose. It's much too fine to be throwin' away, to my thinkin'. Just look at the lace on it. Ya see that *R* there? My missus's name is Rowena. I thought I'd—"

Klaus grabbed it out of his hand and raised it to his nose. Becca's scent filled his nostrils—wildflowers and sweet herbs mingled with her own true scent, earthy yet clean. He groaned, drinking her in greedily, taking her into him, absorbing the very essence of her as if it would make her materialize before him. When he moved his frock coat aside to jam it into his waistcoat pocket, the station master took a step closer.

"You're bleedin'!" he said. "Been pistol-shot, have you?"

"It's nothing," Klaus insisted, tugging his waistcoat closed.

"Look here, there's a surgeon in the common room. He could set you to rights in a trice—no questions asked."

"There isn't time," Klaus responded stalking toward the stables.

Yes, the wound needed tending. But it would have to wait. Such bothersome injuries were new to him, reminding him of his mortality. If he were in the astral—*Fossegrim* still—he would have healed by now, benefiting from the erstwhile mysteries now denied him. Anne-Lise had tried to spare him much of the pain, and to speed the healing with her mystical herbal poultices and drafts and chamomile incense. While her ministering had succeeded to a remarkable degree— an ordinary mortal would have fallen long since—a nagging ache remained, and now *blood*. He had the little cloth bag of herbs Anne-Lise had given him when they left the cottage tucked away in his waistcoat pocket. The first stream he came to, he would make a poultice, but that would have to wait. Benighted time was breathing down his neck, and he cursed the air blue collecting his horse and galloped off with the station master's shouts ringing in his ears.

*Damn! Syl on his throne! Where are you now, Henrik, when I need you most?* he railed at the absent elder as he rode. Surely Henrik would know what to do. Surely he knew what next lay in store. Of all Klaus's gifts, it was his mental powers that he missed most.

"Where I can help you," said that beloved voice, as though the elder stood beside him. "Just as I promised, my lord."

"Henrik?" It was the fever—it had to be. Klaus knew he had one. Not even the wind his motion created riding at such a furious gallop could cool his hot, dry skin. His mind was playing conjuring tricks. Nonetheless, imaginary or real, he nearly lost his seat at the sound.

"Still blasphemous," the elder's voice murmured across his mind. "You can ill afford that in this pass."

"What harm?" Klaus said. "The gods have forsaken me."

"Just so," said the elder. "All the more reason to make a favorable impression upon the one who governs you now."

"How am I hearing you, old friend? No—never mind. It is enough that I do. . . ."

"The gods have stripped you of your Otherworld gifts," Henrik said. "But they have no dominion over the gifts inherent to mortals. I once told you all mortals are endowed, but not all know how to use the gifts they possess. Your mother was such a mortal. You will meet many on your human journey who see and feel and know that which other mortals do not. These gifts you will retain. No Otherworldly power can take them from you. Also . . . though you are denied entrance into the astral, you are not bereft of friends there. You cannot come to us, but we can come to you . . . when it is necessary. Do we not roam this planet freely? Do we not come and go and show ourselves to whom we will? Has that not been so since time out of mind?"

"I . . . I had forgotten."

"Love madness." Henrik sounded sad.

"I will not lose her!"

"Then ride like the wind, young lord. All of her dangers are not in that coach with her. Soon she comes to water."

Becca first glimpsed Lake Windermere wreathed by tall wooded fells at sunset. The wild and beautiful west countryside took her breath away at first sight through the trees. They traveled the fells off the highway, on a track not intended for coaches, she surmised by the way the carriage listed and pitched and labored. Deeply wooded, the access—scarcely more than a path—was sheltered from view of passersby on the lane. Very little of it was on level ground, and the coachman complained again and again that they were at risk of toppling over. The horses were skittish and worn to a lather, their shrill complaints siphoned away on the wind blowing seaward from the fells.

The baron banged the carriage roof with his walking stick. "We should be safe enough from prying eyes to take a respite here," he said to no one in particular as the coach rolled to a shuddering halt. "We cannot go on until the horses are rested. It is still many hours to the border."

"May we get out at least?" said Becca. She craned her neck toward the scenery outside and took a sudden chill. It all seemed bathed in blood. The setting sun ruled the sky and rode the water, a fireball laying down a shimmering band that bled landward from the far side of the lake. Even the tree trunks that stood between were blackened to a deep magenta hue as twilight approached. There was something eerily familiar about the place. It raised the fine hairs on the back of Becca's neck, and her palms had suddenly gone clammy and cold. Though the air was mild enough, a deep, shuddering chill gripped her. And yet she was drawn to it.

"A stroll with your betrothed would not be amiss," said the baron. "You are adequately chaperoned, after all, and by this time tomorrow, you shan't need one."

"My 'betrothed' is not here," she snapped back at him.

"I beg to differ," Pembroke said silkily, laying a familiar hand upon her knee.

Becca slapped it away, ignoring Maud's incredulous

gasp. "You take bold liberties, sir!" she said. "Kindly keep your thieving paws off my person."

"Rebecca!" her father barked.

"No, no, I like a cheeky lady," said the squire. "One has so many missish maidens to contend with these days. They titter behind their fans and bat their eyes demurely to get a man in their clutches, then sour like clabbered cream between the sheets. Wasn't it the Vikings who took no pleasure in their bed sport unless their wenches fought them to a fare-thee-well? Your former intended comes from Viking stock, does he not? You think that he would expect less of you? Your innocence delights me."

"Maud and I will refresh ourselves in private by the water," Becca responded in as unequivocal a tone as she could muster. "My nose and throat are clogged with road dust, and I have not executed a proper toilette since we began this journey."

Nobody spoke.

"Where can we go, Father?" Becca said, waving a wild hand toward the landscape. "We are miles from any sort of civilization in these mountains. Where can we possibly go that the three of you could not run us to ground? There's nothing but water north and south, and the lake is a mile wide."

The baron heaved a sigh. "Make the best of it," he begrudged. "You shan't get another opportunity until we cross the border."

"In private, Father—no prying eyes."

"All right, all right, go!" he said. "And be quick about it. The sun soon sets, and *private* ends before it sinks behind the fells."

There would be precious little privacy. Their captors would surely not let them out of their sight. Her father grumbled something to that effect to the others within their hearing as they made their way through the trees. Becca reached for her handkerchief at the water's edge to plunge it into the blood-tinged water to wash her hot face. But when she groped the little pocket she wore on a cord beneath her frock, and her fingers closed around the conch shell, she remembered. A plaintive moan exited her parched throat, and she sank down on the bank, her head in her hands.

"What is it, my lady?" said Maud. "Oh, fie, and you've been so brave till now. . . ."

Becca dropped her hands into her lap and fondled her pocket. "My handkerchief," she said. "I tossed it out the window at that coaching station yesterday . . . I think it was yesterday. Oh, Maud . . . what if he doesn't come? What if he never finds me?" She dared not say it to the abigail, but how could she live without him now, after she'd given herself to him, after she'd tasted the ecstasy of his passion, after she'd come awake to the mysteries of her sex in those beloved arms? She couldn't confide her greatest fear, that Klaus had given up his immortality for her, and now . . . She couldn't finish the thought.

"I saw you toss that handkerchief," Maud said, kneeling down beside her. "What were ya thinkin'?"

"That he might find it and know I'd passed that way. Silly of me—a little scrap of linen and lace like that? It's likely been trampled under dozens of horses' hooves by now." Tears welled in her eyes again. "He's never going to find me, is he, Maud?" she sobbed.

"Here, now, don't overset yourself, my lady, take mine," said the maid, offering her own handkerchief.

"It isn't the handkerchief, Maud," Becca said, dabbing at her eyes. "It's the hopelessness of it all. If only he would come . . ."

"But I thought ya didn't want him ta come?" the abigail said.

"That was then. It's different now. Father killed Sir Percival Smedley on that dueling ground, Maud— shot him in the back. I saw it with my own eyes. When they took us from that coaching inn, they vowed to do the same to Klaus if I resisted. You know he has been wounded. I feared being the cause of further harm come to him and I thought . . . if I bided my time . . . Oh, I don't know what I thought! Now I'm afraid, Maud. Father is obsessed with what he stands to gain if he shackles me to Pembroke. He will never give in. I do not know how he plans to see this through, but I shan't take another bite of food or a drop to drink, and don't you, either."

"Y-you think he might try to *drug us,* my lady?"

"I certainly wouldn't put it past him. Dear God, I believe he really has gone mad!"

Tears threatened again, and Becca held the empty pocket to her face to cover them, but it wasn't empty. The conch shell was inside, and something else clattered against it. She rummaged deep down until her fingers closed around the aquamarine amulet Henrik had given her. Her heart leapt. She'd almost forgotten. Somehow it comforted her, and she tucked the pocket back inside her frock.

"What are we ever goin' ta do?" the maid wailed.

"Shhhh! You'll bring them down here! Right now, we shall do what we came down here to do—refresh ourselves by the water. The sun sets soon, and they will come for us. We don't want to make them suspicious. That is why I haven't resisted. I'm trying to catch them off their guard long enough to escape. You will have to fend for yourself if that time comes, Maud. Look sharp, and pay attention. If I tell you to run, you must do it as fast as your legs will carry you. Never mind about me. If I don't have to worry over you, I might just be able to get us out of this."

Becca didn't want to alarm the maid with the news that these men saw her as expendable. They hadn't brought Maud along to attend her. She was a liability. They'd taken her so she couldn't set Klaus or any other rescuers on them. They would dispose of her in a trice if needs must, and Becca had no doubts that they would do just that once there was no danger of her telling tales and spoiling their plans. But Becca couldn't worry over that now; it was getting darker by the minute, and a thick mist was rising over the lake.

She got to her feet and staggered to the water's edge. Looking out over the misty expanse, she finally realized why the place seemed so familiar. The indented shorelines formed many little bays, with several distant islands poking their heads out of the mist. It reminded her of the astral archipelago, she realized.

Cold chills brought her to her knees at the edge of the lake. Her legs would no longer support her. Cupping her hands, she bent to scoop up some water, but froze instead. There, hovering beneath the surface— just as her hands were about to break it—yards of seawater green hair appeared, floating lazily on the current. And then a face came clear. But it wasn't Becca's reflection in the lake; it was *Illia's* image gazing back at her, triumphant and regal in all her exquisite glory.

Becca fell back and skittered away from the water's edge, her heart hammering in her breast. It *couldn't* be. Her mind was playing tricks upon her. On her knees, she crept to the edge again, and craned her neck toward the gentle ripples lapping at the river bank. *Sea grass*, of course! Yards and yards of drifting, floating sea grass haloed her own face and not Illia's. She blinked and looked again, just to be sure her eyes hadn't deceived her . . . but no, it was her own pale face staring back at her from the water. Just to be sure, she reached out—once, twice hesitantly—before plunging her hand into the water. She pulled it out again with a fistful of slimy seaweed.

The breath rushed from her lungs in a great sigh of relief, but it was short-lived. Maud's scream spun her around to face her father and the others slip-sliding down the hill. Their demeanor flagged danger. Shoving the abigail out of the way, Pembroke seized Becca just as a pistol shot rang out from behind, turning her to see Klaus on the crest above, a flintlock pistol in each hand, one aimed below, the other trailing smoke into the air. Silhouetted against the blood-colored twilight sky at the top of the hill, he looked like a vengeful phantom. The sight took Becca's breath away.

"Let her go, Pembroke!" Klaus thundered.

"And if I don't?" said the squire, jutting his angular chin. "You've only got one shot left, Lindegren. You cannot do us all with it."

"Just so," said Klaus. "I have accounted for that."

A side glance brought a troop of soldiers pouring over the hill like a swarm of bees. In rapid succession, Maud screamed, Pembroke threw Becca down at the water's edge and ran headlong into two soldiers he hadn't seen advancing. Gildersleeve blanched, his back to the lake and with nowhere to retreat, his frantic eyes oscillating amongst the confusion. Two soldiers laid hold of him, leading him away. Jack Andrews—pistols drawn—made a break to the north, firing, and his long legs took him over the uneven ground until a shot from one of the soldiers' muskets felled him.

Klaus streaked down the hill to Becca's side, and gathered her into his arms. Those strong wonderful arms she so longed to hold her were clasping her to him so tightly she could scarcely breathe, and she clung to him with all her strength.

All at once, he put her from him and took her measure. His strong hands raced up and down her arms, over her shoulders, her throat. He brushed the tendrils of hair from her face, which he cupped in one trembling hand.

"Are you sure you are all right, *mitt kostbart?*" he asked, his breath coming short.

"You are not . . . harmed?"

Becca shook her head. "I'm fine now," she murmured, choking back tears. "I didn't think I would ever see you again. . . ."

Klaus reached to take her in his arms, and she moved to rush into them, when two slender sea-green arms broke the surface of the water and grabbed his legs. *Illia's arms!* Becca hadn't been mistaken earlier: It *was* Illia she had seen beneath the water, but it was Klaus that Illia wanted.

Fighting to keep his footing, Klaus flailed his arms in the air, and Becca reached out to steady him, her hands fisted in his superfine frock coat.

Seizing her wrists, he put her from him roughly. "No, Becca!" he thundered as he toppled into the water. "Stay back! She will kill you!"

Scarcely able to believe her eyes, Becca stood crippled with chills as the vengeful sprite pulled Klaus down beneath the water. She glanced behind. Maud had followed the soldiers and their captives up the hill, evidently to give her a moment alone with Klaus. There was no one in sight. Pacing along the edge, she stared at the churning water waiting for Klaus to surface. He still had his swimming skills; he would always have those, but now, without his Otherworldly powers, he could no longer breathe underwater. He could drown! Was that what Illia wanted? Did she mean to spirit him back to the astral archipelago, where her kind lured mortal men to serve them forever? Or had he made a voluntary choice to join her? Had he sacrificed himself to the sprite so that Becca would be safe from the vindictive creature's vengeance? It certainly seemed so.

Becca pleaded for the sight of him, her eyes snapping back and forth toward the ever widening ripples in the water. He'd been under too long—much too long. His heavy boots would surely weigh him down.

Panic seized her heart like an iron fist. Her breathing had become shallow, and she gulped in air that hung like a bloodied pall over the lake. Calling his name in spasms, she was just about to dive in after him, when Illia and Klaus's heads and torsos surged through the surface of the water as they grappled with each other.

Becca screamed, but her throat was so dry it passed as no more than a squeak. What was she seeing—a ghost? Klaus had gone white as stone, his blue-tinged lips twisted in a grimace, as he filled his lungs with gasps of air in rapid succession, his broad chest heaving. Illia's breathing, however, was effortless. She was in her element. Klaus was hers for the taking. Without his Otherworldly powers, he was as vulnerable as all the other seafaring men the siren Lorelei lured into their lairs. Illia would take him under and either spirit him off to the astral isles, there to enslave him for all eternity, or drown him.

To her horror, Becca watched helpless as Illia seized Klaus by the hair and possessed his lips, meanwhile locking her naked legs around his waist as he tried to push her from him.

"*Noooooooo!*" Becca shrieked, springing toward the river edge.

Tearing his mouth away from the ravenous sprite, Klaus tore at her arms twined around him like snakes. "Stay back, Becca . . . !" he panted. "Do not . . . come near . . . the water!"

"That is right, Becca," the sprite chortled. "Stay back! He wants ye no longer. He has chosen immortality with me, instead of death with ye, foolish chit."

"Do not listen to her, *mitt kostbart!*" Klaus said, still struggling with the death grip Illia had upon him. "Get back from the water!"

Becca could scarcely see them through her tears. He was tiring. He was a strong swimmer, but his boots were weighing him down. If the sprite should let go of him . . . No! She dared not think about that. He was about to make the sacrifice she'd feared. Not while she drew breath!

*Maj!*" she shrilled. "*I command you to set him free!*"

"Foolish mortal," Illia tittered. "Ye cannot use that incantation more than once. Your time is done. He either comes with me or dies in my arms in this godforsaken lake. If I cannot have him, *no one will*—least of all the likes of ye!"

Before Becca could respond, the two were gone, sucked down beneath the surface of the water again. Calling Klaus's name, Becca traveled the bank, her misted eyes straining through the murky red-tinged water, through the swaying sea grass and the distortion of the ripples, searching for some sign of them . . . but there was none. She had never felt so helpless in all her life. Too much time was passing. He could not stay underwater this long without his Otherworldly gifts. He'd told her not to go near the water. But if not her, who? What must be done must be done quickly. There was nothing for it, and she kicked off her slippers, spun around, and dove into the lake.

Fine silt, dredged up from the lake bottom by the conflict, stung her eyes and all but blinded her. It mixed with the seaweed in the eerie underwater darkness, and she could barely see a foot in front of her. Had the sprite taken him already? No! She wouldn't consider that possibility. Needing air, she rose to the surface, her eyes flicking in all directions, but there was no sign of Kraus or Illia. Making matters worse, the light was failing.

All around her the water was suddenly in motion, though there wasn't a breath of breeze. Spinning around, she felt something strike her thigh—something hard. Her heart leapt. Keeping herself afloat with one hand, she reached inside the slit in her frock and gripped her pocket, fingering the little conch shell and . . . the amulet! That was twice now in recent moments that it had attracted her attention as if a living, breathing presence. Becca didn't hesitate. Drawing the aquamarine out, she clenched it in her fist and was set to dive below again when movement on the water caught her eye. She uttered a gasp. The Irrbloss? It was! Bounding and bobbing and skimming the surface, the mysterious lights had begun spinning the ripples into a vortex, as they were wont to do.

Tears swam in her eyes. It was as if she were reunited with long-lost friends. They had never let her down in the past. Their very presence bolstered her courage to dive beneath the surface again. This time, driven by the vortex the bobbing balls of light created, she dove head-first and plunged right into Klaus and Illia, still struggling beneath the whirlpool the lake had become.

Taken by surprise, the sprite lost her grip upon Klaus, and turned her wrath upon Becca instead. Every second counted. Neither Becca nor Klaus dared stay beneath the water any longer. It was plain that Illia meant to keep them there. The vengeful creature's fingers were fisted in Becca's hair now; meanwhile Klaus was struggling to range himself between them. There was no more time, and Becca opened her fist that held the amulet, and drove it into Illia's graceful pointed ear.

A keening siren shriek ripped through the water, and Illia let go, spiraling off into the murky depths. The vortex tightened, spinning Klaus and Becca back toward the whirling surface. Klaus's arms were around her, holding Becca as they broke through gasping for breath, and swam for shore. The whirlpool had calmed when they climbed up on the riverbank and collapsed on the ground, but the Irrbloss remained hovering over the water like curious children.

Breathless, wrapped in Klaus's strong arms, Becca clung to him. Neither spoke. There was no need. Not even Maud's shrill cries as she came running down the hill could enter their space then. They were in a place apart, a place where nothing mattered but that they were together, never to be parted. Illia was gone. The nightmare was over.

# *Epilogue*

"I am sorry for your father, *mitt kostbart*," Klaus murmured in Becca's ear. "There was nothing to be done."

Come fresh from their anvil wedding, they were seated on a rolled-arm lounge in the bedchamber of a rustic though well-appointed four-room cottage that *was* a cottage—one of the many thatched-roof dwellings that lay nestled in the rolling green and lofty climes of the Scottish countryside at Gretna Green for the convenience of newlyweds.

On the far side of the little house, Maud was fast asleep. She'd dropped like a stone the minute she'd finished preparing Becca's bath and assisting with her toilette. She would never know how close she had come to ending her existence in a foreign land.

For Becca, the world was new! She was Countess Lindegren, alone at last with the man she loved, at peace in the arms that meant the world, the moon and the stars to her. Nothing else mattered . . . though still a hint of sorrow lingered when her thoughts strayed to her father.

"He brought it down upon himself, Klaus," she said,

clouding. "Will they hang him, do you think?" Even after all was said and done, how could she bear it?

"That will be up to the magistrates," he said, soothing her with gentle hands. "We must let the law handle it. Your life is with me now, and I will never let anything harm you again for as long as I live."

"Where will we go? What will we do?"

He smiled, dropping a kiss on her brow. "We will go home, my Becca," he said, "to Lindegren Hall."

"It still exists?" she blurted. "I thought . . ."

"It exists in the physical plane now, with all its flaws and dust and falling roof tiles—no more to be cloaked from the view of others, or whirl through the astral gate. We shall have to hire a staff, of course, and if Lindegren Hall is not to your liking, there is a splendid estate in Sweden, also in disrepair, I'm afraid. I haven't been . . . home in . . . many years. Nonetheless, it is quite grand—a castle, uncloaked and waiting, thanks to Henrik. I arranged for that before we left. It's a beautiful place in the north, where half the year is as the dawn, the other half as the twilight, and the *aurora borealis* paints the sky with flashing rainbows. I have missed it so."

"It sounds a place enchanted," she said.

"I think enough time has elapsed that I can safely return. You see, I was found out there, oh so long ago, hence my exile. But that tale is so unpleasant"—he gave a mock shudder—"too bloodthirsty for the ears of a bride on her wedding night." He dosed her with one of his irresistible lopsided smiles, and her heart skipped. She could almost see the Northern lights flashing in his dilated eyes.

Becca's eyes misted, and he folded her closer. "What is it? You're trembling. . . ."

"If we travel to Sweden, we shall have to go by water," she said, "and I no longer have the enchanted amulet Henrik gave me."

Klaus reached into his waistcoat pocket, drew out her handkerchief, and folded it back to reveal the aquamarine sparkling inside. "You mean this?" he asked, handing it to her.

Becca gasped. "But how . . . ?"

Klaus's smile became a grin, and she thrilled at the sight of it. "The vortex spat it out," he said. "I found it on the lakeshore while you were calming Maud."

"The *Irrbloss*?"

He shrugged. "We shall never know if the whirlpool they created dredged it up, or if Illia herself threw it back in her rage. It could repel but not destroy her. Her power is too great for that. Take comfort in the fact that it is returned to you, because we will sail, my Becca, and you must not be afraid."

Becca handed it back to him. "You had best take charge of it," she murmured.

"For now," he agreed, receiving it. He held the aquamarine up and let the hearthlight sparkle through it. "Magnificent," he said. "Even without the enchantment, since time out of mind sailors setting out upon their voyages have carried such a stone for protection from all dangers that lurk in the sea."

Tucking it away, he winced, and Becca stroked his shoulder gently. "All that thrashing about in the water so soon after the wound . . . are you sure you don't need tending? I am an able nurse."

Klaus took her probing hand in his and raised it to his lips. "I do not need a nurse, *mitt kostbart*," he said through a suggestive chuckle and light kisses. "I need my bride in my arms in that bed. With my . . . conversion, the moon no longer rules my mating madness, but I have not lost the fever in my blood. But know this: while that passion is no longer restricted to the astral realm, it shall always be restricted to you and no other." He raised her to her feet. "Now then, let us get you out of that ridiculous nightrail into that grand bed, shall we?"

One by one, Klaus peeled the layers away until Becca stood naked before him in the hearthlight; then he scooped her up and laid her on the bed, his hooded eyes never leaving hers. They glowed with inner warmth, and blazed—just like the fire blazed—as he stood admiring her. That sultry shuttered gaze alone caused a tightening in her loins, a thickening of engorged flesh eager for fulfillment. It was as if he stroked her with his eyes. That caress alone set her aflame. He still possessed *that* magic, if nothing else—the power to seduce with a look, to devastate with a glance. Such power was not of this world. His elders and his gods may have stripped him of his privilege, but they could not strip him of his prowess. She had wed the best of both worlds. He existed on a sensual plane that transcended the two, and he had taken her to live there with him.

Klaus had always seemed as comfortable naked as he was clothed. That had not changed, either. He shed his Egyptian cotton shirt and brocade waistcoat, his inexpressibles and drawers in seamless motions, dropping them alongside the hose and boots he'd tugged off earlier. Naked but for his shoulder bandaged in fresh linen, he touched her with his eyes again. Their gazes locked, he prowled closer and sank down beside her, taking her in his arms with a fluid motion that reminded her of a cresting wave breaking over the shore.

The soft moan that escaped his throat upon contact prompted a similar utterance from her. The mingled sounds resonated through their bodies so severely that Becca's heart skipped a beat as it banged against his hard-muscled chest. Her breasts crushed against him, their dark flushed tips grown tall against his warm, unyielding flesh. He was aroused, and her breath caught as his hard sex throbbed against her. One arm clasped her fast, while he reached with his other hand, tilting her face up so she would meet his eyes.

"Do not be afraid, *mitt kostbart*," he murmured, his finely formed lips lifted at the corners in a soft, knowing smile. "I bring you only pleasure. There will be no pain this time. Do you trust me, my Becca?"

"Y-yes . . ." she murmured, less convincingly than she intended.

Klaus leaned back, studying her, looking deep into her eyes. "Still, you hesitate?" he said. "You wound me, *mitt kostbart*, if still you doubt."

"Oh, no!" she breathed, gripping him tighter. "It is just that . . . I have the greatest fear that I am not skilled enough to. . . to . . ."

Klaus threw his head back and burst into deep-throated laughter. "Allay those fears," he said. Taking her hand, he drove it down between his legs and wrapped it around his swollen member. "See how I live for you?" he murmured. "How I have always lived for you, just as in the 'dreams.' "

"But then, I thought they *were* dreams," she said.

"Silly goose, have you forgotten so soon how we made love at the inn?"

"How could I ever forget? But still, it almost seemed like a dream, and anything is possible in dreams. . . ."

"My beloved little hypocrite," he murmured against her temple, his voice playfully seductive. "All life is illusion, in this world and in the other. You made love to that phantom in your dreams. You gave him your virtue. All that is changed is that now you know the dream is real. I am still your phantom—still the same creature who held you in the waterfall. Do not try to part the veil when you make love to me. Come to me as you came to him. Give to me what you gave him at the inn—your sweet passion. We are one. There is nothing to fear."

He folded her so tenderly in his arms, she was certain she would swoon. Melting against his body, she reached to stroke his face. Every sinew in him was stretched to its limit. The corded muscles in his neck stood out in bold relief, the ridges in his taut middle pressed against her like granite. He was holding back, his rigid member pulsating against her, responding to her slightest motion.

Becca's heart leapt. Their pulses beat as one. Skin to skin, heart to heart, sex to sex—their palpable rhythms were conjoined. It was like a strange primeval dance, the ebb and flow of something more than just their bodies; it was a joining of souls. He had awakened her to pleasures beyond imagining. These were not sensations of the physical world; *they couldn't be*. These were pulsations from the Otherworld, hidden just beneath the surface of their rapture. She could feel it—she could *see* it—she could hear it in his husky breathing, in the way he murmured her name, like a prayer, softly, reverently, his hot breath puffing against her ear, disturbing the saucy curls that had fallen in disarray about the pillow.

The flutter of his moist eyelashes across her temple sent shockwaves of icy fire coursing through her belly and thighs. His long, deft fingers on her breasts, on her sore, aching nipples, seemed to know exactly where to lightly stroke, where to rub and tweak and, yes, to pinch. *Excruciating ecstasy.* Her breath was coming short and labored in involuntary spasms. How much of him was still the astral creature? How much of the supernatural had bled over with him? How much of the waterlord remained? So much of Klaus seemed astral still, even the way he'd gotten into bed, as if he were swimming in water.

All at once her mind reeled back to the way they had made love at the inn, cleaving to each other in furious abandon, standing upright, just as she had seen the astral creatures mate in the very air of the Otherworld. It had happened in privacy, behind closed doors, but what if. . . ? A stifled gasp escaped her throat. The images those thoughts conjured produced a vision so shocking, she answered it aloud.

"We . . . shan't have to do this in *public*, shall we?" she panted. "Openly, I mean, with no modesty, like the creatures in the astral do? There is much of the Otherworld still in you, Klaus. . . ."

He froze in place and raised himself above her, his head thrown back in a mighty guffaw. "Oh, my Becca!" he erupted. "Trust you to know the exact moment to slow my ardor, clever puss. Elsewise, our wedding night would surely have ended far too soon." He laughed again, so convulsed that he rolled onto his back and covered his eyes with his hand. "No, my love," he said. "You may safely lay those fears to rest. I shan't demand that you strip down and pleasure me in the streets. But when we are alone," he went on, rolling over and gathering her in his arms again, "you may prepare yourself for ravishing. I am bewitched. You have enchanted me with magic that surpasses anything the Otherworld has to offer."

"It was a foolish question," Becca said, embarrassed. "It's just that . . . I know what you were. I didn't know exactly what you are now. I didn't know how else to say it."

"You were most eloquent," he replied through another chorus of chuckles, meanwhile bundling her in his arms again. "Ahhh, but, *mitt kostbart*, do not pout. Forgive me, but you are so wonderfully refreshing. I laugh only because you have once more charmed me. In answer to your question, I say again: I am what I always have been, except that I can no longer travel between planes. Whatever Otherworldly gifts I still retain will surface in time . . . you mustn't fear them when they do. Now then, enough of mysterious things! We have our whole lives to sort out such Otherworldly secrets. We must begin again if I am to pleasure you properly. But let us be creative, shall we? The night is warm still, and we are somewhat secluded here." He sprang from the bed and scooped her up in his arms.

Becca gasped. "Klaus!" she cried. "What are you doing?" His eyes were flashing now with something besides passion. There was a devilish gleam in them.

"You have given me a splendid idea," he said. Sweeping her through the cottage door into the starry night, he carried her into the cottage's private, hedge-lined garden, and let her slide the length of him slowly to the ground.

It wasn't a manicured garden, but rather something random and enchantingly wild. The tousled land surrounding the cottage was burgeoning with all manner of fragrant wildflowers—summer's last. Crushed beneath their bare feet, lily and heather, primrose and lavender spread their mingled scents on the gentle breeze. It reminded Becca of the wonderful flowers in the astral realm, and her heart turned over in her breast. Surely he couldn't mean to. . . .

"Klaus, you wouldn't!"

"Oh, but I would, *mitt kostbart*," he said, his deep baritone rumbling through her from head to toe.

His manhood moved against her. One strong arm crushed her close, while his free hand roamed her body and caressed her from arched throat to the full round breast he'd captured.

"I take back what I said before," he murmured against the pounding pulse at the base of her neck. "How fitting that our wedding night be celebrated here, that I take you 'in public, openly, with no modesty . . . like the creatures in the astral do . . .' "

Leaning into his embrace Becca yielded to his kiss. Whatever happened, she and Klaus would be happy. They were together, and that was all that mattered. She replied with another gasp and a troop of throaty pleasure moans as he did exactly as he promised.

# DAWN THOMPSON
# THE RAVENCLIFF BRIDE

As the coach flies up the Cornish coast, Sara sees the end of her journey: Ravencliff Manor. But what sort of man would rescue her from debtors prison by marriage, sight unseen, by proxy? Obviously, a wretch—the same sort of man who lets a strange, wolf-like creature roam his grounds as if it were master. Of course, Sara would have accepted the proposal of the Devil himself to get out of Fleet, so she is resigned to her fate. Then she meets her husband, hair black as sin and a handsome face, and all her assurance vanishes. What strange curse has befallen Nicholas Walraven, and what secrets does he hide? For good or ill, she is now… *The Ravencliff Bride*.

---